THE BURNING MOUNTAIN

Kerry McGinnis was born in Adelaide but has spent most of her life in the Australian bush. She started writing at the age of nine and has published eleven books. These include two volumes of autobiograpy and eight Outback mysteries with Penguin Australia; her fantasy novel 'Far Seeker' was published by Elliot Mackenzie Ltd UK. Kerry's hobbies are reading, music (she's learning the harp), gardening and travel. She currently lives in Bundaberg, Qld.

ALSO BY THE AUTHOR

Pieces of Blue
Heart Country
The Waddi Tree
Wildhorse Creek
Mallee Sky
Tracking North
Out of Alice
Secrets of The Springs
The Heartwood Hotel
The Roadhouse

The Far Seeker Trilogy

Far Seeker

THE BURNING MOUNTAIN

KERRY McGINNIS

THE BURNING MOUNTAIN

KERRY McGINNIS

Paperback

ISBN

978-0-646-80667-9

Designed and Typeset by Keypress Connections
Palmwoods Queensland

DEDICATION

This one is for all those readers who have ever thought,
'Yes, but what if...?'
If they pushed it a bit they'd be writers too.

1

Trader Tranche, merchant of the city of Ripa made his slow way back to his Rhutan homeland along the highway known as the royal road. The road traversed the length of Appella from its southern-most city of Quade, to the pass in the mountains guarding the high plateau before dipping down into the warm fecundity of the Lower Land, long become a satellite state of Appella.

The trader bestrode a grey horse and travelled in a cloud of profanity directed at the pair of mules resisting his efforts to lead them. Tranche was a big, fleshy man, soft in body and unsuited to the task he had undertaken — as the blue turban he wore attested. Blue was the colour of the sea-going traders. The traditional headgear worn by the land traders, leaders of the mainly camel caravans that traversed the larger part of the continent of Belusia, was green. Despite the mildness of the spring day the merchant's jowls ran with sweat and his body ached from the saddle. Ten days on the road wasn't time enough to harden muscles slack from desk work, or to reduce the layering of belly fat laid down by the nervous habit of compulsive eating.

Pausing only to draw breath he damned Sarn anew, as the misbegotten son of a diseased whore, the one to whom he attributed all his present troubles, the least of which were the recalcitrant mules. If Tranche could have been certain of the man's trustworthiness he wouldn't be here in the first place, though given his employee's sudden disappearance, it was as well that he was. That all the bastard had stolen was a horse and saddle might be seen as a mark in his favour — if it wasn't that his failure to take more couldn't also be construed as not knowing where to seek it. Tranche, whose bland, fat man's face hid a suspicious nature, reserved judgement on that point.

It was two days since Sarn had vanished in the night. Two long days of watching for the ambush he momentarily expected, and of packing and physically hauling along the gods-cursed, stubborn mismatch of horse and donkey genitalia that carried his merchandise. Tranche knew himself to be well respected, a valued member of Ripa's Merchants' Guild, partner of Merchant Luka, both once wealthy men.

That was until the installation of Temes, Appella's new king the previous year. He spared a moment to curse him as well. The enterprise on which he was engaged was madness, he knew it, but he also knew he had little choice in the matter now that he was reduced to performing himself tasks that he had long paid other men to undertake. And no wonder — he was getting nowhere bloody fast!

That spurt of irritation led him most unwisely into leaning sideways to lash his rein ends down onto the neck of the mule that had just spread its feet to lean back against the lead rope. It jumped at the blow, barged forward and simultaneously lashed out with its nimble hindquarters. The kick caught the grey horse in the chest. It threw up its head and ran back, the mule kept going forward and Tranche, caught between lead-rope and reins, was dragged from the saddle, and because his arm was entangled in the rope, a short distance after the mule until his head and shoulders collided with a rock.

The second mule seized the opportunity to bolt. Tranche — stunned, winded, bleeding and bruised —

caught a hazy glimpse of a figure darting past him to catch and mount the grey. Both vanished from sight. Groaning, he tried to rise but his head swam sickeningly and his body failed him. Abandoned, injured, robbed — it had to be Sarn's work. His last conscious thought was that Luka had been right. He should have listened to his partner and stayed home.

***

When a little while later, Tranche's eyes opened, the grey horse was back. He could see it hobbled beside the road, grazing unconcernedly. The trader cautiously raised his pounding head high enough to feel the exquisitely painful lump above his ear. His right cheek was scraped raw and his arm ached unremittingly. As he was unbound and not, apparently, under arrest, he made the heroic effort to lift his gaze to discover why this should be so.

Surely they hadn't just stolen the goods and gone, leaving him the horse, which they had first thoughtfully unsaddled? Whoever it was had left the mules' packs too, tidily disposed in a row beyond the fire that crackled nearby. Renewed anxiety leapt in Tranche and he almost missed the figure approaching him with a steaming cup. Not Sarn, or one of Temes's thugs, but a ragged looking youth of the Old Race.

Eyes as dark as Tranche's own met his. 'Drink.' The word came in the Ansham tongue as the stranger offered the cup — Tranche's own, he saw — 'It will help your head.'

'What is it?' The trader's eyes slitted with pain. 'Who are you?' he croaked.

'Nobody — a traveller. And it's just herbs. Your head hit the stone there. It must ache. Drink and rest.'

Tranche obeyed, not caring overmuch if the brew killed him. For an uneasy moment his stomach roiled as the liquid went down, then it settled. He let the empty cup fall and lay back with a groan. Eyes shut he waited and found by insensible degrees that the youth had spoken the truth. The pain was diminishing. The bump remained, his scraped face smarted and his shoulder joint ached as if Bel himself had stuck His trident through it, but he would live. When he was able he rose shakily and took himself to the fire where dinner was cooking. In his pan, he saw, and from his provisions.

The young man stirring the unappetizing mixture he had put together seemed to divine his thought. 'You don't mind?' This time he spoke in Rhutan, his accent was surprisingly good for one from the plateau.

'That's all right.' Tranche eyed the skillet. The dark lumps looked like smoked meat mixed with dried grain and pulses. The grain hadn't been soaked and would never cook. 'That drink — where did you get the herbs?'

'Along the stream.' The lad ducked his head, not meeting his eye. He was slight and wiry in build with a watchful look about him. Tranche guessed his age at around fourteen summers, though there was an air of maturity about him that after a moment's study, and taken with the shadow of hair along his upper lip, had him revising the number upwards. His exposed skin was browned by weather and his dark hair fell to his shoulders. His clothes were worn: tunic, cloak and trousers all bore the stains of hard travel. His only ornament was the plain knife sheath on his belt and the common dagger, its handle bound over with worn leather, which filled it. Casting his eyes about Tranche noticed a bundle of belongings set against a rock together with the traditional hill bow and quiver of arrows. They rested, propped up close to hand, as though they held more value than the sheathed sword that lay below them.

'They did their work,' Tranche said, 'and for that and your help, I thank you. I am Trader Tranche, a merchant of Ripa, on my way home.' An idea was stirring in him. 'And you?' he asked courteously.

'Matto,' the youth muttered. He seemed reluctant to part with information, but the people from these parts were close-mouthed and clannish. Tranche guessed that those from his village, farmers at a guess, or shepherds, met few strangers.

'And where do you come from — or more to the point, whither are you bound?' Tranche squatted awkwardly, his belly in the way, holding his hands to the flames.

'Back there.' A jerk of the head that could have meant anywhere on the plateau. He said boldly like a challenge, 'I'm going through the pass.' He spoke as if it were the gate at the world's end, Tranche thought indulgently. The lad had probably never left his village before. Well, that should make things easier.

He took the plate handed to him and began to eat, scraping the almost raw grain to one side. 'Why's that then?'

Matto shrugged. 'The new taxes. My father died.' He spoke hardily but the merchant heard the pain behind the words and the spark of anger too. 'We worked the sheep but now there isn't even a roof.' There had been difficulty over the taxes then, and Temes' thugs had burnt them out, a common enough practice. Tranche's gaze slid to the bundle, likely all the lad had been able to save. 'So I'll try my luck in the Lower Land.' Matto chewed and swallowed, throat jerking as if he tasted nothing. 'They say it's a rich place.' He stared into the gathering dusk as if he could already see it: a land of orchards and cornfields, with coin for the making, and goods he could only imagine. Silks and spices and costly artisans' works — all there for the earning. 'You're from the city, you said?'

'Aye, but we have taxes too,' Tranche replied temperately. 'Ripa's not as wealthy as it once was. By Bel's scales, it's not! So — a shepherd. What would you do in the city, young man?' He needed the lad but it went against the grain to deceive him. He would be a fish out of water and very likely starve. If he wasn't robbed and killed first. Ripa had its share of desperate citizens these days and that was without counting Temes's troops. 'When did your father die?'

Matto laid down his spoon; his face was thin, Tranche saw and he had eaten with a controlled but voracious appetite. 'Two hands of days ago, I think. Some days I hunt, some days I travel; one loses track of time.' Eyeing the packs, or possibly the food within them, he added diffidently, 'I could drive the mules for you.'

'And when we reach the city? The only sheep there are in the hands of butchers.'

'I can read,' Matto blurted, 'and write. Our master tutored his son and had me taught as well. We were friends,' he explained, 'the son and I. And I cared for the horses too. He was generous — for an Appellan.' The last was said grudgingly.

'Aye. I saw you on the grey. An unusual skill for your race, to ride. But such a generous master would surely have helped you?'

'He — wasn't there,' his eyelids dropped and Tranche saw that this too was a grief to him. 'Things were different under the old king,' Matto muttered.

'And that's the truth,' the merchant sighed. He set aside his plate and seemed to make up his mind. 'How well can you use that bow?'

'Well enough.' Matto spoke hardily and treated him to a stare. 'The men of Ansham are known for their bow skills.'

'So I have heard. Well then, let us make a bargain. Travel to the city with me and use your bow should it be needed. A merchant is a target for every bandit ever born, and the gods know there have been plenty more made this last year. Protect me and my goods and help with the mules. I will feed you; and if your skills with a pen are as you claim, find work for you in my warehouse. What do you say?'

Matto's watchful face stilled in thought. He said cautiously as if it might cause the offer to be retracted, 'I have no horse.'

'Then I shall find you one though it may take a day or two. You were walking anyway,' Tranche pointed out. 'Can you not walk and lead a mule? It will be safer for us both to travel together. The man I was with stole from me else I would not be alone now.'

Matto asked curiously, 'Is the road so very dangerous?'

Like all traders Tranche knew when truth served best in a deal. 'Put it this way: I would sooner the presence of your bow than your help with the mules. And you have seen how needful that is. So, are we agreed?'

'Yes,' Matto said and the deal was struck.

***

Later, lying awake conscious of the night sounds, with the dying coals a ruby wink in the blackness, Tranche wondered at the wisdom of his decision and if he would wake to find his throat cut. He dismissed the idea as fanciful. He was just a boy, for Bel's sake, no older than his own son would have been had he lived. But so were many of the cut-purses haunting the alleyways in Ripa. Any one of them would kill a man for the contents of his pocket. He wished he could hear some sound from his companion who obviously wasn't a snorer — unless he too, was lying awake? To do what? Tranche snorted to himself; this was ridiculous. If the lad had wanted to steal he could have taken the lot while Tranche lay unconscious. He hadn't, so why should he now? Dismissing the matter the Trader heaved his sore body over onto the other hip and composed himself to sleep.

The youth calling himself Matto also lay awake but he thought only of the morrow. He couldn't afford, he told himself, to look back. That life was over and would forever remain so. Henceforth he must become what he claimed to be, forgetting all that had gone before. Staring up at the stars he realised that, save perhaps for Arn and a few of the Old Race, everyone he had known was now dead. It was up to him now to make his own way into the future. At the moment survival was his only aim, but in time, when the rawness of grief had passed, he must find a profession that would allow him to earn his own bread.

He wasted no time on futile dreams of revenge. Temes had won, as he was always bound to do, and there was nothing a simple shepherd boy of Ansham could do about it, except to forget. Rage was useless. Better to start another life in the new persona he had chosen and let the gods take care of vengeance. He watched the uncaring stars until his keen ears picked up the quavering call of a wild dog, then pulled the blanket over his head to block the sound. The heartsick loneliness of it was too close to his own state to bear.

***

Next morning they made a late start and a necessarily slow stage. Matto walked and led the second mule and, slightly to Tranche's chagrin, had little trouble with the animal. The youth paced along steadily with a hand on its neck while the other held the strung bow, its arrows bobbing in the quiver slung across his back. He spoke little but his eyes constantly quartered the countryside. If he was surprised by their leisurely pace he didn't show it, accepting without question whatever Tranche told him. He had plainly taken his master's warning of bandits to heart, keeping a hand on the bow at all times, which, Tranche thought, could be a problem. He cursed himself for overplaying the need for protection and plotted a way to get hold of the quiver. Damage seemed the surest means and when they stopped for the noon meal he directed Matto to unpack the smaller mule.

Matto laid aside his weapons and turned to obey. Tranche had the small blade ready in his hand and it took only seconds to cut through the tough stitches holding the bottom of the quiver together. As soon as it was lifted the arrows would fall through the opening and he'd get his chance. Tranche's hand brushed his breast where the package rode against his heart. Given a few minutes alone with a needle and it would be safe from discovery, even if he was forced to strip at the guard-point — and Bel knew it wouldn't be the first time even traders had been put to that indignity. If they could take our skins, they would. Luka had said that when one of their young traders returned 'taxed' of more than half his merchandise at one of the many guard-points along the royal road.

The stratagem worked perfectly. When the meal was over he stood saying. 'I'll pack up; take the grey to the stream. He didn't drink this morning.'

Matto nodded lifting the quiver belt. Arrows showered through the slit in the bottom as he exclaimed, 'Asher's balls! What —?'

'Let me see.' Tranche wrested it from him. 'The stitches have gone. Go on,' he nodded at the horse, 'get him watered. I'll fix it. I'm a seaman and I never travel without my sewing kit.' He winked at the lad saying jovially, 'Canvas and stitching, that I understand far better than poxy mules.' Unrolling his kit as he spoke he dumped the remaining arrows then glanced up, raising a brow. 'You still here?'

Matto went; by the time he returned the package was stitched securely into the bottom of the quiver. Tranche had replaced the arrows and handed the item over saying mildly, 'Perhaps you should check your gear more often. What if they had spilled like that during an ambush?' Then partly to keep the lad off balance but also because he was curious, he added, 'Do you always swear by the Appellan god?'

'What? Oh,' Matto reddened, silently cursing the slip. 'Habit. My friend — Ninnik,' he plucked the first Appellan name he could think of from the air, 'always did so. I — it is best for those of my race not to use the Goddess's name because officially you know, She doesn't exist.' He spat to add emphasis to anger. 'Asher is a name, not a god.'

'An opinion you would be wise not to voice in Ripa,' Tranche said sternly. 'Remember that if you are to work for me. There one can be made to suffer for anything the king's guards think displeasing to Appella. A muttered curse will do it, a lack of respect, a proud look. Nor does it stop at the guilty party. A warehouse could be emptied to pay for a slight offered by an employee.'

He saw the young man's eyes widen at that and nodded for emphasis. 'We live in difficult times, Matto. See that you don't forget it.'

'Yes, master.' The lad dropped his eyes and satisfied his message had been received Tranche clapped his hands.

'Good. Let us go.'

They reached the inn, in reality little more than a peasant's dwelling providing coarse fare and roughly distilled drink, as the short day ended. There were no beds but the place ran a stable, which, for a fee, customers could share with their mounts. They also dealt in horseflesh, animals either lamed or otherwise injured on the road, which were cheaply acquired, then sold again for exorbitant sums. As a trader Tranche applauded the sentiment, but as a buyer his outraged cries could be heard all over the house before he finally settled on a scrubby hill pony.

The gap-toothed proprietor, grinning with satisfaction, offered to throw in saddle and bridle for a trifle extra. Tranche, wearing the martyred look of a man taken for his last coin, settled in to haggle afresh and eventually the deal was done. The pony had recovered from the stone bruise that had seen her left there and at dawn Matto was sent off to try her paces, and to prove she could actually be ridden.

'I have only this thief's word she has ever done more than pull a cart,' he scowled. 'If she is not dependable I'll have my coin back if I have to choke him for it.'

The pony had a woolly brown coat, stubby ears and a quantity of shaggy mane and tail hair, but proved adequate to the task. Tranche, maintaining his scowl, stood watching. His business used many animals — camels, mules, horses — so the pony, though dear in his estimation, would be a useful acquisition. Matto might use her to deliver messages about the city. The lad hadn't lied about his ability to ride and he carried himself with a greater assurance than the trader had expected for one of his background. If he really could use that bow there might even be a place for him, in a year or two, with the caravans, which now more than ever, needed protecting. True, there had been bandits in the old king's day but half the damned population seemed to have entered the trade now, he thought sourly.

Of course the reason wasn't far to seek. What Temes couldn't tax he confiscated, with inevitable results. Desperate and homeless men were driven to banditry; it was that or starve and their families with them. Still, the worst of this road was behind him now. There were just the guards at the pass to survive, and the rest, as they said on the river, should all be downward sailing.

Matto returned with the pony as Tranche led the mules from the stable, both stretching their necks to lean back against their halters. The trader tugged and swore then the pony took over. She lunged at the jenny mule, ears laid flat, bared yellow teeth snapping at her rump. It was the end of their problems with the pack animals. Both were soon jogging along before the two riders as obedient as chastised children, lead ropes tied up and no thoughts in their head of stopping or straying.

'I would gladly have paid twice the coin had I known that of her,' Tranche said expansively, pleased with his suddenly enhanced buy.

They reached the pass a little before noon, a barren saddle between the peaks with a stout stone building huddled against the flank of the nearer mountain. The day was sunny but a cold wind blew, lifting the white of the permanent snow off the peaks, so that it streamed like smoke against the blue sky and black rock. The building, once a refuge for benighted travellers, had become, under King Temes, a tax station where impost was collected by the guards stationed there. It, and other posts like it on the old Rhutan borders, was manned by soldiers who, lacking the discipline of officers, set their own laws. They stole whatever they chose from the goods inspected, handing out a beating to anyone foolhardy enough to protest.

Tranche reined in just short of the post, while the grey's mane blew sideways and his own clothes were flattened against his plump form by the chilly wind. He eyed his companion who looked suddenly uneasy as if just hit by the realisation that he was about to leave behind all that he knew. Tranche wished the lad looked more the part of a servant, but a glance at his own person reminded him that he was none so smart himself. Catching sight of his ring he slipped it off and pocketed it. No need to make it easy for Temes's bloodsuckers.

'Right,' he said sharply. 'I want you to keep your mouth shut here. Just do as I say and ask no questions. Don't even think them. Act dumb. Unstring the bow too. The guards will not be civil. Annoy them and they'll arrest you, or beat you silly — whichever suits their mood. Got it?'

Startled, by the man's tone as much as his words, Matto nodded. 'Yes, sir.' This was an altogether different Tranche from the easy-going master of their brief acquaintance. The suddenness of the change required some mental adjustment.

'Good.' The trader dismounted, licked his lips nervously and pulled the tunic down over the roll of his belly. 'Drop the *Sir*, call me *Master* instead.'

'Aye, Master.'

'Very good.' At least the lad could follow instructions. Tranche wished his traitorous belly didn't roil so; he rolled his heavy shoulders and strode towards the building, hesitated, then pulled off his turban disclosing thin dark hair. The action seemed to drain his confidence and he shuffled through the door, head and shoulders down as if thinking better of his earlier decisiveness. Matto settled in to wait but Tranche reappeared almost immediately trailed by two tall Appellans, the closest of whom shoved him towards the standing mules.

'Boy!' The bluster of Tranche's tone couldn't hide his nervousness. 'Unpack the mule.'

Matto swung clumsily down but had scarcely reached the jenny when the guard said, 'That'll be mules, sonny. As in both.'

Mindful of his instructions Matto gaped at the man and Tranche's anger hit him like a flail. 'Must I tell you everything twice, you stupid lout? Do it.'

'Yes, Master.' He turned to the other mule, fumbling with the buckles but his slowness angered the guard. The moment the leather bags were off he upended them, showering the rocky ground with cutlery, pans and food. A loaf was mashed under his heel, the flour bag split and a crock of pickled vegetables smashed. Undeterred the second soldier repeated the action with the remaining bags despite Tranche's anguished cry.

'Oh, no sir, please. They will break — my treasures!' He wrung his plump hands. 'Please sirs, I beg you. They are valuable. Let me just find you one to pay the toll —'

'I reckon we can manage.' The larger of the guards grinned, picking out a fine looking dagger, a silver cup and a gold chain with a delicately wrought locket. 'Do for my girl, that.' He tossed it in his hand before pocketing it. 'See anything you fancy Tiv?'

'Reckon I'll have the silk.' His mate pulled a short length through his hands, examining it. 'Ain't enough for the king to miss. Still, oughta buy me a night somewhere cosy.' He stirred the remaining items with his foot. 'Right, toll's paid. Clean this lot up 'less you want a fine for littering.'

'Yes sir. Thank you.' Every inch of Tranche fawned as he bowed saying loudly. 'You heard the man didn't you, boy? You can't be deaf as well as stupid. Pack it up.'

The threat of the fine must have seemed real enough for he hunkered down to help, snatching up broken pots, pieces of wrecked mirrors and spilled dye, tumbling them anyhow into the leather bags. Finally they were done, the mules reloaded and on their way, the two riders jogging behind. Only then did Tranche re-don his turban.

'Don't look back.' He spoke peremptorily just in time to prevent Matto from doing so.

'Why not? You have paid the toll.'

'Which is not to say they can't, or won't, charge it twice,' the trader snapped. 'Did you see much of the king's tax-men in your village, wherever it was?'

'Not a lot,' Matto admitted cautiously.

'Perhaps they were lawful, considerate men, carrying out a distasteful duty?' Tranche suggested. 'Perhaps there were even records kept to ensure none paid more than their due?'

Matto was silent and Tranche went on, the words vibrating with anger. 'No? Well coin and goods are not all they rob us of. They take our pride and dignity as well. We are bled, then bled again. We subsidize the army's wages and fill the pockets of every corrupt bastard in the administration. If you cannot bring yourself to tremble and bow to them you are in for a world of trouble, young man. Remember that when you have more than two coins to rub together and begin to wish yourself back among your sheep.'

2

The pass was long and steep, the bare rock of the mountains edging into the narrow defile as if wishful to close it. Wagons, Matto thought, would have a terrible time getting through in either direction. The occasional scrubby growth clung in narrow crevasses where a handful of soil existed, and in one spot a brave collection of daisies spread gold against the dark stone, their petals shivering in the wind. It was easy to see how a blizzard would pack the narrow corridor with snow. One would be desperate indeed to attempt it then.

With the pass behind them Tranche relaxed and grew more expansive. There would be another toll to pay at the city gates he said, but that should be all — unless they had the bad luck to encounter a wandering patrol. 'Nothing they love more than the sight of a turban.'

'Then why wear it?' Matto asked reasonably. 'If it invites their attention. Do they treat all travellers so?'

'A tinker is as likely to be robbed as a trader,' Tranche admitted, 'but the turban is a form of protection too. A murdered merchant would cause trouble for them, the guild would see to that, whereas a poor man could be slain with impunity. Call it a form of insurance. Once you start at the warehouse you will be given an armband in our House colours. Be sure to wear it whenever you are abroad in the streets.'

He spoke of Ripa then, of its age and proud history

and once legendary wealth. 'That of course has changed now. It all goes to the king. The palace must be stuffed with gold. Our grain feeds his army while our own people go short. Oh, Temes encourages trade and the land is worked overtime, but when the harvest is good a greater share goes to the king. There are always shortages in the city. You will find yourself sadly mistaken in your dreams of an easier life, Matto. I tell no lie about that.'

'So it was better when Cyrus reigned?'

'Elsewhere, yes. Or so they say in the river cities of Appella, Byfield and Nandon for instance — but not in Rhuta. That's because Temes has governed there since our own King Waltu died. Was murdered,' he amended thinly.

'Yes? What happened?'

Tranche sighed. 'I believe the whole thing was engineered, though it may simply have been bad luck. Waltu's daughter was slain and the city blamed the Appellans. Fighting broke out in the city and a number of foreign troops were killed. The king tried to prevent the uprising, and then to protect his people and was accused of treason. Temes crushed the revolt and hanged the king, along with every male in the royal line. So he began his rule with terror and discovered that it works. Now nobody dares oppose him.'

After a moment Matto asked, 'And the queen — did she die too?'

'No. She has gone to live among my people. I was born a Laker, which is what we from the Lake Country call ourselves. She has no power of course but she has her life. Which,' he added grimly, 'is something, given the times.'

'I see.' Matto gazed across the peaceful countryside that just here was given over to orchards dressed in spring blossom, incongruous when viewed against the tale of bloodshed he had just heard. His grandmother lived then. Feeling something more was called for he said, 'But you don't forget.'

'Only a dead man could. Well, you have been warned, young man. Walk carefully in Ripa, speak softly, and whether just or not, pay what is demanded of you. It might not prove the life you have dreamt of, but it is life.'

'Yes,' Matto agreed soberly. 'Does the king permit worship here?'

'Not of the Goddess,' Tranche said directly. 'Her shrine has been torn down. Bel is the god of Rhuta. His temple rivals the palace for splendour. It is very rich — or was until the high priest was arrested. They let him go eventually, but not till his treasury was emptied. I doubt not it was well hidden but none can search like the City Guards.'

'What had he done?'

Tranche shrugged. 'Captain Onli, him they call the Butcher of Ripa, doesn't need a reason. He's head of the City Guards and his prisoners are taken to the Tower, a fortress built into the north wall of the city. Very few of those who enter leave it again, save to be hanged. Of course a high priest is different. Even Onli dare not try a god too far. Besides, why kill the man if he can be made to serve instead? They whisper in the city that much of the information laid against citizens comes from the Temple. Well,' he stopped himself, 'that's enough horror for one day. The times are bad but Ripa has survived for nigh on a thousand years, and not all her rulers can have been just men. We will get by too. Where did you learn our tongue?'

Matto froze for an instant. He had slipped insensibly into speaking Rhutan believing that the trader would have no more than a rudimentary understanding of the hill speech of Ansham. 'My mother,' inventing freely he twisted in the saddle to wave a hand behind him, 'she was from a village at the foot of the mountains. Her people cut her off when she ran off with my father, so I never knew them. I learned it at her knee.'

Tranche nodded. 'That's fortunate. You'll find few with the tongue of the Old Race in the city — save only we traders.' He eased himself in the saddle. 'We'll camp soon. Tomorrow night there'll be an inn, and by all the gods how I am looking forward to a proper bed again!'

***

Two days later they reached the bank of the Great River. It made the Witt seem a mere stream by comparison. Its broad surface sparkled in a sun so warm it was as if they had leapt straight into summer. Rich fields spread across the fertile plain as far as the eye could see. Matto, accustomed to the tiny areas farmed on the rocky plateau, stared in amazement at the springing green on the verdant loam, at the ranked orchard trees, and the long lines of trellised vines already cloaked in greenery.

'You could feed the world,' he declared round-eyed.

'Time was we did. The ships sailed up this river to load our grain, our wine, our oil, and brought back the wealth of nations,' Tranche said regretfully. He shook his head, sighing. 'I have been on such voyages, seen such cargoes brought safely home. There is little profit in it now and I fear more of the world goes hungry than is fed.'

His interest piqued Matto asked eagerly, 'What did you mostly deal in, Master?'

'Ah,' Tranche's sigh was pleasurable this time, 'marvels and the mundane both; that is a trader's life.' He spoke freely, needing no prompting. His work was his passion and Matto heard of shiploads of timber and grain, of salt and sea pearls, and silk and copra. Of ships ballasted with bricks of baked clay; of fur and leathers traded at great risk in the Grasslands by brother traders of the green turban; and of sea shells from Quade (items

Matto couldn't even imagine never having seen one) so fragile that they must travel packed in lamb's wool.

The merchant painted a vivid picture, rich with details of his own experience. He spoke of dangers encountered, of fortunes made, and lost. There were risks at sea as on land: pirates, storms, shipwrecks. Cargoes that went to the bottom with all hands, and others given up for lost that limped triumphantly home long after they had ceased to be looked for. Under the spell of his words the time sped by until the smudged smoke of the city's myriad chimneys became visible.

The river was busier by then, boats plying in both directions, dwarfed by the ocean going ship beating its way against the current, with the afternoon sun dazzling on its white sails. As they drew nearer, Matto saw other vessels under bare poles, warped hard against the docks on the far side of the river. By then the city was plainly visible, the glitter of its tallest edifice, along with the city wall, and the vast spread of buildings beyond.

'How do we cross that?' He nodded at the water roiling past the bank.

'There's a bridge. You will catch the mules and lead or drive them over but first pack your weapons away. Strap the sword under one bag, put the quiver in the other, and unstring the bow. None but the guards go armed in the city. Then follow me, do as I do and keep your mouth shut.'

Matto obeyed using the unstrung bow as a goad to drive the mules before him across the bridge and through the wide gate beyond. The merchant fished coins from the pouch at his waist for the black-clad Guards that pushed themselves off the wall to confront the pair.

'Humble thanks from his Majesty, mate,' the man shook the silver in his fist, 'but you're a bit short.'

'Four animals, two men — that was what I paid when I left,' Tranche replied.

'Toll's gorn up since. That'll be another silver. 'Course we could always take it in kind.' Grinning he nodded at the pack-bags. Stolid faced Tranche reached again for the pouch and then they were through, their mounts' hooves clattering on cobbles. Tranche turned the grey up the first street, cluttered with wagons and blank faced walls of clay brick, and nodded to Matto.

'Catch the mules. You'll have to lead them from here. It's down by the docks.'

Matto had never dreamed a city could be so large. He was to come to know Ripa well but that first day the busy warren of streets and alleyways, of industry and shanty homes that made up the sprawling docklands area staggered him. The afternoon was waning, the streets he traversed already in deep shadow, though far off towards the city centre he caught an occasional flash of sunlight from what he would learn was the roof of Bel's Temple. Little of its light however penetrated to the shadowy bustle around him, where wagons rolled by while men with barrows dodged about their heavy wheels, cursing the mules and their driver for impeding their progress. Boys darted through the throng, trays on their heads or message satchels clutched to their bodies; a cascade of barrels rumbled past like driven geese, two hefty young men directing their progress with kicks and sudden wrenches. The air was rank with the smell of mud, and tar and animal dung, and thick with the shouts and clanging and rattle of business being done and energy spent.

Space in the docks area was at a premium. Warehouses jostled cheek by jowl, their capacious reach jealous of every foot of land. All were walled with a guard on the gate, each with its own dock for shipping and stable areas at back for livestock. Their own operation, Tranche said, had land beyond the city wall where their riding mounts and pack animals could spell between journeys. Matto's first task tomorrow would be to take the mules thither.

'Somebody will go with you,' he added, 'and show you the main routes through the city.'

'Yes, Master.' Matto had a more pressing problem. 'Where will I sleep tonight? I have no coin for an inn.'

'I'll sort something,' the merchant promised. 'Here we are at last!' He greeted the man on the gate as it was swung wide before them. They passed through into a broad receiving yard bustling with noise and movement. Matto gazed around as Tranche stepped heavily down from the grey. A ship warped to the dock for loading moved gently in the current, a pelican perched on its forecastle.

There was a wet smell of fish and mud and rot, and a skinny cat streaked along the riverbank with a fish head in its mouth. The warehouse was vast, a sign: Luka and Tranche, Merchants was fixed above open doors wide enough to take a wagon, the inner space large enough to turn it in. A hammer clanged repetitively in the cavernous depths while bagged grain was being loaded onto the ship. Nearby a team of heavy-footed horses waited patiently in their chains, their dung adding to the aroma of the area.

A sudden yell of alarm from within the warehouse brought Matto's head around to see three men gesticulating wildly and shouting directions at each other as they attempted to corral something he couldn't see. Tranche swore in a resigned way and rubbing his buttocks went off to investigate, calling a brief order over his shoulder as he did so.

'Unpack them. Bring the bags into the office.'

A thin youth, who introduced himself with a sniff as Fatch, came to help. He wore a blue armband and glanced disdainfully from close-set eyes at Matto's ragged clothes and broken boots.

'What are you then — a beggar? Where'd he find you?'

'In Ansham,' Matto said peaceably. 'I was a shepherd. Master Tranche has given me a job here.'

'Yeah? The only sheep here are yokels like you and they soon get fleeced.'

'Leave him alone, Fatch. Hi, I'm Banco.' A second youth hoisted one of the bags onto his shoulder. 'Grab the other one. The office is this way. Don't mind Fatch, he was born quarrelsome. So you're from the Upper Land? Funny, you look like a Rhutan to me.'

'If you're a fair example then most of us do,' Matto replied. 'How long have you worked here? Is it a good place?'

'If you get apprenticed, yeah. I am. When I get my license from the guild I'll be a trader — a green though, I'm not going for the blue, I get sick at sea. I'll be set for life then. What about you?'

Matto shrugged. 'The master didn't say anything about an apprenticeship. How long is that?'

'Five years.' Leading the way into a room full of desks and crowded shelving he dumped his load, waited till Matto had placed his bag tidily beside its mate, then headed back to the yard. 'Course, not every apprentice gets to be a trader; you have to go before the Merchant Guild to get your license, and they're tough. If they pass you you get your turban. I've got two years to go still.'

'I see.' Matto wondered if he could ask Tranche to apprentice him. He could become a trader, earn his living while seeing the world; the idea held an irresistible appeal. 'Well, I'm here to run messages and work at a desk. Who normally does that?'

Banco shrugged. 'Me, Fatch, anyone spare.' He looked his companion up and down. 'You can't go dressed like that though, not if you belong to us. The city is — well it isn't a sheep field. I could lend you another tunic, if you like, while you get that one washed.'

'Thank you,' Matto said gratefully as they gathered up the second mule's load. 'What was that you were chasing before, the three of you?'

'Oh,' Banco started to laugh. 'It was a bird, some great thing like a stork, all pink. Two of them came on the ship. Someone in the city wants to breed them, I think; probably for the king. The hinge broke on the cage and one escaped. Haran was furious! He said we'd get a beating if it got away. It shat all over a bale of silk. He was mad about that too. And every time we grabbed it more feathers came out. Look,' he pointed to tufts of them littered pinkly across the floor. 'You should see it now, no tail, half plucked and a beak like a bent hook, though I think that's natural...'

Tranche's appearance cut the story short. 'Stable the mules, Matto and the pony,' he directed. 'Banco will show you. See there's feed for them. Then come back to the office.' Somebody had already taken the grey away.

'Yes, Master.'

The trader watched the lad take up the lead ropes while Banco gathered the pony's reins and led the little procession away. He returned to the office where his partner awaited him. A short, slim man twenty years his senior, Luka first shut then locked the door behind Tranche. He seldom wasted words and didn't now.

'What've we got?'

Tranche was already opening the leather pack-bag. He spilled Matto's arrows across the desk then inverted the quiver to show the false bottom he'd stitched into it. Two quick nicks with his hand knife released the inner piece and the wash leather bag dropped onto the desk. Loosening the string that held it closed he tipped the pearls into his plump hand. They were of outstanding quality, as one would expect Luka thought, beautifully graded, glimmering softly in the fading light.

He nodded. 'A fortune's worth, but if Sarn knew it means the risk has doubled.'

'I'm aware of it.' The fat trader looked ill. Now that it was over his hand trembled as he fed the pearls back into their bag. 'How soon can the Pride leave?'

'Three days, if the wind is right. We'll not hold them

a moment longer than we must.' Luka set hands to the desk. 'Help me. That lad will be back soon. Who is he? What are we to do with him?'

'I promised him work. He says he's literate and he seems quick enough. A shepherd. His father taxed out of his livelihood, possibly slain, though he wasn't clear on that. We're short a man, and a horse and saddle,' he grumbled remembering. 'He can't be any worse than that thieving bastard Sarn.'

Between them they shifted the heavy desk to come at the safe-box below the trapdoor in the floor, then shifted it all back again. Tranche groaned as he rose from his knees, set a hasty couple of stitches in the quiver and tidied it back into the pack-bag. 'Next time we find another method of delivery. I'm going home. Send the lad over when he returns, Eda can feed him tonight.'

'I'll see to it.' Luka clapped his shoulder affectionately. 'Get you to your dinner and bed, my friend. You've more than earned it.

3

His master's home, Matto discovered on following the older partner's directions, was not in the city's centre but in a neglected looking street behind the warehouse. There was no garden, just a wall around a plot of barren ground with a small dwelling within. Here in its bare, neat rooms Matto was fed by the housekeeper and later slept fitfully through the noisy hubbub that continued far into the night. Lights and drunken voices coursed through the lanes and alleyways from the many sailors' taverns. Dogs barked, somebody screamed — a sound that brought him from sleep to a shivering crouch in the darkness reaching for his unstrung bow before he remembered that his arrows were still back in the mule's bags. Towards dawn there came a low grumbling sound he would later identify as coming from a string of camels yarded up at the back of the stables.

The room he slept in was bare, the windows unshaded by blinds or drapes. Eda cleaned and cooked it seemed, but it was plain that no woman lived on the premises. The table at which Matto had eaten was cluttered with papers and old quills, the mess held down by a horseshoe worn thin and shiny from use. An empty wine flagon served as a doorstop and boots were tossed in an untidy pile in the entrance way. A wife, Matto guessed, would have changed all that, so there couldn't be one. He was grateful for the kindness of the bed and meal. And the small sum Tranche had advanced him to repair his wardrobe.

'We cannot have you dressed like that. Our men stand for the business. Get one of the apprentices to show you where to go and what to buy.'

'Thank you, Master. I'll look for lodgings too; if I may take the time?'

'You can spend your first few days here,' Tranche said. 'The gods know I am seldom home and the city is no place for green lads. Best find your feet first.'

Matto had flushed at that but had sense enough to recognise good advice when it was given, and to take it.

***

Over the next dozen days Tranche found himself well satisfied with his new employee. He was quick and intelligent, and considering his background, amazingly literate. He spoke well too; and his manners had not been learned in a shepherd's bothy. Tranche, hovering between caution and suspicion pondered these facts, weighing them against the lad's account of his Appellan benefactor and the sheer happenstance of their first meeting, then dismissed the matter.

Such attributes could only be an asset to the business; besides Matto's interest in his work was real; he copied and filed quickly and neatly and aboard the brown pony, clattered about the city delivering messages and bills of lading to customers, and carrying back orders word perfect to the office.

Keeping a discreet eye on his recruit Tranche also approved his frugality, though the lad had no coin to waste at present, and good sense. He kept away from the taverns frequented by the soldiers, and behaved as obsequiously as anyone could wish, when accosted by the City Guards. They liked to bait the young ones, the merchant knew, but Matto was unfailingly patient and polite in his responses. His good sense showed itself also in his choice of companion, the older of the two apprentices who, on one of his rest days had shown him about the city. Matto had returned full of it that evening, with a great number of questions about the god's temple which he had visited, and the palace that they had rowed past.

'None of us see the inside of it these days,' Tranche observed. 'Time was the Guildmasters of every guild did. They formed part of King Waltu's Council. None enter now save Temes's people, and slaves of course — another practice the city never knew before. If you are curious about our royal master you will have your chance to see him at the River Festival.'

Matto paused his fork. 'What's that?'

'A religious observance. The king's barge leads a procession of boats up river on the day of the summer solstice. To celebrate the gift of the river. This year there will be a fee for each boat.' Tranche's lips twisted. He was a natural actor and his malleable flesh and soft, doe eyes spoke volumes more than his tongue. 'So naturally all the guilds are obliged to enter. In the old days we drew lots to host the day. We'd deck the boats with flowers and bunting while the high-priest blessed the water on which the fields and the commerce of the city depends. All the guilds held their own feasts with music, and bonfires. There'd be dancing in the streets...' He smiled nostalgically. 'It was a day for hand-fasting. Many couples made their vows at the River Festival.' His smile vanished and abruptly he pushed his plate aside. 'I doubt it will be so this year.'

'Not with the City Guard,' Matto agreed.

The lad was quick; you never had to spell things out for him. None spoke openly of the Guards' practices but all felt the threat of their presence. And somehow, despite this absence of talk, stories of Captain Onli still circulated. Everybody knew that torture was commonplace in the Wazzit Tower, that grim fortress on the north wall. And they knew that the king placed no restrictions on his Guards' behaviour; that even wellborn young women could vanish off streets the Guards walked and never be found again for all their family's wealth (however reduced these days.) Even that when some unfortunate died in the Tower, Captain Onli threw back his head and bayed, like a mad dog, at the moon...

True or vastly exaggerated the whispers added to the city's unease. Doors were bolted at dusk, and those lacking doors to close behind them sought the company of their fellows in alehouses, often no more than a roof with a bar crammed beneath it. No, Tranche thought, there would be few Ripans eager to light bonfires, or dance the night away in the streets this summer.

The Festival duly came and went, a poorer showing than the previous year, the merriment more manufactured than genuine. Luka and Tranche's boat was well back in the flotilla, modestly garbed out with goods from their warehouse, cotton in place of silk, wood where silver had once shone. The partners stood on the foredeck along with the House Traders, Haran, Jensa and Ramie, and a handful of business friends not obliged to provide their own vessel. The apprentices, Matto, and the rest of the workers filled out the seats behind.

The river was choppy in the wake of the other boats, and the wind blew strongly, fluttering the bunting, which, Tranche saw with mild irritation, was getting soaked. When, the priest's part completed, the king's barge turned to sail back past the convoy the huzzas, as each boatload snatched off their hats, sounded forced and thin. He saw Matto staring, forgetting, or perhaps unaware that he was expected to cheer, but it hardly mattered, unless an informant was watching, for the king wasn't. The lad stared hard at the royal profile but when majesty did glance their way Matto had turned away. Another breach of protocol that Tranche should mention to him but probably wouldn't. He himself gazed stolidly back until the gilded barge had passed, his mobile actor's face blank.

***

The original few days of Matto's stay were long past but Tranche made no mention of it and so he continued to live in the bare little house until both had insensibly come to accept the arrangement as permanent. Several times Matto had offered to find a room elsewhere but nothing had come of it; either the rent was too high for his wages, or the distance from the docks made it impractical. Listening to him explain his third failure to find somewhere else, Tranche had shrugged over his papers.

'Don't worry about it. Your being here doesn't bother me, nor is Eda complaining. Stay, unless,' he cocked an enquiring eyebrow, 'you want to go?'

'No, Master,' Matto said. 'I am more than happy, only I don't want favours. The rest of them must pay rent and I —'

'That's easily fixed,' Tranche interrupted. 'I'll dock your pay a suitable amount. Will that content you?'

'Yes, thank you.' Matto, having listened to Banco's grumbles about the cost of rent in the city, felt happier. He needed to fit in here and was aware that his apparently favoured status had made him a target for resentment among some of the single workers. Fatch, for instance, who had never needed a reason to dislike him. From the start Matto's industry had shown the other up, and that he had a neater hand and a quicker intelligence didn't help either.

Fatch had a poor memory for orders and prices, and Matto's dockets and loading manifests were always legible, which could not be said of the hen tracks the other youth produced. The apprentice seldom missed an opportunity to sneer, his jibes mostly aimed at the slavery status and ignorance of a race whom he referred to as sheep-shaggers.

'Squatting on a hill watching sheep, that's all your lot's good for. Not surprising really they get round to shaggin' 'em. I suppose they'd die of boredom else. What d'you call a city where you come from, boy? Three huts and a privy? Bet you'd never ever saw a cobbled street till you got here.'

His close-set eyes gleamed with spite and something close to hatred. Matto sighed. It was Bart all over again, without the beatings. Banco remonstrated with his junior once or twice but it made no difference. 'Ignore him,' he advised. 'He knows you're already better at the work than he is. It's jealousy, that's all. He probably also knows he'll not get his turban and he's taking that out on you. Pay him no mind.'

Matto heeded the advice though he doubted it would make any difference. Fatch was a bully and a sneak, not above sabotage or tale bearing when he could manage it. Papers Matto had worked on had a habit of getting mislaid, and stock take numbers of warehouse quantities altered. The second time it happened Luka called him into the office, a scowl on his face, the offending list in his hand.

'It's not like you to be careless, Matto,' he said sternly. 'This won't do! We need an accurate count. The Guards have only to learn we are a box or a bale out and we'll have them in here performing their own stock take, and you know what that means.'

Matto did; it cost a merchant, on average, a wagonload of goods for putting the Guards to that sort of trouble.

Luka shook the paper angrily at him. 'You have added it thrice, and by my calculations none of the totals reached are correct. What is the matter with you?'

'May I see it, sir?' Matto seethed as he studied it, knowing instantly who was to blame. He said flatly, 'It is my list, I made it, but the figures have been altered. See here, I make my fours and twos differently to those. Somebody has sought to make mischief for me and replaced my sums with others of their own devising.'

Luka peered at the paper, then with a jerk of his head at his partner showed it to him. His eyesight, Matto realised, was no longer keen for it took Tranche but one glance to verify his clerk's claim.

'It's as he says. They've plainly been altered. Somebody is making trouble for the lad, or,' he chewed his lip and shot a glance at Luka, 'could it be something more? An excuse think you, for a raid? Do you have any idea who could be responsible, Matto?'

He shook his head; tale bearing wouldn't help. 'None. And I will make a practice in future of bringing such accounting straight to your desk, Master. I want no act of mine causing trouble for the House.'

Coming out of the office Matto saw Fatch hovering nearby. The other smirked at him as he went on his way affecting not to notice. Thereafter he was careful with his work, locking papers away in the files, or carrying them direct to Tranche's office. It didn't stop ink bottles upending themselves in his desk, or quills being unaccountably broken, but Matto, quietly mending the damage, told himself it was only petty spite. And the gods knew he had survived far worse in the world he had left.

***

A year to the day of his arrival in the city with spring again breaking across the land, Tranche offered Matto an apprenticeship. He had first talked the matter over with Luka, whom he knew disapproved of the fact that Matto still shared his home.

'I'm doing him no favours,' he said when Luka brought up the subject, as he knew the latter was bound to. Haran their chief trader was present also. 'He pays his way, and it's convenient for us both. He's a likeable lad with a good head on his shoulders. I admit I enjoy his company and Eda has grown fond of him too — he livens us both up.'

Luka said carefully, 'Of course you are lonely my friend, and your heart is empty. Surely after all this time you should look around you for a wi —'

Haran interrupted him, saying bluntly, 'He is trying to say that we don't want to see you hurt. What do you know of this young man anyway?'

'That he will be good for the House,' Tranche snapped. 'And before either of you go there, he is neither my catamite nor a substitute son! He has a good head for business and that is all that concerns me. As it should you. His training will recoup effort wasted on Fatch. He will fail the board as sure as sunrise! And that leaves only Banco unless we find another. So I am proposing Matto. If you have a better candidate now is the time to say so.'

***

He got his way and in due course Matto signed his articles. The lad seemed genuinely thrilled by the opportunity, however long and tedious the road to trader might be.

'It's five years,' Tranche had warned handing over the paper. 'That can be a lifetime at your age.'

Matto's thoughts however, had already skipped across them. 'I shall have twenty-one summers by then. Thank you, Master. Do apprentices go with the caravans as part of their training?'

'Of course. How else shall they learn? Banco

accompanies Haran on his next trip. Your turn will come, never doubt it.' He blew on the ink and folded the paper away then moved by a generous impulse, flipped a coin across the desk. 'Go to the temple and make an offering to mark the occasion. Be back here by the noon bell.'

Waving off the lad's thanks he settled back to his paperwork, one ear cocked to the clamour of the yard where a wagon was loading, while a Guard, shadowed by Luka's unyielding presence, inspected the cargo that had come ashore that morning. The House would be robbed by the duty imposed of course, but that was a merchant's lot these days. Not, he thought indulgently, that it would worry the lad. It was something he himself had almost forgotten — the simple enjoyment of small things. An outing, a break in the day's toil, perhaps even (one couldn't be sure with boys) the spiritual balm that reverence could bring.

***

There was no thought of reverence in Matto's mind. For all he had lived a year in the city it was only his second visit to the temple of Bel. It was strange now he came to think of it, but the Goddess had not come to him once since his arrival in Ripa. He wondered if it meant that She had no power where another god ruled, or simply that She had found a worthier vessel and he no longer mattered to Her. The thought piqued him but only a little. He was Matto the shepherd lad who, against all odds, was now firmly set on the path he had chosen; a freedom beyond the reach of princes.

He dutifully bought an offering with the coin Tranche had provided, then toured the temple, studying the images of the god, eyeing the giant tapestries his mother may have worked on, and observing the movements of the red-robed priests. Duty done he made his way back

40

to the docks and while short-cutting through the alley that ran behind the stables met Fatch, barrowing a load of manure and dirty straw, on his way to the midden on the strip of wasteland at the alley's end.

Fatch seemed always to assume that his seniority granted an automatic superiority over younger or unapprenticed workers, but one glance at his scowling face warned Matto that he'd heard of his promotion. He spat, 'You sneaking little weasel! So that's why you're his bum-boy, eh?'

Matto stopped dead. He said disbelievingly, 'What?'

'You think we couldn't work out why the fat man kept you in his house? Right handy to his bed, weren't yer? Usual practice where you come from, is it? Change from sheep I reck —'

In the back of Matto's mind a voice rasped, *What are you waiting for, lad? That's a weapon you're holding. Use the bloody thing!* Rissak. Well, he had no weapon save his fists but they, coupled with rage, were sufficient. Fatch, approaching the end of his apprenticeship had twenty summers, and though his weedy frame was wiry from work in the yard, he had never drilled with a weapon. Matto hit him before he finished speaking, and again while he gaped in shock. Blood spurted from his nose and a tooth gashed Matto's knuckles.

'Keep your filthy tongue to yourself,' he hissed, 'or next time I'll cut it out. You hear me?' He gave Fatch a violent shove that sent him staggering into the barrow, which tipped beneath him, landing him in the dung and scrapings of the stable. Glaring, Matto pulled down his tunic and stalked away. Swearing obscenely the other rose slowly and aimed a furious kick at the barrow. Part of his ire was directed at himself that he had neither said a word, nor lifted a hand in his own defence. But who knew the sheep-shagging foreign bastard would go off his head like that? He had seemed an easy mark, willing to let anything pass. Fatch sniffed blood and spat, vowing to make the little turd wish he'd continued that practice.

***

Banco left with Haran for Meddia, much to Matto's envy. The caravan carried salt, and great rolls of dried fruit: plums, peaches, apricots from last summer's harvest, as well as ceramics and woollen goods. Meddian sumpter laws were strict, Tranche explained, there would be no call for silk or luxury items, though the Meddians mined and exported high quality jade and ingots of raw tin. The fact was no secret, so the guards that accompanied the caravans were doubled on trips to the northern kingdom. Every destination was different, which meant the successful trader must balance cargo and travel requirements to the needs of customers, and the terrain involved.

Without his friend's company the time that was Matto's own dragged. He sought permission to take Wren the brown pony, out on his own account, and after several false turns found his way to what had been the goddess's shrine beyond the city wall. Nothing was left of it save an obstinate seep of moisture forcing its way through the mound of smashed rubble atop where, Matto presumed, the spring had once flowed. Yellow bindweed was growing over the piled stone, the delicate flowers a counterpoint to the savagery that had destroyed the holy place.

The destruction angered him, the emotion forcing open the door on the past that he had hitherto kept tightly shut. Next time he had a spare half-day he took a ride up river, hiring one of the many boatmen that plied for trade from points along the city-side bank. Russa was a river rat, one of the many young men from the shanties in the poorer part of the city earning a precarious living on the water; passenger or cargo, it made no difference to him.

'Where to?' he asked, spinning the boat about with a careless oar. "S double going upriver, mind.'

'I don't mind,' Matto said. He sat silent throughout the ride, gripping the splintery gunwale as Russa drove the boat upstream. It plainly needed effort against the current and Russa didn't rest on the oars for fear of losing the headway he'd gained. They moved away from the sprawl of the docks, following other craft tracking sluggishly upstream, passing those moored to stout posts or pulled up into river mud. The waterway was huge; Matto appreciated just how huge as he was rowed beneath the bridge and came eventually to a more peaceful stretch of bank backed by trees, and the shape of a large building.

'Is that the palace?'

'Yeah,' the boatman grunted, "tis.'

Matto eyed it carefully, studying the details of its facade. He now recognised palms, and seeing their upright form as they had appeared in his vision, looked for the terrace where he had glimpsed Taba and his mother. He had been born in that palace, he reminded himself as the walls slid slowly by. Seventeen generations of his family, which no longer existed, had lived in it.

There! Just where the steps jutted onto the bank was where the kingfisher had flown up with the fish in its beak. He listened raptly as if he might still hear an echo of girlish laughter, but there was only the slap of water against the hull, and the slow creak of the oars. At least his grandmother still lived, even if he could never know her. He —'

'How far we goin'?' The boatman broke into his thoughts. 'O'ny I want to see some coin up front 'fore too much further.'

'Not that far.' Matto rallied his wits. 'In fact anywhere here will do.'

'You mad?' Russa stopped rowing to look at him. 'There's a whole comp'ny of Guards in there and they don't care none for trespassers. Be the Tower if yer caught anywheres round there.' He jerked his head at the bank.

'Oh — well, further along?'

'Barracks,' the man said succinctly. 'Beyond that the on'y place you can land is outside the wall.'

Matto bowed to the inevitable. 'All right then, take me back.' There were two landward gates in the city wall but using them was always a gamble depending on the temper of the Guards posted there. It might cost a copper coin or, on a different day, a manhandling by someone resentful of his duty.

The boatman swung his craft about. 'New to the city, ain't yer? Talk like you come from up along.' The tilt of his head indicated the distant mountains. 'Plenty o' your sort come, thinkin' the livin's easier in the city, but it ain't. I'll tell yer that for free.'

'No,' Matto agreed. 'You're right about that.'

4

Spring rain swelled the Great River, flooding the fields outside Ripa. The froth of orchard blossoms sent the bees delirious, while fishermen pulled long faces over empty nets. A furious river, turgid with mud, didn't help their catch. Some, as they did each year, hired themselves out as farm laborers, while others turned to ferrying boatloads of firewood to the city. It was an enterprise laden with hazard given the state of the river and, as usual, a few paid with their lives. In the taverns where soldiers and the City Guards drank there was renewed talk of war with the Black Country still stubbornly refusing the overtures of King Temes to open its borders to trade with its powerful neighbour.

South-east in the Grasslands the barbarians were stirring again, moving out in waves from their winter camps onto fresh spring pastures. When their horses strengthened the border raiding would begin. Meanwhile Temes made his dispositions that would serve both to contain them, as was necessary, and at the same time purge the army of those elements he saw as being least loyal to himself.

He had already got rid of most of his father's generals and now dispatched company after company of what had been the King's Own to the frontier with orders to pursue, engage and destroy the enemy. The youngest of Cyrus's generals, recognising the order for the death sentence it was, dared to question it. He was arrested, stripped of his rank and hauled in a metal cage to the edge of the Seas-of-Grass to await his fate, as a way of encouraging obedience in his men.

Banco, with the Meddian trip under his belt, went south that spring, again with Trader Haran, leaving an envious Matto and a furious Fatch behind. Fatch's apprenticeship was over; the Merchants' Guild had denied him his turban and he had become just another yardman at the warehouse, hoisting bales from the bowels of ships, rolling and stacking barrels, and mucking out the stables. Matto himself, as the green of spring turned to the dust and rising heat of summer was, though only in his second year, thrilled to be detailed off to accompany a caravan to the Lake Country.

Well, caravan was pitching it a bit high, he thought. Call it twenty mules led by Trader Ramie and the journey no more than ten days. The cargo was grain (mules were as strong for their weight as camels), pottery and salt. Not the most exciting stuff but trade was the lifeblood of nations, and men needed more than silk and precious gems for daily living. He accepted that, as he did his own quite minor role in the caravan.

'We're not expecting trouble,' Tranche though still looked worried. He rubbed his fleshy face and sighed. 'But there are poor men out there. Desperate men,' he amended. 'Every day it seems more are being squeezed from their livelihoods.' He sighed again. 'Well, we have families to provide for too.' He meant in the abstract, Matto thought, for as far as he knew Tranche had no one. 'So you will go along with your bow and I'll pray you return without finding the need to draw it.'

'Yes, Master.' Matto could scarcely contain his delight. The day seemed all at once brighter. 'Shall I take Wren?'

'Gods no! Ramie will have someone find you a horse. Give him your bow until you are out of the city, and again on your return. There'll be a City Guard riding with you.'

Matto stared. This was a new departure for caravans. 'Why?'

'The money is better?' Tranche suggested dryly. 'At least it is regular if he steals a bit each day. Well, he'll not get much benefit from this cargo, that is one comfort.'

They left on a bright morning that promised heat, clearing the city gates without undue delay. Ramie had a way with him, hailing the Guards with cheerful familiarity as he paid the toll, railing good-naturedly against the weather.

'Your mate back there is soon going to be wishing himself in your shoes, believe me. It'll be a scorcher today. I wouldn't object to a nice shady gate to sit in myself, 'stead of wearing my tailbone out dragging this lot around.' He flipped an extra copper to the closest Guard. 'Have a drink on me when your shift is done. Imagining it will cool me down.'

'Works for me,' the Guard grinned and waved them through.

It was a hot journey but Matto was acclimatized by now and heat didn't worry him. His exposed skin was as tanned as any of his countrymen. It was only the Appellans who turned red and broke out in rashes from sultry days when the sweat ran freely and not a breath of air stirred the somnolent city. The Guard riding with them grumbled all the way, his face burned crimson by the first evening. He complained about his posting and plainly preferred the easier duty of patrolling the city streets. Matto learned from his litany of complaints that though assigned the task by Captain Onli himself, the merchants were paying for his presence.

That first evening, with Tranche's words in mind, Matto took himself off a little way from the camp and set up a target. He shot off a score of arrows, grimacing when he missed. His aim was off; it had been a long time since he'd practised. Collecting his arrows he tried again; the light was going but his aim, he was pleased to see, had improved slightly. Three quarters of his arrows now quivered in the target, the rest having missed by the slimmest margin. Satisfied he unstrung the bow and walked forward to pull them free.

'That's nice shooting.' Ramie, unseen by Matto, had come silently to watch. 'Tranche said you were good.'

'And out of practice. There are men of my race who wouldn't have missed at twice that distance.'

'Well, that's good enough for me.' Ramie nodded at the bow. 'Have you ever killed a man with it?' he asked bluntly.

Matto stilled and forced his eyes wide. 'By the Mother! No, of course not.' He looked down at the weapon in his hand. 'We were only allowed it to defend the sheep. I have killed a wolf,' he lied, hoping he sounded like a vainglorious boy, 'and that is just as dangerous a prey.'

'I would argue with that,' Ramie said mildly, eyeing the bow curiously. 'And all the shepherds carry them? I wonder the king permits it.'

'Wool is the staple product of the high plateau,' Matto said. 'While there are wolves the sheep will need protection.'

Ramie laughed and clapped his shoulder. 'Spoken like a trader, lad. Let us hope we meet none of the two legged variety on this trip.'

He had his wish. The days passed uneventfully; Matto continued his evening practice but there was no call for his skill. They reached the last camping ground on the Lake edge on the fifth day, and spent another one there exchanging cargo, and seeing what little the country had to offer. It wasn't much. The lake system was vast but very little of it was visible for the water's surface was dotted with large floating islands of reeds. They grew as thick as the hair on a man's head, and more than half again his height, and were in constant movement, shifting about at the pull of the wind and hidden currents. The lake's edge was fringed with a band of stunted willows, and the only visible building was a sort of way station, half tavern, half warehouse, set opposite a small pier that jutted out into the lake.

Here they were met by three Laker men who oversaw the unloading of the cargo and spent several hours with Ramie in the smoke scented room of the tavern, dickering with the trader over their own cargo. Matto had wondered what the Lake Country produced that would interest Ripa. It proved to be tanned hides, and bales of soft, alpaca weave, and the smoked meat of the waterbirds that rose from the surface of the lake in vast quantities to wheel raucously against the sky. There were egret plumes as well, and jewelry made of tiny polished spiral shells. He saw it all back in the city for Ramie's trading was done in private.

Matto and the others, with half a day to fill, went swimming, save for the City Guard who baked on duty, hating the rest with his eyes as they splashed and yelled like children in the cool water. What he was actually guarding none of them could work out as he prowled about the tavern walls like a hungry dog convinced that the ones inside were getting his share of the meat.

The return journey was also uneventful. At the noon camp on the last day Matto surrendered his bow and quiver to Ramie and saw it packed away. The City Guard was saddle sore and pushed to the front of the caravan as the river came in sight. He was first across the bridge and through the gate, with a scowl for the Guard who inquired after his trip. He immediately peeled away from the column, heading back to barracks. Ramie shrugged as he paid the toll.

'He didn't seem to enjoy our company — or maybe it was the mules.'

'Maybe he's just dry,' the Guard responded. 'They drink water those Lakers, or grog?'

'If you'd call it that.' Ramie grimaced. 'Piss weak ale only. I tell you it'd be a penance to live there. Fish is all right in moderation but three times a day? I'm glad to be home.' He stayed chatting until the last mule had passed him then stretched himself. 'Right lads, have a drink on me.' Flipping them each a coin he said, 'I'm off to the Temple. Maybe Bel can arrange that my next trip's into Appella. At least the wine is potable there.'

He caught up with the heavily laden column before they reached the docks and stepped tiredly down from his horse, waving a sullen Fatch over to take the animal. Others came to unload the mules while they, with burdens removed, immediately sought a soft patch of ground in the yard on which to drop to their knees and roll, kicking their bodies over and back, before surging back to their feet. Matto, finished with the bags came to collect his bow that Ramie had tucked under his arm.

'I'll leave it in the office for you,' he said. 'Take the mules through to the stables first and give them a handful of grain. You did well, Matto. There mightn't have been any call for it this time but I'm thinking your shooting skill would make you a useful inclusion on some of our longer trips. I'll talk to the partners about it.'

Excitement coursed through Matto. He said, 'But I'm only in my second year. I thought apprentices had to wait until their fourth before they could travel with a real caravan?'

'That true, but I'm talking about guard work, not trading. Master Tranche might consider you too young, but there's no harm in asking. Off you go now.'

Treading on air, Matto went. He didn't mind the journeyman work in the office, or the physical labour and message carrying that the job entailed, for the promise of future travel made it all worthwhile. That such a time might almost have arrived was too wonderful to take in all at once. Of course it all depended on Tranche who had originally hired him as a guard anyway. He'd been two years younger then so he could scarcely cavil now at his youthfulness, Matto thought. Whistling, he slapped the closest mule's flank and herded them towards the stable.

Both Luka and Tranche were waiting in the office. Ramie nodded to them, locked the door behind him, then dumped the bow and unceremoniously spilled arrows across the desk.

'Worked like a charm,' he said. 'Mind, I was lucky at the gate both ways.' He pulled the lining up on the quiver and digging the tip of his dagger into the stitching, removed the gems. 'The coronation necklace,' he said, displaying it.

Tranche touched the chain of diamonds with one finger and drew an appreciative breath. 'Bel's revenge,' he breathed. 'That should buy a few swords.'

'Trouble is, gold's getting tight in the city,' Luka observed. 'I think when Haran brings his lot in we might have to look overseas for a buyer — if we're to get the value of the jewels, I mean.'

'We can't afford to accept less, but it's a risk. If the ship were lost...' Tranche paused. 'What about Matto? No problem there? He's quick, you know.'

'His first thought was for his weapon but I sent him off to stable and grain the mules. Told him I'd bring the stuff in and he could collect it later.'

'Let's get these out of sight then.' Luka laid hands on one end of the heavy desk and when Matto appeared to collect his bow he found the office door standing open and Tranche putting away his papers. Outside the wide stretch of river flashed beaten gold in the setting sun, with a foreground of silhouetted gulls topping the mussel encrusted posts about the dock.

Matto glanced quickly around. 'Trader Ramie has gone then?' He sounded disappointed.

'Mmn?' The merchant glanced up from his task. 'Oh, Matto, there you are. Yes, he went home. Your bow's in the corner there. Did you enjoy the trip? What did you think of the Lake Country?'

'There wasn't much to see. I thought there'd be a city on the water, or a town at least, but it was all reed thickets. Where do the Lakers live?'

'They're there,' Tranche assured him, 'just not at the lake's edge. You have to take a canoe and a guide. It's easy to get lost amid the reed islands. Originally they built on the water for defense; it's pretty hard to mount a cohesive attack on an enemy you can't reach, let alone find. The fact that the islands shift about in the current doesn't make it easier — or the size of the lake system. It's vast, you know.' He closed a drawer and turned, dusting off his hands. 'That's it then, time I was locking up. Captain Stark is due tomorrow; we had a bird from Deems to say he'd reached the port. So we'll be in for a busy day. Don't forget your bow. Off you go then. I'll wait and lock up. Tell Eda I'll not be long.'

***

For the first time that same year, the streets of Ripa saw occasional ragged remnants from the King's Own. There weren't many; most either still served or had died in the Seas-of-Grass. Some, whole companies it was said, had deserted and these faced death by hanging if they were caught. Those haunting the streets and taverns of the city however were the maimed and the sick, their soldiering days behind them. In King Waltu's time the temple had succoured the needy, but these men followed a different god. Neither Bel's priests nor His overtaxed citizens saw any reason to be charitable.

'Let their precious Light feed 'em if the king ain't about to,' was the wisdom of the taverns. 'They should go back to their own land.' Seventeen years of occupation, Ramie thought, hearing the growled agreement to this proposition, and the ordinary Rhutan had still not accepted the annexation of their country. It heartened him and he lost no time reporting the sentiment to the merchants.

'Talk is cheap,' Luka observed. 'There's a deal of difference between what you say to your mates and actually acting on it.'

'True enough,' the ever mercurial Tranche interposed, 'but for every three that say it there's one will really mean it. I think it's a hopeful pointer and we should maybe exploit the opening it offers, feed the resentment until it becomes hope.'

Luka shook his head vigorously. 'Not yet. It's much too soon. When the time and the weapons are ready, another two, perhaps three years... Let us not ruin everything through haste. Every man that knows is another mouth to blab and we must never forget Captain Onli, whose spies are always listening.'

Tranche shivered, his upbeat mood instantly dampened. 'Bel's curse on him and his works! I count myself as bold as the next man but the mere thought of Onli turns my bowels to water. May he burn forever in Bel's pit!'

'Aye,' Luka agreed soberly eyeing his fellow conspirators. 'We carry on as we are then, agreed? And it might be worth our while to check out these new beggars. There might be something we can use —'

Ramie frowned. 'Cripples? Those I've seen are well past wielding a weapon, sir. Of what use could they be? There is the question of loyalty too.'

'To whom? Certainly not Temes. If they can't fight themselves they still have experience and knowledge of how it should be done. These men were the cream of Cyrus's army, remember. Let me look into the matter. In any case they cannot be left to starve. Perhaps the other guilds could be asked for help there too?'

5

Banco returned, toughened and changed from his experiences, as autumn was fading into winter. His caravan had been all the way south to Port Chard, then on to the garrison city of Quade perched on the rocky shore of Belusia's southern-most point. On their return they had given the fighting along the border land (where heavy Appellan casualties were reported) a wide berth, heading instead up the centre of the country through the cities of Byfield and Nandon to the old eastern border of Ansham. From there they had travelled directly east to the port of Providence and followed the coastline, dotted with fishing villages and hamlets, north to Deems, and thence up-river to Ripa.

It had been a marvel of a trip, a real eye-opener, he told Matto over a tavern meal that first night, face flushed with enjoyment as he described the highlights to his friend. They'd been attacked twice by bandits, both lots being successfully repelled by their guards. The first had been a full ambush in hilly country where a man had no view ahead.

'Haran didn't hesitate,' he said admiringly. 'I never saw a string of camels quicker off their feet. The men had them down and their legs tied before you could blink. See, the thing is, if the first rush fails and you can get your men organised to defend your beasts — and believe me Haran can! — well the bandits' next move is to try running them off. You can't defend the main caravan and chase runaways at the same time. If they manage to get away with two or three camels, well that's success for them, and maybe, depending on the load, a damned disaster for us. It was an education for me to see a real trader operate. I mean it's no good learning to assess quality and barter for goods if we can't hold 'em, is it?'

Matto, who had been looking forward to speaking of his own journey, forgot about it. How could a mere trip to the Lake Country compare with what his friend had done and seen? He said, 'Was Haran happy with the trading?'

'He seemed so.' Pushing his empty plate aside Banco glanced across the lamp lit room with its low ceiling and smoky atmosphere and lowered his voice. 'It's getting tougher. The king really is squeezing the margins now. Every city there's a toll to enter, another to leave. Fees for setting up in the market squares, fees for grazing... About the only places you can get into, and out of, without paying are the little villages. Ansham was the best for that. They still stick to the old rules of hospitality. A couple of shepherds came into the camp one night bringing us a sheep for our meal to welcome us. Can you imagine that? In Ripa they'd be charging you for everything, including the bleat. And the gate tolls here are the steepest of all — for their own merchants! Haran's got a trick for that though, too.'

'What does he do?'

'Loads the really valuable stuff onto this cranky old bull camel. The handlers hate the old brute and with good reason. His bite could maim you. So when we got back we struck a pair of thieving Guards, not that that's so hard! They said they were gonna examine the loads, make sure we weren't smuggling. Haran just shrugged and let them at it. They got a couple of camels down and spread their bags about and all the while the traffic's building up behind us. The old bull was next. He changed their minds pretty quick, I can tell you.' He grinned, youthful face alight. 'He wouldn't kneel and kept moaning and slobbering, and snaking his head at 'em. In the end they gave up and let us through. Probably cost another silver but it was worth it.'

'What was his load — the bull?'

Banco's eyes glinted as he grinned. 'Jade from Media. We got it in Deems. I tell you Matto, I've learnt a lot from just one trip. You will too when your turn comes.'

In the meantime Haran had passed the contraband goods (rubies this time: necklace, tiara and ear drops) to the partners, saying cheerfully, 'It went without a hitch. I had salt and pottery on the first two beasts with just a little sweetener, a couple of really nice ivory boxes inlaid with pearl shell. We're seeing a lot of good stuff coming onto the market now times are so tough. Anyway the bastards took 'em but they gave up the quicker for it. Reckoned the old bull wasn't worth the risk.'

'I'll get a bird off, let them know they've arrived safely.' Tranche spoke from the floor beside the strong box as he stowed the goods away.

'And we'd best think of another way next time,' Luka suggested. 'They could have forced your men to unpack him.'

'Aye.' Haran's face sobered. The risks were never far from their minds. Tranche mopped his face at the thought and penned the message in a minuscule hand. They were careful but each conspirator was aware that a single tiny slip, just a breath of suspicion in their long game plan, could land them all in the Tower. It was, if you dwelt upon it, a paralysing thought. And a timely warning of the fact came next day when Matto, returned from delivering a message, all but rode down Haran as he emerged from the stables.

'Sorry, didn't see you there.' The lad was pale as if in the grip of shock. His hands shook as he busied himself unsaddling Wren and putting her into her stall. He dropped the bridle and seemed to take a long time picking it up. It was odd behaviour for one usually so composed and Haran's attention was caught. He propped himself in the doorway and watched the youth dip feed for the manger.

'That's too much oats,' he said mildly, 'you'll overheat her. What's wrong? Trouble with the Guards?' The lad should have the procedure off pat, the trader thought. Bel knew they had drilled it into all their staff. Be respectful, answer their questions, and hand over whatever was demanded.

Matto's jaw clenched. 'I just saw three men murdered. I was at the Smiths' Guildhouse picking up a letter of credit.' He looked vaguely at the satchel, its strap presently slung across the saddle seat. 'I'd not been there before; I didn't know that street takes you past the Tower. The Guards were bringing them out. Their hands were tied, and they'd been beaten to a pulp — they could scarcely stand. The Guards —' he looked sick, 'they threw them onto a cart, like they were sacks of grain, then pulled nooses over their heads. I didn't realise the ropes were tied to the gate lintel... It was all so quick. One of the Guards smacked his blade on the horse's rump and it jumped away. The men were pulled off the cart and left to swing. One of the Guards was laughing.' He patted the pony blindly, the only sound in the silence the crunch of grain between her jaws.

Haran said evenly, 'It's been going on for a while. I thought you'd have known. Temes put his stamp on the city when he took over from his brother, before the old king died. Those men probably spoke against him, or had something he wanted — daughters perhaps, or gold, or property. Or they might just have been Onli's victims; he doesn't seem to need a reason.'

Matto's quiet demeanour had vanished. His dark eyes blazed as he cried, 'They are Temes's subjects. A king has a duty to protect —' The vehement words were bitten off as he drew an audible breath. 'Sorry. I'm being naive, aren't I?'

'Idealistic.' Haran's tone was judicious. 'A bit odd, considering who you are.'

Cold touched Matto's spine. 'What do you mean?'

'Just that I thought the Old Race had no time for kings. Your grandfather would probably have spat on anything Appellan in a crown. My advice lad? Forget what you saw, you can't change it. And if you can't forget, a cup or two with a friend after work, usually softens the edge of memory.'

Haran left the stable in a thoughtful mood; the exchange had put to rest an unacknowledged doubt he had sometimes nursed about Matto. Spies were everywhere in the city and it wasn't to be supposed that the partners' business didn't harbour at least one. He wondered how, or if, he might discover the identity of the executed men. It probably wouldn't help, but in the deadly game they pursued against the crown you couldn't tell when even a name might prove useful. Someday, the gods willing and their luck holding, this city would rise against the tyrant oppressing it, for wronged men held long memories.

***

That evening, following his mentor's advice Matto joined Banco in the ale house behind the ships' chandler. It was a drinking place for sailors and river rats, more suited to their purses than the tavern two streets over that the merchants themselves tended to frequent. The walls of the house had shifted a little over the years, and the smoke blackened ceiling beams sagged in one corner, but the lights were well polished, and the food hot and filling.

The room was always well supplied with customers and loud with talk.

Matto gazed around to check that no guards were present then told Banco of what he had witnessed. For a little while they sat in silence considering the grisly tale. There was no point in words; talk wouldn't alter what had happened, or cure the cancer of Temes's deeds. Banco tapped his companion's hand bringing Matto back to the moment.

'Best forget it,' he said low voiced, lifting his tankard.

'I know.' He sought for a change of subject. 'Summer after next you'll be drinking with the traders. I'll have to find someone else to share a table with.'

'If I get my turban,' Banco demurred. 'It's no sure thing you know. The guild's standards are high.' He had grown taller and broader in the two years of their friendship. Sitting there in the neat apprentice tunic they both wore he looked a man grown compared to the unfinished canvas of his younger companion.

'You will,' Matto said. 'What then? Will you head off and base yourself somewhere south, or stay in the city?'

Banco eyed him. 'You seem very certain — have you heard something? What aren't you telling me?'

Matto flung up his hands. 'Nothing. If you weren't so dumb you'd know you'll make a great trader. So — will you stay? I shall miss you if you go.'

'Of course I'll stay in Ripa.' Smiling a little Banco turned his cup. 'I've met a girl. But keep that to yourself.' He flushed a little. 'If I get my turban we shall marry, but I haven't said anything to her yet.'

'Right.' Matto digested this. Banco was his elder by four years. He would have twenty-two summers when his apprenticeship ended; time enough to be setting up his household. His mother Matto knew, lived in the city, and there was a married older sister. Knowledge of his friend's plans made him feel suddenly very alone. Which reminded him of something Haran had said about Temes setting his stamp on the city. Banco would have been a child at the time but he must have heard talk about the deaths of Ripa's royals. Perhaps he could learn more from him than the sketchy outline that was all he he had ever heard of the fate of his family.

Repeating what Haran had said, Matto asked, 'What did he mean he put his stamp on the city?'

Banco glanced about. 'Not here,' he murmured, 'outside.' He drained his cup and stood. Matto followed him out, exchanging the smell of sweat and ale for the all-pervading odour of camels and molasses. A wagonload had been delivered that afternoon, and one of the barrels had smashed when it toppled from the vehicle. Banco began to walk through the moon shadowed street, his voice a murmur in the night.

'King Waltu's daughter was murdered. I had what? about five summers at the time so I don't remember much about those couple of days though the adults have never forgotten. The city was in an uproar — you have no idea Matto! Fighting in the streets, houses alight, soldiers smashing down doors... My mother and sister and I were in the cellar. My father's decision. We stayed down there for two days and two nights and when we finally came out he was dead. I remember my mother screaming and neighbours in the house...'

'Of course a great number of others were dead too,' he said flatly. 'That was the day Ripa changed. Oh, some will tell you it happened when Cyrus, the old Appellan king, rode through the city gates, but that's not true. Not wholly. Temes was responsible for killing our king, and for what followed too.'

'What happened with your father? Do you know?'

'He was caught up in the fighting, like so many others who died. He was a shoemaker,' Banco said bitterly. 'He belonged to the Leatherworkers' Guild. He had awls and knives; he didn't even own a sword, but Temes's killers cut him down regardless. Him, and bakers, and fishermen, and beggars, and water-carriers. They hewed their way through the city; then they hanged the king and his eldest son, and a few other men from the royal house, but that was only the beginning.'

'There was more?' Matto asked in disbelief.

'Aye, there was. Ripa was under martial law and things were very tense. The old Council was disbanded, some of its members, all influential men of course, arrested, then Temes declared an amnesty. There was to be a parade in the main square, and he'd address the citizens so no further misunderstandings could occur between them and his men. Our dead had been buried by then and business was resuming. Everybody thought it was over, that Temes's gesture was the beginning of a new stability. You don't have a royal house in Ansham so you probably don't understand how deeply we were affected by the loss of ours. They, the royals, were Ripa's, well Rhuta's really, stability. Waltu was a good king, law-abiding, just... While he reigned you felt that things were well — stable.' He laughed, an abrupt sour sound in the night. 'We none of us knew then how stabilizing a force terror could also be, you see.'

Matto swallowed. 'I don't think I'm going to like hearing this, but go on.'

'Nobody else will tell you,' Banco said. 'We don't speak of it to outsiders. It's the secret at the heart of Temes's grip on Ripa. I was there but I remember only the noise. My mother hid my face in her gown and covered my ears but I still heard. We had to attend because the soldiers came through the streets banging on doors, telling us to go. After what we'd already lived through nobody was arguing. Some, the more sanguine I suppose, saw the gathering as an opportunity, so there were food stalls and hand carts amid the throng, as if it were a festival we attended. A section round the central fountain had been roped off.' He stopped to clear his throat, pausing against a weathered post on the riverbank.

'The first comers moved into it, perhaps seventy odd people,' he said, voice suddenly husky, 'the rest filled the Processional Way and backed up through the streets. That was the first time any of us saw the City Guards. They were created that day. They marched into the square, the people shrinking back to let them pass. They positioned themselves about the roped enclosure forming a human wall and everybody fell silent as Temes began to speak.'

His voice cracked and he stopped, raising his face to the sky. 'It's harder than I thought, saying it. He said — that bloody monster said — of course I didn't understand at the time but my mother repeated the words to me years later, he said he didn't want to be unnecessarily harsh, so after the late disturbance, that's what he called it — the massacre of our citizens, the deaths of our royals — he was making an example to serve as a guide for us. Then he signalled the Guards who drew their swords and cut down everyone inside the rope. Men, women, children — every living soul. Sometimes I hear the screams still in my sleep. There was nowhere to run except at the guards, so they all died.'

Matto croaked, 'Merciful Mother! Why?'

'To teach obedience. He said some of us might feel we had a grievance but henceforth judgement would be the province of Captain Onli of the Guards — as it still is. As you have seen today.' He began to move again. They had long since passed Matto's turning and Banco lived in the opposite direction but neither fact seemed to matter.

Matto shook his head, mumbled, 'No wonder Haran told me to forget.'

'Yes. All Ripa remembers though, as we are meant to. And if you are ever tempted to forget then you may well be dragged off to face Captain Onli. And you don't even know the worst of it yet.'

'The worst? You mean there's more?'

Banco nodded grimly. 'It's never spoken of in the yard but Tranche's wife and son were inside the rope. It was put there to catch the more affluent citizens, those for whom the mob automatically make way. He only survived himself because he'd gone to a market stall to buy his son a drink, and he couldn't get back through the crush.' A dog snarled from the shadows and he looked around, suddenly aware of their surroundings — the gleam of water and the narrow street with black alleys leading off. A good place for knife-work and robbery. 'Gods! Where are we? I didn't realise — Come on, let's get back.'

6

Matto didn't leave the city again until the following year. He'd waited hopefully whenever a trading caravan left but Tranche never offered him the chance to join them. Then out of the blue one day his master announced that Captain Kcno was sailing for thc Batlin Islands and if hc wished he could travel down river to Deems aboard it, for the experience.

'For if you gain your turban,' Tranche said, rubbing his sagging jowls, 'most of your work will be on the seas. Might as well learn if you're subject to the sickness now.'

'What sickness is that, Master?'

'The motion of the waters. Some men heave their guts out from the moment they step aboard. I never did but I've known others all but die from it.'

Matto it turned out was also impervious though the one passenger who shipped with them illustrated the truth of Tranche's words before they even met the sea. It proved an easy passage. Told to make himself generally useful Matto lifted and pulled to order, cheerfully coiled ropes and helped holystone the deck. The Island Spirit was a small coastal trader and seldom ventured far into the ocean.

Her seamen were a good-natured lot and Matto's actual duties for his House consisted only of overseeing the cargo's arrival, and checking it off against the manifest. He had hesitated over taking his bow until Tranche encouraged it.

'Certainly, take it. A ship's no safer than a caravan. Pirates, bandits — where's the difference? Except that ships cost a deal more than camels and can be fired besides. The sailors are useful fighters but an extra weapon never hurts.'

There had, however, been no call for defensive measures and Matto had enjoyed the trip, as he did the two days spent exploring the port city once the Island Spirit sailed. He visited the markets, fell into talk with a sailor waiting for a berth in an outbound ship, and roamed the seashore, so different to the familiar riverbank, his senses filled with the sight, sound and smell of ocean.

His return trip to Ripa was slow, aboard a small, decked boat that fought its way upstream with much tacking, and when the wind finally failed, labour at the oars. The blisters on his hands were still raw when he carried his gear into the office to report to Tranche. The merchant wanted to know everything about his trip; no detail of what he had seen or heard was too small to interest him, from the price of dates in the markets, to the number of ships tied up in the harbour, along with their house flags and points of origin.

When Matto eventually ran dry of words, his master nodded. 'Good, that's good. You notice and remember things. Information is a crucial part of our business, Matto. Half a trader's skill lies in collecting it and in knowing how and when to put it to use. It's a commodity, like anything else. A bit of information a customer can benefit from might well clinch you the deal. Sometimes it can even be important enough to sell outright. You did well. Now, leave your gear — yes, I know you've just got back, but nobody's had time to check the birds today and I'm expecting messages. Just see to that, will you, then you may take the afternoon off.'

He waited until the office door closed, locked it, then picked up the quiver and carried it to the desk.

***

Banco's apprenticeship ended and Tranche bought the wine with which the entire workforce drank to his future. Luka presented him with his turban, the traditional gift from master to successful apprentice. It was green and seemed impossibly long but Luka wound it expertly into place while Banco sat in a blaze of happiness, on an upturned keg. Afternoon had turned to evening when the party ended; there had been food and speeches and quite a bit of wine, and jovial attempts by the younger men (vigorously defended against) to wrest the new acquisition from its owner.

When the gates were locked that night Banco and Matto left together, but not this time, for the alehouse. The new trader was going to see his girl. A little drunk on wine and excitement he shook hands solemnly with his companion and walked off, singing a love song whose words he kept losing. Matto listened to his voice fade knowing their friendship must now change. Henceforth they would spend less time together. Banco's betrothed as much as his new status would see to that. His new duties would take him beyond the yards and the docks, and his work would be shrouded in secrecy. Confidentiality was the traders' creed. Deals were never discussed with outsiders, which Matto realised, he had suddenly become, and must so remain, until he gained his own turban.

He would miss Banco, Matto reflected, listening to the frog chorus from the river and the endless slap and suck of water against the jetty pilings. He had been a good friend, the best he'd known since Rissak. Still, in another two years, given ordinary luck, he too would be wearing the turban. It was a worthwhile calling, a satisfactory way to spend one's life. Matto seldom allowed himself to visit the past but found himself wondering where he might be now, if his and Tranche's path had not crossed... Perhaps the Goddess had arranged it so? The thought made him uncomfortable. Like Jekka, the little half-man who had healed and ultimately saved him, he believed he had done with that part of his life.

He was in his own country, in the city of his birth, and if it suffered under its rapacious king, it was still possible to live happily in obscurity — if one was careful. There was even satisfaction of a sort, a certain grim irony, in moving freely about unrecognised beneath his enemy's very nose. Matto had caught several glimpses of King Temes since that first river festival, but even if they met face to face, he knew that his uncle would see only the apprentice, and not the nephew he believed long dead.

It was like faith, he thought, bending his steps towards the lane behind the stables, you saw what you wanted to. He had visited the temple with Banco soon after his arrival in Ripa, finding only the cold memory of power amid the drifting sacrificial smoke and the greed in the eyes of the red robed priests. Everything there had a price, and the cynicism of it all shocked him, yet Banco's belief had been plain.

'It is splendid, is it not?' his friend asked, pointing out the details of carving and craftsmanship, the skilled needlework in the huge tapestries that depicted the attributes of Bel. 'It will be your first temple of course. You have no shrines, they tell me, in Ansham?'

'They are forbidden,' Matto said, gazing about him. 'It's all very fine but it seems — empty to me. You worship Him, but do you feel His presence here?'

Banco, he remembered, had laughed at him. 'Are all shepherd lads as simple? The priests are here, why would the God be?'

'Yes, of course.' He had dropped the subject then.

Perhaps it was just city sophistication sharpened by commerce but he couldn't help compare Banco's careless attitude with the simple piety of Berta's votive bowl, or Dura's whispered prayers, in a land where both were outlawed.

***

That year the bandit raids multiplied until they posed a real threat rather than just an added aggravation to the travelling caravans. Men taxed out of their farms, army veterans without livelihood, the desperate homeless from the cities, all turned to theft to live. Lawless society begat lawlessness and under Temes's reign the strong preyed on the weak, and the weak, if inadequately armed, went under. No prudent caravan master took his beasts from the security of his guarded premises without a contingent of armed men. It was costly, but so were lost cargoes and dead camels. The merchants swallowed the increased call on their purses as they did the constantly increasing levies, but not without bitter, though private, grumbling.

The whole of Rhuta grumbled, but furtively, beneath its breath. Tranche sometimes imagined he could hear the city, like the muted whisper of subterranean cisterns filling, but nothing was going to change things. The reason was simple: next to gold the greatest currency Ripa's citizens possessed was information. The city was riddled with Onli's spies.

Men were recruited for the task but anyone could report an overheard conversation, an incautious criticism. Informers flourished so that Ripa's very exhalations reeked of suspicion and distrust.

According to Haran matters were not as bad in other cities removed from the seat of power, although it was hard to judge in Meddia, where paranoia of a different kind had always ruled.

It meant, had Tranche dared dwell on it, bowel loosening twists of fear at the risk he and his partners ran, for any fresh contact in business or among their own workmen, could already be in Onli's pay, or considering how to become so.

'Informing is the growth industry of our times,' he remarked sourly to Luka. 'It wouldn't surprise to find there are spies set to watch even the Guards.'

'I would bet on it,' Luka agreed, 'but it's not all bad. You might say it actually affords us protection. Onli, whom I'm sure would torture his own mother for the pleasure of her screams, can't think anyone would be mad enough to plot against him in such a climate of suspicion.' He eyed his partner with concern. 'You are wearing yourself out. No ships are available so maybe you should take the next caravan out yourself; get away from the city for a while? I could manage here.'

Tranche, remembering that now distant trip with the mules, shuddered. 'I think not. There's worry and there's masochism.' He dismissed the idea. 'The timber from Barat is on the dock. I have a wagon coming to shift it to the timber yard though their last bill is still unpaid. Ramie should be back anytime too. He's been gone a moon or more, but at least trade is brisker now that talk of war with Barat has ceased.'

'Some good has finally come from the Grasslands then,' Luka observed.

Tranche grunted agreement though they had lost a caravan and four men to a raid from the barbarians there the previous year. So bold had the tribes become that Temes was forced to dispatch an army to quell them. It wouldn't last. Even Cyrus had never done more than hold them in check, but the necessary intervention had made a limited trade possible again with Barat. Luka took a folded length of green cloth from the cupboard against the wall, and began to wind it about his head. 'Get the timber loaded,' he said. 'I'll go have a word with the man about his bill. Don't worry, I'll see the account is settled.'

He would too, Tranche knew. Their debtor would see the turban and remember the consequences of defaulting. The guilds were all powerful in the city; they could blackball the timber yards business if they chose, ensuring its proprietors could neither buy, sell, nor deal with any other guild in Ripa. It would be good to think that the rest of Rhuta's problems could be solved so easily.

7

Haran conveyed yet another lot of jewelry to the safe box under Tranche's desk. He had lost count over the years of the value of the goods that had briefly resided there. The trick was not to hold them a second longer than was needed. Even so he fretted over every moment they were there. Luka had offered to take them to his home but Tranche wouldn't hear of it.

'And if they were discovered there? You have a daughter to protect, man, and grandchildren. What have I to lose?' The reminder silenced his partner.

'Things will settle down,' the younger man added, 'and at any rate the queen cannot have much more to send. Besides, nothing actually happened. A close call, yes, but nothing was discovered.'

It had cost them a camel, a small price considering the alternative — their lives, their business, and the hope they all lived for. It had been one of those unforeseeable accidents of fate, a troop of soldiers travelling late when any decent commander would have already had them camped or in barracks for the night. Instead they had almost blundered upon the two Lakers transporting the latest shipment of arms. The men had just time enough to kneel the beast in the scanty shelter of a gully and pith it with a dagger before they were discovered. The sharpened point entering behind the animal's ear had severed the spinal cord so that the beast died with one convulsive jerk, the sound covered by the hooves of the troop.

The two smugglers had crept off, returning cautiously later to find the camel and its load undiscovered. So secrecy had been maintained, the weapons saved and subsequently recovered. It had been, Tranche thought, a salutary reminder to them all just how thin and perilous was the knife edge they trod.

Haran, cleaning his nails with the point of his dagger, said, 'I think this lot should be the last. We shouldn't accept another stone. They must keep something back to run the country with once we've reclaimed it. Besides, the risk grows every time.'

'Frankly it's always amazed me that Temes didn't go after the collection the moment he took over,' Tranche said. 'He may never have seen the royal jewels, but wouldn't he expect them to exist?'

'He had the temple treasury, which included plenty of gems for the wealthy gave them freely,' Luka reminded him. 'Perhaps he thought they were the crown jewels? After all he knew about the Princess's connection to the temple. And the quality wasn't lacking in the stuff he took, as I have cause to know. I gave gems myself when my son was born.' Luka's boy had died on his first trading trip, falling from the rigging of a ship.

Haran, taking up a handful of dates to munch, returned the talk to the present. 'I've the last of the goods ready for Meddia, but the escort is short a guard. There are men enough to choose from but none I would vouch for; too many have either served with the City Guards or the army. There's Fatch, but he'd never be my choice.'

'Matto can go.' Tranche waved away a hovering fly. The wine in his cup glowed ruby in the light from the heavily barred windows. 'His bow's as good as two swords by all accounts. If we could lay hands on a dozen more and the men to use them, we'd have an escort to reckon with. Yes, take him. The experience will do him good.'

***

Meddia lay to the north of Rhuta, a harsh, highland country with pockets of fertile land amid the rocky hills that, rough though they were, never quite achieved the status of mountains. The Meddii, as judged by the cosmopolitan traders, were an austere, inward looking race. While they had not, like Barat, closed their borders to outsiders, they were an insular people with harsh laws that even Cyrus's comparatively benevolent rule had not weakened. Meddii that fell into debt could be sold into slavery. Their sumptuary rules were strict and no Medic, as the healer-priests were called, could leave the country. The capital city of Hafran, built on a rocky crag over looking the River Palt, bore a grim and joyless aspect.

Matto, absorbing this brief digest as he rode beside Haran, eyed him in surprise.

"So why do we trade with them? Tranche once said that the best customers have an interest in what is new and different. That doesn't sound much like the Meddii to me.'

'Did I not mention their wealth? That's why. Our House doesn't deal in slaves but they are the basis of Meddia's economy. The country's rich in tin, jade and silver — the reason Cyrus took it over — and the mines are worked by slaves. Myself, I think it explains the harshness of their laws for the mines take a heavy toll on human life, so there's always a need for more labour. It takes very little to get yourself arrested there, so be warned. Avoid the gambling cribs and brothels, they're illegal anyway, but any place where arguments turn to fights can be dangerous, for the City Watch is everywhere.'

'I will remember,' Matto said soberly. He fell back, bow in hand, to ride on the wing of the long caravan, while Haran, eyes slitted below the folds of his turban, turned his thoughts back to the endless plans and speculations that were a large part of his working life.

The bandits attacked the following day. Haran had time only to curse as the low ridges to either side of their route erupted with screaming men charging towards them with maximum noise, intent upon cutting the leading camels free, while killing all that opposed the endeavour. It was a common pattern of attack. Half the band to harass the column, leaving the rest to get away with whatever beasts they could wrest from the train. The remainder would then disengage from the action to form a rearguard behind the stolen animals, already lumbering for the horizon.

The best defence was for the handlers to sit their beasts down, forming a bulwark of flesh and cargo as cover for the men. It wasn't an easy maneuver to accomplish in the midst of an attack. Camels were unpredictable but if it could be managed losses were generally light for the bandits were reluctant to kill the animals they needed to transport the stolen goods from the scene. If foiled they usually abandoned the attack to try again later, but that wouldn't happen today, Haran thought, for the train was already panicked, the camels bellowing and lashing out with their lethal hind feet. Fear jolted his heart and he cursed, a rich stream of invective calling down the wrath of all gods on the heads of the sons of whores presently trying to kill him. His bellowed orders coincided with the practiced swing of his blade at the closest bandit, as he checked frantically on his escorts' activities.

The man he had swung at ducked, but not low enough. The blade opened his scalp, the force of the blow making him reel as his face was sheeted with blood. His horse bolted into the train, the collision knocking its rider from the saddle. An arm's length away another bandit hacked at the rope strung between the beasts, panicking them into a trampling mass. The bull camel at the head of the now tangled string roared as he skittered sideways, pulling the beast behind him off balance. The outlaw grunted as Haran's blade took him between neck and shoulder, a shower of crimson erupting as the flesh parted. Panting in fear and fury, the blood roaring in his head, the trader ripped his mount about to take stock of the screeching and dying behind him.

It was immediately apparent to him that the fight was going their way. He had five armed guards, six counting Matto, against at least fifteen, but the young man's bow had turned the tide. Matto was on foot, halfway up the ridge, shooting down at the tide of men below. He needed the elevation to pick out his targets, Haran instantly saw, and was afoot for accuracy. For a moment he watched the still figure pull and release the bowstring, saw the hand rise to snatch another arrow from the quiver, before nocking the bow again. It was done as calmly as if it were hares he was shooting, and every arrow was finding its mark. Haran saw a man fall shot through the throat, another shriek as an arrow found his thigh, pinning it to the saddle beneath. The trampled vegetation contained wild sage; the strong reek of it rose to choke his breathing with overtones of blood and the stink of his own fear, as he narrowly avoided being spitted on his way to Matto's side.

One of the bandits had seen the bowman's vulnerability too, and slamming spurs to his mount plainly gambled on closing the distance between them before the archer could target him. Haran shouted a warning that went unheard, but Bona, leader of the escort, also realised the danger, and with a lively appreciation of Matto's value angled his horse to charge from the enemy's left. It gave him an immediate vantage over the attacker, forcing the man to swing clumsily backhanded at him. The force behind the blow, which missed Bona, left his body wide open for the riposte that followed. The man's horse shied wildly, all but ripping the sword from Bona's grip as he tugged it free. Matto yelled a breathless, 'Thank you!' as he released again. The heavy thud of the arrow finding its target drowned amid the background clamour of the fight.

It couldn't last. Whether Bona had killed their leader, or through fear of the deadly bow the remainder of the gang suddenly broke and fled. A badly wounded man fell from his saddle and was dragged; Haran heard his thin scream, abruptly silenced by a frenzied hoof as the dust rose behind their going. He slumped in his saddle, mouth parched and hands trembling now that it was over, taking deep breaths as he let the reaction bleed away before straightening again, once more in command.

***

Riderless horses skittered about, some trotting and whinnying after their departed companions. The camels milled and bellowed, one kicking in its death throes. The cook, a cheerful, bandy-legged veteran of the road was dead, and two of the handlers were hurt, one badly, his arm almost severed at the elbow. His moaning put men's teeth on edge and the sight of the exposed bone was sickening. Haran, organising an impromptu camp, dealing with the wounded, posting lookouts, though he doubted their assailants would be back, knew they had been lucky. Seven of the bandits were dead — eight counting the dragged man. It could have been them; would have been them, he amended, without Matto's bow.

***

Later, he asked, 'Where did you learn to shoot like that?'

'All Ansham shepherds use the bow. There are wolves to protect against.' Matto had recovered a handful of arrows and was spinning the point of each on his palm, checking the shafts for damage and straightness. Wooden shafts hitting bone or metal could warp out of true.

Haran said mildly. 'Do they all stay as calm as you? Your first fight too. One would almost think you'd been trained.'

Matto's hand jumped suddenly, the fingers trembling so that the arrow fell from his palm. 'Sorry, what did you say —? I think it's catching up with me. I feel a bit —'

'Sit down. Of course you do, you've killed men, one at least of which was trying to kill you. Look, you did well, lad, but next time, if there is a next time, I'm detailing someone off to guard you. It didn't take 'em long to twig it was you they needed to stop. So from now on when trouble hits you'll have a mate to watch your back.'

Matto didn't appear to be listening. He was gazing blankly about him, before turning to look guiltily at the trader. 'I've lost my horse,' he blurted. 'Sorry. I — I should've tied him up. I just jumped off and —'

Haran snorted amusement. 'Bel's balls!' He shouted, his shoulders shaking with sudden cathartic laughter. 'We've six or eight of theirs in exchange and we're still breathing, aren't we? Don't be fretting over a poxy horse, lad. It's all right. Bloodletting takes you that way sometimes — especially when it's your first. You'll be fine again soon.'

***

There were no further attacks. The dead cook had been an Appellan, a follower of the Light but Haran knew enough of their customs to oversee the construction of a pyre. Lacking the actual words of their god's service he gathered the men of the caravan about the fire to utter a generic prayer designed to send the cook's soul on its journey into the shadows. Then they continued their own with the slaughtered camel's load spread among his brethren. The two wounded men were deposited, to recover or die, at the next hamlet — a poor enough compromise but the best they could do for them.

'I'd like to have got them into Meddia,' Haran muttered, as they left. 'Those Medics are unbelievable, they can near as dammit raise the dead. But it's a full two days travel and neither of them would stand that.' The second wounded man had a hole in his side where a sword's tip had punched in below the ribs. 'They can't leave the citadel. The healers, I mean. Some damn law of the head-priest. Makes no sense to any normal man but a lot about the Meddii don't. Seems to me they've only got one law and it covers everything: Thou shalt not.'

***

Matto laughed. He seemed to have recovered from the effects of the raid, Haran thought. To be certain he said, 'Yesterday... You're not worrying about the men you killed? Because you shouldn't. Their shades might come into your dreams for a while and the best way to stop that is to forget about them.'

'I already have.' Matto's face hardened into something older than his years. 'They got what they deserved for trying to kill us.'

A shout from behind punctuated their words. Both riders hipped about, hands snatching automatically at their weapons but they weren't under attack. The shouter was on foot, trousers about his ankles, pale buttocks on display as he stumbled frantically away from the bush where he'd squatted to relieve himself. His mount, reins loose and ears pricked was snorting as he backed up nervously from the coiled serpent visible between them, its upper body raised to strike.

'And that's another thing about this part of the country,' Haran grumbled. 'Watch out for the snakes. The bloody things are deadly.'

***

The citadel of Hafran was as stark and grim as Matto, from Jekka's stories about his birthplace, had imagined it to be. The healer priests wore grey gowns that matched the chilly grey rock from which the city was built. Meddia had been under Appellan control for more than twenty summers but their presence had done little to change the place. An Appellan governor ruled from the abbey where the priest-king had once reigned, and a section of the impregnable wall about the citadel had been razed. The barracks, built at the time of Hafran's defeat, were possibly the newest construction in the city. A precaution and a sign, like the removal of the wall, that their overlords intended to hold that which they had been at such pains to take.

***

With the penalties for crime so drastic (there was no reprieve from the mines, once sentenced a man served for life) the presence of the military might have seemed redundant but their duties were less those of soldiers, than of a city watch as Matto was to learn. On an evening five days after entering Hafran, three of them swaggered into the tavern where the caravaneers were taking their evening meal. Haran, seeing the door open to admit them, muttered to his tablemates, 'Here's trouble. Sit tight.'

The tavern was small and timber built with undressed roof beams and a sanded floor. What tables there were had already been filled; the trio of newcomers looked about then strolled over to one occupied by four men. All, farmers by their looks, rose immediately. Three swallowed their ale and left; the fourth, glaring around the room, found space on a backless bench and called the server for a fresh pot, his words slurring drunkenly.

'He's asking to start something, the fool,' Haran murmured.

The server made matters worse by holding onto the fresh pot. 'I'll see your coin first, Jemet.'

A brief argument ensued from which the clearest words to emerge were the drunken man's. 'A pox on your ale, you thief. That weren't the price yestiddy.'

'Yeah?' the server retorted, 'Well it is now, chummy. 'T'ain't my fault if the king raises taxes —'

'Then a pox on the king, too,' roared his incensed customer. 'I'll warrant he don't go short —'

He got no further for the trio of military had coalesced about the bench from which the other patrons were hastily scrambling. The room went still as a soldier drew back his arm and punched the fuddled man, a solid blow to the jaw then another hard jab to his middle. Jemet sagged, collapsing until his chin hit the bench. Two of them grabbed his arms and hauled him outside. Everyone froze until the door slammed behind them when the talk resumed, but softly, as if all present feared to draw attention to themselves.

Haran drained his wine and glanced about the table. 'We're strangers here, boys, and leaving tomorrow. Suit yourselves but I'm for an early night.' Matto and a couple of the others rose with him and followed him out, each avoiding the others' eyes. It was shameful Matto knew, but there was nothing they could do. Every one of them was powerless against the might of the king. Tonight's scene, or something like it, was a daily occurrence across the occupied countries of the empire, where the military held power over civilians. To intervene could land them all in the mines; they would be beaten whatever the outcome, (there were always more soldiers) imprisoned, the caravan and its goods confiscated and their lives would be over...

Tonight's little episode was nothing anyone of them hadn't seen or heard before, but it still didn't sit well with Matto.

He brought up the matter at the noon camp next day. They were still within Meddia but Haran had nevertheless posted lookouts, as much for military patrols as bandits, though it was hard to know sometimes, he jested sourly, which of the two stole the most. It was a clear, windy day with a sparkle on the sun dried grass and the first hint of autumn in the air. Matto snuffed at it appreciatively as he dropped down off his horse into the lee of a boulder to hunker beside the trader.

'The man that was beaten last night,' he said abruptly.

'The drunk?' Haran eyed him, preparing to be patient. 'Look, we both know it happens, but what can we do — particularly as we don't belong here? Their laws are harsher than ours so we can't afford to get involved. You know that.' He cleared his throat, pricked by shame for his words, which were as cowardly as the deed that had brought them forth. Matto however scarcely seemed to be listening. His eyes were fixed frowningly on a camel's jaw as it ground its cud, first right then left, the gaze of the beast's absurdly long lashed eyes as remote as a mountain top.

'I saw him this morning,' he said, 'the drunk. He was behind the barn, pretty badly beaten. A stable hand was cleaning him up, I think he was a friend. The man could hardly speak but he mumbled something about them paying for it — when the Prince comes. That's what he said.' His dark eyes glanced questioningly at Haran who cursed under his breath, remembering then that Tranche had once said it paid to listen to what Matto picked up.

'You sure?' He let skepticism colour his words. 'You'd have thought they'd have kicked the drink out of him,' he jeered callously. 'What prince? The royal line is Temes. He took care to make sure of that — though I'd be glad if you forgot I ever said so.'

Matto waved the remark aside. 'That's what I heard. That they all died in Ansham. Which makes it odd, don't you think, that people shouldn't know it here? They know the latest rise in the price of grain, that a new governor's been appointed in Quade — why not old news such as that Smerdis and his sons are dead?'

Haran shrugged, his face giving nothing away. 'The man could be addled in the head, I suppose. Pretty well has to be to say what he did, even if he was drunk. And you could have misheard him. Look, never mind that. I wanted to talk to you about a plan Bona's come up with.'

'Well, Tranche had thought of it, too. They're both very impressed with your bow. I can see myself it's the best deterrent we've got so I was wondering how difficult it'd be to get a handful more of them? You told Bona you make your own arrows so can you make another of those?'

He nodded at the weapon Matto carried across his back, the taut string tight over his chest, and listened to his own voice, hardly registering the lad's answer, nodding where appropriate, while his thoughts ran furiously on, weighing the risks and advantages of this new intelligence.

It was bound to happen of course. They had all known it. You could swear men to secrecy but the truth would still trickle out; through a drunk's rambling, or a man's desperate need to salve his pride, or the belief that the friend you confided in was safe, and could hold his tongue... But somebody hadn't and the whispers had begun. It wasn't entirely bad, he judged; only the desperate would place credence in it, witness Matto's reaction, but those who did could become assets when the time was right. Besides, broken men needed hope, a symbol to believe in, and the truth they had striven to hide for so long might well provide it. Just as long as it didn't get them all killed first...

8

Overall, the Meddian trip proved a profitable one, despite the loss of the cook and the two wounded men. The one with the stab wound to the body had died, the other had survived though it would be a long while before he resumed work; nor would he be travelling again with a caravan when he did, for a man needed both hands for that. A Hafran merchant had paid handsomely to have certain papers delivered to a confederate in Deems; and at Yalk, a highland town that lived on the products of the mulberry groves, and where the river was permanently stained with dye, they had the pick of the new season's silk.

Haran made a pouch of a length of it to hold the merchant's papers, and bound it to his body beneath his tunic. He had considered using the quiver again but the papers were too bulky, and the mere fact of it being hidden would tell against them if it were discovered. They were business papers of no interest to a Guard, which wouldn't prevent them being confiscated, particularly by an illiterate one, but he had been paid for confidentiality and delivery, and he meant to fulfill the contract. He was pleased too by the silks: they were amazingly fine, so light they could be threaded through a finger ring. And the dyers in Yalk were known as the best in the whole of Belusia.

Matto was intrigued by the whole spinning and dyeing process and had spent a portion of his wages on a sample, a wisp of silky iridescent colour as light as spider's silk.

'You want to hang onto that,' Haran advised, casting a critical eye over it. 'There's a flaw in the weaving there, see? But small, hardly noticeable; you'll get a good offer for that if you're canny.' He grinned, 'Your first trade. That's permitted under guild law — if it's only one item and not sold to a recognised business.'

He thought of it again in Deems and meant to ask the lad if he could help him find a buyer, but Matto had vanished from the tavern where they'd been putting up for the few days of their sojourn, and didn't reappear until the final breakfast. Later, riding out of the sprawling port city with its crowds of crying gulls, he remembered to ask, though by then he had formed his own idea as to the silk's destination. Obviously pleased with himself, Matto met the enquiry with a shrug.

'I gave it to a girl. She was very nice.'

Haran laughed. 'They all are, the joy girls. Travellers' comforts we call them. Pity. She'd have settled happily for coin, you know. You could have doubled your money with that sample.'

Matto regretted only that she had been left behind. Filette was pretty and young, a fisherman's daughter, spending her first season at the inn. She had never, she told him, been with a man before. If it were true it was a first for both of them, but they had managed, and it was only afterwards when she lay in his arms in her narrow bed under the eaves, with their clothing strewn on the thin rug, that he remembered what Rissak had said that day as they rode back from Cran's smithy. *A prince's seed is not as other men's...* Well, he was no longer a prince, and when she had stirred and opened clear, hazel eyes to smile at him he had kissed their lids and then her mouth, repeating it to himself: *I am not...*

They had moved together again then, with more certainty this time, in the excitement that built to sweet, shuddering release, with the hazy knowledge that there was still tomorrow night, and another after that before they must part. Now he yawned, heavy eyed in the saddle, not in the least regretting the silk. Haran warned him to keep his eyes open and his wits on the job, then let him be.

As it happened Haran had good reason to be thankful that the papers he carried were on his person and not in the quiver, for on the last day into Ripa they were joined by a troop of soldiers, led by a hard eyed Appellan officer. They turned up at their noon camp and accompanied them to the city, leaving no opportunity for Matto's weapon to become part of the cargo. The trader had no chance to issue instructions but was glad to observe the lad slipping the string from the bow, and stashing the frame beneath his saddle flap. There was nothing he could do to disguise the quiver though. Watching the officer study the camels as if deciding how many loads to examine, he was momentarily encouraged to see him glance aside as if deciding against spending the time. The man wanted details of where they'd traded and what they carried, then his eye was caught by the feather shafts protruding above Matto's shoulder and held out an imperious hand.

'Show me that. Where did you get it?'

'He's part of my escort,' Haran spoke before Matto could, blessing the gods that for once the smuggler's space in the bottom was empty.

'Did I ask you? Well, boy?'

'From Ansham, sir,' Matto replied. 'I used to guard the sheep, and now I work, as my master said, as an escort for the caravans.' The officer dumped the arrows, examined one curiously, then ran his hand down into the quiver. Feeling something there he frowned, causing Haran to utter a silent prayer as the soft kidskin was yanked inside out. Tranche, he immediately saw, had done a poor job the last time he had secured the cover, or perhaps the skin had torn from repeated stitching. One side gaped open as the Appellan looked from it to Matto, his face hard.

'What is this? Looks like a false bottom to me.'

'No, sir.' If Matto was surprised by the alteration to his equipment, Haran thought, he wasn't showing it. Scarcely pausing, he explained, 'I keep my spare tips in there, sir. You need extras because they're barbed you see, and you can't always cut them out. There should be one there now...' He trailed off as the man shook the quiver to no effect. 'Damn! Sorry sir, it must've fallen out when you upended it...' He dropped to his knees, sifting the loose dirt through his fingers, saying apologetically. 'It takes an age to shape one. I hope — ah!' He had twisted around, both hands busy and now rose beaming with relief to proffer the missing article to the officer. 'I found it.'

Haran breathed again as the man turned it in his fingers, grunted dismissively, then flipped it back to its owner, tossing the quiver after it. 'Right,' he said making towards his mount. 'We'll ride with you to the city, Trader. Leaving now. I'd as lief make it before dark.'

They arrived just as dusk was bleeding into the landscape and a river breeze stirred the smoky flambeaux lighting the Guards at the broad city gates. Later, with the camels unloaded, yarded and fed, the company dispersed, save for Matto to whom Haran said privily, 'I'd like a word. Come to the office when you're done here.'

The look the apprentice gave him was hard and unfriendly. 'I'll come now,' he said. 'I'd like a word myself.'

Luka and Tranche were waiting in the office. They greeted Haran and looked surprised to see Matto follow him in, bow and quiver in hand.

'Well, how was the trip?' Tranche came forward to

grip his chief trader's arm in greeting. 'Matto! Why are you here? I would have thought there were tasks enough awaiting you in the yard.' He spoke mildly but it was still a rebuke.

'I am here,' his apprentice, snapped, 'for an explanation about this.' He tipped the arrows onto the desk and reached into the quiver to invert it. 'This,' he repeated, flicking the false bottom. 'Nobody else but you has had the opportunity to meddle with my gear. It could have got me arrested today. Right now I could be in the Tower, answering Captain Onli. Yes, I work here, but does that give you the right to risk my life?'

He couldn't have said which outraged him more — the danger, or Tranche's betrayal. Memories of their first meeting came to him then, of the two thugs searching the mules at the head of the pass, goods smashed and scattered, but the quiver on his back unnoticed. And previous to that the quiver bottom torn and Tranche mending it. Had he unknowingly carried something past the guards that day too? As he had obviously done — how many times since?

'Ah,' Tranche's gaze flicked questioningly to Haran who shrugged and rubbed his jaw.

'A troop rode with us the last bit of the way. They picked us up at noon before we had packed the weapons away. We fought off an ambush on the way north so I wasn't taking any chances. The officer in charge got curious, asked to see that,' he nodded at the quiver. 'Either you didn't stitch the bottom too well last time or the kidskin's torn. And Matto's right,' he added grimly, 'we could all be in the Tower now if he hadn't come up with an explanation to satisfy the man. You did well there, lad.'

Matto ignored the praise to repeat, 'Last time. So, just how long have I been risking my neck for you?' He looked at Tranche. 'It was from the beginning, wasn't it?

That's the reason you hired me! Not for the mules but to bring something out of the Upper Land.'

'No, son, no,' Tranche protested. 'It was mostly for the mules. And you wouldn't have been in any danger. I told you to act stupid, remember? So if the goods had been found they wouldn't have bothered with some dull peasant boy.' He sounded upset. 'They wouldn't have hurt you.'

'Apart from a good kicking perhaps,' Matto said bitterly, 'that could easily have maimed me. I thought you were helping me.'

'It hasn't done you any harm,' Luka observed dispassionately. 'You have a position, a wage, a place to live. None of which you had before. And the need for what we are doing has passed. Stitch up the bottom again and there's an end to it.'

'An end to it! You used me,' Matto cried furiously.

'Yes, we did, and I, for one, regret it. It has preyed on my mind but thankfully no harm has come to you from it.' Tranche held the young man's hot gaze. 'You won't be involved again, Matto. You have my word on it. Can we leave it there? We'll talk later, if you wish, at home.' He took the desk knife and with a couple of strokes cut the false bottom free. 'There, best not carry it out tonight though. There are Guards on the docks.' He laid the quiver aside, went to the door, opened it and stood waiting. A moment later Matto found himself outside, still angry but with nothing left to say.

Within the office the three men exchanged glances. 'Will he keep his mouth shut, do you think?' Haran asked. 'He thinks on his feet, I'll give him that.' He told them about the arrowhead, adding, 'He must've had it on him but I never saw him palm it.'

'He's quick, and loyal,' Tranche protested. 'I'm certain we can trust him.'

'Because you want to,' Luka was blunt. 'Are you sure

you really know him, my friend? You called him son and if that is how you see him then you have lost all objectivity. It is our lives as well at stake here, remember.'

Tranche flushed. 'A slip of the tongue. I have heard Haran address him as lad. Besides, he cannot give away what he doesn't know.'

'You said there were Guards here — why?' The question came from Haran.

Luka's face was grim. 'Something, or somebody slipped up, I suspect. It's the second time they've come. The first was to search the Bouncing Bucket. The ship had scarcely tied up before they were all over it. They've been poking around in the warehouse today. Not an organised search but demands to open this and that. I suspect we've an informer in our workforce. Realistically, it would be strange if we hadn't.'

'Well it couldn't have been Matto,' Tranche pointed out with some satisfaction, 'he's been gone for the past three months.'

It didn't necessarily follow, Haran thought. A man could go to the Guards and if they judged him useful enough they could delay an investigation till he was safely out of the way where no finger of blame could point his way. How much did they really know about Matto? He had appeared out of nowhere and he never spoke of his past or his family; he never for instance quoted his dead father, or mentioned the Appellan friend with whom he had allegedly shared lessons and sport. Which reminded him of something. He told his partners about the drunk in Hafran that the soldiers had beaten up, and Matto's account of his ramblings. Tranche frowned over it, chewing nervously at a thumbnail, but Luka took Haran's point.

'It was always going to come out sometime. But should it reach the wrong ears they'll not believe it. Why should they? You say Matto didn't?'

'Not for a moment. Or so I thought then.'

'Well, it's happened. What about the ambush you mentioned? Anybody hurt. Much lost?'

Tranche poured the wine waiting on his desk and the partners settled to hear their trader's account. Haran took his cup with a grunt of thanks and lifted it to his mouth.

'Aah, the taste of home... We lost a camel and three men. They killed Stone — the cook,' he amplified, 'and two handlers were badly wounded. I had to leave them, they were too hurt to travel. One died, spear to the body. The other lost his arm.'

Luka winced. 'And our losses?'

Haran tipped his hand. 'Not too bad, the beast carried woollen goods mostly. We fought 'em off fairly quickly. Might have been a different story without Matto's bow. He's bloody deadly, accounted for half the bandits himself. Stood and shot like a veteran, cool as you please. Ramie once told me he'd killed a wolf and I took it for a boy's boasting. Not any longer. If he was older I'd say he'd had military training — but that's not possible. His people are nominal slaves to the Appellans, have been forever. You don't find them in the army.' He drank, his gaze turning speculative, then set down his cup. 'So what do you think is behind this attention from the Guards?'

Luka shrugged. 'Take your pick out of three possibilities. Either they're onto what we're doing, or somebody — a rival House perhaps? — is making trouble, or it's just routine suspicion. Not forgetting that it's the Guards' task to keep the city edgy; a frightened population is less of a personal risk to the king, after all. If that's the case I doubt we have much to worry about because local affairs won't have Temes's attention now he's involved again with Barat.'

Haran frowned. 'In what way?'

Tranche sighed. 'He has the ridiculous idea he can

force the country to open its borders to him. He's after their gold of course. Guildmaster Feric was hauled up to the palace to sign a paper on all our behalf, demanding the right to unrestricted trading. The thing is farcical — or would be if it weren't going to provoke a war. Because it is worded as an ultimatum, Feric said.'

'I sometimes wonder if Temes is actually mad,' Luka mused. 'Of course the guild has no doubts on the matter. Still, it does have the advantage of focusing the king's mind beyond the city.'

'Not Onli's though,' Tranche muttered. He glanced uneasily at the shut door. 'Best open that; closed doors suggest plotting.' He did so, setting it wide so the three men could see out but only Fatch was visible, sweeping up spilled grain in the lantern's glow. The rest of the workforce, including Matto, had gone.

'For Bel's sake!' Tranche sounded exasperated, 'what are you still doing here?'

The man glowered at him. 'Cleaning up. Foreman said I wasn't to leave till it was done. I didn't spill the bloody stuff,' he muttered, 'but who gets to clean it up? Fatch of course.'

'Well, leave it now and get off with you,' the merchant replied irritably. 'We'll be locking up in a moment.' He watched his worker slouch off and sighed. 'I'll see him past the Guards then head home. Are you two coming?'

'Shortly,' Luka called. 'I'll lock up.' The two men watched their friend hurry after Fatch and Haran spoke what was on both their minds.

'He's feeling the strain. I've not seen him this jumpy before.'

'It's having the guards here. Myself, I think it's the smell of money draws them, but it is unsettling and now with this business of Matto... He's far too fond of the lad, and was, right from the start. Having him live in his house, putting him up so soon for the apprenticeship.

I'm not saying the boy's not earned it, he'll make a fine trader — but calling him son was no slip of the tongue, whatever he pretends. It doesn't take a genius to see that's how Tranche thinks of him.' He sighed, swept the wine cups and bottle aside from the desk and tidied them away. 'And on top of that there's this rumour of the Prince circulating in Meddia of all places. Are you quite sure —? Hold though,' his look sharpened and he bit at his lip in concentrated thought, 'you didn't hear it yourself, you said?'

'No. Matto told m —' Haran's voice faded. 'Bel's scales! You don't think that he —?'

Luka's thin, patrician face with its high brow and long nose was unreadable. 'Was flying a kite to see what your reaction would be? It's possible. Anything is these days, that's the damn trouble! Who in this city could not be approached to earn a little extra coin? And we know nothing about him really, except that he comes from Ansham. From the first it struck me as odd that a boy raised there should speak our tongue with a city accent. I daresay if you ask him he will claim to have learned it from a Rhutan — and it might even be the truth.'

Haran's face was a study. 'You should have spoken out before he became entrenched here, then! I've no more wish than any to end my days in the Tower but there is more at stake here than our lives.'

'And if I am wrong? Tranche would never forgive us. No, we must watch young Matto, where he goes, who he sees, but we cannot breathe a word of it to Tranche. He wouldn't listen and besides, I couldn't do it to him. The man has suffered enough. Well,' he extinguished the light, leaving the room patterned with moon shadows as they moved to the door, 'it must wait until tomorrow. Where did I put that damn key?'

It was found and they stepped out into a night made light by the disk of the full moon rising beyond the river, and made their way to the gate.

9

Over the following days Haran kept an unobtrusive eye on Matto's travels about the city. When possible he watched who he met and spoke with, but saw nothing to further rouse his suspicions. The lad did his work and for all Haran could see, kept well clear of the Guards. Which he was bound to do, of course, if he was in their pay. They'd meet secretly if that were the case, probably at night when his time was his own.

Cursing his suspicious nature Haran extended his surveillance to the evenings, learning only that there was a girl Matto visited in the Street of the Weavers. Not exactly a prostitute but one who would welcome a young man with a coin to spare, to her bed. Another night Haran wasted an evening following the apprentice to Banco's house. The new trader was married now but the two of them had always been friends, and nothing was more unlikely than that the newest member of their House would plot against his own business interests.

Trudging home through a shower of rain Haran decided that distrust was the curse of the conspirator. It was fed by fear, while the knowledge of clandestine activities caused one to see danger in every shadow. Enough was enough, he decided. He had learned nothing to the lad's discredit because there was nothing to learn. If there was a spy in their House he had been looking in the wrong place for him.

Then, the following day, while walking to the markets where many a traders' commissions were won, he stumbled upon Matto getting himself beaten up in an alleyway. Haran had no weapon; none but the Guards and military went armed in the city. He shouted, and snatching a stout stick from the load of a surprised peddler of wood, charged into the alley. To his surprise the two assaulting the apprentice stood fast and glared at him. Matto, disheveled and bloody faced, reeled back, one hand pressed to his thigh. His clothes were covered in muck, for the alley served as a dumping ground for all manner of rubbish. He was limping but Haran could see no weapons in the others' hands, nor any blood beyond that from Matto's nose.

'This be a private argument,' one of the young men stated bellicosely, but it was plain from the way he eyed it that he recognised Haran's turban for what it was, and understood the power of the guilds. Both assailants were of an age with Matto. Almost sulkily the speaker added. 'This one has a long nose on him. We be teaching him that private talk be just that.'

'I think it's over — the talking and the lesson,' Haran said coolly. The second man, silent till then, nudged his friend urgently.

'Come on Tan, leave it.' Without further ado they backed up then dove suddenly out of the alley's mouth and were lost in the passing traffic.

Haran tossed the stick aside. 'What was that about? You do realise the Guards could have turned up? They arrest brawlers.'

'It wasn't of my choosing,' Matto flared, adding more moderately. 'Thanks, anyway.' He straightened his clothes, grimacing as he rubbed his leg.

'Are you hurt?'

'No, no I'm fine. A kick, that's all. I'll have a fair bruise to show for it tomorrow.' His lips moved, more flinch than smile as he took a step. 'Good thing they weren't minded to kill.'

'So what was so private?'

Matto shrugged his tunic straighter and smoothed the sleeves. 'I overheard something they said, asked them about it. The taller one said they couldn't talk there and led me here; then both set upon me without a word. It was lucky you came when you did.'

'As you say. So what didn't they wish to share?'

Matto hesitated, a frown on his face. 'It was just like in Meddia. They spoke of a prince. They were making plans to leave the city and join him, so they believe he's real enough. They called him the Prince — no name. I was curious to know more. Well,' he shrugged, 'Banco told me what happened here when the Appellans came, and after the uprising. How your own king and his family were wiped out for breaking faith with Cyrus. So who is this mysterious prince? An imposter, a missing third cousin that Temes somehow overlooked in his killing spree?'

'How should I know? When times are hard men dream up heroes to do what they cannot manage themselves. The only princes we are likely to see are those from Barat, supposing they have them there, and I doubt their intent will be to right our wrongs. They're far more likely to enslave us.'

Matto's interest, as he had intended, was diverted. 'Then you think there will be war between them and Temes?'

'You might as well say us, for the Black Country won't differentiate,' Haran grumbled. 'Yes, it's inevitable given that madman in the palace. We may kiss such trade as we have there, goodbye. And expect another tax hike to boot. Wars are ruinously expensive and not just for the losing side.' He jerked his head towards the street. 'Come. Where, by the way, are you supposed to be? Never mind. You'd best walk back with me and clean yourself up. You can't appear at a client's door looking like that. You smell worse than a ship's bilge, too. Brawling in the street is not what the House pays you for.'

Matto flushed and obeyed, trying to minimize his limp.

***

A few days later the trader again led a small caravan to the Lake Country, using Matto's bow as an excuse to include him. 'Better, if he is a spy, to have him under my eye,' he told Luka privily, 'and out of the way. The next shipment will be delivered to the meeting point while we're gone. Then it might be wise to halt them for a bit. At least until we see how matters go with Barat.'

Luka, laying his quill aside, nodded. Temes was gathering his northern army to fling against the unknown quantity that was Barat. They would be marching west within a dozen days and any unit finding itself short of rations or mounts would commandeer whatever they came across en route. It would be a disaster for them all should this include the arms delivery. He pinched the bridge of his nose considering the mountain of gold that Temes must already have spent upon his current enterprise.

Temes was a ruinously extravagant monarch. Between his jewels, his favourites, his new pleasure boat (its cabins rumoured to be covered and padded in cloth of gold) it was small wonder that he grasped at any excuse for war. Only the treasures of another country could fund his insatiable greed. But it was his ability as a war leader that Luka most questioned. If there must be war he found himself wishing that Cyrus were in charge. He said as much now, brow creased with misgivings for the future.

Haran agreed. 'He'll likely find he's bitten off more than he can chew. I hope it chokes the bastard — or a

Baratan fighter does it for us. I'd be first to stand him a drink.'

'Before or after he enslaved you?' Luka asked dryly. 'They're not fond of foreigners in Barat.' He smoothed his silver hair and considered. 'No, the best we can hope for is that they will maul him into an early withdrawal. It's madness! His southern forces are tied up in the Grasslands. Those that aren't collecting tolls and taxes, that is. His army's discipline is non-existent, he's slaughtered half his generals and Cyrus's Green Corp, which was the backbone of his strength in arms, scarcely exists. An early withdrawal might be too much to hope for — it could be outright defeat. And where would that leave the Prince? I believe he can reclaim his throne, but not if Temes has already lost it. By the time he is ready to move we could be conquered again, and already the vassals of Barat.'

'You had better not mention it to Tranche. He's got enough worries.' Haran gazed gloomily at the pile of invoices the merchant had been working on, then sighed and rose. 'Well, we still have cargoes to deliver. War just makes it harder, that's all.'

***

Luka's hopes proved a correct forecast of the outcome of hostilities between the two countries. All was fury and excitement at first; then the shortages began, prices rose and there were fewer soldiers in the city. Six moons after they had marched off the spring rains saw the now demoralized troops retreating in a manner that uncomfortably resembled a rout. The king himself had never been a fixture on the battlefield where the weather remained mild enough for year round campaigning. Withdrawing to Ripa after a few weeks in the field he left his generals the task of prosecuting the war where the

99

enemy's cavalry (entirely unforeseen, they had expected infantry) fought on ground of its own choosing. The mounted horsemen were deadly in a charge in open country, but worse as small pickets striking out of the mists then vanishing like wraiths back into the densely wooded country.

To the harried troops, attacked by day and night, startled from sleep by the flash of spears and the unholy howling of the black-faced demons that fell upon them, the land itself was against them. Barat's narrow passes and jungle clad mountains, where snakes slithered and spiders as big as a man's hand bound their webs between the trees, made the men uneasy.

Tales of strange and deadly animals in the forests, whispers that their black skinned foes ate the captives they took, and the silent deaths of comrades sleeping within arm-lengths of their fellows, fuelled their fear. Then there was the sky that periodically glowed red beyond the forest as though, far away, some giant's hearth perpetually burnt, intending who knew what end for those foolhardy enough to invade this secretive land?

Many of the soldiers were green, unblooded recruits, more accustomed to dealing with civilians than a savage and vengeful foe who launched silent night raids to knife sentries, and when they attacked openly did so like dark, screaming demons thundering out of a waking nightmare.

Within a moon of their first encounter with the Baratans, the demoralized troops were close to mutiny. The generals drew their forces back and, too afraid of their king to admit defeat, deployed the men pointlessly across the perimeter they had established, wherever possible avoiding engaging the enemy. When forced to defend themselves, lacking in both experience and will they inevitably lost the encounter.

Supplies ran short as the mild winter dragged on, and the rate of desertion grew to the point where the generals became more concerned with curbing this type of loss, than fighting the war. If caught, the deserters were hanged, but the ranks still thinned, men melting away into the night, or from the ends of marching columns. There was desert country between them and home, but they were more afraid of the enemy than their officers, and willing to risk the waterless wastes to escape both.

*****

Back in Ripa life was little easier for its citizens, particularly in the merchants' compounds along the docks where the City Guard seemed to have taken up residence. They boarded and searched every ship that tied up, and could be found at all hours poking about in the warehouses lining the riverbanks. They examined incoming cargoes, inspected all the stored goods, even demanding that camels in the process of loading be unpacked and their wares searched again.

'What in Bel's holy name are they looking for?' A compatriot of Luka's exploded. 'They've had half my riding mounts and a season's supply of silks — a fat lot of good that will do the army — and still they keep coming back.'

'Tell me about it!' The partners' business had lost horses to the army too. 'They're like blowflies round a carcass. By the way, are you missing any birds?'

The man frowned. 'I'd have to check. To be sure we've not had so many arrive lately. Why, are you?'

'I daresay it's hawks,' Luka said carefully. 'Either that or orders are falling off due to the unrest. Perhaps our customers don't care for the uncertainty war brings to the roads.'

'You're right there,' his companion replied feelingly. 'The bandits were bad enough, Bel knows! But now the roads are chockful of deserters if half the talk in the markets is right. That's something to look forward to when this madness is over.'

'Aye,' Luka said. The threat of the noose would ensure the deserters joined the bandits for how else would they live? He sighed. 'Trying times indeed, my friend. Let me know about your birds, won't you?'

***

Tranche's fears were not so easily dismissed. 'They know something,' he fretted, mopping at the nervous sweat that sprung afresh to his face as he wiped it. 'They must have got the birds and cracked our cypher. Certainly they didn't get through, either of them, or why would the jewels have been sent? We expressly told them not to risk it again!'

'I know,' Luka soothed, 'but even if they got the message they will never break the cypher. If they had we'd already be in the Tower. But you know Onli won't move against us without proof. The guild would not stand for it.' Even their megalomaniac king, he thought, knew that the city needed its merchants to survive, particularly now when the war seemed not only less likely to contribute to his resources, but to completely drain them. It was protection of a sort, the rest depended on their ability to bluff if out should it come to questions. If they were caught with incriminating evidence of course, then they were doomed, and their enterprise with them.

'Somebody's pointed them at us — at all of us,' Haran growled. 'Maybe to make it less obvious in order to spread the suspicion over who's the spy?' His distrust of Matto, which though it had eased through lack of proof, had never completely died, flared again, but he didn't voice it. 'And when I discover who it is...'

'We can't stay shut up in here.' Tranche, unheeding, stopped his restless pacing and hurried to the door, 'It reeks of conspiracy.' His hands shook as he pulled it open, saying loudly, 'I'll have the order logged out this afternoon then.' He dropped his voice. 'We can meet at my house tonight, work out what to do.'

Luka shook his head. 'There's Matto... Better to use my cellar. We should shift the gems too. It would only take one Guard exceeding — actually,' his voice quickened at the sudden thought, 'if I were Onli that's exactly how I'd handle it.'

'What do you mean?' Tranche's eyes widened in alarm at his tone.

'Turn a couple of men loose with orders to search the building. If they find nothing he can punish them for going beyond their remit. If however, they do turn something up then the guild's culpable too —'

Haran swore. 'You're right! It's so bloody obvious when you point it out. So we shift them tonight. If only those damn birds had got through we wouldn't be holding them. We should — I dunno, bury 'em somewhere?'

Tranche nodded, his stomach twisting nervously. Yes, I'll return after dark, or stay late. I own I'll be glad to have them gone. It seemed an acceptable risk before but now their presence here terrifies me.'

Luka gripped his shoulder. 'Courage, old friend. Remember: we are but three hard pressed, innocent traders with the weight of the city's commerce on our shoulders, struggling to pay for the king's ill-advised war. Let us so act.'

***

At another time with less at stake Tranche might have thought his partner omniscient for at mid-afternoon the Guards arrived to carry out the scenario Luka had outlined. He had been down at the wharf, detouring on his way back to the premises of a shipping agent, to discuss another cargo. Bulk loading, like grain, travelled by ship, as did the huge casks of Rhutan wine, their sheer weight ruling out the use of camels. Returning to the yard he immediately noticed the absence of Guards, and his heart lightened. Perhaps they were finally satisfied and the business would now be left in peace.

He had taken only a step into the building when this hope was dashed and his heart paralysed by a sudden grip on both his arms.

'And here he is,' a voice declared at his shoulder. 'This way if you please, sir. I think you're wanted inside.'

Numbed by terror, his mouth too dry to protest, Tranche moved woodenly towards his fate. The miniature satchel on his belt, in which reposed the keys to his yard and office, contained a pellet of poison. He would take it sooner than face Onli's torturers. He was not a brave man; he knew that only hatred and a huge anger had brought him this far along the road he had chosen, but he would die rather than give up his friends, which he also knew, under torture he would do. He embarrassed himself with his timidity, hating the nervous sweating and twitching that he couldn't control. It cost him so much more to do what Haran and Luka, both equally at risk, managed so easily, but he would play it through as long as he could, then cheat the Appellan dogs at the last.

The decision brought him a little comfort that was lost again in the shock of seeing the office door with its shattered lock. Books, papers and shelving littered the floor. Two men were systematically destroying his files, ripping them apart to join the growing heap on the floor.

'What?' he cried, genuinely outraged. 'What are you doing? How can I operate — Those are customers' records!' Dropping to his knees he plucked distractedly at the detritus. 'Why are you doing this to me?' Tears of shock stood in his soft doe eyes, only half his distress acted. 'The guild shall hear of this!'

'Don't reckon they'll want to know when we find what we're after.' A tall Guard dropped the last file and stared across the destruction he'd wrought, surveying the room. From the edge of his vision Tranche was aware that a half circle of workers had gathered beyond the outer door. Luka, he remembered was out. His foreman wore a look of shock, Matto stood blank faced in the background, while Fatch who was closest stared avidly, and with satisfaction he thought, at the ruined files he had once worked on. Nobody spoke, but given their position, for they too were about to be tainted with the charge of treason — Tranche didn't blame them. He wouldn't risk it either.

The man had finished his scrutiny of the room. 'Only the desk left,' he said. 'You two, tip it over. See what's underneath.'

"S a heavy bastard of a thing,' one of them grunted, heaving experimentally at it. For a brief moment Tranche allowed himself to think it was the desk itself they wanted but after smashing the drawers the spokesman turned unerringly to the floor. Peeling the rug aside he shot a look at the merchant, still on his knees amid the drift of torn records. His smirk froze Tranche's blood. They knew then. The whole performance had been a charade, played out for his benefit. Somebody, Fatch for sure from the look of enjoyment on his face, had betrayed them. He let his hand slip towards his belt while his gaze clung in morbid fascination to the Guard's face, as if he must witness his own destruction there before he truly believed it. Take it, his mind screamed, now, while there's time. And still he delayed, rolling the pellet in his fingers, while his heart jumped sickeningly with each beat.

'Well,' the Guard grinned. 'Hidey hole, eh? That's more like it. I wonder why you'd need that, an honest man like you?'

Tranche surprised himself. His voice came out firmer than he could have hoped. 'Any business needs a secure place from time to time. There's nothing in it; just a client's papers of credit. You could have just said what you were looking for instead of —' He waved a hand over the room's wreckage. 'It will take days, a moon even to —'

'Won't be your problem, sunshine,' the man retorted cheerfully, 'you'll be occupied with Cap'n Onli.' He hauled the trapdoor up.

Tranche shut his eyes and brought his hand to his lips — and paused there as the Guard swore. Forcing himself to look rather than pass out he stared into the safe-box. The wind went out of him like air from a punctured bellows and the pellet dropped from his suddenly nerveless fingers. The box was as empty as he had claimed, save for the papers. There was no corded bag, no gems. The world seemed to stop and just in time to prevent him from blurting out something stupid, a new voice broke into the litany of oaths the Guard was uttering.

'What in Bel's name is going on here?'

It was Luka at his imperious best, the green turban like a crown of fury, his icy glance skewering the suddenly sweating leader of the coterie. 'Are you in charge here, and responsible for this? Is the guild aware of your activities? By fire and water they will be made so! What is the meaning of this wanton destruction? Who ordered it?'

The Guard captain, enraged at being wrong-footed and perhaps a little afraid at having found nothing to justify the damage done, shot Tranche a look of loathing and struggled for a civil tone.

'Sorry sir. Information was laid — seems it was wrong. Maybe the lads were a bit enthusiastic like, carrying out their duties.' His glance skittered over the smashed drawers and shelving. 'Here, you two. Stand the desk up. A mistake, sir. We'll be off then.'

'A mistake too far,' Luka said coldly, 'as you will soon discover. Not so fast.' His glance fell on his watching men. 'Matto, Fatch! Get in here. I want a record of this. You will make a list of every bit of damage done and this man here will sign both sheets. One for the House, one for the Guildmaster when I register a complaint.'

The Appellan scowled but didn't quite dare walk away. Luka folded his arms and waited while his two employees examined and listed the wreckage. Matto eyed the files helplessly. 'What of these, Master? How can we tell how many...?'

'Estimate,' Luka snapped, 'and if you cannot find it list the coins from the cashbox too. There were fifty silvers in there yesterday.' The money was kept to pay off the carters who transported goods to the docks.

When at last it was done and the lists duly signed, Luka waved his two scribes out on the heels of the departing Guards. He shut the door behind them, grimacing at the smashed lock, then stepped closer to grip his partner's shoulder, which had begun to shake. 'Are you all right?'

Tranche ignored him. He wandered across to kneel by the safe-box. 'Great Bel! They've gone!' Lifting his right arm he studied the tremors wracking it. 'I had the poison at my lips — it was that close, Luka! Then I heard him swear. I opened my eyes and the box was empty. I dropped it somewhere here.' He fell to his knees, and began pawing through a drift of papers.

Gently,' his partner said, face registering concern. 'What did you drop?'

'Why the poison, man! It's here somewhere. I must find it.'

'No.' Grasping his shoulder Luka drew him to his feet. 'What we must find are the gems. They didn't simply vanish, my friend. Somebody found and removed them. Somebody knows. The question is: who?'

'Yes, of course. I'm sorry.' Tranche shook his head as if to clear it, brown eyes wide. 'I'm not thinking straight. The shock — I was terrified, Luka. Utterly terrified. I almost shat myself —' The door opened as he spoke and Matto stepped in, closing it quietly behind him again.

'Get out!' Luka roared. 'By the gods you presume too much, young man! You are an apprentice not a partner. You cannot stroll into your master's office without even the courtesy of a knock.'

'It's all right,' Tranche began, but the older man cut him short.

'No, it is not! The time has come for a little straight speaking. Somebody —' Abruptly he bit the words off and, nostrils flaring, drew an audible breath. He schooled his tone before he spoke again. 'Just go. We have serious matters to settle here.'

'Is finding this one of them?' The apprentice pulled a corded bag from beneath his tunic and set it on the desk. 'Sorry for butting in gentlemen, but I thought you'd want it back.' Turning about he headed for the door.

10

The breath of the two men went out in a gasp. Tranche said, 'How? What —?' and could manage no more.

'Wait!' Luka said.

Matto, hand reaching for the door, looked at him. 'I thought you wanted me gone?'

'No. Please, come back. I don't know how... But you need to explain yourself. I owe you an apology, it seems. We are deeply in your debt, Matto, but —'

Tranche was more direct. 'How did you find out about the safe-box?'

Matto's stiffness vanished into apology. 'I saw you open it one evening, years back. It was late, everyone else had gone and you hadn't quite shut the door. I was coming back to ask you something, and I just caught a glimpse — so I left again.' He shrugged. 'We all knew you kept gold and notes of credit here, so I guessed the safe-box was partners' business that you wouldn't want me to be aware of. Which is why I never said anything. I wondered if Fatch knew though. He blames you,' he told Tranche, 'for not getting his turban; says you didn't support him. He's always hanging around the office, so it seemed likely.'

'You don't get on with him,' Tranche said. 'You never have.'

'No. He's a sneaky little git, light fingered too. It crossed my mind to wonder if he's the informer. Well, somebody plainly is! The Guards seem to know too much about us: when ships are due in, what valuables are in the cargo... Then yesterday I actually saw him meet with one of the Guards. Not by chance either. Fatch had apparently been kicking his heels for some time because he was angry with the man for being late. I smelt a trap in the making and it occurred to me that maybe he'd planted something for them to find. So I checked the office while you were down at the ship, and luckily for us all, remembered the hiding place under your desk.' He nodded at the bag. 'I'm guessing that's the sort of stuff you were smuggling in my quiver?'

'Thank you Matto. That was well done, you've saved all our lives by your action. But all you have told us is the how of it. Not the why.'

The apprentice stiffened. 'Is loyalty not enough? I work for the House; and Master Tranche has always treated me well. He has given me a place and a future. I don't forget that the day we met I had neither.'

'Yes, it was odd that. I have always thought so,' Luka said meditatively. 'That you should meet him of all men, just where and when you did.'

'No odder than a respectable House smuggling gems,' Matto shot back. 'I am not the one breaking the law here. Are you going to explain — or do you still not trust me?'

Tranche opened his mouth but Luka cut across him before he could speak. 'We two cannot make that decision alone, but come with us now to my place and we shall see.' When Matto hesitated he waved an expansive hand. 'Hold onto the gems then — will that satisfy you? Hide them under your tunic and we shall go to oh, buy replacement furniture, Bel knows we need it! Make some notes of what's needed in case we are stopped and questioned, though I doubt that we will be.'

Matto did as he was bidden, slipping the cord through his belt and tucking the bag out of sight. He took the paper on which Tranche had scrawled down some jottings and a few measurements while Luka opened the broken door to call to Fatch and the next closest man.

'Aye, Master?'

'You two, clear this mess up,' he responded irritably, a man whose temper was clearly on the stretch. 'Take out the broken wood and box the papers. They will all have to be pieced together, sorted and where possible salvaged. Bel's tail! What a bloody shambles. You have those measurements, Matto?'

'Yes, Master.'

'Well, come on then. We haven't all day!' The two left, the turbanned head and its dark haired companion bobbing from sight through the gates. Tranche, watching them go, swore suddenly and kicked his chair across the room, just missing the clerk, who jumped in surprise. Fatch said, 'Master?' his voice jerking upwards on the second syllable.

Tranche ignored him. 'I need a drink.' He started towards the cupboard where the wine was kept, remembered that it was kindling and the flask a stain on the floor, swore again and left the office, heading for the sailors' tavern on the waterfront.

***

It was the first time Matto had been to Luka's home. It was set back a little from other houses in a better section of the city, and like the palace itself the grounds ran down to the grassed river bank. It also included a small jetty. Keeping a boat meant that its owner could leave the city, as one could from the palace or the docks, without passing through the city gates — an advantage that could only benefit a smuggler, Matto decided. They entered by a side door, Luka waving away the servant that came to meet him.

'Tell my daughter I am occupied,' he said.

'She is from home, sir,' the man responded.

'All the better. I have business to discuss.'

He led his guest through the well-appointed house. There were rugs on the floor, paintings and mirrors on the walls. Matto caught a glimpse through an open door of a glass cabinet holding a glazed ceramic bowl that, even at a swift glance, was beautiful. It was not the home of a poor man; and he must have been even wealthier once before Cyrus had appeared at Ripa's gates. Was it to regain this wealth that he had taken to smuggling, Matto wondered? And was surprised by how deeply he was disappointed by the idea.

In a windowless room containing a long bench, books, a brazier and a shabby looking armchair, Luka motioned to the younger man to help him push aside the heavy bench. A trapdoor beneath gave onto a steep flight of steps leading to a roomy cellar furnished with wine barrels. A rough plank table stood in the centre, some chairs, and a lamp. He lit the lamp, waved Matto to a seat and held out his hand. 'The jewels, if you please.'

Matto handed them over. He gazed about, eyeing the wine casks and, incongruously, a shelf of cheese-wheels, while Luka watched him, the bag of gems on the table between them. It was very quiet, Luka didn't speak again and no other sound penetrated the walls. Matto was aware of a growing disquiet. The thought came to him with a little frisson of alarm that he had blundered upon knowledge the merchant must wish he didn't possess. He could be killed here with nobody the wiser. Nor did he doubt Luka's ability to order it, should he feel the need. Tranche's sweating fear back in the office saw to that.

Whatever the two were up to it was no game and the stakes were high. The lamp burned without a flicker and the air smelled vaguely of cool stone, old wine, and the faint fusty odour of cheese. Matto held himself still, thinking back over those moments in the office. He asked the question Luka had least expected.

'What did you mean that it was odd — my meeting Tranche, of all men? There was nobody else to meet. We were alone on the road that day.'

The merchant took a moment to shape his answer studying his apprentice's face. Either Matto knew already, or he didn't. Either way it scarcely mattered now, he knew too much for them to release him.

'So you weren't aware he'd lost his son? That the boy would have been your age, or near it, when you met?'

Matto looked puzzled. 'How could I? The man was a stranger to me. But it's not news, Banco told me that years ago.' He paused putting it together, and a slow flush mounted his cheeks. 'Wait — you think I knew it then, and played on it to have him take me on? That is the most despicable thing I ever heard! He needed help, so I helped him. It cost me nothing, and afterwards he was kind and helped me in return. That's all there was to it.' He sprang to his feet. 'For the record, Master, I have been loyal to him and your House, and I'll not sit here and listen to this. You do him no honour either, to think him so easily gulled.'

'Sit down!' Luka rapped out. Behind them the trapdoor swung up and footsteps descended, two sets of them. Then daylight vanished again leaving only the lamp's glow to show first Tranche and then Haran. The latter carried cups and a basket from which ends of loaves poked.

'I'm starved,' he announced emptying bread, onions and a skin of dark sausage onto the table. 'Is that cheese just for decoration?'

'What? No, help yourself' said Luka, plainly thrown off his stride by the interruption. Matto slowly resumed his seat as the whole became blindingly clear to him. Not a vision, over the past few seasons he had ceased to even think of the Goddess, but a sudden coming together of disparate rumour and supposition into a whole picture.

'The gems,' he exclaimed, 'they're nothing to do with the House, are they? You were smuggling before I ever came onto the scene, under the very noses of the king's men. You're buying arms for this prince you pretend doesn't exist. Of course! Who is better placed than merchants with contacts outside the country, and ships — no wonder the Guards were searching them! You're probably the only ones who could pull it off. And here I was thinking you just wanted to be wealthy again the way you once were!'

There was a moment's frozen silence. The sound of Haran's knife sawing at a loaf, stilled. Matto glanced from Luka's blank face to Tranche's surprised one, and then at Haran's, its stilled watchfulness the most dangerous of the three. His hand dropped by instinct to where his dagger was sheathed at his belt, hovering there as Haran began placidly sawing again. 'And if we are?' he asked.

Matto laughed, a short, derisive sound, shorn of all humour. 'Good luck to you. But I would be wary gentlemen, of your would-be ruler. So desperate a gamble and all based on lies! Who is he? Some scion of an Appellan noble with ambitions for the throne?'

'Prince Darien is the rightful heir of this land,' Luka corrected coldly. 'He is the son of the late Princess Leona and Prince Smerdis, King Temes's elder brother. He is unknown save to the army he is gathering, but he is the legitimate heir, the one Cyrus himself nominated as his successor.'

Matto was shaking his head before he had done speaking; he studied the faces of the three conspirators, men he had liked and respected, men to whom he owed a debt of gratitude, and knew he couldn't keep silent on this issue. His life as well as their was involved. The Tower was so close to them all he could almost see the shadow of the noose swinging above their heads. Temes's retribution would be terrible, and he would be swept up in it, he thought despairingly, along with every man that worked for the House. It was Onli's way. All would be judged guilty by association.

'He cannot be. The Princess had but one son and his name was Marric. You have only to ask in Ansham to establish that. It is where he lived and died, was murdered rather, on the king's orders, along with his father Smerdis, and Smerdis's other son.'

'That's the official story,' Tranche agreed. 'It's the one the Princess planned. She was a seer, you know, she could see what was to come. Of course she didn't plan the lad's death. That was a tragedy. My sister is a priestess of the Goddess. She served Leona and was chosen by her to be Darien's foster-mother, to have the raising of him. The Princess bore twins and he was the first-born. My sister took him from the birthing bed and reared him anonymously. The other twin was the official baby, the one they smuggled from the city the night of the revolt. And you are right in saying he died. But Darien is in the Lake Country with his grandmother, Queen Quan. And these,' he upended the bag of gems so that they rolled out onto the bare boards amidst the food, 'are the last of Rhuta's royal jewels. We have been selling them bit by bit over the years, to finance the arms that will bring Darien to his rightful throne.'

Luka cleared his throat in a pointed fashion. 'Well done, now you've told him everything; was that wise or even necessary? We are here, remember, to make a decision.'

Haran looked up from his bread and sausage, dark eyes fixed on Matto. 'Tranche believes that Fatch is our spy, but I think there's a very good chance it's you. No,' he raised a hand as Matto spluttered a denial. 'Save it. See, the thing is, you knew about the safe-box, which is not so good. Then today you moved the jewels in time to prevent their discovery, a point in your favour one might reason, and intimated that Fatch is tight with the Guards. But we only have your word for that, and how do we know that Onli isn't playing a long game here?'

'Maybe you really are the spy and the two of you hatched this plot between you.' He scratched his ear lobe with the tip of his knife. 'Be simple enough, wouldn't it? He tears the place apart, fails to find anything, you return the goods to us once he's gone, which makes you seem loyal and above board. Then, like my associate Tranche just did, we spill the whole plot and you trot back to Onli and get us all arrested. It all seems a bit pat to a suspicious bugger like me.'

Tranche said, 'Matto would never — He's proved his —'

'Yeah, well, you might be willing to risk your life on him, my friend, but I'm not,' Haran retorted. 'You had to give him the Prince's bloody locality? Even if we believed him there's no letting him go now. Besides, he knows a sight too much about the dead twin for my liking. A simple shepherd lad? Where would he even get his name from?'

'I'm from Ansham, of course I know!' Matto cried furiously, the irony of his position not lost on him. Only by admitting to his real identity could he convince them of his innocence, and that was the last thing he could afford to tell men already in the shadow of the Tower. 'And there was no twin! Be damned to that for a tale. This Darien of yours is an imposter. If you must risk your lives for your country don't do it for a scheming mountebank who has no more claim to the throne than you have.' He had never expected to have to defend himself against his own supposed death. Possibly the only living person who could identify him was his uncle; and in that event he would be dead in truth. He started to rise. 'I will have nothing to do with this madness.'

Instantly Haran was standing, the knife, still with a smear of sausage fat on the blade, in his hand.

'Sit down. I haven't said we'll kill you but you can't expect us to let you walk out of here with what you've learned. So you'll be taking a little trip to the Lakes with us. Let's call it a precaution. Tranche, you'll have to leave too. Just for a bit till we see which way Onli jumps when this one,' he nodded at Matto, 'disappears.'

Matto folded his arms. 'What are you going to do, drag me there? Because you'll have to. I want nothing to do with this business, any of it.' He glanced at the steps, measuring the distance, then sprang, his wiry form closing the gap even before his falling chair clattered against the stone floor.

Haran was quicker, thrusting out a leg to trip him as he landed and following it with a punch that had the considerable strength of his shoulders behind it. Matto's mouth opened involuntarily as the air rushed from him and his face smacked against the floor. Tranche was on his feet shouting as Haran placed a knee on his captive's labouring chest. He reached for the cord with which he'd come provided, and while Matto gasped and whooped, lashed his wrists together. He waited for the younger man's breathing to ease then hauled him to his feet, steering him back to the chair which he set back on its legs.

'If we're still keeping tally,' he announced conversationally, 'that counts against you too.' Then reeled back with an oath as Matto's skull made violent contact with his nose. Blinded by pain he lashed out with his boot and more by good luck than judgement, caught the side of his attacker's bad leg. This time Matto stayed down, teeth gritted against the sickening waves of pain, his head ringing from its second contact with the stone floor. Blood poured from Haran's nose to spatter his clothes. He righted the chair once again, heaved the supine body up by a handful of tunic and slammed him into it.

'Now we're square,' he growled. 'Try that again and it will get personal.'

Tranche was plainly unhappy about the course events had taken, Luka, stroking his short beard non-committal. They listened as Haran, voice muffled by the cloth jammed against his nose, outlined the plan he'd devised. 'The Lakes is the best place for him. The Prince has the manpower to guard prisoners, and the time. We have neither, so we hand him over and let them get the truth from him. And right now the Lakes is the best place for you too, Tranche, till we see how the wind's blowing. As far as the House knows you'll have taken ship to Deems. Nothing unusual in that. The Alpen Girl sails tomorrow so if things turn bad we can always say you changed your mind and stayed aboard for the voyage as trader for the trip. Meanwhile Luka creates a fuss with the guild over the Guards' unlawful search, and the damage they did. They have nothing on us yet so it could all blow over, in fact it probably will. If, that's to say when it does, you can return.'

'And, if we're to believe him,' Luka nodded at the glowering Matto, 'what about Fatch?'

Haran scratched his cheek. 'Wait and see? We've only his word for it Fatch ever met with a Guard. If he did, if he's the spy... Well, us pretending ignorance could give us an advantage; we could plant false information...' He frowned, thinking about it. 'Nope, too dangerous. Still, turning him off, if he is the spy, could rouse suspicion too. If Onli were to think we'd rumbled him as an informer it might make him wonder what we've got to hide.'

He speared a wedge of cheese with his knife and considered the elder partner. 'Now might be a good time to send your daughter out of the city for a bit. A visit to a distant cousin? As distant as you can find, perhaps. Just as a precaution.'

Luka fingered his beard. 'You really think it necessary?'

'Wise, anyway. And that just leaves you and me. We should stay, and dispose of these somewhere safe.' His gaze rested on the bag of gems. 'We can't use them now the army's all over the place. And I reckon this should be our last private meeting, too. Time to go quiet for a bit I think.'

'I agree,' Luka said. 'Tranche?'

The plump merchant nodded unhappily. 'Yes, it all makes sense, except this business with Matto. I don't believe —'

'It doesn't matter what you want to believe,' Haran broke in. 'You're the one that told him where the Prince can be found. That alone means we can't let him loose! You heard him say he doesn't want any part of it. That's only a step from deciding to inform on us. Listen, it's simple — either he's for us or against us. Look at it this way, if he's as innocent as he claims the Lakers can keep him for as long as it takes, and I'll be the first to apologise when they let him go. If he's not, well, we've far more pressing worries than a dead spy.'

Matto's blood chilled at these words. How in the Mother's name was he going to prove he wasn't a traitor without revealing the truth, when doing so would certainly seal his fate? The last thing this bogus prince could risk was the real heir turning up to ruin his plans. This Darien didn't even have to believe him. Even a hint of his true identity would be cause enough for him to order his death. He listened as the discussion moved on to House business, orders received, goods on hand, as if they were sitting around in Tranche's office over an everyday meeting, and his fate just another item on the agenda. Haran's attention however, he noticed, as he strained surreptiously at his bonds, never strayed far from him, nor did the knife leave his hand. If he could speak with Tranche alone, Matto thought, reason with him, there was a chance he could talk him round. But there seemed little likelihood of that.

He had been blind. The whole thing became so obvious once you knew about the smuggling that he wondered he hadn't worked it out for himself. Not what was going on exactly — that was beyond belief! — but that something was afoot. The talents of the three men meshed together as smoothly as the motion of a ship turning into the wind with every rope and square of canvas playing its part. Luka plainly provided the intellect behind their desperate venture, Tranche the emotion fuelling it, while Haran did what was necessary. And if that included slipping a knife into Matto's ribs, he wouldn't baulk at the need.

No doubt they made a formidable combination, witness the fact that they had carried on undetected for years, but they were still hopelessly outclassed Matto knew, both they and their pseudo prince, by their enemy. If they mustered every Laker man to fight, Temes's army would still outnumber them by thousands. Which hardly mattered to him, Matto admitted, as he'd either be dead or so deeply implicated by then that he'd wish he was when the inevitable happened. He closed his eyes raging, silently at his situation. His head throbbed and his face itched where blood from his split scalp had dried and tightened the skin. Knowing the futility of it he continued to wrestle with his bonds, while feverishly pondering his options.

Fixated as the three men were on their prince, they wouldn't believe his claim to be another. Anyway he had no proof and a secret told was no longer safe. The other way was to wait, let them prove him a spy. Which might be a painful course if the false prince's men resorted to beating the truth from him, and, even lacking a confession they might still kill him, just to be on the safe side. They were playing for the highest stakes, and his, he guessed wouldn't be the only death meted out for the cause. Given what he now knew of Haran's deviousness it wouldn't surprise him at all if Fatch also were to be found dead in an alley some day soon. Well, no one deserved it more, but it was little compensation all the same.

The third option he had was to wait and be ready to take any opportunity that offered freedom. Where he might go if he could get away was another matter, but he would face that when he came to it. The talk at the table had ceased. He opened his eyes to see them rising, the conference over. Haran looped a length of cord about his bound wrists and showed him the dagger, now wiped clean of cheese and sausage.

'Right, young man.' He nodded at the steps, 'Up you go. Nice and steady. We're taking a boat ride and you'd be wise not to try anything. Even if my blade misses your throat you'll not swim far with your hands tied.'

PART TWO

11

The two men riding through the humpy ridges of the Lake Country drylands saw the anomaly in the landscape and angled their mounts to investigate. They approached cautiously for the country was particularly unsafe at present as the burnt out farmstead they had recently seen, attested. Deserters from Temes's routed army, bandits, disgruntled soldiers making their bootyless way home — all took what they wanted by force of arms, as the death and destruction at the farm holding proved.

Hands on their weapons the men, garbed in identical blue tunics over grey trousers, were suitably wary as they neared the tumbled body. They'd seen similar tricks before to bait an ambush, and habits learned in frontier fighting tended to stay with a man. So Nannik sat his saddle watchfully, eyes flicking between scrubby oak and rocky outcrop, while Osram dropped lightly to the ground, drawing his blade before stepping forward to investigate the body.

When he saw his partner drive the weapon back into its scabbard and break into a run, Nannik kicked his mount forward. 'What?' he called, trotting over.

'It's a child.' Osram's voice was shocked. 'Lord of Light! Who's responsible for this?'

His words roused the girl; she seemed at death's door yet at sight of the man looming above her she gave a wordless shriek, dry mouth gaping wide while her hands, swollen from the cord bound tightly about her wrists, scrabbled uselessly at the hard earth, trying to thrust herself away from him.

She was very young, not even on the cusp of womanhood, but the front of her torn and filthy gown was bloodstained in a way that could only mean one thing. Osram, who for all his ferocity in battle had a gentle side to him, looked away from it, suddenly ashamed of his sex.

'Here.' Nannik offered his knife. The child, who could scarcely, he thought, have ten summers behind her, shrank back, dark eyes dilating with terror. She tried to scream but only a rasping sound passed her blood caked lips. Her dark skin held overtones of grey as Osram cut her bonds while Nannik fetched the water-skin from his saddle and fed a slow trickle of liquid into her.

'She's from Barat,' he said wonderingly. 'How, under Asher's Light did she wind up here in the desert?' The border was at least seven days ride away. That she had been badly used was plain enough — her bare feet were raw and swollen, and despite her dark skin it was easy to tell the bruises on her face and upper arms. Her nose seemed to have been broken too. So she had been beaten and raped but the rest was harder to read. Either she had somehow escaped her captors with her hands still tied, or she had been deliberately dumped in this waterless wilderness to wander until she perished.

'It's all right, little one,' Osram soothed. 'We won't hurt you.' His words seemed to freeze the girl. She stared with dilated eyes as if at a snake. A smile didn't help either. Seething with outrage he said, 'Bandits? But what would they want with a child? Army deserters? If I get my hands on whoever did this I'll castrate the bastard myself.'

'More likely slavers with a coffle for Meddia,' Nannik said thoughtfully. It was illegal, slaves were supposedly debtors or criminals, but the trade went on, while throughout Rhuta the Guards did nothing to halt it.

The poor, the unlucky, the defenseless could all find themselves snatched out of their lives, chained and then sold into an unimaginable future. 'It would account for her hands being bound.'

'Not for the rest,' Osram argued. 'Slavers want undamaged goods. We'd best feed her something. What have we got?'

'How about this then — she was taken, managed to get away from the coffle, and had the bad luck to run into somebody best avoided?' Nannik suggested busy at the saddlebags. He softened bread in the last of their wine and held it to the child's lips. 'More water,' he said, watching her weak efforts to chew, 'then we'd best head for the shrine. The Sisters will know what she needs.'

Though a little revived by the food and water the child's torn feet couldn't support her. She struggled, screaming, when Osram lifted her then suddenly went limp as consciousness fled. In the saddle he gathered her to him, carrying her light as an injured bird in his strong arms. Asher knew she resembled one, he thought anxiously; she was as weak as a new-hatched nestling. Her head lolled against his supporting arm, the cracked and bloody lips parted to show the dry pink cavern of her mouth, the thin stuff of her gown scarcely lifting over the flat, childish chest.

***

'How's she doing?' Nannik broke the long silence, easing himself in the saddle, glad that the shadows had finally lengthened towards late afternoon. The horses still stepped tirelessly forward but they wouldn't reach the Lakes much before sundown.

'Weaker, I think,' Osram fretted.

'Maybe I should ride ahead — tell them you're coming?'

'It won't get her there any quicker. Besides, I might need your blade if I run into company.'

'True.' The past days had shown them what the rabble of a demoralised army could do. Even Osram, hampered by his charge, would be easy game, his mount alone temptation enough for disgruntled deserters to risk attacking an armed man. Nannik resumed his silent squinting scrutiny of the barren land as the horses clopped briskly on.

They reached the shrine on the lake shore as the setting sun turned its waters to a blaze of gold. Nannik shouted, then dismounted to take the child's form from Osram's aching arms. His call brought a tall woman clothed in the white garb of a priestess. She asked no questions but casting a quick look at their burden led the way into a quiet interior where she bade him lay the girl on a bed there. Water plinked musically and there was a smell of crushed herbs on the cool air. Digesting Osram's rapid account of finding the child the priestess nodded once then ushered them out again.

'Be sure we will do all in our power for the little one. If the Goddess wills it she will live. Know that you have earned Her blessing in your care for Her child.'

'Well,' Nannik stretched until his shoulder muscles cracked then scrubbed a weary hand over his face, pausing to smooth the fair mustache on his upper lip, 'that's that sorted then. We'd best get the horses seen to and report in. Darien must be wondering by now what's befallen us.'

'Aye,' Osram yawned widely. They were two day's overdue. 'And a poor enough report to bring him. A lost child, five dead Lakers, a burnt out farmstead, the butchery of that travelling family and what — fifteen recruits, was it?'

'We can't take the credit for that, they recruited 'emselves. Looks like they beat us back here too. See the grey?' They had come to the gate of a field beside a stabling complex where several dozen horses could be seen. Nannik jerked his head at one. 'That's what he was riding, the bandy legged fellow with the squint. If they continue coming in at this rate we'll soon be running short of feed for the animals.'

'Nobody ever said that raising an army was cheap. But Darien seems to keep finding the funds, though Light knows how! I dunno about you but I'm dying for a brew, and something to prise my belly off my backbone.'

'You're getting soft, big man. Back in the Grasslands I've seen you go two days just on the sniff of a meal.'

'About the only advantage terror gives you.' Osram turned his mount loose to wander off and roll, scratching its sweaty body against the hard soil. 'That's something for the Prince to remember, too,' he added soberly, 'because afterwards, whoever wins the war that's coming, the barbarians will still be there in their Grasslands, waiting for the victor. Just like always.'

'Very true, my friend, but that's tomorrow's worry.' There was a boat awaiting them at the end of a narrow jetty. They dropped into it with the ease of practice, taking a little longer perhaps, than a native Laker would have done, to find their balance, then sent it skimming across the extended reach of water, weaving through the drifting islands of reeds until they were lost to sight from the shore.

***

It was dark on the river. Moonlight touched the rippling current with moving fingers of silver, but bank and jetty were solid black. Tranche stepped into the boat first, setting it wobbling. Matto, shoved from behind and still with bound hands, fell clumsily into the fat merchant's grasp and then Haran followed, catching the painter thrown to him as Luka cast off then pressed the buoyant vessel away with one foot. Shuffling his backside onto the plank seat, Matto suggested, 'If you free my hands I could help row.'

'Or beat my head in with an oar,' Haran agreed shortly. 'We'll manage without your help.'

'Suit yourself.' The shoulder shape that was Matto shrugged. 'You do the work then.'

A light wind blew on their backs where the dark, shapeless mass that was the city lay speckled with light. The temple, unmistakable by its height, was lavishly lit, the glow from the torches planted either side of the entrance showing clearly in the night. Haran, facing the city as he rowed, traced a line north from its brightness but failed to locate the Wazzit Tower. It brooded in obscurity, somehow the more threatening for the darkness that hid it from sight. He snuffled through his tender nose and wondered about Matto.

Was he right in his suspicions? The young man had been a useful, reliable servant of the House, dependable, attentive to his work, but hadn't there always been an element of secretiveness in the way he seldom spoke of his past life? Haran had never heard him mention his family, or the friends he must have had back in Ansham. Today's business with the search and his removal of the gems — that was all a bit too pat, somehow. And he had attempted to escape.

That definitely counted against him. Had he seen the web of circumstantial evidence, for it was no more than that, Haran admitted, closing against him and panicked? That single act counted most heavily against him, and brought no credit on himself either, the trader thought. The young bastard had caught him unawares, right enough. His own fault. He should have expected it for if his suspicions were correct Matto was going to his death at the Lakes and must know it to be so.

It was a hard pull upstream and a long time since the trader had worked a boat. He heard Tranche's heavy breathing and felt the tightness in his palms that would be blisters later on, then the ache starting up in his shoulders. For a long time there was just the squeak of rowlocks, the ripple and suck of the water against the boat's skin and an occasional groan of effort from Tranche. They were midstream, working their way gradually against the current for he needed to recognise the place where he had arranged for the horses to be waiting.

Sweating, feeling his back muscles begin to tighten, Haran's thoughts returned to worry at the enigma of their captive, who seemed content to bide in silence. It argued a degree of control remarkable under the circumstances, and yet another mark against him. He was halfway tempted to free the young bugger and make him row, but it would be madness. He could attack them, or deliberately overturn the boat and drown them all. A wise man took no liberties with the Great River; even Bel, deity though he was, probably had a healthy respect for the power leashed within its current.

Slowly the bank drew nearer; the sound of water and the creak of the oars became gradually overlaid by the croak of frogs, and the sleepy quarreling of ducks roosting on the mud banks of a small, willow-grown island where they were safe from marauding dogs and foxes. The jetty he sought was close, just upstream of the island.

'Not far now,' he grunted to his rowing mate, the breath coming hard in his throat. 'Keep an eye out.'

It was Matto who spotted it, the first words he had spoken since his offer to row. He added to them as the cord he was being led by tightened, pulling him up the weed-slimed steps.

'The cord's too tight. My hands are numb.'

'Remind me to apologise later.' Haran boosted him onto one of the horses, waiting saddled and provisioned, as he had ordered. Fleetingly he wondered what the handler he'd entrusted with the task had made of it, and hoped he could hold his tongue. He mounted his own horse, took Matto's reins and led off across the open country between the fields of unseen crops, and past the darkened farmsteads that dotted the arable land. It would be a hard ride but he calculated that they could make their destination by dawn of the second day. Tranche's hurried protest, that surely they could at least loosen the lad's hands now they were off the water, he ignored.

They stopped once to relieve themselves and make an unhurried meal while the horses grazed on the edge of some farmer's fields. Matto's hands were freed to enable him to eat, but not until his ankles had been bound and secured to a tree. He bore it without complaint save to observe sardonically, 'You are earning yourself a lot to apologise for, Haran.'

'We'll see about that,' was the truculent reply. Tranche, plainly unhappy, murmured something placatory that Matto brushed aside.

'Tell me about your sister,' he said. 'The one that supposedly fostered your prince. Why would a priestess of the Mother be serving the Seer of Bel? Doesn't that seem just a little unlikely? If she's your sister why does she follow the Goddess, anyway?'

'She was the Oracle, not the Seer. Though not at the time. The Princess was ejected from the Temple of Bel before her marriage,' Tranche explained. 'As for the rest, we are both, my sister and I, Laker born. I told you that when first we met. Neither of us have ever worshipped Bel. King Waltu's brother, who governed the Lake Country then, married a local, so there were those in the royal court who were followers of the Lady, as we call her here. So you see it is not so surprising, after all.'

Matto eyed the merchant's heavy face, lit fitfully by the light of their small campfire. When had he last really looked at the brown, doe eyes and now sparse, dark hair? Take away the fat and the years — he said, 'I remember now, but you look like a Rhutan.'

'So do you,' Haran interjected, anxious to keep any understanding from developing between the two. 'Maybe you are one, and not from Ansham at all.'

Matto ignored him. 'You were saying — your sister?'

'It was because she was an outsider that Ananda came to serve the Princess. The high priest had Named her, which meant that the temple women who attended the pregnancies of the high born women, were prevented from doing so by their vows. It was a great scandal — you can have no idea. Had the father not been Cyrus's own son she must have died then by the high priest's hand; and few would have blamed him. You have to understand, she was the Oracle of Bel, close to the godhead, and holy above all... and that he was a foreigner only made it worse, and an Appellan at that!'

Tranche shook his head, lost in the telling of the old tragedy. 'Only Cyrus's intervention saved her life. He married her to Smerdis, which pleased nobody, but it protected her, for a while. Long enough to birth her sons. Perhaps she knew what was to come, she was the Oracle after all, and that's why she did what she did, hid Darien away to await his time. Of course there were others involved too, there had to be — all Lakers. The Lake Country has ever upheld the rights of Rhuta.'

'And when your sister returned to the Lakes, presumably unwed, and with a child, after what — a moon, possibly two — nobody asked awkward questions? Babies don't appear overnight,' Matto pointed out, adding with a malicious glance at Haran. 'I was a shepherd, remember? I know how it works.'

Tranche wrinkled his brow. 'Why would they? The Lady's priestesses don't wed. Their rites celebrate the sex act between men and women; they all bear children if they can. The Prince was simply accepted as a result of such a union. None of the Goddess's Babes, as they are called ever know who their fathers are.'

Matto pounced on the admission. 'In fact, you have only her word then that she isn't your Prince's real mother.'

'Are we fools?' Haran demanded harshly. 'There is an independent witness to his birth and a document in Princess Leona's own hand attesting to it, and that of his brother Prince Marric.' To Tranche he said brusquely. 'Enough. Ignore him. He's trying to create doubt where there is none. Put out your hands.'

This last was addressed to Matto. Resignedly he complied, his wrists were rebound, he was hoisted into the saddle and the journey continued while the stars wore away the blackness of time. In the grey light of dawn Haran, who had been searching the landscape, found the barn he was seeking, a dilapidated structure on the edge of a fallow field, with an equally tumbledown farmhouse beyond. Tranche leaned his bulk on the sagging door to force it open and they entered the cavernous darkness which proved to be supplied with hay, water, and a rough circle of fire-blackened stones. Matto was again tethered by the ankles to a sturdy roof upright, then Haran stripped the gear from the horses, and spread the saddle cloths to dry, while Tranche disappeared to collect the makings of a fire.

'One of your smugglers' hideouts, is it?' Matto asked from where he squatted against the post as he chafed his swollen hands, wincing with pain as the blood returned to sausage shaped fingers. He eyed the length of light chain securing his feet, knowing there was no way he could get it off. The wire securing it had been crimped with shoeing pincers taken from the forge in the back corner of the barn. All contingencies, even that of replacing a lost shoe, were catered for in the barn whose inner structure, he now saw, was actually stronger than its appearance indicated. He didn't expect an answer and didn't get one.

It had been a long ride and all were weary. Tranche prepared a quick meal then doused the fire, rolled himself into his cloak and went to sleep on a pile of hay, his snores disturbing the silence. Matto yawned and wished he had his own cloak. He tugged a bundle of hay towards him, making himself as comfortable as he could, ignoring Haran who was inspecting the feet of the feeding horses. Eyes drifting shut he humped onto his side, remembering another barn and a winter on the plateau. Only Rissak had been with him then and both had been fleeing for their lives... He sighed a long exhalation. Perhaps the death Cran had foreseen for him was finally about to claim him? The thought came and passed, his mind taken up with digesting the extraordinary story that Tranche had told.

Loathe though he was to believe it, Matto had to admit it still held the ring of truth. Which might just mean that the man himself believed it, not that it was true. Because if it was, then surely Taba would have known. She had been there in the palace when he, and if it were so, his twin, was born. So why would she not have told him? Therefore it could only be a farrago of lies.

Tranche had said his grandmother still lived. Surely she wouldn't lend herself to a hoax of this nature, unless — he paused to consider a new thought. Unless her hatred of Rhuta's oppressors was so great given what had happened to her family, that she had agreed to it to seek revenge? If the fake prince was Laker born, perhaps even a remote connection of the Rhutan royals? Taba had been a Laker and she was Waltu's niece. So, an overlooked third cousin say, with some actual claim to the throne? Matto could accept that. As if he had a choice, he wryly reminded himslf, but somehow even in his own present straits, it seemed important that his rightful place should not be usurped by a mountebank seeking only his own advancement. Worn out he slept on the thought.

***

Sunlight poked diffused fingers of brightness in through a section of holed wall. The chain clinked when he moved and a feeding horse snorted and shook itself, its tread heavy on the floor. Matto dozed, drawing up his legs and a vague picture of water-sheeted rock came to him, but he couldn't place it. Was it the Cave of the Mother to which they had carried Taba, or the flat beside the creek where the blue horses had fallen with him?

The memory brought a brief, vivid image of Rissak as he had been that day, and he sighed in his sleep with regret and old pain. It wasn't often he allowed his thoughts to dwell on the past but when he did let himself remember, the loss of his friend was still sharp. He opened his eyes to diminished brightness and the sight of Haran doggedly keeping watch. It must be afternoon then. He muttered a curse at his captor and rolled over, dozing off again, the rest of the day lost in jumbled dreams that fled even as he tried to hold them.

***

When he woke the barn was dim, lit only by the fire that Tranche was tending. The holes where the sunlight had shone were greyed over and there was a savoury smell of cooking meat. Haran slept in the hay, the ends of his turban over his face. The barn smelled of smoke and horse dung, and the sharp odour of urine where the horses had staled in the scattered hay. Hearing the chain rattle Tranche glanced up from his cooking.

'You want to piss, help yourself. The horses have been before you.'

'What time of day is it?' Matto rose; his chain didn't reach to the trough but he turned his back to avail himself of the man's suggestion. 'I'm thirsty.'

'Just on dark.' The merchant fetched him water, saying awkwardly, 'I don't believe it, you know. That you'd spy for Onli.'

'No? But you're going along with him,' Matto nodded at the supine figure, 'in delivering me up to this imposter you all believe in,' he said coldly. 'You think this prince is going to let me live when I know his claim to the throne is a lie?' He slumped wearily back to the ground, the hopelessness of his situation suddenly overwhelming. 'I've served you well for five years, Tranche. I saved you from the Tower, remember? What part of that makes me a spy?'

'Your damned smooth tongue. Hold it or I'll gag you.' The surly words came from Haran whom their voices had roused. He yawned, sat up and pulled off his turban leaving his head looking strangely naked as he rose to go and splash in the trough. 'Save your arguments for the Lakes. If you're as lily-white as you claim no harm has been done. If you're not you're their problem, not ours. Either way talking now isn't going to help. Eat up and we'll be on our way.'

***

The night was a repetition of the previous one. The horses, no longer fresh, went less willingly. Haran spelled them at midnight while they shared the last of their food — stale bread and meat tainted with the musty odour of the leather in which it had been carried. Matto's bound wrists throbbed as they rode, his reins firmly in Haran's grasp. If his mount had been fresher, he might he thought, have tried frightening it into bolting, taking his chances with the dangling reins and the darkness, but that was the counsel of despair. It would only confirm his captor's suspicions and gain him nothing. And if he did get away he'd be lost in a waterless wilderness with no way of freeing the hands that were now too numb to be of any help to him.

By imperceptible degrees the dark lightened, the stars paled and the sun's first rays crept up the sky behind them. A smudge of taller growth appeared in the distance causing Tranche to straighten his slumped shoulders with a groan of relief as the band of willows filled the horizon.

Their mounts, scenting journey's end, quickened their paces across the bare ground for they had long since passed from the fertile farmland into desolate ridge country where the scrubby bushes barely reached above the horses' knees.

Dry gullies marked the crease of the ridges, and the few trees were thin and parched looking in contrast to the green willows fringing the enormous body of water they could now see stretching before them. A breeze blew off it, rich with the scents of mud and rotting vegetation from the islands of drifting reeds. A threnody of noise, the morning chorus of bird calls, the splash and squawk of ducks and divers, and the high ki-ki-ki of hunting hawks came faintly to the three riders.

Clustered on the near bank, the complex of warehouse and stables Matto had visited before proved to be unattended. The buildings were locked fast, and nobody came to answer Haran's shout.

'Doesn't matter, there are boats.' He unsaddled, turning the horses into the small fenced enclosure beside the stable where there was feed and water. Choosing the broader beamed boat Haran hauled Matto into it before settling again to the oars. Tranche's soft palms cringed as he gripped his own pair, uttering a soft, unconscious grunt of discomfort with each pull.

'I could eat an ox, and sleep for a week,' he mumbled, punctuating the words with a huge yawn.

'Well you'll soon be able to; maybe not an ox but perhaps a duck,' Haran said. 'Our young apprentice won't be so fortunate though, unless he's as innocent as he claims.'

'Your nose is swollen,' Matto retorted with enough satisfaction to earn the glare he felt on the back of his neck. But his heart raced with fear. His hands now that he could see rather than just feel them, were every bit as bad as he'd imagined — puffed and purple looking, the pain adding to his inner apprehension. He was damned if he revealed his true identity, yet unable to prove his innocence if he didn't.

Matto watched a kingfisher dive and emerge again, shedding silver droplets from its wings. A family of water hens sped out of a patch of rushes at the lake's edge, necks outstretched and tails bobbing, and the air was thick with a cloying scent that he eventually realised came from the flowering plumes on the reeds. He wondered how Haran knew where to go — it all looked the same to him, the vast expanse of water, its wavelets dazzling with reflected sunlight, broken into a maze by the drifting islands of reeds, some as large as a house, that towered above them. He saw the whiskered face of an otter for a moment before the heavy beat of wings pulled his eyes skywards to a flight of swans overhead. It was hard to believe that thousands of people lived somewhere out here in this watery realm of plenty.

The boat ride went on and on. Once Matto smelled smoke and heard a hum as of the distant voices of men calling to each other but Haran didn't, as he'd expected, row towards them. Rather he seemed to use the rising hum of human occupation as a navigational aid, angling the boat more sharply to the left until the sounds faded behind them and there was only the gurgle of waves slapping the hull, and the rustle of wind in the reed tops.

The boat itself was made of reeds, he realized, and waterproofed with pitch. He could see the blackness through the tightly woven skin. Banco had once told him that the Lakers built their homes from the same material, together with the pontoons they floated upon. They fed their milch goats on the succulent tops, and crafted their furniture from its stems, while the rotting mats of vegetation that supported the islands provided a rich humus for their gardens. He wondered how they cooked without torching such flammable homes, and if many of the children of such dwellings drowned.

At last, unable to bear the suspense any longer Matto cleared his throat. 'Wasn't that Laketown back there?'

'It was,' Haran agreed.

'So where are we going?' He knew these men, his mind insisted. It was nonsense to believe they could abandon him amid the reeds, or simply drop him over the side. Of course they weren't about to murder him! His heart jumped with the thought. And yet, and yet... If they believed he threatened their cause and their lives, why not? Temes, as he had cause to know, played for keeps — why shouldn't those opposing him adopt the same methods? It was a relief when Haran answered, even if his words carried little comfort.

'To the Prince. You'll be the army's prisoner. They'll get the truth from you; they have a short way with spies. And if you should be one my lad, then they'll make you wish that you'd never been born. So you'll be more than ready to welcome your death when it comes.'

12

And suddenly they had arrived, a couple of oar strokes shooting their craft clear of an obscuring reed bank to reveal long lines of floating buildings secured together to form a pattern of streets, so that a man might walk the length of them without descending to the shallow canoes tethered, like waiting mounts, at every pontoon's side. The watery canals between them sparkled, here and there smoke spiralled into the clear air, and a man's voice came faintly through an open window. A standard of some sort, showing a white swan on a blue background with what could be a tower in the lower corner, flapped in the breeze above a central building. And it was here that Haran steered the boat.

When it nudged against the water-darkened post Tranche, with a dexterity belying his girth, stood to grasp the mooring ring and secure the painter. Of course, Matto thought, watching his former master adjust to the lively motion of their craft, he was Laker bred. He licked dry lips trying to prepare himself while overhead a sentry in a blue tunic over grey trousers, stamped his boots and challenged them.

Haran shipped his oars and rose, more carefully than his companion had. 'Tranche and Haran from the city. We've a prisoner for interrogation; and we need to see the Prince if he's available.'

The sentry, of whom only his face was visible, stepped back from sight. 'Come on up.'

As before Haran went first, towing his captive. It wasn't an easy climb without his hands, which were now so numbed as to be useless, but the pressure on the leading cord at least prevented Matto from toppling backwards. The platform, once he arrived on it, he found to sway to a slight constant movement that kept him on the edge of balance. The sentry vanished inside the building to report and in the few moments of his absence Matto stared about, noting the military precision with which the buildings were aligned.

Barracks, he supposed, and mess halls, an armoury — all that was necessary to house and field an armed force. He might be an imposter but Haran's phony prince seemed to operate to a high standard, however pretentious his aspirations. Cyrus, he thought mordantly, picking out the distant familiar stamps and clangs of drill exercise, would have approved.

Chiming in with his thoughts the door through which the sentry had vanished suddenly opened to disclose a scarred, and eye-patched Appellan, who greeted his captors with a roar of good humour.

'Tranche you old villain! Well, the Prince will be pleased to —' his voice sharpened suddenly, his attention caught perhaps by the other's expression. 'What is it? Something's happened?'

'You could say so, it might be nothing, but...' Tranche's voice faded into a meaningless mumble. Matto, forgetting, took an impetuous step and was almost yanked from his feet as Haran jerked the cord tight. He barely noticed, his mouth had dropped open and he swayed, hands held before him like a supplicant as the earth reeled about him. There could be no mistaking that voice! He had to swallow to moisten his tongue and even then his voice creaked as if from long disuse, as if it was he who had died.

'Rissak! Is that you?'

The man with the eye patch and the face split by a puckered scar that pulled his left cheek awry exposing two teeth on the side of his mouth, turned and stared, moving his head slightly the better to study the figure before him. His shocked recognition was equally as great.

'Marric!' It was a question that, repeated, became affirmation. 'Marric! May the Light slay me if — You're alive, lad!'

Haran stared, stupefied. 'You know each other?'

Face paper white the young man who called himself Matto shook his head. 'I don't understand. Five years ago I saw you dead. I said the rites for you. It had been my shame ever since that I dared not build your pyre...'

'Thank Asher for that then,' the ghost before him quipped. The old familiar dryness of tone, the grin, horribly misshapen though it now was — Marric's heart swelled making his eyes smart. He achieved an answering smile as he shook his head. 'I should have known a mere troop couldn't kill you,' he said thickly.

'And I you, lad.' Smiling, shaking his head, he reached to embrace Matto before noticing his bound wrists. His gaze swung to Haran, a crack of displeasure in his tone. 'Why is this man bound?' Snatching a knife from his boot he cut the bonds with some difficulty, so deeply were the cords sunk into the swollen flesh.

Haran, looking uncertainly between them, said defensively, 'He's — we believe him to be a spy. One of our own men. We couldn't not act so we've brought him here for the truth to be sifted.'

'Spy my arse!' Rissak barked furiously taking in the condition of the hands Marric was cuddling to his chest. 'This man you've been ill-treating is a royal prince. He's Darien's twin brother. Spying? Is it likely? For the king who's been plotting his death since the day he was born?'

Haran was speechless. Flustered but vindicated Tranche said triumphantly, 'I told you Matto wouldn't —' But Marric, bent double over the agony of returning circulation had no sympathy or words to spare for either of them.

Tranche, given the other man's certainty, was eager to acquit his late employee of spying, though not about to accept his new identity. He said, 'You're wrong, Rissak. He cannot be who you claim he is, for he told us himself that the younger prince was murdered by his uncle.'

'Well of course he did, seeing Ripa's the last place on earth he would want his identity known. God of all fools! I thought city folk were supposed to be quick. Come away in, lad. The Prince is in a meeting but he'll be glad enough to postpone it when he knows the reason.' He shook his head, studying his old pupil, 'You've grown, changed — but not that much. I can hardly believe it is you.'

Marric, still rubbing his wrists, said wryly, 'If that is all you're a lucky man. I can't believe anything I've learned lately, save never to trust a damn merchant again.'

Inside the door was a short entrance that led to a large council room from which a man's deep voice could be heard, interrupted once by a woman's lighter tones. The inner walls were unadorned, a common practice, Marric would learn in Laker dwellings, for the uniform grey of the tightly bundled reeds woven in two directions created their own ornamental patterns. Just now, his head reeling, he was in no condition to notice much, but gathered an impression of a dozen seated figures, of bright floor rugs below a large table littered with the detritus of all meetings: paper scrolls, inkpots, quills, a scatter of wine goblets and lists shared between three of the men nearest to him. Then his breath froze in an audible gasp, and he stared in shock at the speaker, the young man at the far end of the table with the bright rays of morning light bathing his face.

'Tardi!' The name exploded in his head even as reason told him it wasn't possible. But this man with his red hair and high brow, with the arrogant ridge of nose and well-sculpted lips below the bright gleam of blue eyes, was how an adult Tardi would have looked. Any doubts Rissak's words had not dispelled immediately died. Twin or not Darien was, indisputably, a descendant of Cyrus, one time Great King of Appella. Temes himself could not meet this man face to face and deny it.

As in a dream he heard Rissak break the news of his own identity, and the clamour of exclamations it invoked from all present. It was noise, no more, all he registered was the hated face coming towards him. He had a moment in which to dissemble, to hide his instinctive antipathy, before Darien had seized his arms, laughing incredulously, shooting questions which, his wits adrift, Marric answered somewhat at random. He made his swollen hands the excuse for not returning the hearty embrace with which he was welcomed. He longed to escape, to give his disoriented mind a chance to assimilate what his eyes told him. He desperately craved privacy in which to shake off the shock of the encounter.

Rissak spoke for him. 'You haven't changed, lad,' he said with his hideous smile. Switching his single eye to Darien he beamed his satisfaction. 'I told you he was always a quiet one.'

Prince Darien (and yes, he looked a prince, just as Tardi had, Marric admitted to himself) laughed, his brilliant gaze measuring their differences. 'How could I ever have recognised you? I imagined you as red as I am. To see us who would even think we were brothers?'

At that word the shackles of hatred were loosened a little and Marric could answer him. 'So, it is true then that we are twins? Nobody had ever even hinted to me that you existed.'

'It's true, Prince Marric.' It was the woman, whom he now noticed for the first time, who spoke. She was trim and comely still, though her fair hair was touched here and there with silver, and webs of tiny lines creased the fine skin about the corners of her eyes. Hers had been the voice that interrupted Darien's, which made her a person of importance. Marric tucked the thought aside.

She said, 'I am Ananda, Priestess of the Mother. I was present at your birthing. I held you, and your brother before you, when you were born. It was your mother's wish that I foster her eldest son here, in secret. She was the Oracle of Bel as I am sure you know. She saw the future and planned it all as a way to keep him safe. I think I would have known you though, had I reason to look closely. You have the look of Leona, something in your brow and eyes — though hers were grey. I see nothing of her in Darien,' she cast him a fond look, 'but there is no question that you are her son. Rissak told me that you also have her gift?'

It was a question, he saw; she sought confirmation, perhaps unwilling to take his ex-bodyguard's word for it. He wondered if she would resent him for the gift, if such it was, then suddenly didn't care if she did. For the first time he noticed that Tranche was also in the room, looking decidedly startled. He had got more than he'd bargained for in his apprentice. Marric didn't give a damn about that either. The anger swelled in his head while his thoughts dipped and fled like birds drinking. He nodded brusquely at the woman. 'Once. Not for years now.'

'Perhaps there has been no need,' she suggested kindly.

'Perhaps,' he said indifferently. 'So, why did Taba not know I was a twin? For I swear she didn't. She would have told me the truth if she had known it and then —' What? he wondered. Given him the choice of perhaps blurting it out, adding another to Temes's murder list?

'Because nobody was meant to know. Not even the queen. Leona believed it to be the only way to safeguard Darien — to ensure he lived to claim his inheritance and free the land. Nobody would suspect a child of the Sisterhood, not when there was another son for the world to watch. Only she and I and her maid knew that she carried twins. She was a strong woman your mother; she loved her country, and she did what she saw was needful.'

Marric breathed in, face inscrutable as he rubbed absently at his wrists. 'Really? And what if I had been a girl — how was she to proceed then?'

Ananda regarded him calmly. 'You must remember who she was, Prince Marric, the power she channeled. Of course she knew her unborn babes were sons.'

'Of course,' he agreed, keeping his tone light. The room he saw had emptied, only the family remained. Tranche and Ananda, he supposed they were family, himself, Rissak and Darien. Haran seemed to have disappeared; he would deal with him later. 'One forgets,' he addressed Darien, 'the God's hand in all this. Or the Goddess's. I have, I think you will agree, played my part as useful bait quite well brother, managing both to keep your enemies busy and my own skin relatively whole the while. Not without help of course,' he nodded to Rissak. 'Now it is up to you to perform your part.'

A cup of untouched wine stood on the table. He reached for it and saluted Darien. 'A twin toast then — doubly suitable, wouldn't you say? Let us drink to our mother's foresight and care; and to the downfall of our uncle.' He swallowed, the taste bitter in his mouth. Darien, whose smile had slipped a little found a glass and drank too, then lifted it again.

'And I would drink to my brother whose presence beside me I have missed life long.'

'And I am afraid you must miss a little longer,' Marric manufactured a yawn and lowered the cup. 'Your pardon but I would sleep, if I could. The last couple of nights have not been exactly restful.' It was childish but he no longer cared. Tranche looked unhappy, Ananda thoughtful, and even the gods he thought, would have trouble reading Rissak's face. He remembered the stones which he still carried, forgotten for years now, in the bottom of the pouch that was part of his belt and wondered if his friend still juggled. His bow, he recollected was back in Ripa, and Haran, of course, had his dagger. He would demand it back but he thought he'd rather fling it into the lake than hand it over to Tardi's double.

Ananda turned murmuring apologies for thoughtlessness; of course he must be weary and hungry too. He should accompany her now and she would see to his needs. Tomorrow would be time enough for talking, once the wonder of his appearance had really sunk in for them all... Excusing himself punctiliously Marric followed her out, leaving silence behind him.

Rissak was the first to break it, his words colliding with a rushed apology from Tranche who was wringing his hands. 'My lord, I am so sorry. But how could we possibly guess? He has been with us for five years and I —'

'Of course you couldn't know, Uncle,' Darien said. 'And think, had things not fallen out so we might never have known. Nobody is blaming you for suspecting him.'

'I fear Matto will,' Tranche said glumly.

'He has more on his mind than that, I think,' Darien said stolidly.

Rissak spoke gruffly into the renewed silence. 'Give him time, my Prince.'

The blue eyes were blank with dismay. 'He hates me. I saw it in his face the instant our gazes met. He hid it immediately — he doesn't show much, does he? but it was there. Why? He doesn't know me, and we are brothers after all.'

'It wasn't you he saw, but Tardi, your half brother — a right little shit. Now him he did hate. A redhead too, Tardi, and now I think of it the spit of you, and mean as a nest of snakes. But don't worry, he'll come round, he was never short on sense and he'll work out you can't help how you look. I think it's the rest of it that's sticking in his craw right now. It's a pity the Lady Ananda hadn't been the one to tell him about you. She might've put it better than a man would.'

'You mean he resents my claim?'

'Light save you, no! Marric never wanted the throne. His father disowned him over it — what do you think that does to a lad? And now he's just been told his mother virtually did the same. You heard him. He called himself bait and from where he sits it must certainly look that way.' Rissak winced at this thought and drew circles in the spilled wine where his cup had slopped.

'Think about it. His life has been at risk from the time the Lady Taba fled with him. Yes, he lived in a palace, eventually, but so do boot boys and kitchen hands, and most of them suffer less abuse than he survived. It can't have been easy, even without that little turd Tardi. Then his foster-mother is murdered and he's crippled...'

He sighed, remembering as he met the intent blue gaze. 'He was just a boy but he handled it well. Then or later, I never heard him complain about his lot. I admired that in him. I knew I'd never turn him into a soldier but he always made the best of whatever the gods threw at him. But now he's thinking all that didn't just happen, it was planned — by his mother, because she must've known what the consequences to him would be when she had you spirited away. His life at hazard, do you see, my Prince? To keep yours safe. Of course he's angry. He wouldn't be human if he wasn't.'

Darien bent his head dismayed by what he'd learned. 'I do see, yes. I hadn't thought. When he first looked at me

I felt he was in some ways older than I. No wonder then.'

'Experience marks a man, as does betrayal,' Rissak agreed, 'but some of it's the Goddess. Bound to be, I'd reckon. Though he said that's stopped, didn't he? The visions cost him great pain when they come so count yourself lucky, my Prince, that you are not similarly gifted.'

'It seems I must count myself lucky indeed,' Darien murmured staring blankly at his wine.

Tranche whom the two men had forgotten, protested, 'But it wasn't like that! It was the Lady's plan, not the Princess's. She was only trying to safeguard the throne and both her sons — as she would have, had she lived.'

'That may be so,' Rissak countered, 'but right now how it was, and how it appears to onlookers is just so much dung. What it must seem to Marric is that the throne and one of those sons mattered to the Princess much more than the other one did.'

***

Marric kept to the room he had been given until night crept like a coverlet over the lake. He had slept eventually, the angry turmoil of his thoughts yielding to the demands of his body. Ananda had taken him to a room fitted out sparsely as a bed chamber for, he would have guessed, an officer in Darien's army. It was a bare but functional space, with a simple hand-pump in a tiny adjoining alcove that filled either basin or hip-bath. He had sluiced away the sweat and dust of his travels, eaten the plate of food Ananda had brought him then, after a struggle to remove his boots with his still puffy hands, stretched out on the bed.

The food he'd eaten had lain in an indigestible lump in his stomach, keeping company with his anger. The priestess had done her best to soften it; speaking of

Darien, reiterating their happiness at finding him alive when for so long they had thought of him as dead.

'Your grandmother will be thrilled,' she had said gently in the face of his stony courtesy. 'She lives with us — my daughter and Darien and me.'

'I shall look forward to meeting her,' he had replied politely, the coldness of his words belying their content, 'after I have slept.'

She had left him then and he had lain chewing the cud of his bitterness until sleep claimed him, to be awakened by a lamp carrying servant, or possibly given his hostess's calling as high-priestess, a novitiate, come to bring him to dine.

They ate in the same room where his arrival had earlier interrupted Darien's council. The long table was set for six and it was here that Marric met his grandmother, already seated, a stately dame with an upright posture and silver hair. Her face was carved with lines that seemed to soften as her eyes hungrily searched his face. She half lifted her arms then let them fall back to her lap as he bowed stiffly before her. 'Madam. Taba often spoke to me of you.'

'Did she, grandson? I am glad. Little Mouse. I have kept her memory bright in my heart these twenty years. I grieve for her still. As I am sure you must. She loved you greatly.'

'That,' he said woodenly, 'I never doubted.'

'Sit down, Marric,' Ananda said hospitably as he nodded greetings to the rest of the table. Tranche was present, but not he noticed, Haran; Rissak also and Darien, blue eyes guarded but hopeful, an empty seat beside him.

'My daughter,' Ananda said seeing the direction of his gaze. 'She will be sorry not to have the news but we are keeping it close for now. You may trust the officers who were here when you arrived, not to speak of your identity.'

He thanked her, asked what was proper and managed to return civil answers to his brother's questions. He learned too of Tranche's efforts on his adopted nephew's behalf. The jewels it seemed, were yet another example of his mother's foresight. She had sent them to the Lake shrine the day she knew herself to be pregnant, securing the future for the son who would someday need a war chest to fight for the throne he had been promised. Queen Quan on the night her husband died, had also managed to secrete the larger portion of her royal jewelry and carried it with her from the city.

'Very practical,' Marric commented dryly. 'Goddess inspired or native wit, I wonder? I expect it hardly matters. So what forces have the gems bought you to date?'

'Eight thousand men under arms, and we are still recruiting. It has taken time. The gems had to first to be smuggled out, which has been down to Tranche and his friends, then all the weapons brought back in. It has been an enterprise fraught with the danger of discovery at every turn.' Darien's cautiousness relaxed a little and suddenly he exclaimed, 'It was you, wasn't it? It must have been! The shepherd boy who helped my uncle get a parcel of jewels by the toll collectors in the high pass? Hidden in a quiver or some such object, was it Uncle? Did he never tell you?'

'I discovered it for myself, much later.' Marric recalled the bleak, windswept station, the casual brutality and greed of the two soldiers collecting the toll, the sick roil of his belly fearing that he would be somehow discovered for who he was. 'No, he didn't tell me. There seems no end to what I wasn't told.'

Tranche said quickly. 'Really, there was very little risk, Ma — Prince Marric.'

'Possibly. If I had not been fleeing for my life at the time,' Marric replied, keeping his tone even.

Darien, sensing the subject was better left, quickly began to speak of his army, built it appeared, about a core of Rissak's old comrades — those who had survived the punishing campaigns in the Grasslands, designed by Temes to decimate those of his father's troops whose loyalty he suspected. Queen Quan (he could think of her no other way) contributed little to the talk. Her glance moved frequently between the two young men, her expression one of sad resignation.

The meal ended at last and after a short interval when the board had been cleared, and the dish of nuts standing beside the wine was down to shells, Marric rose. He had scarcely touched his glass. Ananda and the queen had retired earlier, followed by Tranche who, unless he had napped during the day must be badly in need of slccp. He certainly looked it and Marric felt a momentary twinge of compunction for his old master, though not enough to soften his anger. He was tired of being used.

Darien, returning his twin's 'goodnight' sat on, slumped dispiritedly in his seat, tilting the lees of his wine in the lamplight as the door closed behind his twin. He sighed, his lips tight.

'How much time will he need?' he asked softly. 'This is killing me, Rissak. For the Lady's sake! He is my brother.'

'I know, my Prince. But it has only been a day. That is not long in which to forgive a lifetime of deceit.'

***

Much later that evening Marric, who had spent the intervening time sitting in the starlit darkness before his borrowed door, heard approaching footsteps and looked up to see his old bodyguard coming towards him. He carried cups and wine, which he bent to place on the floor before easing himself down alongside Marric, grunting himself comfortable with his back against the woven wall.

The fall of light from the lamp pole on the pontoon's edge cast the wreck of his face into shadow making it possible to believe him the old Rissak, unchanged by the years. He poured without speaking and passed the cup across. Marric took it and said what he had been thinking.

'Cran was right after all, that day — just wrong in his interpretation.'

Rissak thought back. 'Oh, aye — the shadow he spoke of? You mean what he saw was really Darien?'

'So it would seem. The night Jekka died was when I finally believed he'd been wrong about me. Up till then it was always in the back of my mind, but when I walked away from there leaving you both for dead, I ceased to believe. I forgot his words altogether. Jekka said it was nonsense anyway, but on the trip here I remembered them again. And I wondered if the shadow had finally caught up with me. But Jekka was right all along. I begin to understand why he raged against the gods.' He turned his head to the black water about them, its ripples patterned with gold where the lamplight fell. 'Taba lived here, you know, as a small child — a few years only, but it was her home.'

'Aye. It's peaceful and you get used to the movement.'

Marric sipped his wine then remembered and pulled the pouch of stones from his belt and passed them to his companion. 'Here. These are yours. Do you still juggle?'

Rissak poured the stones into his palm, turning them slowly as if reacquainting himself with their shapes. Then he tipped them back into the bag and tossed it to Marric. 'Keep them. You need two eyes to juggle; the stones are never quite where you think they are with one.'

'What happened to you that night, Rissak?' The question came abruptly. 'Who helped you escape death? Somebody must have.'

'It was Hemma the village headman.' Rissak stretched out his legs crossing one booted foot over the other. 'The soldiers killed his son, that's why he came, why he saved me. They found us because we'd been seen, and somebody talked. Hunters chasing that damn bear, I expect.

'When the troop reached the village they took the quickest way to the truth. The boy had only six summers. They used a knife on him to make Hemma talk, then killed the child anyway when they had what they wanted. Later that night the man went to the glen to see for himself what they'd done.' He shrugged. 'Grief, fury, hatred — more than a match for superstition when it came to it. The child was his only son. He should have hated me as being the cause of the boy's death, but he saved me instead.' His hand rose to his hidden face and Marric guessed he was tracing the scar there. 'Have to say his sewing weren't much. I suppose he'd seen Jekka treating wounds that way.'

'They can't have gone back, the soldiers,' Marric mused, 'or they'd have noticed your body had gone.'

'They did — in the morning apparently. But Hemma had thought of that, too. He carried me out on one of their horses, then returned and made a pyre of the bodies. I gather he used the wood I'd cut for for Jekka — even so it must've taken him the rest of the night. Did it all without help too. Only his old mother, who had some skill in herb lore, ever learned I was there in the village until the day I left.

'Of course it was near a moon later before I knew anything of the aftermath. When I asked if the troops had come back he told me about burning the dead. I asked if he'd found your body but he couldn't tell me. It was the middle of the night and he was mad with grief. Even if he could have been positive it still meant nothing. Temes would have wanted to be certain so had they got you, they'd have packed you off, dead or alive. Of course this was all long afterwards, a full season had passed.' He sipped at his cup. 'Spring had come round again before I was fit to travel.'

It had been spring too, Marric remembered, when the soldiers came. He said, 'So from there to here — how did that happen?'

Rissak shrugged. 'Fate, luck, the gods — call it what you will. When I quitted the village I took the pass as we'd planned, and picked up escort work here and there. Told 'em I'd been discharged from the army but I could still swing a blade. I had the idea that if, by some chance, you'd got away, you'd be in Rhuta.' He drank, refilled their cups. 'I suppose I couldn't admit my race was run — Cyrus, the throne, you — all gone. Anyway, this day I ran into a hunting party from the Lakes, they go after the desert deer round here when they want real meat on the table, you know, and I saw Darien.' He paused, remembering. 'I'd have recognised that face anywhere.'

'Tardi to the life,' Marric agreed flatly.

'In looks only, lad,' Rissak said mildly. 'And he can't help that.'

Marric ignored that. 'What of his bid for the throne; can he win?'

'Aye, I believe so. He's a leader. Men'll follow him, like they did Cyrus. They want to please him and the right man can do much with that. And they believe in his cause — that's important too.'

'And he has about eight thousand to stand against — what? Thirty thousand fighting men would you say that Temes could field these days?'

'Not so many,' Rissak said judiciously. 'The army's scattered clear across the country from the Grasslands to Meddia and Rhuta. There's a good number tied up with the southern barbarians; he daren't shift those. And he's lost the Green Corps. That's ten thousand of his best fighters gone alone. We're recruiting and training all the time. And, best of all, his lot have just suffered a defeat in Barat. That won't do much for their morale, especially when Temes is through hanging the generals involved. The rank and file is deserting in droves as it is. Our men,' he added grimly, 'have been cleaning up the results of that. It's good training for them and Darien both, but it comes dear at the cost of people's suffering. He feels that, the Prince. He will make a good king, Marric. If you cannot trust him yet, then you may trust me when I tell you so.'

'Because you are his man now?' The instant they left his lips Marric wished the words unsaid. The hurt he felt at this final betrayal was something not for others to even guess at.

Rissak was silent for a moment then his voice came evenly from the darkness. 'Aye, lad, I am sworn to him now. I thought you gone and —'

'I'm sorry. That was unfair,' Marric said quickly. 'You don't owe me an explanation. It's the task Cyrus gave you after all. Not his fault he'd also been lied to. He would have approved of my brother in a way he never could have of me. If a spirit that has crossed the Bridge can know anything of what passes here, then he must be well pleased with you. And with the way matters have gone. One can see the god's hand at work in it, which isn't to say one has to like it,' he added levelly, 'but there are compensations. That you still live is one of them.' He yawned ostentatiously and got to his feet, clapping the other man's shoulder as he did so, an uncharacteristic act for him. 'I have sleep still to make up, so I'll bid you goodnight.'

'Aye, I'll see you tomorrow lad,' Rissak returned. He watched Marric vanish through the door, feeling the pontoon rock gently beneath him as his boots crossed the floor. Presently, tipping the rest of his cup into the lake, he swore softly and comprehensively before leaving, heavy hearted, to seek his own rest.

13

Contrary to what he had told Rissak it was long before Marric slept. And when he did, for the first time in a long while, he dreamed. He had spoken the truth earlier in that not once, since entering Rhuta had he been troubled by visions. In the early days he had made one visit to the site of the Mother's shrine outside the city walls where some devout farmer had, long ago, put aside land for the use of the Goddess and her devotees. The shrine had been razed, the spring there filled in, and though he had stood in silent concentration for an age, he had felt nothing of Her presence.

He had left the place, scarcely knowing whether to feel disappointment or relief, and She had not touched his life since. So, like Jekka, he had allowed himself to believe that he was done with the gods — or they with him. But once, he thought now with a touch of weary bitterness, as he bunched his pillow and stared upwards into darkness, he had also believed that he had a future as a merchant.

The dream was as highly coloured as a painting into which he had somehow wandered. He stood somewhere high, cloaked by a mist, which by turns, shrouded and disclosed his surroundings, a verdant, mountainous countryside where great trees grew. Marric had never seen such trees, forest giants, their trunks bedecked with growths of ferns and flowering vines. Beyond them a mountain burned like a fiery furnace vomiting streams of red-hot liquid whose glow reflected from the underside of the smoke clouds hanging above it. In the dream he felt the wind on his face but not a leaf in the picture stirred, and no sound broke the stillness. The whole scene might have been painted, and himself a coloured statue within it save for the wind's caress and the despair that filled his heart.

***

He carried the memory of the dream with him through succeeding days, puzzling over it as he found his place in the new surroundings to which, he had to assume because of the dream, the Goddess had brought him. Darien was courteous and unrelentingly friendly, and gradually Marric found what he knew to be his unreasonable dislike of his twin, somewhat lessened. It wasn't, he frequently reminded himself, his brother's fault that their lives had taken the paths they had.

Their parents, on whom the blame could justly have fallen, were dead, which left only his grandmother, and to her for some reason he could not articulate even to himself, he would not bend. Quan met his polite indifference stoically, only observing one day when he found himself alone with her, 'I see your father in you, Marric. I find that strange. You have your mother's face, insofar as a son can, yet Darien who resembles her not at all, is most like her.'

'Indeed Madam. You would know best I am sure.' He had found the item he had returned for. Picking it up he turned to leave.

'Yes,' she mused as if he had not spoken, shrewd eyes assessing him. 'He could not forgive either, or admit a mistake. Appellans — an arrogant race. How different things might have been if he had made the effort. You were not the only one deceived, you know. I learned of my other grandson's birth only after the rest of my family were dead.'

Brought up short by the words he stared at her. He had imagined her the brains behind the whole deception.

'Obduracy,' she said, 'a family trait, and coupled with arrogance.' She shook her head, adding, 'You are already older than your mother who loved you more than you could possibly know.' Back straight she walked away from him, regal in bearing with her crown of silver hair.

***

He met some of Darien's officers, learning to recognise them among the throng that came daily to consult with his brother. There was Nannik, an Appellan, brown of face and hair, his hooded eyes shrewd. Osram of the same race, a fair giant of a man, his strength a byword. Buka, a Laker who seemed squat beside his taller confederates; he had a dark, steady gaze and a recent injury to his right ear where the lobe was missing.

Sedak was willowy and fair — another of the displaced Green Corp. He was a handsome man with a languid grace that hinted at an expertise with the blade at his hip. Listening to him speak of weapons took Marric's thoughts back to the drill yard at Valleyford.

'Have you taught blade work?' he asked.

'Aye, Prince Marric.' He eyed his interlocutor's belt, bare of all but a plain handled dagger that had been returned to him. 'You carry no weapon yourself?'

'I was brought here a prisoner,' Marric answered dryly. 'Anyway, I prefer the bow, though mine is back in Ripa.'

'Not for long.' Rissak had overheard. 'Haran is fetching it for you even now. Meantime you should have a blade. I'm sure that Sedak here would partner you for practice. He's one of our best.'

The other put up his brows at that. 'Care to name those better?'

He and Rissak had laughed while Marric forced a smile to cover the pang that Rissak had not offered his own services. He accepted the blade he was brought and belted it on. None went unarmed in this floating military camp; even Ananda wore a short dagger at her girdle. Marric had still not met her daughter whose absence nobody had commented on, but on the third day since his arrival, the high-priestess came to find him, paddling swiftly down the long line of pontoons, to the one where the men did their drill.

It was a broad floating platform and Marric was standing to one side in the company of Rissak and Nannik, watching Darien fight two-handed with blade and dagger against two men at once, his efforts cheered on by an audience of a hundred or so. His twin, Marric realised, was a formidable swordsman, his athleticism matched by timing and judgement. Catching the look of pride on Rissak's face he felt a momentary flare of jealousy but thrust it aside. It was good his old mentor, who had suffered so greatly in Marric's service, should finally have found the warrior he deserved to follow. Then Ananda called to him from the water and he bent low to receive the message.

The drill platform was a good distance from the Commander's Camp, which was how Darien's dwelling was styled. It was quicker, Ananda told him, to boat than walk it. On the Lakes canoes were used much as horses were on land.

They halved the time it took to move between points, and soon he was following her own nimble steps up onto the pontoon and into an airy living space within the house to which he had not previously penetrated.

It was a pleasant room with rugs on the floor, and a scatter of small tables on one of which rested a silver fruit platter and a bronze lamp. Beside it were comfortable woven chairs padded with bright cushions.

At his entrance a woman sprang up with a little cry, and came swiftly to throw her arms about him. There was no time to think, only to see that she was well past her middle years, that her dark curls were threaded with grey, that she was slightly shorter than him. Her voice when she spoke was somewhere between tears and laughter.

'Oh, my boy! After all these years and past hope... I never thought to see this day.'

***

The cadence of her voice was so familiar, as was the scent of lavender that his heart momentarily seized. He said stupidly, 'Taba?'

She laughed and kissed him, her thin, fine-boned hands holding his face as she stared into his eyes, her own brown orbs sparkling with unshed tears. 'I'm Khat, dear boy, Taba's mother. When Ananda came to tell me you were found, and actually here! Well, it was as if the Lady had answered all my prayers.'

Marric took her hands and gave them a brief, gentle squeeze before letting go. 'Then you know that she is dead these many seasons?'

'Yes,' she said simply. 'My little bird. They are all gone now my children, but you were her babe. She raised you and now you have come home to make an old woman happy. Sit here by me, Marric. I would hear all of it, or as much as you care to tell me. Of you and my daughter and your lives together.' She patted his hand smiling Taba's smile at him so that he suddenly wanted to cling to her and weep. 'There is no hurry. We have days and days in which to talk and remember her.'

'I'd like that.' The sober young man with the still expression and eyes older than his years gazed at her, throat working as he swallowed, and Lady Khat took and cradled his right hand between her own two in wordless comfort. 'I will,' he said, 'because she loved me. And that was all the more precious because she was the only one who did.'

'No girls then? Not even one?' Khat smiled playfully at him though tears were welling over her lower lids.

'Yes, of course. But that was different — passing fancies. She rests in a mountain cave — a shrine to the Mother, in the company of the true kings of Ansham. But first,' he tore his thoughts away from the past to remember his manners, 'may I get you something? Some wine or other refreshments?'

Khat shook her head, her cheeks were damp but the smile never left her lips. 'I need nothing, dear boy. Look at you! I can hardly believe you are here, so handsome with your mother's beautiful bone structure!' Marric blushed and she laughed. 'I'm sorry. I'm sure Taba would have mentioned your looks to you could she but have seen you grown. Tell me about — oh, your tenth summer — that will do for a starting point.'

Marric found her extraordinarily easy to talk to. They spent the rest of the morning together while Khat, her smiles mingling with tears, learned of her daughter's life as Marric built for her a picture of their time together in a foreign land. It eased his heart to speak of his foster mother, and if something of Rissak's steadfast devotion to him, and his boyhood love of Dura crept into the telling, that too was balm for the pain of losing both. When at length he ceased to speak Khat sighed.

'And Yonti? My youngest. I have always assumed he perished for he never returned, and even our friends on the plateau could find no trace of him.'

'Taba believed he was killed in the mountains, protecting her, holding off the soldiers who were hunting us. She fled into a blizzard but he never caught her up —

or so she told me once. I am so sorry,' Marric said gently.

'Don't be.' Her thin, veined hand touched his. 'It is an old grief, but mine is no worse than Quan's; we both lost husbands and children on that terrible night when my daughter left us. Only Darien was left, and now beyond hope, we have you as well. Truly the Lady blesses us!' Her eyes, so like Taba's dwelt lovingly on his face. 'Try to be kind to your grandmother, Marric. Remember, none of this was of our choosing. Yes, she sent you both away that night, and though ultimately that decision led to Taba's death, it is because of it that you are alive today.'

He bowed his head at the gentle reproof. 'I will remember. Thank you for coming today,' his throat, he realised was tired. When was the last time he had talked so much? He couldn't recall. 'And now we must take something. I am parched and surely it is near time for the noon meal?'

'Yes,' Khat agreed, 'and then Darien will find somebody to take me home.'

'I would offer,' Marric's rare smile broke across his face, 'but it were wiser not to. We should both of us end up in the lake.'

'You will soon have the way of — ' The rest of the words were lost in a woman's long drawn shriek, and his own burst of coughing as the smoke rolled over him.

'Marric!' cried Khat as he stumbled and fell. She thrust herself up from the chair, wide eyed with alarm as his body began to convulse. 'Ananda!'

...the fire was in the thatch, the roar of it growing louder, almost drowning the women's panicked screams. There were figures in the smoke, running, grabbing, shouting harshly as they manhandled their captives. Two of them seized a brown haired girl, flung her to the ground and tore at her clothing as she bucked and wrenched in their hold, shrieking with terror. The impatient fist of the man astride her snapped her head sideways, and she lay dazed, blood leaking from her nose as he thrust into her. When he was done the second man took his place. Hens screeched and ran in the madness, and a black child, crazed with fear, darted into a building already on fire. The roof fell in a shower of sparks that whirled above the blazing mountain and an imperative voice cried, 'Go! Go now! Save her!'

***

Marric came to himself lying on a rug on a platform of reeds that moved gently beneath him. He was surrounded by a circle of booted feet and there was a woman kneeling beside him. With an effort that brought the sweat to his brow he forced his strengthless arms to push his body into a seated position, and to lift the intolerable weight of his pounding head. His stomach heaved and he locked his jaw shut, swallowing the bile. There was no time for that. He had to get up, had to go to their aid.

A voice, Darien's, said, 'Marric?' It was questioning, dismayed, but Rissak was quicker to understand. He hooked his arms roughly about him and hauled him to a chair. The woman — it was the high-priestess, he thought blearily, had vanished along with the Lady Khat. He wondered how long he had been out.

'Speak. Tell us.' Rissak's face was urgent, the single eyes demanding, understanding that some emergency had occurred. 'What did you See, lad?'

'The shrine,' he panted, eyes half shut in agony, 'the women there... under attack. Now, or soon. Must go — get the women away.'

Darien bent above him, a hand gripping his shoulder, ruddy face pale. 'This comes from the god?'

'From the Mother. There's no time —'

'We're leaving,' his twin said, turning at once to issue rapid instructions to the cadre of officers with him. The shrill blast of a horn cut through Marric's head then Ananda was there with a cup.

'It has only steeped a little so I made it stronger. Drink it off then chew the herbs. It will help,' she said crisply. He did so, gulping the brew down as he swayed to his feet.

Rissak frowned. 'You're not fit. You should stay.'

'Can't — I must reach her.' He could see the burning roof, the moment it began to dip and fall above the defenseless child. Then Ananda's cry turned every head to where she stood, stricken suddenly pale, both hands pressed flat to her breast.

'Merciful Lady, Fenny is there!'

Darien swore and paled in turn. 'I'll get her out if it's the last thing I do.' He turned to shout an impatient order, Marric cried, 'Wait!' and then he was tumbling down into the light boat behind his twin, eyes cringing from the brilliance of sunlight on water. He watched as a fighting force was swiftly marshalled and twenty men set off, like horses spurred to a race, with Darien's boat in the lead.

They took a barge in tow, large, flat, and heavy in the water, despite the help of a fitful wind. Trying to imitate his twin's actions, Marric clumsily plied a second paddle, beginning to understand Darien's plan. His head was starting to clear, so he spat out the last of the masticated herbs; they had worked, lessening the ache, which seemed to help his thinking. They couldn't simply carry the women away in the little boats, there were far too many of them. As well there would be the children at the shrine, and those occupying beds in the Healing Centre — hence the need for the barge.

As if reading his mind Darien, seated before him, turned his head without ceasing to paddle, the muscles of his shoulders bunching with each stroke. 'You couldn't tell how many...?'

'No. Nor when it will happen. Only the order: Go now! So the raid must be imminent. They fired the buildings before they started in on the women.'

'Yes. Well, no smoke yet.' His twin's voice was calm as his head tilted to search the sky. He said tightly, 'We spoke only yesterday of how to evacuate the shrine should the need arise. Odd that this has come so soon after.'

It wasn't, Marric knew, it was ordained. He kept the thought to himself, wondering instead why the child he had been shown was so important that the suffering of the brown-haired woman he had seen raped didn't matter, so long as the former was saved.

His breathing deepened as he laboured at the paddle, his mind straining ahead of the dead weight they were dragging. He felt like roaring in frustration at the time it was taking. To the right and left he could see the little boats struggling onwards, grim faced rowers bent above the paddles. The one man aboard the barge had a sail rigged and darted endlessly about adjusting it, trying to capture every capful of reluctant breeze. Then smoke burst in an explosion of roiling black above the still distant willows and Marric knew that the time the warning had won for them had just expired. The rowers knew it too; a shout of despair went up before Darien's voice overrode it.

'Paddle for your lives, men! With the Lady's help we will do it yet.'

They obeyed, and now a short jetty, like the one Marric had seen back at the warehouse at the other end of the lake, became visible. They strained towards it, slowly, so slowly — then the leading boats were shooting away to either side, their momentum halted by skillful paddles, and the barge settled hard against the pilings with a force that made them rock.

Darien leapt out into knee-deep water and charged for the bank, shouting crisp orders. Two men peeled off to stay with the barge and secure it, while the rest followed him at a run up the sloping bank through the fringing willows.

The noise hit Marric first; excited yelling, the crackle of fire, and the screams of women interspersed with mad, wild laughter. The raiders, some of them anyway, were drunk. Then the Laker party burst out of the screening foliage, weapons in hand, into a scene of chaos.

***

It was a large complex they faced for the shrine had stood there for centuries, being added to as the decades passed. There were extensive gardens with their attendant, open fronted sheds, and even a small stable as if the place were a farm. Which in a way it was for the priestesses produced their own food.

There were hens and pigs, and milch goats and a dovecote (its inhabitants on the wing at present). The shrine itself was quite large, an airy, open-sided building and beyond it were many others: kitchen, dormitories, laundry, stillrooms in which herbs were stored and distilled; rooms where the sick were nursed and the children taught; a whole busy little village and half of it already on fire.

The raiders had come primarily to rob but drink and the lure of women had overset this. The sober amongst them had run a cart out of the shed and were busy stripping gardens and pens of what they contained. The hens had escaped in the confusion and now fled squawking amid the running women and pursuing men.

The stables had either caught fire or been torched and the two horses within battered at the walls in terror, their screaming cutting through the babble of noise outside. The reed walls gave suddenly to the assault upon them and Marric jumped aside as the animals bolted past, one with a burning beam across its back. The horse, bucking wildly, cannoned into another building dislodging the beam, which instantly set light to the new dwelling.

Unaware yet, in his sodden state of the Laker's arrival, a raider chased a hen, swiping at it with his blade until blinded by the low rolling smoke, it flew in to the new conflagration. The man staggered to a stop then, laughing uproariously. 'Ish cooking ishelf for me,' he bellowed happily. He was still laughing when Sedak ran him through.

***

Marric glimpsed the brown-haired girl of his vision being pulled to her feet by a Laker and pushed on her way towards the barge. She fell after a few paces and stayed huddled on the ground, too shocked or hurt to continue. She was probably safe enough, he thought, as battle broke out around him. The raiders would be too busy saving themselves now to bother her again, and he hadn't time to stop. The smoke was as heavy as fog and harder to breath as he sought desperately for some reference point to identify the building into which the child had fled. Then a raider ran at him, teeth bared in a snarl, his sword leaping like a live thing for Marric's throat.

Marric blocked desperately, ducking and slashing, the moves that were once daily practice coming rustily back to muscles and mind. Dodging an overhead swing he saw, from the corner of his eye, thin black legs below a short shift that fled past behind his opponent's back. The momentary distraction almost cost him his life. He saw the blade coming at the level of his navel and flung himself aside. It was so close a thing the point of the blade sheared through his tunic but the raider had over extended himself and before he could recover, Marric's sword entered his exposed armpit. Yanking the blade free he ran after the child.

She had vanished from sight but he sprinted into the closest building and through it like a whirlwind, slamming doors back as he shouted, but no answer came from within. The second building he tried was a dormitory, its roof already well ablaze, the far end of it beginning to crumble. Unheeding of the heat and the screams behind him, lungs burning, reddened eyes tearing, he plunged inside and found not one but three people, amid the smoke and roar of encroaching flames.

A young fair-haired woman was shouting at an old one who clung stubbornly to a bed frame refusing to be moved. The child was behind the pair, crouched against a chest, embers from the burning thatch dropping around her. She tensed at sight of him, poised to run again, blind to the fiery danger in which they all stood.

The girl, hoarse from smoke and desperation, wrestled fiercely with the old woman's grip. 'Help me!' she cried, but Marric dared not take his eyes from the child.

'In a moment.' He had to do this slowly. Nerves on fire with the need for haste he sank to his haunches holding her frightened gaze with his own as he laid his weapon down and, as slowly as he could manage, held out his hand. The stillness slipped over him and he smiled into her eyes, which were as dark as his own, watching them widen as the sonorous words welled unbidden from some unknown source inside him. 'Come, my little one, there is nothing to fear from me. I am here to take you home.'

Dimly he heard the end of the roof fall in. The old woman screeched and the girl cried out in fear and fury. He held his breath, then the child rose and came to him and took his hand. He stood sheathing his sword with his free hand, and with a roar the world came rushing back.

The roof would go at any moment. Brutally he broke the old one's grip and threw her, screeching and kicking, over his shoulder. Still clutching the child's hand he pushed the girl before him, all three running for the door as the roof finally gave way.

14

Outside a blessed gust of wind shifted the smoke for a moment and they stopped, panting, eyes tearing and burning, to cough and breathe. The old woman, set on her feet again, clawed at Marric until the girl pulled her away.

'Stop it, Essa! I'm sorry,' she gasped. 'She's addled in her wits, poor thing. How did you know to come?'

'It doesn't matter.' He drew his sword again. 'Can you hold the child too, and follow? There's a barge to take you all to safety.' The fighting was still fierce, the clash of arms continuous, punctuated by fierce grunts of effort and the cries of the dying. He wondered how many raiders there were, and wished uselessly for his bow. A quick glance showed the immediate vicinity to be clear, and he jerked his head for the girl to follow. She came trustingly, holding her charges close by either hand. They had covered perhaps a dozen paces in this wise when the two raiders rounded the corner of the building before them.

They were dragging a woman between them but dropped her at sight of him and brought their blades up. She lay where she fell, her face covered, but he recognised the brown hair. 'Run!' he shouted, the curt command intended for all four of them, and to the blonde girl, 'Don't lose the child!'

None of them heeded him. The fallen girl stayed

where she was while the blonde opened her mouth and screamed with an intensity to make men wince, although Marric, mounting a desperate defense against two blades, had no time to listen to what it was she was screaming. The building helped. Get your back against something if there's more than one — a tree, a wall, a comrade... Rissak's instructions from long ago. The wall in question was warming up but it kept his second opponent from circling about to get behind him.

On the other hand he couldn't retreat. He took an early slash to his forearm, felt the jar of his blade as he blocked a thrust from the left, and the thud of the wall against his back as, disengaging, he parried the second blade. He was tiring, the unaccustomed weapon heavy in his hand. He wished the girl had obeyed him and run; the child could still be lost, as his life was about to be. Rissak's words echoed again in his head, a fragment of his interminable weapon's lore: Any man'll step back from steel in the face. The trick is to be ready to take advantage of it...

Lifting his blade Marric drew breath and thrust it, yelling, at the man on the left, scarcely feeling the hot sting of steel across his ribs. His opponent recoiled as Rissak had promised.

He had time for the breathless wish that his old mentor could have witnessed the move while his angled blade thrust home beneath the collarbone, then the second raider was on him. He would have died, should have died then, only the girl's screaming had done its job and brought help at the run.

His savior was lithe and fast, bare head darkened with sweat and soot, blue eyes cold with furious murder. The raider fell and he whirled, seeking the next foe, only lowering his blade when he saw that there was just the women, the child and his twin, panting for breath over his weapon.

'Marric,' he reached to steady him, asking urgently, 'Are you hurt?'

'Fine,' he gasped. 'I'm fine, just a cut.' Blood had leaked over his hand and more stained the waist of his tunic. 'Thank you brother. Another moment...' A sob of relief and gladness cut him off and he turned to see the blonde girl drop the child's hand and hurl herself at his twin.

'Darien, oh, Darien!'

'Fenny! Praise the Lady! I've been searching all over —' His left arm went round her slim body to pull it close; he dropped a kiss on her hair, dishevelled and soot-streaked though it was. 'Those men didn't — ? You're not hurt?'

She shook her head, mumbling something into his chest while he petted and soothed her, speaking across her to his twin. 'Marric, can you get them all aboard and count heads? Fenny will help, she knows the women. There'll be the wounded too — and the dead. Make the best speed you can.'

'Yes, of course.' His arm smarted fiercely, but the momentary exhaustion had passed. He put up his sword. 'What of the raiders?'

'I think we have them all, or nearly so. Kenta took their horses off, a good move. Any we've missed are on foot and we'll soon have them too.' He toed the ribs of the man he had killed. 'We have lost three of our own and the shrine is a shambles, but that can be put right given time.' Noticing that the girl in the dirt hadn't moved he dropped to his knees beside her. 'Is she dead?'

'No, terrified.' Fenny knelt alongside him. 'Brede? It's all right Brede, you are safe now.' But the blank stare in the wide eyes didn't change, nor would the girl speak. Marric felt someone beside him, then the child's thin fingers stole into his.

'Come along, little one,' he said gently and found a smile for her. 'What is your name?'

She stared at him, eyes questioning and puzzled, but made no reply.

Brede, in a catatonic state, was carried to the barge where other women waited, or were still arriving. There were fifty-three in all, most of them dedicated to the Lady. Of the rest some, widows or ill-treated wives, had come to the shrine seeking shelter, while others had occupied beds in the infirmary.

One or two like Marthe, a robust woman of middle years, simply earned their living there. In Marthe's case tending and butchering the pigs she bred. There were a dozen children of all ages, not counting the homeless stray rescued from the Drylands a moon ago. Seven men had been wounded in the fighting and there were the bodies of the three who had been killed.

With all safely aboard at last the barge was pushed off. Smoke continued to stain the sky behind them while a lone cock crowed repeatedly, asserting dominance over what was left of his flock.

Marric found a spot on the crowded deck for himself and the child who pressed herself against his legs as if she feared abandonment. He watched the small boats link themselves up again and begin the long, slow return tow until Fenny, the high-priestess's daughter, he reminded himself, appeared suddenly at his side and made herself mistress of his slashed arm.

'Let me bind that for you, you're losing blood. I don't know you, do I? How are you called? Have you just recently joined us?'

'I'm Marric. And no you don't. I arrived a few days since with Tranche.'

Who would be her uncle, he realised. Some perverse instinct stopped him from revealing his connection to Darien. 'Look, the cut can wait. Besides, it really needs washing first.' She was very beautiful, even dishevelled and daubed with soot and sweat. There was a scrape on the rounded swell of her forearm and he had the absurd desire to tend it.

'It will get it.' She smiled showing even white teeth. 'Don't worry, the shrine trains us well. One should always stop the bleeding before doing anything else.' She spoke didactically as if quoting. 'And your side — is that hurt too?'

'No,' he spoke abruptly, 'the skin's hardly broken. I will see to it later myself. Sorry,' he'd been curt, he realised. 'I didn't mean to snap.'

She inclined her head, then glancing at the silent child beside him observed, 'Saba's taken to you, I see. How do you come to speak her language?'

'Is that her name?' He looked his surprise. 'What made you think I do? She's Baratan, is she not?'

'It's what we call her, and yes, we assume she's from the Black Country but nobody here speaks her tongue. Only you did, at least she came to you, which is most unusual, so she must have understood you, although I didn't. She's deathly afraid of men. She was found almost dead poor little mite, and brought to us to heal. She had been shockingly — abused.' The hesitant use of the last word conveyed her meaning. 'She won't even go near boys her own age, but as you saved her life, and mine — Did I thank you for that?'

'If that's true it was my pleasure, my lady. And that feels much better, thank you.' Marric flexed his now bandaged arm and smiled into her grey eyes. She smiled back, teeth white and even between red lips. The rest of her face was smudged with soot and dirt, around which her fair hair straggled in disarray, but he thought he had never seen anything prettier

Marric opened his mouth in search of something clever to say but was prevented by the old body he had carried from the burning dormitory, who chose that moment to have a seizure. By the time her breathing, and the efforts to save her, had both stopped, the barge had reached what proved to be the army's infirmary where the Lady Ananda stood waiting to meet them.

***

That evening Darien held council with his captains. He included Ananda who had come directly from the hospital with a report on the wounded. Tomorrow the funerals for those killed would be held, and alternative housing found among the civilian homes, for the women and children of the shrine. There was none to spare in the army encampment where space must be preserved for the constant incoming trickle of recruits.

A summary of the day's events made for grim hearing. A fourth man could be added to the tally of the dead for the Goddess had called him, Ananda reported, and he would not last the night. Another might lose the use of his sword arm. The remaining six would recover in time, as should the women who had suffered assault and rape, save perhaps for Brede whose mind was presently beyond recall. The Lady's warning had prevented a greater catastrophe, and the structural losses at the shrine could always be made good. Its treasures were safe, even if the bulk of the livestock and stores were either lost or damaged, and the gardens trampled into ruin.

Darien was less sanguine about the raid's effects. It had, he told them soberly, shown up the vulnerability of their base. It was all very well to take the war to Temes as eventually they must, but doing so meant leaving Laketown open to similar raids with none to defend it. And the obvious course of splitting their force to leave half at home would surely doom them to a quick failure. Neither could they carry the population with them. Given the disparity of numbers between the two forces mobility was their chief advantage, and one they must retain.

So other means of protection had to be canvassed and a chance word from his brother, here the table turned to stare curiously at Marric, had given him an idea he thought worth pursuing.

Sedak, raising a skeptical eyebrow, was first to speak. 'And how is this to be done? The lake itself will not stop them for long. I dareswear as many craft ply the Great River as we have here. Temes has only to order the Ripan boatmen fetched —'

But Rissak, the first to understand, was nodding, a grin stretching his ruined face. 'Aye, lad. You're thinking of the bow: pick 'em off at a distance.' Then his face fell. 'But where are we to magic archers enough from? It'd take months to train them, and first you need the bows, and the wood to make the arrows...'

Marric, unaware that any remark of his had influenced his twin's thinking, said cautiously, 'Bows would work well, that's true. Had you archers enough you could stop any water borne invasion. But before the men to use them you first need the bows. Making them takes time and skill. Time for the wood to cure and glue to set.' He glanced round at the faces about the table and lifted his shoulders at the hopelessness of the prospect. 'In the Upper Land they use hornbeam and juniper. Here you only have access to willow and I have no idea whether or not it's suitable.'

'Have you made a bow yourself, Prince?' Sedak asked.

'No,' he admitted. 'Arrows, yes. Those I can craft. My bow was made for me by a man truly skilled in the art. The shepherds of Ansham all —'

'And they are who we must enlist to our cause,' Darien broke in. 'Not just the shepherds though, any man of Ansham who is willing to fight. And the more bowyers among them the better. And I have been thinking brother,' he bent an eager gaze on Marric, 'that you are the man to convince them of the rightness of our cause. Surely they would wish to throw off the yoke of their slavery? They are slaves, my uncle tells me?'

It was half a question. 'Me?' Marric asked amazed. 'Well,' he considered, 'all right, I do know them and,' with a glance for Sedak, Osram, Nannik and Rissak, 'I'm not Appellan, which is in my favour. But the Old Race haven't served under arms since Cyrus's grandfather defeated them. As to slaves — they are and they aren't.'

He paused then seeking how best to convey the apartness of Arn's people. 'They live as they always have, save that they own nothing and their labour is for their overlords, but they are not sold as slaves commonly are. Yes, they are a conquered people and yet, when you know them, they are not. They hate their oppressors but go their own way. Their loyalty is to themselves only. You cannot coerce them. Their overlords have tried these hundred seasons or more and failed.' He appealed to Rissak. 'Can you see Cran taking up arms beside your people?'

'We are one people here, with one aim, to rid ourselves of tyranny,' Darien stated.

'That is easy to say,' Marric observed quietly, 'when you own the land you stand on and are free to worship your gods and follow your own king. None of which the Old Race can do.' He nodded at the seated Appellans. 'You have enlisted a thousand or more of the Green Corp, you told me. See it from their side. A thousand descendants of the men who took their land and freedom, who tried to outlaw their Goddess and stifle their culture. Why would they even listen to me if I came to them on your behalf?'

Rissak nodded unhappily. 'He is right, my Prince. They are a people very like the wind, impossible to order.'

'They would listen for reward. Every man is open to self interest.' Darien ignored the interjection. 'Self-rule, free worship, the boundaries of their land restored. Would that be enticement enough?'

Nannik frowned. 'But sir — how do we know we can

trust them? Cyrus found their loyalty suspect after all. It is why he forbade them to serve under arms.'

'My grandfather didn't need them,' Darien replied bluntly, 'we do. We must take the risk. Between us we shall hammer out an agreement acceptable to them. We have the Goddess in common after all. However tenuous it is a bond, and where feasible such bonds must be forged into unbreakable chains. They must, else we cannot survive. Today's events have shown me that.'

15

The following day Haran returned to the Lakes. He arrived at mid-morning shortly after Lady Khat had sent a young man in a boat to invite Marric to her home. Berra, who introduced himself as Khat's grandson, was a typical Laker, dark-haired and short of stature, with the broad shoulders of a rower.

'Your pardon for the summons, my lord,' he said shyly. 'I was to tell you that Grandmam has taken a chill, else she would have come to you.' He eyed Marric curiously and ventured. 'Your foster-mother was my aunt, but I never met her.'

'I'm sorry for that,' Marric responded. 'She was a wonderful person.' He climbed gingerly into the craft, working it out. 'So you will be her brother's son? How is it that you survived? I thought that all Taba's male relatives were killed.'

'Aye, my lord. My father was Bugle. I never met him either. He died two moons before I was born, so my mother told me.'

'I see. Well there is no need to 'lord' me, Berra, we are cousins of a sort, I believe. Besides, I am only recently become a prince again. I was an apprentice to a merchant in Ripa before I came here. Is your grandmother really ill?'

'Well,' Berra replied, 'she says she is perfectly able to be rowed about; it is my mother who refuses to let her take chances with her health. So I was sent to fetch you.' As all the Lakers seemed able to do, he was picking an unerring route between the reed islands following apparently some map fixed in his head. 'Grandmam said you grew up on the high plateau — what is it like there? I have always wondered.'

'Different.' Marric trailed his hand through the cool water, snatching it back when it touched something hard. He had a momentary glimpse of a ridged shell then the terrapin was gone, lost in the depths. 'There are rivers, but no lakes like this, and in winter the snow lies for moon upon moon...'

The journey passed quickly as Marric spoke of life at Valleyford, and the visit that followed did too. Khat's daughter-in-law, Marric suspected, was more interested in meeting the 'lost' prince than preventing Lady Khat from unwise exertion on the water, but she was pleasant enough, plying him with food and drink, and questions. He did his best to answer them and asked some of his own. She had a married daughter he learned, and Berra was a year younger than he himself was. Looking around he thought that the house, though comfortably enough appointed, was small, not at all what Marric had imagined for the widow of the brother of a king. He tried to picture Taba here with — what was it? three growing brothers, and couldn't. It was Khat herself who corrected him.

'Oh no, this is Marla's home,' she indicated her daughter-in-law. 'I have lived with her ever since the killings. I couldn't stand the silence of my own place. Of course my little bird had flown early. She was only nine when she went to Ripa. After — when only we women and the children were left...' She shook her head, pressing her lips together and he saw the sadness in her, bone deep, ineradicable.

'Now Mother,' Marla said, 'it does no good to —'

'Yes dear, I know.' Khat smiled at her and went on to

ask about his bandaged arm, which led to a discussion of the raid upon the shrine.

'Darien believes they were a band of deserters from the army that went to Barat,' Marric told them. 'Masterless men but no less dangerous for that. If he's right it does mean the king wasn't behind the attack, which is good news. I gather that Darien's force is not quite ready yet to challenge Temes.'

'The Lady protect him,' Khat said automatically. It was plain that his twin was a favourite here. 'Have you talked with your grandmother yet, Marric?'

'Not yet,' he admitted, adding hastily, 'But I promise you that I will. This very day if I get the chance.'

Her smile that reminded him so much of Taba's broke across her face. 'Thank you, my dear. And now I think Berra had best take you back. I find I am a little weary after all.'

He bent to kiss her hand and then her cheek, bowed to Marla and thanked her for her hospitality, and was soon once again seated in the reed boat, being borne swiftly back the way they had come.

'Are you not in the army, Berra?' Marric asked as they threaded through the floating islands. He had wondered about this when they first met.

The young man's shoulders stiffened. 'No,' he replied gruffly. 'Of course I wanted to enlist, but the Prince forbade it. It is not fair of him! Every jack of them,' he waved the paddle to encompass the tidy lines of floating homes anchored either side of watery streets that bustled with craft, as an ordinary town might with pedestrians and carriages, 'will follow him to war and I alone cannot.'

'But why should that be so?'

'Because of my father and his father. My grandfather was brother to King Waltu and I am the last of his line. If Prince Darien should fall in battle I am his heir —' He broke off, forgetting to paddle then the boat rocked as he hipped about to stare in astonished delight at Marric. 'No, by the Lady, I am not! Dolt that I am not to have realised — ! You are now the heir, my lord! Why did I not think? Ah,' his sigh was rich with satisfaction. 'He cannot stop me now!'

'Indeed,' Marric murmured. Darien wouldn't stop him either. The fervor with which his twin had come to his rescue at the shrine had dissolved the last remnants of his hostility, but in any event, he told himself, he was bound to join any cause that opposed Temes. He shuddered to think what would befall the population of the Lakes should the rising fail. Lady Khat, his grandmother, Fenny — all would be swept up in the conflagration that would follow defeat. It was unthinkable that he should not play his part and he could best begin, he thought practically, by persuading Arn to help them.

He must talk the old man into spreading the word among the bowmen of Ansham that their skills were needed to prosecute the coming war. The old priest had the influence if he would only use it on their behalf, for archers were the best single way to help redress the disparity of size between the two armies. All the training and courage in the world wouldn't prevent a tidal wave of numbers rolling over a numerically inferior force.

Still pondering the problem when they arrived back at their starting point, Marric thanked Berra for his service. He made a creditable job of leaving the craft without falling into the lake, and was instantly hailed by name.

'I see you are finding your boat legs, Prince Marric.'

Haran came to his feet from where he had been squatting, caravaneer fashion, with his back to the wall of the building. He bowed stiffly to Marric, offering a brief glimpse of his turban's top. His nose was still faintly bruised.

'As you say,' Marric observed neutrally. 'What brings you back?'

'The Prince's business. Also I wish to apologise for how we — I — treated you. Although it was of your own making. Why did you not simply tell us the truth?'

'Why did not you when you were using me to smuggle stuff?' Marric retorted. 'Or did you reckon that treason was more dangerous than my position, should anyone have learned my true identity?'

Haran sighed, tacitly admitting the truth in Marric's words. 'Well, if it is any consolation, Prince, you are a loss to the House. The first thing Luka said when I told him was: *Damn! There goes the best apprentice material we've had in many seasons.* He sends his abject apologies for doubting you. And this.' He bent to retrieve the long package wrapped in a loosely woven cloth. Marric stripped it off to reveal his bow and quiver of arrows.

'Thank you,' he said, adding honestly, 'there is a part of me will miss the House. I enjoyed my time with it, and my journeys with you. You taught me a lot, as did Tranche and Luka. My brother is lucky in your support of him.'

Haran's wary look dissolved. He nodded, essaying a small grin. 'Thank you, and you've quite a way with you when in a corner, Mat — er Prince Marric.' Delicately he touched his nose.

And now Marric smiled. 'Then I apologise also. Now has anyone seen to your needs? How did you get here and how long have you been waiting for me?'

'A little while. As to how there's always a hidden craft at the landing place. I paddled myself here.'

'But how did you find it without a guide?'

Haran snorted. 'I find my way through mountains and deserts. Why should water stop me? Where is everyone, anyway?'

'Darien will most likely be with the wounded, or he might have gone to oversee the salvage at the shrine.' The trader's blank look reminded Marric that the man knew nothing of yesterday's raid. 'Come inside, I'll send for wine and food; there is much to tell you.'

When Darien, flanked by Rissak and the two young Lakers who served as sentries and messengers for the Prince returned, bringing a clatter of boots and deep voices that broke the peace of the place, Marric excused himself and went in search of his grandmother. The family quarters were on the pontoon moored behind the rooms where Darien met and sometimes dined with his officers and immediate family. Queen Quan's more secluded rooms had been made homely and welcoming with garden plants spilling from large urns along the front of the house platform, and a long reed seat scattered with bright cushions and shaded from the afternoon sun. It was here he waited while a servant went to inform the queen of his arrival.

Instead of having him conducted to her presence, Quan came herself to meet him, a stately figure, not over tall but slim and erect for her years, with the quiet certainty that age and position had given her. He rose at her approach finding her almost his match in height.

'Marric. This is a surprise.' She settled herself at one end of the seat, indicating the rest with a wave of her hand. 'Please, be seated. How may I help you?'

'Grandmother, I trust you are well?' He bowed carefully and sat, a little startled when the seat moved beneath him with a gentle, gliding motion. Quan caught his surprise and smiled.

'Ingenious, is it not? It rocks. I find it soothing and often sit here of an evening. So,' she nodded at his bandaged arm, 'yesterday's raid? I understand the consequences would have been far worse without your warning.'

'It is the Goddess you must thank for that, not me,' he demurred. 'I have not — it was my first vision since my fifteenth summer.'

'Which tells you what?' Quan prompted. Her manner was not cool so much, he thought, as contained. She was nothing like Lady Khat whose warmth lay close beneath the surface, which was not to say that Quan was without it. With her, he judged, it would always be a matter of head over heart. Perhaps they were more alike than he had imagined.

'That I am meant to be here?' he hazarded.

She considered his answer. 'Possibly. One does well,' she cautioned him, 'to regard the Great One's messages warily. You received a warning, which was acted upon, and lives were saved. But was that all? It is rare to find matters as simple as that. I have never myself been troubled, Bel be thanked! by visions, or godly interventions, but from what I have seen of how things went with my daughter, it is seldom that simple.'

'No.' Marric agreed, studying his hands. 'I think, that is to say it's possible, that the warning principally came for a black child I rescued from a burning building. It was her I saw in the vision. She was the one, I believe, that I was meant to save. I don't know why she is important, or what part she will or may, play in the future. Only that I suspect she is somehow crucial to Darien's cause. If that's what the vision is about.' He looked into her face, his own troubled. 'How did my mother do it, how did she know what it all meant? What if I am wrong? The child is just a waif the men found in the desert. She is without speech and we have no clue to her identity. The men who brought her in suspect she escaped from a slaver's coffle. She cannot even tell us her name.'

'And yet your goddess wanted her saved?'

'So it would seem.'

'Then you have done your part,' Quan replied. 'And if more is required then doubtless it will be shown you. So, tell me, Marric, have you brought yourself to think more kindly of your family?'

He flushed, and reflected that the queen was also very direct. He answered truthfully. 'Yes. And I regret my earlier behaviour. It was childish of me to blame you. I am sorry for that, Madame.'

'I would rather you continue to call me Grandmother.' Quan said. 'And it was an entirely natural mistake, for one who never knew my daughter.' She reached to pat his hand but didn't let her own linger there as Khat's would have done. 'From the time she was five summers old there was little that mattered to her in her own life that Leona didn't organise for herself.' Her smile was faint and reminiscent. 'I am sure there must have been times when even Bel wondered at his choice of mouthpiece.'

Marric seized the opening. 'Please, will you tell me of her, Grandmother? What she was like? Taba always called her more than pretty, she was beautiful, she said. Of course I believed her, but when I grew older I sometimes wondered if that was what she thought a son might want to hear of his mother?'

The queen nodded, her smile a little sad. 'Oh, she was beautiful, very. And clever, quick to grasp a point. And bold, too bold for her own good. Leona was all those things. And her father's darling. She would have been so proud of you two boys. It breaks my heart to think — It was Temes, his men anyway, who took her that day. His own secretary confessed it to me. But I am almost certain that the priests of Bel killed her. Fevran the high-priest was her enemy.'

'Taba said as much. She told me how he hated her.'

'She was right,' Quan said, 'but she didn't understand. Mouse — we called her Mouse — was an innocent in the true sense. So loving and gentle. She believed Fevran hated Leona for the blasphemy she'd committed, but it went far deeper than that. It was thwarted lust that drove him, not hate.' She lifted her brows. 'Do I shock you, grandson? We all have sexual natures and your mother's beauty was such that men desired her at sight. Even priests.'

Her sharp gaze lost its focus turning inwards as she remembered. 'They brought her to us, the ones who found her body, and we washed her, Mallow and I. Her hands were still bound and her beautiful face —' She stopped to breathe deeply. 'And in her mouth was a lump of flesh. She had bitten her killer, torn and worried at him while he beat her —' She stopped to breathe again and Marric leaned towards her.

'Grandmother — don't! Let it rest. Let her rest. I should not have asked.' He touched her arm. 'Please. It distresses you.'

'Of course it does!' Quan snapped. 'She was my daughter. And you will hear it Marric, for the same reason Darien did. Fevran still lives, but with a crippled hand that he cannot use. Tranche told me so many seasons back. It was his flesh your mother tore, and when Ripa falls to our army, as it will, as it must, then we will be avenged upon her murderer.'

Coldness filled Marric steeling his heart, sheathing his limbs. Quan saw the change and nodded. 'Yes. It is right. Even Waltu, Bel bless him, would not have forgiven this. And that is without considering everything that followed from it.'

Marric, grappling with sudden conjecture, barely heard her words. He said slowly, 'This has made me wonder — well, I did so at the time but I ended by dismissing the matter because Taba's warnings made me think the plots at Valleyford were all about me. But when you take them all together it doesn't really make sense. A slave girl wearing Taba's cloak was killed — to make me the more vulnerable she thought. But why involve her?

'Any man with a blade could have taken my life whether she was there or not, and I doubt my father would have lifted a finger against him. And the poisoned fruit the hawker brought... Was it not more likely that she, rather than I, would eat it? I was not even living with her then, and a casual question to anyone could have elicited the fact.' His dark eyes were like stone as they met the queen's gaze. 'Can Fevran also have been responsible for Taba's murder?'

'I would put nothing past that vicious little adder. She was your mother's confidante, and your protector. Leona had every right to scorn him but ah,' the queen looked old of a sudden, less regal and frailer as she bent as if in pain, bony hands rising to cage her mouth, 'at what cost to us all.'

'Let him enjoy his vengeance while he may,' Marric said grimly. 'I will kill him myself when the time comes. You may be sure of that, Grandmother.'

Quan's eyes glittered as she touched his hand. 'It is strange how the generations repeat themselves. You are like my son Tomas, quieter perhaps, for he was a joyful boy, while your brother has all Leona's fire and flamboyance. The two of you will go far together. Thank you for coming today, Marric. Another time I would hear of your life, and tell you of Mouse and Leona's girlhood, but just now I would like to be alone.'

'Of course.' He pressed her hand and left her there rocking quietly on the seat.

16

Fenny was with Darien in the meeting room when Marric returned, working together over a paper marred with ink blots and many lines crossed through and rewritten. He was scowling, muttering over the wording, red hair rumpled from where his hand had repeatedly run through it.

'No, it is too little.' Fenny took the quill from his hand and leaning in against his shoulder dashed the nib through the last line and wrote it anew. 'There — what is wrong with that? You are not the bargainer here Darien, but the supplicant. You wish to have what they may not want to give.'

Darien considered the line carefully, rubbing his knuckles against his jaw, then his hand rose to encircle her neck pulling her face down level with his, the golden head beside the red one. His face had lightened of its scowl as he kissed her cheek.

'You are right of course. Thank you. The fighting, the organising I can manage, but this capturing of words... You are far better at it than I will ever be.'

Marric coughed to announce his presence, wishing he had not seen the intimacy between them. Fenny, glancing up to note him there in the doorway, said lightly, 'Another reason to thank the Lady for bringing your brother home. Who better than one trained by Tranche to handle such affairs? Merchants are nothing if not diplomatic. The successful ones anyway.'

'True. Marric will you give me your opinion on this? It is a broad proposal for the Old Race, setting out the changes we would make for them, in exchange for their allegiance. What do you think?' His nails clicked restlessly against the table's surface as he watched his twin read. 'Of course the problem will be finding someone with sufficient influence over his fellows to deliver it to. It's not as if they have any form of government. Haran will carry it for us but I own, as the thing must be done in secret, that getting it there will be the easy part. Who to address it to — that is the problem.'

'Mmn.' Marric skimmed quickly through the draft proposal, which promised a reinstatement of the original boundaries of Ansham, self rule, religious rights, and reimbursement for land now occupied by their Appellan overlords.

'Well, we cannot simply kick them off it,' Darien said, judging at the speed of his brother's reading. 'You do see that? It would sow the seeds of further troubles. If it didn't immediately start another war! But of course the original owners should have some recompense. We would have to set up a court of royal justice I suppose, that could decide on payment; and enforce it where necessary. What do you think?'

'It seems fair.' Marric went back and read it again. 'I agree about the compensation. The land the nobles have taken comprises most of the arable areas of Ansham, and there's little enough of that. Might you not suggest that instead of an outright payment, they should be taxed annually on their occupancy? It would save endless administration and resentment, and fund a treasury for the country, while still providing work for the Old Race whose livelihoods have come to depend upon the nobles. I agree that you cannot just give the land back. The social upheaval would be too great, and your justice system swamped.'

Fenny beamed at him. 'There!' she said triumphantly taking back the paper. 'You see, Darien? You could not have a better advisor. Shall I put it in?'

'Yes,' Darien was nodding enthusiastically. 'It is a far better way of handling the matter. Thank you Marric. Now if only you could solve the rest so easily Haran could be on his way tomorrow.'

Marric nodded. 'Actually, I can. The man to seek out to receive this, the one with authority over his people is someone I know well. He is their high priest who, in another age, would also be their king. It would however, be a waste of time to send Haran. He would not even find him. I will go.' Light fractured for an instant behind his eyes and he caught a whiff of snake and knew then that this too had been ordained. He nodded at the written-over sheets. 'If you wish I can transcribe that into Ansham tonight, and leave in the morning.'

Darien was shaking his head. 'No!' he said forcefully. 'You cannot! You are speaking of Valleyford, of returning there, are you not? You escaped alive from it once; there is no way you can go back. I won't allow it.'

'It is not for you to allow me anything.' Marric's voice was wintry of a sudden. Resentment bloomed in him and he fought to dispel it, knowing that fear for him had prompted his twin's words. In a more conciliatory tone he added, 'This is a thing that I am bidden to do. You mustn't, in fact you can't, stop me. Arn will speak with no one else. That I can guarantee. If Haran goes in my stead he will lose his labour and you a possible ally.'

Darien glared at him jaw visibly clenched as he bit back on speech. His chest heaved with a deep breath, then his shoulders relaxed and he breathed out, the ire fading from his expression. 'Very well then, but you will be careful? I beg you will take no chances, brother. I could not bear to lose you again.' The glimpse of fear in his eyes jolted Marric. 'And please, you must not go alone. I will send Rissak —'

'No.' The refusal came before he'd time to think but he knew it was right. Rissak wouldn't offer himself, which was the only way Marric could accept his service. Seeking to soften the abruptness of his refusal he said, 'His place is with you. Besides he would be at more risk on the plateau than ever I could be.' He picked a face and name at random from the officers he had met at Darien's table. 'If he is willing I would have the big man — Osram.'

'Yes, an excellent choice.' Darien looked relieved. He called and one of his Laker guards stuck his head through the door. 'Find Osram for me. Tell him he is needed.'

'Yes, my lord.' The man departed.

'Thank you. Well, I'll get started on this.' Marric retrieved the paper and had turned to leave when Darien's voice stopped him.

'I beg you will forgive me, brother, for the unthinking way I spoke to you. I have become too accustomed perhaps to giving orders. I do not seek to order you — never think it! It was just —' he opened his hand smiling a little crookedly. 'You are dear to me, you know? I have followers enough, but none as precious as you and Fenny are. Promise me that you will take care?'

'You may be certain of it,' Marric avoided Fenny's eye. Of course he had known from the start, he told himself, before he had even met her. How was he to forget the way Darien had looked when he swore; *I'll get her back.* And the way he had snatched her to him when he found her amid the burning buildings? He sought words that would reciprocate his twin's affectionate declaration but envy had stolen his generosity of spirit. 'I promise that I shall stay safe,' he said flatly, 'if only to spite Temes.'

En route to his room Marric passed a servant and asked for quills, ink and paper to be brought to him. It was a while since he'd had cause to translate anything. Most of the records he had dealt with in Ripa had been in the Rhutan language. The tongue of Ansham had similar roots but he must make no mistakes. The gods knew it would be hard enough to convince Arn, or at least, he amended, for Arn to persuade his people to agree to the proposal when to do so would mean joining causes with some of the hated enemy. Even his embittered grandson who had ached for rebellion might refuse to listen. If he kept his mind on his task he could surely banish the vision of his brother with his arm about Fenny's neck as he kissed the silky skin of her cheek. And when they were alone, what else? He refused to let his mind go there.

The smallest movement glimpsed in the corner of his eye as he stepped through the door to his room and the paper was fluttering floorwards, his sword half out, before brain and sight caught up with his reflexes. Rissak, he thought sardonically would be proud. He shoved the blade home again and let out his breath seeking to gentle his voice to the startled child backing away before him.

'It is all right, little one. What are you doing here?' The interrogative note in his voice brought her hesitantly closer. She said something, staring at him expectantly, dark eyes enormous in her dark face. Her lips were plump, bow like, they trembled and parted, while she squeezed her child's hands into fists, then spoke in a soft rush of words. He shook his head slowly, opening his hands to mime incomprehension. The dark eyes flashed, her voice rising imperiously as if in demand but as his brow wrinkled in perplexity, the expectant light died from her face. A single tear trickled down one dark cheek.

'Saba.' Marric squatted before her watching her face as he pointed to himself. 'Mar-ric,' he said distinctly, repeating the name several times. Then he pointed to her, 'Saba?' exaggerating the lift in his voice so she would recognise a question. 'Me Mar-ric. You — Saba?'

She was intelligent. 'Mah-ric.' The delicate hand almost touched him then she pointed to herself and shook her head violently as she mouthed the name he had called her.

'Not Saba then.' Marric nodded and smiled that he understood, then repeated the pantomime of naming himself before pointing again to her, his brows raised interrogatively.

'Amtee,' she enunciated, and when he parroted it carefully, nodded.

'Good. I am Marric, you are Amtee. Now, Amtee, I have work to do, so come with me.' He held out his hand and the child shied back but followed him obediently from the room, hands tucked behind her. Marric had thought to deliver her to a servant but it was Fenny he came across first.

'Oh, there you are, Saba,' she scolded. 'I've been searching all over — where did you find her, Marric?'

'She was in my room. Her name is Amtee by the way, but I'm afraid that's all I could learn. It's a thousand pities we cannot spe — Wait!' Marric shook his head. 'I'm a fool! Where is Tranche, do you know?'

Fenny was eyeing him in surprise. 'I can find him if you wish. Why? What have you thought of?'

'I sometimes forget that in his younger days he was a trader. Mostly at sea but he would certainly have gone also to Barat. Therefore he must have learned a little of the language, for how could he trade without it? Traders seem always to have a handful of words of every country they visit. Can you ask him to try with her? If he only speaks a little it might still be enough to help her learn our tongue.'

'Of course!' Then her enthusiasm died. 'Only she won't stay in the same room with a man.'

'She came to me,' Marric pointed out. 'Fenny, I feel that this is important. I can't tell you why because I do not know myself. Just that it is. If she truly will not sit with him face to face, can he not talk to her from behind a screen, so she need hear only his voice?'

'It's worth a try,' the girl agreed looking down at the

girl who, Marric noted, had taken her hand without fuss. The child's bright gaze shuttled between their two faces, her brows knitted into a frown as she tried vainly to glean from their expressions, the burden of their speech.

'Thank you,' he said, the words sounding stiff in his own ears.

'I am glad to help however I can.' She smiled coaxingly. 'You know Marric, that Darien really appreciates —'

'Yes, of course,' he broke in, 'but I must beg you to excuse me now. If I am to have that proposal ready in time I should get back to it. Thank you for your help with Amtee.' Not waiting for an answer he turned back to his room.

***

They left at dawn the following morning while the ducks were still waking, and before the first fingers of sunlight had touched the lake's surface. Osram's large bulk in the boat obscured Marric's forward view and he had to twist about to see his brother's craft behind him. Darien and Rissak towed the third boat containing the supplies and saddles. They wove their way swiftly through the reed islands where unseen creatures plopped wetly out of sight at their approach. The first rays of sunlight were touching the willows as they pulled in at the jetty before the warehouse and stables. A Laker came to meet them leading two mounts and a pack mule, that hung back on its halter rope and was roundly cursed for doing so. In no time they were loaded and ready to depart. Feeling self-conscious about it Marric grasped his twin's forearm and was instantly pulled into a quick hug.

'Travel with caution, brother,' Darien urged, and to Osram, 'See that you bring him back safe to me, you hear?'

194

'Aye, sir.' Osram right arm thumped across his chest in the old Green Corps salute. 'I'll do that.'

'Take care, lad,' Rissak slapped his shoulder. 'You're as well guarded as you can be with this big ox. Just don't try gambling with him.'

'I'll remember.' Marric smiled with true affection at his old mentor. 'You too. Don't start the war while I'm gone, will you?'

Darien laughed, sunlight on his uncapped head. 'We're not quite ready for that yet. Bring me a deal with this Arn of yours though, and that could change.'

The two stood watching them ride off, the mule resigned now to its fate, jogging equably beside Marric's bay mare to leave Osram free to defend them both at need.

Rissak blew out his breath glancing sideways at Darien. 'He'll be all right, my Prince. He's tougher than he looks and the gods are with him.' As he spoke his fingers, unbidden, made the sun sign. Angrily he caught the gesture and deliberately closed his fist.

'Aye,' Darien muttered. 'And I do not forget that they were with my mother too — for a while.'

***

Marric carried his bow and a full quiver of arrows, and slung across his chest was the strap of the satchel holding the translated proposal. He had made two copies, each of which Darien had already signed. Enough, should he be caught with them on him, to get him hanged for treason, he thought, while scuppering Darien's cause before it was even launched. Getting it past the guards at the pass would be their first major challenge.

He mentioned this to Osram who shook his head, flicking blond curls about, a tolerant smile on his face.

'Don't be worrying about that, Prince Marric. We'll not be taking the pass.'

'Not?' He narrowed his gaze. 'I thought it was the only way through the mountains?'

'Only official way, maybe, Prince. The way we'll go is the smugglers' route. Rougher but shorter. And private, if you don't count the odd mountain goat or eagle Prince, and I don't reckon they'll be carrying tales to the Pretty Boy.'

Marric grinned at him. 'That's a name I haven't heard since I left the plateau! Rissak called him that, too. And you needn't Prince me every sentence, Osram. My name is Marric. So, tell me — How did you wind up in my brother's army?'

Osram it seemed, along with most of the Green Corp now enrolled in the Laker Prince's cause, had defected from the useless struggle against the barbarians when a popular general, who had refused to sacrifice further troops by marching them to their deaths in the Grassland, had been beheaded on Temes's orders.

'It was one senseless death too many,' the big man said. 'It was plain Temes wanted rid of us. He'd already had Lendl, another general sent naked in a cage for the barbarians to slaughter. They flayed him, poor bastard.' His face darkening as he spoke. 'Calls himself a king! King of the Black Apes maybe. He knew our loyalties had lain first with Cyrus and then to the Corps. We felt none for him, not once he started murdering us. That's what it was, cold-blooded murder! So we quit, those of us who still lived. Less than a quarter,' he added, falling silent at the memory of comrades lost.

'And so you found my brother?'

Osram shrugged. 'Nah. First I ran across Rissak. Hardly recognised him, but he knew me. He hooked us up with Darien.' He shrugged. 'We are soldiers Pr — Marric. Where else were we to go? The choice was slim, a life of banditry, or a legitimate cause to fight for? If Temes catches us —' He shrugged. 'We all have a price on our heads.' He rumbled a deep laugh from his belly. 'You would be surprised how motivating that knowledge is! The Pretty Boy shames his father's memory. Besides, some few of us knew that he was never Cyrus's choice of heir.' He glanced across at Marric. 'There was talk it was you. Even Rissak believed it before —'

'Aye,' Marric agreed abruptly. 'So did I, but that was before I knew of my twin's existence. Now, tell me more about this smugglers' path.'

***

They reached it late the following day and it was as steep as Osram had promised. They came upon it in the dark having spent the last of the afternoon laying up in a copse where the animals could feed. Earlier they had taken to the woods to bypass the isolated dwellings scattered among the foothills. It was grazing country this far from the Lakes, for the ground was dry and rocky, unsuited to the plough. Here and there, where over the centuries mountain streams had carried silt to the bottom lands, small, hard-scrabble orchards of cherry and apple had been planted, but mainly all the travellers saw were incurious stock that lifted their heads to watch them pass by, the chain links on the pack-bags clinking to the mule's steps.

Daylight found them halfway up the mountain on a track made only, Marric thought, for and by goats. Watching the sure-footed mule pick its way along it he fervently wished he were riding it instead of his mount that trembled and snorted, needing to be coaxed every step of the way. Mules climbed like mountain goats, their narrow hooves finding purchase where a horse's broader ones slipped and skidded. Osram dealt patiently with them, his large form which should have been clumsy, as deft and neat footed as the pack mule's.

197

'And how do you know about this route?' Marric asked when they paused to eat. He stretched his weary body, aching from the tension of effort. 'You surely weren't smuggling yourself?'

The big man grinned. 'Nah. I was one of Cyrus's scouts. It's a good way to learn country. The trick is to watch for animal pads. If they can go there chances are a man can too — if he's up to no good.'

The route got no better. Marric's leg, which rarely troubled him now, ached from the strain of climbing for they spent as much time out of the saddle as in it. His limp came back; it would settle again he knew, but he was just as glad there were none to observe his hobbling gait. He doubted, after all this time that it would give him away, for the army must consider him long dead, but he'd sooner not have his belief put to the test.

'That's the worst of it,' Osram informed him when the ground finally levelled out. He nodded to the east. 'The pass is that way. There shouldn't be a soul closer than a good day's ride in that direction, which would just about bring you to the royal road. We're maybe three days travel from Valleyfield here. Next trick will be finding your man without getting ourselves noticed.'

Marric's neck prickled and he spoke with sudden certainty. 'I doubt that will be a problem. He knows we are coming.'

'And how is that?' Osram demanded, but Marric, gaze remote, simply shook his head. The big man sucked his teeth but asked no further questions on the subject as they made their camp and cooked a meal over the small fire-pit that Osram dug, using an armful of branches to shield the flames from sight.

'Though you are quite certain there is no-one to see,' Marric observed dryly.

'Yeah well, a bit of caution never comes amiss,' his companion replied.

That night the ache in Marric's leg kept him from sleep, and when he finally drifted off he dreamed of travelling on the Great River following its serpentine curves towards distant mountains. Only the dull gleam before him, he realised, was composed of scales gliding smoothly across the landscape. His heart began to pound as the night fled silently past until at length he stood again amid the mist shrouded trees, with a red glow lighting the far clouds, and the shadow of fear and loss freezing his heart.

17

On the plateau the two men continued their journey swiftly, but with caution.

They travelled overland, choosing secluded camps, and giving the villages and the flocks they sighted a wide berth. 'For we are in Ansham now where not even a rabbit moves unnoticed,' Marric advised.

Osram sniffed disbelievingly. 'I told you I was a scout. I'll warrant not a soul has seen us pass.'

Nevertheless that evening as they unpacked in the shelter of a grove of trees and were picketing the animals for the night, the mule's long ears suddenly twitched and he snorted a raspy warning. A figure stepped out from beneath the trees to confront them causing Osram's hand to fly to his sword hilt. Marric, crouched to kindle their small fire, made a hand movement to stay him. He kept very still, his gaze on the lean, bitter-faced man before him. He would be past thirty summers now, he thought, and had not lost a jot of his youthful intransigence. Rising to his feet he nodded a greeting, which Keelin ignored.

'Grandfather said, come.'

Osram was regarding him with raised brows as Marric dipped his chin in reply. 'Yes, I've been expecting to hear from him. It is good to see you well, Keelin.'

The shepherd ignored the pleasantry, simply turning on his heel as if expecting them to follow. Osram startled, said, 'What, now?' He made a move towards the horses but Marric shook his head, and grumbling under his breath the big man followed on foot. It was a long walk with only the starlight and a young moon to guide them. After a short while spent stumbling over the rough ground, Osram muttered, 'This is madness, Marric. It could be a trap. Who is this man, anyway?'

'He is the grandson of a king — who incidentally, is the man we go to see. The same man being also the high priest of his people.'

'An outlaw then. What concerns me is how he knew we were coming?'

Marric said patiently for it was important for the success of their enterprise that Osram understood, 'An outlaw only by the laws of Cyrus and Temes. But please remember that Cyrus is dead now, and if my brother succeeds he will change the laws. Are you supporting Temes or Darien here? As to how he knew — in the same manner that I knew about the attack on the shrine. He whom we go to meet is a man of great power. You will look at him and see what all Appellans see, a seemingly simple, unlettered shepherd, but don't be misled. Arn is far more than that. Just remember that everything hangs on this meeting. If I cannot win his support then we have wasted our journey.'

'And we could not have ridden to see him in daylight?'

'Why should we? They walk, and it is we who are the supplicants here. Your race is no better than theirs Osram, but your belief that it is could well jeopardize everything, so please, mind your words.'

Osram stumbled again, rumbling an oath as he did so, but afterwards held his peace.

Keelin led them in silence until a glimmer of light showed at a little distance ahead. He gave the call of a nightjar, the sound so realistic it was moments before Marric realised it had come from him. He stopped and turned, motioning them with a jerk of his head, to walk forward. 'They await you,' he said, and stepped back, vanishing into the night.

'Now what?' Osram muttered. 'Is this some fool's errand?'

'No. Keep your hand from your weapon,' Marric retorted sharply. 'Remember, these people have no reason to trust you.' His eyes, long accustomed to the low light, picked a path for them and he trod confidently forward to the doorway of the hut from which the glimmer of light had escaped.

Inside five men were seated on a woven mat that covered the dirt floor. The structure, Marric thought after a swift glance around, was new, built for this purpose. It was roofed with brush piled over green saplings, and more brush bundles had been woven between uprights to form the walls. There was a doorway with a hanging cloth but no door. The whole thing could be swiftly dismantled, and would be he thought, the moment the meeting ended. Arn sat in the centre of the arc the five men's bodies made, and Marric was not entirely surprised to recognise Cran there too. The others were unknown to him. He gave them all a formal greeting in their own tongue, then directed his words to the old shepherd.

'I am glad to see you, old friend. And you Cran. This is my companion and protector Osram.' He folded his legs and sat, first removing the bow from his shoulder and setting it aside. 'I thank you all for coming together this way. It has saved us a deal of time.'

'Which grows short, my brother,' Arn murmured. 'You are well, Prince Marric? It has been a while and a while since we parted.'

'It has.' The lamp provided little illumination. Arn adjusted the wick and his features were thrown into sharp relief, the deeply seamed face and prominent nose and brow. His cheeks were thinner, Marric saw, but the power in the glance of his deep-set eyes remained unchanged.

He wore his shabby shepherd's apparel, and sat with his skinny shanks crossed before him, the tattoos plain on his wrist as he moved his hand around the circle, naming the men present, all of whom had travelled many days to be present, he said, at the meeting.

There was an air of wariness in the hut. The men responded, unsmiling, to the introductions and when Marric, seeking to relax them, asked Cran how Berta did, Arn rebuked him brusquely.

'We have but this night to settle matters. Therefore let us speak only of them. These men put their lives at risk by being here.'

Osram scowled at him. 'So does the Prince,' he said laboriously in their tongue, 'and he has come a sight further.'

'Enough Osram! You have the right of it, Arn. Very well then let us speak of what brings us here. There is no need to rehearse the injustices you suffer, and have suffered, under Appellan rule. Or the tyranny of the present king's reign. My brother, should he succeed in taking the throne, will change the unjust laws we now have. He will be a firm friend and strong ally of an independent Ansham —'

'In exchange for what, the blood of our young men?' growled a grey haired elder from the left of the circle.

'Yes,' Marric agreed steadily, 'and that of the Lakers, the Rhutans, and not a few Appellans, also. It is the only way this thing can be done. We need archers — and you are the only people to use the bow. Your men are our best hope of success.'

The man laughed jeeringly. 'And then this brother of yours, whom none of us have even seen, will do what for us exactly? As little, I warrant, as possible.'

'Peace, Matla,' Arn said. 'We have discussed this. Let the Prince speak. When he has done so then is the time for talk.'

'Thank you.' Marric took a breath. He could practically

feel Osram fulminating beside him, and placed a warning hand on his leg. He didn't know how much the big man understood of the quick exchanges, but obviously enough to read the temper of the meeting. 'My brother Darien has given the matter much thought,' he began, and with a silent prayer to the Goddess slipped into the start of his prepared speech.

***

It took most of the night and all Marric's skill as an advocate to persuade the men to agree to the Laker Prince's request. Arn, he thought, was committed from the start but the others had to be convinced. They stopped at midnight to eat, Arn fetching out from a satchel thrust through the doorway by an unseen person, the flat bread and ewe's cheese that was a staple of the region. Many a time the child Marric had shared this shepherd's repast on the hills about Valleyford. Now, passing round the flask of rough wine, he took the opportunity to speak with Cran, who grasped his arm in friendly fashion, asking how he and Rissak had fared that long ago winter, and where his old friend was now.

'He is no longer with you?'

'No, he serves my brother now, the Laker Prince in whom he has found the warrior he always hoped I would be,' Marric admitted ruefully. 'He's my twin, the shadow you foresaw. But how could any man have guessed that?'

'Her ways are strange indeed,' Cran agreed. 'But the Goddess has smiled on you for your leg has healed, I see. Rissak is well too?'

'Now, yes. He all but died that winter.' He gave the briefest sketch of that spring night when the soldiers had found them. 'That he survived is truly a miracle. I mourned his death until a moon ago when we met again. He recognised me at once, even with one eye.'

Cran laughed. 'Aye, that is Rissak. And he will fight in this war you are brewing?'

'Yes. As will I. Temes is a monster, Cran. He must be stopped. He has the blood of thousands on his hands. Even his own people have turned against his atrocities.' He indicated Osram with a sideways tilt of his head. 'Most of the famous Green Corp were among his victims. All that are left have become the backbone of my brother's army. And in Ripa —' he shook his head at his inability to condense the history of horrors the city had known.

'His reign is built on sadism and terror. I doubt even he knows the number of those killed on his orders. You have yet to feel the full effect upon the plateau, but mark my words, unless we stop him now you will.'

'The more reason to join forces then,' the smith said in his placid way, 'and hopefully before the taxes cripple us completely. Matla is the stumbling block. He would have all Appellans thrown out of Ansham as the price of agreement, and the land redistributed, but that is impossible. Too many generations have passed now.'

'And you will need the revenue they bring in to run the country,' Marric agreed. 'We must have unity Cran, for our numbers are not so great as yet. It is the only way we can win.' Memory teased at him, then returned with a tiny shock of recognition. 'So that is what it meant!' he murmured aloud.

The smith cocked an enquiring brow. 'Something I should know?'

'No — well, yes, I suppose. I have just recalled the first vision the Goddess sent me. She showed me the world, like a bubble in my hands. The Upper and Lower Lands, I could see it all. And then She showed me Tardi my half-brother — only I see now that it wasn't him. It was Darien! I was very young; all I took from it at the time was that Tardi would be king someday, just as he always said he would.'

'Then tell Matla, for surely this proves that this is all, even to your coming here this night, the Mother's design,' Cran urged. 'He is a stubborn man, who carries hate like a burden, but even he cannot stand against Her divine will.'

It proved to be the lever they needed. There was more discussion of ways and means and timing, but once a consensus had been reached only the conditions were left to quibble over. Matla was unlettered but first Cran and then Arn, squinting to make it out in the poor light, read aloud Marric's carefully translated document whilst the latter explained, where necessary, the reasoning behind the clauses. Even so the morning star was halfway to its apogee before the last signature was made — in Matla's case a forked mark like a deer's antler, with a cross through it.

'It is well,' Arn said, standing to watch him laboriously transcribe the sign. He ambled to the doorway and made the fluting call that Keelin had given to announce their arrival. Marric folded his copy of the agreement away and drained the last of the rough wine from the flask.

His back ached from sitting so long and his eyes were gritty with weariness. He wasn't looking forward to the long trek back to camp, but Cran and the others were rolling up the floor mat and gathering their belongings, obviously readying themselves to depart. The young men standing sentry would, he imagined, swiftly dismantle the hut and by full daylight it would be as if the meeting had never happened. It was the way of the Old Race who wrote the history of their actions on the wind and the movement of the water.

Stepping outside he finally had time to speak briefly with Arn. 'How did you know when you sent Keelin that I even lived?'

'I have seen you, my brother,' the old shepherd replied, 'in the flame and the water when I watch the world.'

'When I was a child — did you know of my brother then? I'll swear that Taba didn't.'

The old man returned his look, his gaze calm and wise. 'Only that a shadow stood always at your shoulder. Some,' his glance slid sideways to where Cran stood talking to Matla, 'saw death in it, but the years teach that much of what we guess is wrong. And if it is not, then our unmaking, when it comes, should do so unannounced. It was not for him to tell you.'

'I asked him to. But will you tell me now if you know anything of a black child and a land where a mountain burns? I see it constantly in my dreams.' He said nothing of the dread those dreams aroused in him.

'No,' Arn replied.

Marric waited and when he said no more, asked: 'Does that mean you don't know? Or that you won't tell me?'

'It means it is your task to fulfill, my brother.' The old man's tone was austere and Marric flushed at the rebuke. Regaining his composure he abandoned the subject and asked instead after Dura.

'She is well; married and with a fine son.'

'Is she happy?'

'As women are who have young to care for.' His head moved slightly and next instant Keelin was there, a shadow in the starlight, his step as silent as dew falling. He jerked his head at Marric.

'Come.'

'Yes. May the Mother be with you, Arn. Thank you for the meeting.'

The old shepherd inclined his head. 'We have changed our world a little tonight, you and I. My people will not forget it. Travel safely, my brother.'

'Wonderful are Her ways,' Marric agreed. 'Stay well, old friend.' The thought came to him then, like an arrow from the dark, that he would not see Arn again. He kept it from his face, and Arn being who he was, sought to banish it also from his thoughts, for a man's unmaking, the old man had said, should come to him unheralded.

18

They returned as swiftly from the plateau as the terrain permitted, Marric more than glad to leave the smugglers' path behind him. Ascending it had been bad enough, but coming down, he discovered, was even worse. His bad thigh trembled with strain on the steepest pitches and his heart thudded every time a loose stone rolled beneath his feet.

Darien greeted them warmly when, weary and stubble faced, they stepped from the boat some ten days after they had left. They hadn't encountered a soul on the return trip, which wasn't to say, Osram told Rissak, also on hand to greet them that they had passed unremarked.

'You are back so soon? The venture failed then?' Darien rubbed his jaw, his disappointment plain. 'Well, it was always a long shot but worth the effort.'

'On the contrary,' Marric grinned at him, 'they have promised two thousand archers if the campaign starts this season. Which it must do, for once that many men leave the plateau it will signal plainly to the enemy that something is up.'

'Two thousand!' Darien's eyes blazed with a fierce joy. 'Brother, you have worked a miracle. How did you do it and so quickly? I had reckoned a moon at least for meetings and discussion, and then they still have to agree —'

'They knew we were coming,' Osram said. He flicked an uneasy glance at Rissak, his fingers spoking out in the sun sign. 'They are an unchancy people to deal with. I don't know how, but they knew why we were there before a word was said.'

Marric yawned. 'I told you, man; their high priest hears the Goddess who sees all. We left a bird with them, Darien. Arn will release it on the day the archers leave, but the journey will take them longer than our return did for they come on foot, and they must hunt their food as well. Time enough at any event for you to organise provender and quarters for them here. Their leader is called Keelin. You will need all your diplomacy in dealing with him. He is both proud and bitter, and he hates Appellans.'

'Thank you Marric. I am forever in your debt for this. But enough for now. Come away in, you must eat and rest before we face the next problem, which may not be so easily solved. Did you guess when you asked Tranche to speak with her?'

Marric's gut clenched and he forced a slow breath before asking, 'What? Is it Amtee — what's happened?'

'Later,' Darien threw an arm across his shoulder. 'After you have eaten. I will call the captains so we may take counsel on it together.'

***

It was almost dusk when they met again in the main room. Darien, flanked by Rissak, sat with the other captains about the table. A seat had been left for Marric and he pulled it out, returning the others' greetings: Nannik, Sedak, Osram, the Laker whose name he kept forgetting. All greeted him with a familiar respect that warmed his heart. They had heard news of the success of his mission to Ansham and were eagerly discussing it when Darien called the meeting to order.

'We have another problem on our hands and it could be a tricky one, gentlemen. You all know of the black child that Osram and Nannik found and saved in the desert lands. Since then she has lived with the Sisters of the Shrine, but she cannot speak our language so she and her circumstances have remained a mystery to us. My brother,' he looked at Marric, 'asked my uncle to speak with her, reasoning that a merchant learns many tongues. It worked.' He looked unhappy that it had, saying heavily, 'I think I preferred ignorance to what he has discovered.'

'And that is?' Marric's neck hair rose.

Darien opened his hands with a grimace. 'Of course Tranche's knowledge of her language is rusty and incomplete but he has pieced her tale together over many days. Amtee, to name her rightly, was kidnapped from the city, though how remains unclear, and was then taken to a place on the border of her country and sold to slavers. Somehow she escaped from the coffle — Tranche isn't sure, but thinks she got away in the night — and she was wandering crazed with thirst when what she calls the other men found her.'

He drew a breath, his face hardening. 'You know what happened then. They left her, tied and half dead, which is how Nannik and Osram found her. What you don't know is that she is the grand-daughter of the Manata of Barat. That, it seems, is how their king is styled. We have on our hands, gentlemen,' he said grimly, 'the kidnapped princess of a sovereign nation recently at war with our own — for the Baratans will make no distinction between us and the army of Appella. And if that isn't bad enough she has suffered assault, rape, and near death, at the hands of our countrymen. It is grounds enough for another war were she discovered here.'

'Then she must be returned and swiftly.' As Marric spoke the inevitability of it settled over him like a fowler's net. He could thrash about, and thrust this way and that, but the only path open to him was the one that led to the mountain. He wondered, with a little frisson of fear, what it was that awaited him there.

Darien frowned at him. 'According to Tranche she said that you, yours is the one name she seems to know, told her you had come to take her home.' It was more question that statement.

Marric sighed. 'The Goddess told her, not I. It was during the attack on the shrine. I cannot, after all, speak her tongue. But it means that I must do as the Mother has promised.'

'No.' Darien said, 'I need you here. Nannik can take her, or Sedak. With some women to serve her, priestesses perhaps, and a guard for consequence and safety.' He stopped for Marric was shaking his head.

'Darien, she has been raped, abused in body and mind. She fears all men save me. I only got her out of that burning building because when the Goddess spoke to her in her own tongue She used my voice. It built a bond that caused her to trust me. I am called to go. I don't know why, only that I must.' He expected an argument but his brother was staring at him.

'You used my name.' Marric flushed at the wonderment in his tone. The sight brought his twin to an awareness of their audience. Reverting to business he said slowly like a man seeking to understand, 'You mean it's like the warning about the raid?'

Marric tried to answer honestly. 'Not exactly for I cannot see what is required. But there is a compulsion upon me.' Choosing his words, he added carefully, 'Nothing is plain save that as Her servant I am bound not to disobey. To do so would be to court death.'

His twin's eyes widened. 'You truly believe that to be so?'

'She is the Goddess,' Marric said. 'I know it.' The men about the table were silent and he saw defeat in his brother's face.

'Then you must go,' Darien said.

***

Time probably mattered now. Marric sought out Fenny whom he had not glimpsed since his return, to learn where Amtee was now housed. Child or not she was a princess and would need to be told of the arrangements made for her journey. He proved to be correct in this assessment. Fenny smiled gladly upon him then went on to confess ruefully that in his absence the silent, frightened child had become a little despot. Tranche's limping tongue apparently enraged her and though her wishes, when they could be understood, were being fulfilled to the best of Fenny's abilities, she was plainly accustomed to much better.

'You can't blame her,' Fenny explained with a smile whose openness sent his heart racing. She wore blue today and her fair hair shone like silk in the lamplight. 'Apparently we have done everything wrong since she came. She has had no veil, no head covering, all sorts of lowborn people have touched her. She has had to sleep without privacy or guards. Now that she can, in a fashion, make her complaints known there are no end to them.

'Apparently, in her own land, her maids or slaves — neither my uncle nor I can quite decide which — never stray from her side. So now she demands that as well. I daresay she feels safer that way, but it does mean you will have four of us to protect and humour on the journey. You did tell her, she swears you did, that you are personally taking her home?'

'Yes, in a manner of speaking I suppose I did, but —'

'Then you must do so. She is depending on you. I —'

'Of course I will take her — escort her. But not you! It could be dangerous and Darien would never permit it.'

'On the other hand Amtee demands it. Poor you,' she said drolly, 'you are barely home from Ansham. How did that go by the way? We had not looked to see you back for ages yet. And now, it appears, you must saddle up again. Don't look so alarmed. My uncle will travel with us to interpret, and two priestesses, Ema and Kata, and guards of course.'

She laughed then. 'Mother says we should have a sprinkling of duchesses and at least one princess to give Amtee consequence, but as there are none in our society, she must make do with the high-priestess's daughter.' She smiled devastatingly at his horrified expression. 'Come, it will not be so bad, it might even be fun. Only think how few people have seen inside Barat.'

'No,' he said flatly. 'We could be attacked. You must not risk yourself.'

'But a little girl and two other women may?' The grey eyes flashed in sudden temper. 'It will be far more dangerous for Darien's cause not to return the child. What if her grandfather were to learn of her presence here? He would certainly think we had stolen her and would instantly declare war on us. Conflicts have started over less and nations been lost thereby! According to what Amtee says, the royal women of Barat are guarded like jewels. Anyway, it is my decision. I go out of love for Darien and my country, and because as a woman it is all I can do to help him achieve his dream.'

Marric swallowed further protest, along with the mad idea that nations counted for little when weighed against her life. Amazingly he found that Ananda shared her daughter's views, and if Darien had fought against them he had done it privately and lost. Only Marric seemed to appreciate the awful danger he could be taking her into, but nobody heeded his protests and arrangements went steadily ahead for their departure.

Osram, who would again accompany him, organised the baggage train and Darien produced two eager young Laker soldiers to help guard the party. It all happened so quickly that on the morning of the fourth day they were packed and ready to leave. Their party consisted of five men, three women and the Princess, now swathed from head to foot in coloured silks. Tranche wore his blue turban, Marric's wardrobe was borrowed from his brother's best, and the Lakers sported their sky blue and grey uniform.

In their baggage they carried the flag they would display once they reached the border, a formal gesture this towards their embassage. Nor had a kingly gift for the Manata been forgotten. It was an emerald from the royal jewels that would, Darien said regretfully, have clothed and armed a regiment, and likely fed them for a month besides. He and Rissak accompanied the party to the shore complex to see them off. At parting he held Fenny fiercely to him for an instant, then took his twin's arm in a hard grip.

'She is dear to me so bring her safely back, brother. And yourself too. The sun and the moon on your path, and may the Lady watch over you all.'

Rissak clapped his shoulder. 'Keep your eyes peeled, lad. If you run into trouble leave the blade work to Osram.'

The two stood to watch them mount and ride off. Darien raised his hand as Marric swung his horse about, flashing them a strained smile. They waited until the party had dwindled from sight into the dusty girth-high brush of the drylands then silently took their places in the boat.

'Osram is as good as they come, my Prince,' Rissak offered after a space. 'He will keep them safe. You know that.'

'Yes.' Darien plied his paddle.

'And your uncle is used to dealing with foreigners. Those Laker lads are well trained too.'

'Yes, gods damn you, I know!' Darien said violently. 'I am not denying it. But however safe he may be doesn't change the fact that he is still out there, taking the risks that should be mine.'

Wisely, Rissak held his peace and paddled.

***

Having the women to consider meant that Marric could not travel with the speed that had governed the journey to Ansham. He had been vaguely surprised the women could even ride, but a moment's reflection showed him that, boats apart, the saddle was the Lakers only means of transport. Lake Town had no carriages or wagons. Fenny and the two priestesses were capable horsewomen; it was Amtee who was the novice, constantly slowing their pace. Also she demanded time each morning in which to bathe and dress, and when tired or out of temper, time in which to recover.

Tranche, with only a layman's grasp of her tongue, which naturally didn't include the high flown language of court, was the one who suffered most from her tantrums. He was not allowed to face her when they conversed and in any case his skill didn't extend to compliments. His bald questions and answers however, were seen as insulting, as were his unwitting trespasses on subjects, deemed by Baratan court teaching, to be impolite. Fenny, seeing her long suffering relative driven again at a noon stop from Amtee's presence by the child's high scolding voice, sighed and rolled her eyes.

'Life was certainly easier when she was a nameless waif. He's the only one she can speak to and the little hussy treats him like a dog.'

'I think she's frightened,' Marric said, his gaze devouring the line of Fenny's throat and the arch of a fair eyebrow.

'Not a bit of it. That's plain, old fashioned temper that should earn her a smacked bottom.'

'I know, but underneath she's desperately afraid. Think about it. According to what Tranche says, girls of her station live in seclusion chaperoned every step of the way. The shame of what has befallen her must be bad enough but when she's home again, and it becomes known — what then? The very way she was clothed and housed at the shrine was so different from what she demands now, that it probably broke a hundred taboos. How many men and boys have seen her face, her bare limbs? Add that to the assault on her person — Will she be blamed for it, ostracized, cast from her home? Of course she's afraid.'

Fenny's attitude changed as she considered his words. 'You are right, of course. Poor child.' She cast a curious look at him. 'Is it the Goddess that makes you so intuitive, Marric? Men are not usually as perceptive, not where children are concerned.'

He shrugged. 'We were all children once, and anyone who suffered then or was unhappy can recognise the symptoms in another.' Glancing at the shadow-line he rose reluctantly to his feet. 'Time we were moving again.'

Riding on, the bow hanging ready on his shoulder, he recalled her words and the way she had looked at him, then folded the memory away with the others he had collected. He repeatedly told himself that he would not sit with her during the noon breaks, nor allow himself to ride beside her, but after the shortest period of abstinence his resolution usually failed. She seemed to welcome, at least she never repudiated, his presence. But, here for Darien's sake as she had plainly told him she was, why would she not be kind to him for the same reason? She would be his sister-in-law. The thought was so painful he jerked his mount's head about and spurred forward to join Barb, the younger of the Lakers, presently riding in the lead of their little party.

***

Crossing the drylands they needed to fit their daily stages to the available water. The country lived up to its name but there were wells, one or two deep rock holes, and one evening Osram shed his tunic to free his shoulders and dug a soak in a sandy river bed, spading away the dampening grains until the water seeped through to fill the hole he had made. He bailed out a supply for the camp before leading the animals down to drink.

Amtee was forced to forego her bath the following morning, and made her displeasure felt all day. Fortunately there was a plentiful supply at their next camp. Fenny rinsed out some of the Princess's clothing, laying them over the bushes to dry so that the area about the royal tent took on a festive air. The display of her garments to the public gaze however, brought on another stormy session with the Princess for the long-suffering Tranche.

***

The attack came later that same night, the bandits, they later surmised, having trailed them from the soak. They burst upon the camp, riding at a fair clip in the moonlight, the drumming hooves alerting the men sleeping about the fire, granting them precious seconds in which to scramble away from the dying light, before the raiders hit the camp. There was neither time nor need for orders. The Lakers, Barb and Stoner, vanished into the low scrub fringing the waterhole. Tranche went in a stumbling run to protect the tent in which all the women slept, while Marric pressed his back against a sturdy tree trunk and nocked his first arrow. Waiting for a target he spared a quick glance about for Osram but the big man had disappeared.

Their attackers were not expecting resistance; speed and the shock of night raids had worked for them in the past, immobilising their targets long enough for lethal blows to be struck. There were eight of them but three were dead before the rest realised that the archer was there, while the one who raced knife in hand to slit the tent, ran straight onto Tranche's unseen blade. Stoner, guarding the horses, got another, and Osram accounted for the one who elected to fight. The remaining two fled, pursued a little way by Barb.

Amtee, waking to the sounds of slaughter, was terrified. She screamed incoherently at Tranche when he attempted to comfort her, breaking into hysterical sobs until Kata, comfortable, middle-aged and talkative, gathered her up and smacked a kiss on her brow.

'Come, you're safe enough now, pet. Couldn't the big one there kill a wolf with his bare hands? What's a few little bandits to him, now?' The words might have been unintelligible but the tone comforted. Fenny, fighting her own fear gave a shaky laugh and applied her energy to getting the girl soothed and settled again. Marric's arrival achieved more than either woman's efforts, his simple presence having a calming effect on the child. Amtee, forgetting all her previous taboos about his sex seized his hand, holding on tenaciously until her sobs quieted and she eventually slipped into sleep. Marric waited, crouched beside her pallet until her eyelids had fluttered closed, then rose stiffly to his feet.

'Thank you,' Fenny murmured.

'Are you all right, all of you?' In the dim light of the lamp one of the women had kindled he eyed her anxiously.

'We're fine,' the girl assured him, 'and my uncle, praise the Lady. What of the others?'

'Not a scratch,' he assured her over his shoulder as he ducked quickly out of the tent. His relief at her safety was such that it was all he could do not to seize her in his arms to assure himself that she had taken no hurt. 'You should try and rest. I doubt we'll be troubled again. Certainly not tonight.' He could conceive of no circumstances in which the two who had escaped would return.

She followed him out to place a gentle hand on his arm. 'And you. I have seen you standing watch each night. If you are sure they won't return you should all rest.'

So she had noticed. He smiled at her, resisting the urge to brush back the hair that shadowed her brow. 'Perhaps we will. Go on now, try to sleep. Morning will be here soon enough.'

***

By dawn the men had dragged the bodies of the bandits from sight and scuffed dirt over the spilt blood. Breakfast was made and eaten without speaking of the night's events though afterwards Marric took Kata aside to assure her that she need not fear for her safety. 'As you have seen, Sister, we are in good hands with these men.' His gaze, the priestess noted, was on Fenny as he spoke, and she thought the words of assurance were meant for her too.

If he had expected alarm he got none. The motherly woman said comfortably, 'I know it. The Lady cares for her own, Prince Marric, as I am sure you are aware.'

They packed up the tent, loaded the mules and began another day's travel, drawing ever closer to their goal. The once distant blue of the mountains had become tree clothed humps, and for the past two night they had been able to see a strange glow reflected on the clouds, emanating Marric guessed, from the burning mount that for so long had troubled his dreams.

19

Day followed day with the party on high alert but there were no further attacks. It was more than twenty summers since Tranche had been this way, and then only once, for his trading travel had mostly been done aboard ship. Still, his memory for country was good and at length he guided them out of the trackless drylands onto the road leading to the border. It was a sobering sight for scattered along it was the detritus of a retreating army: overturned wagons, abandoned packs, the carcasses of horse and mules, and even the occasional human corpse.

Altogether it was a grim reminder of their possible reception for they were attempting to visit a land their king had attacked, and by which he had been roundly defeated. They could expect to meet with hostility from the border guards, Tranche warned Marric. They might well be lucky to even make it to the compound where the traders had traditionally transacted their business, let alone past it. Or, he added lugubriously, they might as easily be killed on sight, before they had a chance to make their purpose known.

'Well, get the words ready to ensure that we aren't,' Marric retorted shortly, aware that Fenny could overhear their conversation.

'And you had better make it quick,' Osram observed, squinting at a dust haze in the distance. 'Unless I'm mistaken there's company coming our way.'

It was a patrol of three mounted cavalrymen. They had dark, unfriendly faces above green and brown uniforms, and a bristle of weapons including a nasty looking spiked metal ball on a chain. Amtee pulled her scarf even higher, leaving but a slit for her eyes. Tranche flashed an agonised glance at her, which she ignored then, nervously clearing his throat, launched into a halting speech.

They didn't listen. The obvious leader of the little group ranted at them, forcing his mount forward until his thrusting face sprayed spittle at Marric. His free hand gripped the haft of the ball and chain and he swung it whizzing past the Rhutan Prince's face to the accompaniment of another tirade. His action elicited an angry roar from his followers, both of whom flourished wicked looking curved blades.

'Wait!' Marric barked as Osram's hand moved to his side, and to Tranche, dry-mouthed beside him, 'Try again.' The merchant raised his hand placatingly but Amtee chose to intervene, speaking sharply without looking at the men, the disdain in her childish treble clear.

There was a moment's silence then one of the men laughed and said something back that caused Tranche to shrink and close his eyes.

'Light above!' Osram swore. It wasn't difficult to guess what the speaker's words implied. 'What if he lays hands on her?'

'Wait!' Marric commanded again, his nerves at a stretch. It would mean their death to resist now, but perhaps they would all be slaughtered anyway? The only thing he could be certain of was that raising a weapon would doom their task before it began, but if these men were to touch the women, what then? Conscious of Osram's gaze upon him he held himself still and silent as the seconds crawled past and all but gasped in relief when Amtee spoke again.

Her tone was icy, and her dark eyes shot fire above the concealing scarf. The man who had spoken jerked suddenly erect then fell from his horse as if shot, groveling at the feet of her mare. The other two stiffened into ebony statues, and Marric saw a bead of sweat appear upon the closest man's brow. A final imperious barrage and the prostrate man rose and motioned them forward.

Marric bowed deeply from his saddle towards Amtee, before nudging his mount forward. She inclined her head gracefully back as their subdued captors led them on at a gentle pace, their silence and rigid spines speaking eloquently enough of the trouble their behavior had brought them. Doubtless they would be disciplined, which was a shame Marric thought, but preferable to he and his party being spitted. Punishment (if it were severe enough) would breed resentment, which they might try to visit upon those they would see as responsible for bringing it. Tranche had been able to tell him little enough of the Manata of Barat, but none of what he had learned suggested leniency. The man was a tyrant in any language. Osram seemed to share his views.

In a low voice he said, 'I wouldn't be in those poor buggers boots.'

'No. Nothing else was going to work though. It could've turned really nasty back there. What's that up ahead? Some sort of wall?'

The trading compound looked what it was, a stopping place for transients who would fulfill their business here and leave. Small, single-storied houses, secure sheds, and adequate stabling for animals surrounded a vast covered market area where traders could display their own wares, and haggle for the exotica offered by native Baratans. A colourful flag flapped loosely above the gate entrance and too late now, Marric thought of theirs, still folded in the packs.

His own fault, he should have kept it handy. The patrol might have accorded them more respect if they had come visibly as an embassy from the Lakes. Well, the chance was gone now. Guards opened the gate. Marric stared about him with interest, noting how the forest had been cleared back beyond the timber wall enclosing the compound, with the result that the sun beat cruelly down on the exposed wooden dwellings. He found himself wondering how they kept the ground so bare, for the weather was steamy, promising rain. Barat was a fertile country, tropical where Rhuta was temperate, and for the past handful of days the sere drylands heat had gradually given way to a sapping humidity that brought the sweat springing to their skins.

One building was obviously a barracks. A soldier, an officer from his cap and collar badge, strolled from it, calling something to the patrol soldiers. He stiffened at whatever they replied then bowed deeply to Amtee, averting his eyes from her form. She ignored him but allowed her mare to be turned by one of the guards and led away followed by the other women whom the officer waved impatiently after her.

Marric relaxed. They would find her the best accommodation, then send word to the Manata that his grand-daughter had been found. Two more soldiers, summoned by the officer's shout, mounted and came at a trot towards the gate, and it was only then that he realised the women were being shepherded back towards it.

'Hey!' He spurred his horse only to find himself blocked by the three men of the patrol. The gate was opening again, and Amtee, her voice suddenly shrill, was objecting, pointing back towards Marric and his men, while the hand on her mare's bridle dragged the animal inexorably forward. Fenny, a hint of panic in her tone, cried, 'Marric!'

'Stay with her!' he shouted, trying unsuccessfully to force his way past the men of the patrol. 'Say something! Stop them!' he yelled at Tranche, but the shouting only brought more guards who drew their weapons and ringed them around. Resistance was plainly hopeless. Osram looked to Marric but he shook his head and dismounted, motioning to the others to do the same. The big Appellan tensed for action, looked sideways at him for a lead.

'What now? Maybe we should've —'

'No. We talk — well Tranche can; the rest of you look harmless. I imagine they're only following standing orders, no foreigner to leave the compound. Still, they can hardly take the Princess's women from her. Ask for water, Tranche, ask their names. Anything till they settle down. I can't believe they aren't curious as to our purpose here. Talk, and convince them we're harmless, then we'll see what to do next.'

He was glad to find his strategy working. After what seemed a lengthy exchange for such a simple request, one of the men sheathed his blade and went off to return with a pitcher of water. They all drank gratefully and Tranche, mouthing careful syllables interspersed with long pauses for thought, eventually turned a haggard, sweaty face to Marric.

'I think, I'm not certain, but the burden of what he's saying seems to be that we cannot travel in the high-born's company. They don't like at all that she has been with us. So now we have to travel separately. They are very suspicious of our involvement but I don't know the word for rescuers. Still, they're taking us to the city too, but first they'll bring us food. We'll rest in the house there,' he pointed at the nearest building and the officer, whose eyes had never left Tranche's face, nodded vigorously, 'and eat. Then he'll take us.' He wiped his brow blowing out a long breath. 'I think that's right.'

'Well done,' Marric clapped his shoulder; he bowed to the officer and smiled. They had all put up their weapons and the tension was markedly less. The man snapped an order that dispersed his men, smiled in return and beckoned them to follow.

'How far is this city?' Osram asked.

'I don't know do I? Does it matter?' Tranche said irritably. 'I'm getting about one word in five and guessing the rest. We wait in the house, we eat, he comes, we go. That's it.'

'You've done wonders,' Marric told him. 'If we have to wait let's do it in the shade.' His tunic was so sodden with sweat that a breeze brushing across the compound sent a shiver through him like the touch of a ghostly hand. The Baratan officer however seemed impervious to the sun's strength, for his limbs and dark face were dry. Marric studied him frankly, for he had not known that a human skin could be so black. A rush of dizziness combined with a cold sweat on his face induced a sudden nausea that was gone a moment later. Too much sun, he thought. Shade had never looked more inviting as he led the way into the building. The relief of stepping into the cool dimness was like plunging his heated body into a mountain pool. He turned his head to speak to Tranche but something that felt like a stone wall crashed into it, his legs crumpled beneath him and he fell into blackness.

***

Banco was dead. Marric stood above him in the dimness of the cell, mourning the broken body and what fists and clubs had done to the once handsome face. A barred door opened and a voice giggled obscenely, then ululated on a high note, like a dog baying the moon. The skin of his neck prickled as the hair there pulled erect. He spun about, his breath coming short, trying to pierce the darkness to see whatever it was that threatened him, but the only light was dim and diffused and being quenched by the dark waters below. He rose through them choking, and clawing at the weight pressing the breath from him, only to sink again into inky gloom where all manner of spectres crawled, wearing the faces of people he had once known.

He was desperately thirsty but he knew that if he opened his mouth he would drown. His arms moved and he moaned as the pain burst through his head. The light was brighter, as if the clouds had cleared from the moon's face. He had walked in it by the river once, he remembered with his friend, who was now dead. The knowledge sent a jolt of horror through him — what it meant, what it would lead to. He whispered Banco's name and somebody said, close to his face, 'He's coming round.'

They gave him a mouthful of water, which was difficult, because all their hands were bound, and by degrees he came to himself enough to realize that he lay on the fouled straw in a stable where a dim light filtered through overhead planks. Staring into an empty stall he saw Darien, the red hair a little subdued by grey, frowning over a scroll he had spread before him.

He wore a cloak and a light diadem of gold, and a brazier burned near his feet. He was a score of summers older and he held the throne. Marric bent his will and his throbbing head to project the question: When? but received no enlightenment. He called his brother's name with such purpose that the figure in the vision lifted his head, and looked questioningly about. Then a voice he recognised as Osram's said, 'He's dreaming still.' Something wet spread over his face and he licked feebly at it as his senses returned to him.

It was the morning of the second day, they told him. He had been unconscious since the previous noon, the only one of them harmed because, Osram reported bitterly, 'The bastards held a blade to your throat and disarmed us.' Lacking horses and weapons, their hands securely bound before them they were pushed helpless into the stable.

'We're still alive,' Marric croaked. His party had saved him some food, bread and pulses of some sort that had been cooked into a tasteless porridge. He forced himself to chew and swallow. It was the only food they'd been given. That and one pitcher of water between the five of them. Marric had the last of it. It helped a little but left him craving more. Resolutely he put the thought aside.

'That's the good news?' Stoner asked dolefully. 'How do we know these black men aren't cannibals? They say —'

'Because they'd feed us better if they were,' Marric replied gravely, 'stands to reason.' It raised a laugh from the older men, even Stoner giving a reluctant smile. Tranche added something in Baratan.

'Means: Pass the salt,' he explained. 'What do we do now, Marric?'

He replied soberly, 'Pray. I mean it. I'm sorry Tranche: Banco is dead. Very sorry, he was my friend. Onli had him in the Tower. Please tell me he didn't know anything about your operation?'

There was a moment's shocked silence. Not for the death so much, three of those present hadn't known the man, but for Marric's ability to state it as a fact. Tranche paled. 'Oh, poor, poor lad. And he's married with a child. Lady of mercy, why?'

Osram made the sun sign, the spoked fingers of his sword hand rigid over his heart. He said slowly, 'Because they thought he knew something — or did he?'

'No! He was never involved, he was only a boy for Bel's sake!'

'He was older than me,' Marric said dryly. 'That apart — what else?' He had not missed the sudden stricken look that had crossed the merchant's face.

Tranche sounded wretched with remorse. 'I don't say he did for he never mentioned it, but he may have seen part of an arms shipment on board the Seabird once. He wasn't supposed to be in the hold but he came looking for me with some message just as the mate opened the bales to show me the goods. He could have seen the blades.'

'Then Luka and Haran had best have good bolt holes for they'll need them,' Marric said grimly. 'It won't take long for the City Guards to —'

'Something's happening!' Barb had wriggled about to set one eye to a knothole in the stable wall. 'There's a party of riders just come in. They've stopped at the barracks. The captain who met us has come out — and hey! he's getting a right bollocking! Listen, you can hear it.' They could too. Marric's eyes, full of surmise, met those of his companions. A man's angry tones came clearly to them, then Barb was shuffling back from his peephole, his swollen hands held out at the end of his bound wrists as he hissed urgently, 'They're coming over.'

Osram huffed out a breath. 'Finally! I thought the child had forgotten us.'

It was much more probable, Marric thought, that nobody had listened to her. Relying on her ability to convince her grandfather of their good intentions towards her had always been the weak spot in his plan. They had already lost a day and there could be many more delays yet before they could leave. Time hadn't mattered greatly before Banco's death, because Darien hadn't been planning an immediate move against Temes, but Banco's torture had changed that. Whatever he had known Temes most certainly knew now also.

In a hurried undertone to Osram, he said, 'We must get word back. Warn Darien. Depend upon it Onli will have linked Banco back to Tranche. Temes could be marching on the Lakes within days. Or sending spies, though a column of troops to reconnoiter is more his style.'

The big man's face was stolid, hiding whatever dismay he felt. 'Your god showed you this, too?'

'Goddess. And no She didn't, it's just commonsense, man! If you get the chance remember where you're needed most. Carry the message. I can look after my —'

There was no time for more. The door slammed back against the wall as it burst open and a man shot through the air to land on his face among their feet. An angry voice snarled something and squinting painfully against the sudden incursion of light, Marric saw the silhouette of several men looking in at them. The man who had been thrown, one of the patrol that had picked them up, stayed on his knees, crawling to them each by turn to cut the bonds from their hands. His own shook so badly he was in danger of inflicting further damage, but at last it was done and their abused flesh began to burn and ache as the blood returned to numbed fingers.

The newcomer, furious as he was, was plainly important. His clothing proclaimed the fact as did the way the troopers jumped to his orders. Large, well built and some years older than Marric, he carried himself proudly and owned a deep, melodious voice that now enquired, in fluent Rhutan, 'Who, among you, is Prince Marric?'

'I am he.' Marric stood shakily, conscious of looking less than impressive. Blood from his head wound caked his hair and had dried on one side of his face; he rubbed his wrist over it as his hand was still too numb to obey. 'Who are you?' he demanded imperiously, 'And why have we been imprisoned? We came in peace to return your princess, and are treated like criminals for our courtesy. Why?'

'Because there has been a terrible mistake for which these stupid, brainless dogs,' the newcomer glared at their hapless guards, 'these dung eating animals, will be flogged. You have brought my sister back to us and this is how we repay you?' He wore a green tunic over a white shirt, loose trousers, and riding boots spattered with dust and mud. His weapon, a curved sword, hung at his side. The tunic was stitched with gold and he wore a thick golden torc about the base of his dark throat. The guards cowered from his flashing glance, the threat of a flogging obviously real.

'Forgive me,' he bowed to Marric. 'Allow me to present myself. I am the Manat, or as you would say in your tongue Prince, of Barat. Grandson and heir to the Manata. My name is Doku. The moment we heard Amtee's tale I set off to bring you to court, for my grandfather would see you himself. It is true that our countries have been at war, but to treat a prince thus —' He glanced at Marric's hands, the dried blood in his hair, and scowled anew. 'These dolts do not deserve to live.'

Osram growled, sotto voce, 'Immediately? It's the second day.'

Shooting the big Appellan a quelling glance Marric said, 'We are honoured you have come yourself, my lord. I am Marric, as you have heard. The younger grandson of Rhuta's last legitimate king. The man who presently holds the throne, and has made war upon your country is a usurper, whom my brother would replace, will replace,' he amended. 'This, our gods have shown to me. I would have you know that the recent attack upon you was none of my brother's doing.'

Duko waved a dismissive hand. 'These things we can speak of later. First we must see to your comfort. You must bathe and rest, food will be brought to you, and a healer shall attend to your hurts. Tomorrow, if you are recovered enough we will return to the city. The Manata requests the favour of your presence.' He bowed deeply again and turning snapped something in his own tongue at his men.

'Wait! That is, a moment more please, my lord. What of the women who were with the Princess? They are safe, unharmed?'

Their host looked momentarily affronted. 'You need to ask? We are not savages!' Marric held his gaze and his silence and the man gave an infinitesimal nod. 'Of course. You have no reason to think otherwise. Know then that they are well. The Lady Fenny was most concerned for you all.'

'Thank you.' The relief he felt was almost painful; it weakened his knees and he was suddenly lightheaded so that Osram beside him, seeing him sway took an unobtrusive grip of his elbow. Tranche's breath went out in a gusty sigh behind him and he locked his knees but dared not risk another bow. All he craved just then was a cool, dark place in which to lay his splitting head.

***

By the time they were reunited with their baggage, and had bathed and eaten the last of the daylight was gone. The meal had been excellent, as had the wine. The Manat did not return but the healer, a thin man with slender hands whose right ear had been cropped close to his skull, visited their quarters to examine and salve Marric's head where the skin had split from the force of the blow that had felled him. His gentle fingers felt their way across his patient's skull while he stood with closed eyes, chanting beneath his breath. Finished, he beamed upon Marric, and gabbled something obviously meant to reassure, before smothering the cut with a green paste, and applying the same to his scored wrists. Then he bowed deeply, head almost touching the wooden floor, and departed.

Marric kicked off his boots and lay down. He had inspected their quarters, which, if hardly luxurious, were clean and comfortable. The view from the open window showed the lighted barracks where, he assumed, Doku was spending the night. Osram who had come to see how he did, cocked his head as something yammered in the forest beyond the wall. In the silence that followed they both heard the sounds of the guard's boots moving past the main door.

The big man jerked his head at it saying laconically, 'I tried it. It opens — we're not prisoners.'

'No,' Marric agreed, 'but we have neither horses nor arms.' The latter had not been returned with their luggage. The only blade they had between them was his dagger, which had been out sight beneath his tunic when he was knocked unconscious. 'And as we cannot leave without the women,' (a brief burst of joy at the memory of Doku's words: *The Lady Fenny was most concerned...*) I would say that we are prisoners of a sort. Best get some sleep. The gods only know what tomorrow will bring.'

20

Marric found himself unable to take his own advice. Tossing sleepless in the warm darkness he remembered his dream of Banco's death, and wondered if anyone had yet carried news of it to his wife. He had no doubt of the validity of his seeing. It had been a true dream. What had his torturers torn from his friend? What agonies had he suffered at the hands of Onli and his sadists? Were all who had worked for Luka and Tranche now in danger of similar treatment? He feared for Luka. How long would his elderly body be able to withstand what they would do to him? Was his brother's cause to fail before it was launched?

Closing his mind to the images that tormented him he thought of Fenny instead, but even her memory could not anchor his thoughts. As could not the knowledge he had been shown of Darien, in years to come, as king. His twin would succeed then while he, where would he be? The icy worm of fear was back gnawing at his guts. Something — something to do with the burning mountain awaited him. He was certain of that in a visceral way that he couldn't shake. Was that why the Mother had granted him that glimpse of the future, because he wouldn't live to see it firsthand?

The gods don't lie. Jekka had said that. But they never showed the whole truth either and he sensed that something darker lay in wait, some purpose he was meant to fulfill whose end he couldn't descry. He recalled the little hunchback's bitter words of the gods' capricious ways with the lives of those who served them, and was deeply, coldly, afraid. It would be easier to stand in the battle line with his countrymen and see death coming from a clean blade, than to twist alone here upon the worst that his imagination could conjure.

Then it came to him that this was his battle, his alone, as Arn had hinted. The only one perhaps, that he was fitted for and which might even be vital to the outcome of the whole desperate enterprise that winning the throne had become. Strangely, the knowledge calmed him, and after a while he slept without the torment of further dreams.

The following morning the whole party, led by Doku's escort, pounded from the compound and was well on their way by the time the sun lifted itself above the surrounding forest. The Manat proved genial company. The previous day he had been stiffly embarrassed, mortified by his countrymen's behavior, but now he asked about their journey hither, although he must have heard the facts of it firsthand from Amtee or, had he chosen to do so, the three Rhutan women.

Today he was set on learning about the conditions in Rhuta, about Temes and his usurpation of the throne. Marric answered freely, seeing no reason not to, finding in Doku a mind as quick and apt to rule as his twin's. The Manat displayed the same firm grasp of tactics, and was withering in his criticism of Temes's failed campaign against his own country.

'So your brother, this Prince Darien, should win the encounter, given luck,' he mused. 'Luck is ever the soldier's friend. And you, Prince Marric, you will fight also in his cause?'

'I am no soldier,' he sought to turn the subject. 'You have an excellent grasp of our tongue, Prince Doku. May I ask how you acquired it?'

'From the application of my tutor's stick.' His dark skin made his teeth seem very white when he smiled. 'It was an unusual decision my father took. He was less traditional than the Manata. One should understand one's neighbours, he believed, lest they become one's enemies. And how true that has proved! So he had a tutor found for me and I learned. He will teach my son also.'

'Yet Princess Amtee did not?'

'Of course not — she is female. Our women live in seclusion, they have no need to learn foreign tongues, especially enemy ones.' His voice had cooled at mention of Amtee.

'We are not enemies. At least the faction that I represent, are not. We were horrified when we finally learned the Princess's identity.' Marric remembered something then. 'You said you were the Manata's heir? Then your father —?'

Doku's gaze hardened. 'He was killed in the war with your countrymen.'

Marric suppressed dismay. 'Ah, I am sorry.'

'Yes. The Manata had four sons, enough one would think, but now only I and my own baby son remain in the succession. My sister no longer counts for what man of rank would have her now, despoiled as she has been? She can never marry, my little sister, nor know the joys of children of her own. Something else your countrymen have taken from us.'

The dark face was closed, unreadable. Marric said inadequately, 'I am more sorry than I can say for the misfortunes your family have suffered. I will carry my brother's apology, his deepest regret over these matters to the feet of the Manata, but you understand it was not our doing.'

'I do, yes, but I doubt my grandfather will.' Doku said bluntly. They were walking the horses now, their escort, including Marric's party having dropped back, to allow the princes to converse in private. 'His anger is very great. He is old and his grieving is bitter, not only for his son but also for the posy of his heart whom you have returned to us dishonored and soiled. It is not your fault, you say, but a king stands for his country, does he not? And the shame he feels belongs also to his nation.'

Marric tried to see where this was going. He said, 'Shame doesn't come into it — not for her. Outrage yes; hatred for the slavers, and for the men who abused her afterwards. I do not say this in mitigation. Nothing can excuse what they did, but they had no idea of her identity, so it was not meant as an insult to the Manata or to Barat.'

Doku didn't bother to refute it. Their way passed into shade then back into bludgeoning sunlight. A curtain of rain glimmered in the distance where the forest had thinned to farmland, to terraced slopes covered in a green scrawl of growth. Sweat crawled down Marric's ribs, sticking his clothing to his skin, the flat planes of Doku's high cheek-boned face glistened wet, and the rank smell of heat rose from their mounts' damp hides. Doku said thoughtfully, 'They said you killed men on the journey here, to keep her safe?'

Marric shrugged. 'They were bandits. Many such infest our land now. Under Temes's reign the law has become lax. He hangs the innocent but thieves and murderers flourish.'

The Manat nodded pursuing his own line of thought. 'Blood is a powerful symbol to us. To shed it for another is to become brother to the one you save, another son to his mother. But to kill a man is to become the enemy of his kin.' His gaze weighed the slighter figure riding at his side, his look half curious, half regretful. 'I have never known it happen before, but by our laws you have become both. My brother, for what affects my blood kin affects me also, and the slayer of my sire. Is that not peculiar?'

And so at last the Mother's plan was made clear to him. Marric drew a long breath to slow his heart and steady his voice before he spoke. 'So, I am to be the scapegoat then.' His hands were cold as if all the blood had fled from them. 'Symbolically guilty of your father's death, though I wasn't in any way involved in it? And what else? A sop for the pride of the men who failed to guard their princess?'

'Royalty stands as the symbol of its people. By that reasoning their crimes therefore, are yours.' Doku spoke as one reasoning aloud. 'In this instance strictly speaking, they are your king's, but you are here and the Manata is not inclined to leniency. Believe me, Prince Marric I regret it, for your actions have as I said, made us brothers in blood. But I cannot gainsay my king. You may be assured that no harm will come to your party. They shall return unhindered to your own country, though my sister it seems, is much attached to the Lady Fenny, and would wish her to stay.'

'She cannot. She is to be my brother's bride,' Marric said curtly. 'And she is, besides, the daughter of our high priestess.'

'Then Amtee must part with her. She will be sorry. As I am for your situation but there is nothing more I can do about it. I have already spoken to my grandfather urging that my sister's rescue should cancel out my father's death, but he is adamant that the sentence is carried out. He is old and he has lost his last son and somebody must die for it,' he finished simply.

In the end, Marric wondered numbly, was it no more than that? Not the whim of the Great Ones carelessly discarding a tool no longer needed, but the blind rage of an old tyrant taking revenge upon a foreign stranger?

It hardly mattered he supposed; either way he would die.

***

They reached the city a little before nightfall after a hard day's riding, having changed horses twice along the way. Barat, despite its forests, seemed quite densely populated. Small villages and quite large towns were folded into the landscape, and the road they followed had been a busy one. Osram and the rest of the party exclaimed cheerfully over the vibrant vegetation and the occasional glimpses of forest life in the form of fleeing shapes amid the trunks and branches of the huge trees. Tranche, casting a merchant's acquisitive eye over the goods displayed in the various markets they passed, asked numerous questions of the escort, often reining aside to stare until he was impatiently collected up again.

Doku sent a man to buy melons at one of the stalls and these they devoured with their noon meal, the creamy flesh cool and sweet, satisfying their chronic thirst. By then the city was visible in the distance, a great sprawl of buildings astride a wide, muddy river, where boats with coloured sails plied their business. The city was unwalled, a strange sight to Marric's party, and back-dropped by the distant volcano. Fascinated by the sight of it, Marric turned to Doku.

'What causes the fire? Does it always burn thus?'

'It is the home of our god. And the eruption is how he created the land,' Doku said. He bowed his head as he spoke, touching two fingers to his brow and heart. 'Many, many lifetimes ago, more than one can number, before man was, the Fire God lifted the mountains of our land and delved the fertile valleys deep to make a place for His people. And lest we forget His majesty He reminds us now and then, by opening His sacred mountain to display His awesome strength. It is beyond magical for the very stone burns! The place is sacred to Him. Only the priests may go there.'

'I have seen it in visions sent by my god,' Marric said, 'but even our traders who are far travelled, have never spoken of witnessing such a sight.'

'How should they? Foreigners come but seldom to our land, and the god may remind us but once in a span of lifetimes. There are grandfathers who have never seen it happen before. Of course,' he added, 'there are lesser gods, of forest and field, but the God of the Mountain is the greatest, His name too sacred for outsiders to know. And what of your god, Marric? Will your spirit, so far from its home, find its way back to Him?'

'Mine is the Goddess who gives life. She is with me always, wherever I go.' Marric hoped it was true. To turn the focus from himself, he said, 'Osram, the big man, his god is Asher of the Light, and in Ripa they worship Bel of the River, but my Goddess is the oldest of all. She is the Mother, the One who gives life and decides the manner of our deaths. The Light, we are told is for the day and knowledge; and Bel binds the harvest to the rivers, the land, and the seas; but the Mother is everywhere for She holds dominion over earth and air and water...'

He went on speaking because it was better than the silence of his thoughts that only fostered fear. The road unrolled before them, its verges fringed with splashes of scarlet where wild poppies grew. They reminded him of blood and he hastily lifted his gaze to the workers chanting in the fields. Sparkling, short-lived showers blew over them as clouds crossed the high vault of the heavens, fluffy white against the background of the roiling greyness and the flickering fire at the volcano's summit.

It was as if he existed in a clear bubble that sound penetrated, with the whole of the busy world already half removed from him, in the way it was whenever he stood in the stillness of the space between the worlds, when the awesome power of the Mother ripped him from himself.

As the day wore on the city grew, until finally they

were riding through its streets, gazing about at a myriad of black faces and handsome buildings of brick and stone fronting the broad thoroughfares. One of their escort had produced a standard and spurred ahead to ride in the lead, ensuring a rapid passage for them through the busy streets. The people drew aside, bowing them on. In this manner they traversed the bustling hives of markets and squares, where shopkeepers vied for custom with the many street-sellers. They passed the larger official looking buildings, and came to a vast walled complex that was the palace enclave. It was part administration area, part barracks, Doku explained. The closed section to the right with its high latticed walls through which gardens could be glimpsed, was the royal women's' quarters, and at the very heart of the enclave, surrounded by elaborate courtyards, lay the palace itself.

'Where is the Lady Fenny housed?' Marric asked as he dismounted. The building before them was solid enough to serve as a prison for all its carvings, and the curving steps before the grand entrance. There were also, he saw, guards stationed at the wide, double doors. 'I should like to see her first.'

'You may satisfy yourself as to her wellbeing tomorrow,' Doku said blandly. 'She is with my sister and it is too late now to disturb them.'

'You said she was worried. Would it not be a kindness to reassure her tonight by facilitating a brief visit?' For a moment he thought he had gained permission for his host was nodding.

'You are right to remind me, Prince Marric. I will have a message conveyed of your safe arrival here.'

'Thank you.' It was pointless, perhaps even counter-productive to protest. Osram, who should have known better, was also impatient, and put a blunt question of his own.

'My lord, we are needed at home. How long before we might leave?'

Doku spoke with a chilling hauteur. 'Your prince has an audience with the Manata in the morning. Following that you will be escorted back to the border. I trust that will be speedy enough for you?'

'Indeed it will. Thank you,' the big man replied, unperturbed by irony.

The moment they were alone inside their allotted quarters Marric rounded angrily upon him. 'Will you mind your tongue, man? We need his goodwill. The gods know there is none to be had from this Manata of his.'

'Sorry sir. Straight question — where's the harm in that? Seems to me if they mean it and intend to deal fair with us they would give us back our arms.' He slapped his empty scabbard, his gaze narrowing as he ran Marric's words back through his head. 'What have you learned about the Manata then, sir?'

'Oh, for Light's sake, stop *siring* me!' He would have to tell him. Keeping the big man in the dark would only lead him into trying something stupid tomorrow, and possibly getting the whole party killed. What would become of Fenny and her two companions then? Marric sighed and jerked his head at Osram to accompany him. He chose the closest room, shutting the door and leaning back against it to prevent interruption.

'The audience in the morning — it is to be a trial, followed by an execution. Mine. Keep your voice down,' he hissed as the Appellan let out an angry roar. 'I'm to be formally blamed for the death of Doku's father who was killed in the war, as well as for what befell Amtee. There is no appeal. I gather the trial is not to settle the question of blame, that's already decided, but as a means for the king, the Manata, to vent his spleen.' Seeing the other's face he added swiftly, 'It's not Doku's fault. He has already tried interceding. It didn't work.'

'Asher's bloody balls!' Osram exploded in an angry mutter. 'So he says! We can't —'

Marric cut him off firmly. 'I believe him. Look,' he said rapidly, 'I knew when we left the Lakes that I rode to my death.' It was almost true; he had known something then and it would lead to less argument to present it now as a fact. 'There is nothing you can do about it. Your task is to get the others home and warn my brother about the manner of Banco's death. Luka, if he is not already dead, may be in great danger. I cannot say how, but Darien will win the battle, though he needs every man possible at his side to achieve it. Send Stoner and Barb ahead with the message, and get the Lady Fenny safely home and you will have done all I could ask of you.'

Osram's face had changed from fury to incredulity. 'Light's blood! You expect me to ride home and tell your brother I let them execute you?'

'You have no choice; just as I have none. To put the matter at its plainest, the Mother has made it clear to me that Darien will have the throne but the price is my death.' And in his head he suddenly heard Taba's beloved voice: *Your name comes from an old Laker legend. It means Sacrifice.* So, not his mother's as Taba had believed, but his own. He said steadily. 'It is Her will, Osram. You cannot save me, and if you try you could well jeopardize the future I have seen for our country. Therefore, tomorrow you will keep a still tongue in your head and when it is done get the rest of them home, do you understand?'

'But —'

'That was an order, captain! I said do you understand?'

'Aye, Prince Marric, I do.' Osram, stiff as stone, saluted him in the fashion of the Green Corp before wheeling about like a man on parade. Marric stepped aside from the door to let him exit then sank tiredly into a chair. Unclenching his jaw he glanced around at the quite luxurious accommodation that was complete with its own sunken bath. You couldn't fault it, he thought. If nothing else his last night would at least be comfortable.

21

Sleep was long in coming but when it did it was of his mother that Marric dreamed. He had no memory of ever having seen her in the flesh but he knew her at once. Princess Leona stood in the forecourt of the great temple of Bel where he had once wandered with Banco, his curious gaze taking in the glazed tiles with their images of fish, and sea flowers and other curiosities.

Leona smiled lovingly at him. There was a table beside her on which a lute rested, a handful of bright ribbons tied about its neck. There was no other in the scene, just the sunlit court, the table and the lute. She was very young, but then she had died as a girl, he thought. She was lovely. Neither Taba nor his grandmother had exaggerated the beauty of her grey eyes, or of the lustrous hair that framed her face and spilled over the shoulders of her gown.

He said, 'Mother!' and she stretched a slim hand towards him across the table.

'My darling boy. You have become a man.'

He said wistfully, 'I missed you.'

Her smile was tender. 'I know. Be strong tomorrow. I love you, my son.'

The dream faded but the happiness it engendered stayed with him until he woke and remembered, then it was wiped from his thoughts and he rose heavy hearted, his guts a-squirm with fear. Clean clothing had been provided for his audience with the Baratan ruler; he dressed mechanically and forced himself to eat with the others, then took Osram aside for a final word.

He had decided last night on the rightness of his decision and, having made it, had felt the last of the resentment he had harbored against his twin drain from him. It left him lighter of spirit, in the same way his dream had. Leona had loved him, and he now knew that the pattern of his life had not been of her choosing any more than his approaching death was of his. He and she alike, had served as they must, and there was comfort of a sort in the knowledge that their fates had been settled before either of them were born.

'Here,' Marric pulled the dagger from the sheath at his belt, marveling at the chance that allowed it still to be in his possession. 'Take it. Wear it under your tunic. When you get back give it to Rissak. He knows its significance to me. Tell him — tell him it is as it should be, he will understand — and for him to give it to Darien. Will you promise me that, Osram?'

'I'm to hide it from this lot,' the jerk of the big Appellan's head took in the world beyond the locked door, 'and see Rissak gets it and say: *It's as it should be.* And give it to Darien. I can do that. Mind, he's just as likely to bury it in me, the Prince is, when he learns I came back without you. Look sir, I've been thinking. When the guards come for us we could rush 'em, take hostages. We'd have a bargaining point then. We —'

'And they already have a greater one,' Marric snapped. 'They have the women, for Light's sake! Do you wish to tell your prince you lost the Lady Fenny as well? Forget it. I have told you the throne hinges upon this. So you will let matters run their course. Understand?'

'Yessir,' Osram answered dolefully.

'But thank you,' Marric forced a smile as he clapped the tall man's shoulder. 'You've been in battle, man. It's no worse than I imagine that to be. It's the waiting that's the hardest, and the imagining. Dying itself is easy.'

'As you say, sir.' He struggled with himself then blurted, 'Only my orders were to keep you safe. I know fine well your brother would rather lose the throne than you.'

It was a different approach but the appeal could only be refused. 'It's not his choice. It's my death, or thousands. If he fails to best Temes there will be such a slaughter that men will weep to remember it; the wives, the sisters, the children of every Laker will die. I know my uncle and this I can guarantee. So enough! I will hear no more.'

There came a clatter of boots from outside and a scratching at the door as it was unlocked. Marric braced himself but it was just one man. He saluted, seemed to count them, then stood at attention beside the door through which a spear of sunlight entered. Marric called to Tranche.

'Ask him where the women are,' he instructed. 'Tell him the Manat said we could see them this morning.'

Tranche visibly girded himself, cleared his throat and launched into hesitant speech but it did no good. The man listened, shrugged and turned his gaze away from his interlocutor.

Tranche raised his palms apologetically. 'Either he doesn't understand what I'm saying, or he doesn't know the answer.'

'Never mind. I'll raise it with Doku. That sounds like him now.' He drew a breath and straightened, schooling his face. They might kill him but he was damned if he would let them see him afraid. The brilliance of the morning's light pouring through the doorway was momentarily blocked by the shape of their host, who was accompanied by an escort of a dozen soldiers, their boots loud as a drumbeat against the wooden floor.

Doku bowed politely to Marric, ignoring the rest of the party. 'Good morning, Prince. I trust you had a comfortable night?'

'I am well rested, thank you. However you did say that I could see my countrywomen this morning?' He made it a question, glancing past his host and the guards as if their bodies might be obscuring them from his sight.

'I believe I said they would be reassured by seeing you,' Doku replied pleasantly. 'And so they may. That', he waved at the tall building behind the lattice work fence, which lay opposite, with arches that opened onto a second floor balustrade, 'is where they are. They will see you pass below them on the way to the palace. Naturally they cannot attend the audience, and even if it were possible you would not wish to distress them by having them there. Such matters are not for women to witness. The Manata awaits your presence. Shall we go?'

Seething, Marric followed him outside. The distance was short, not requiring them to ride, or perhaps his captors feared that given a horse he might attempt an escape. His eyes scanned the women's quarters but the window embrasures were deep, and the arches filled with morning shadow. He had, he realised then, only Doku's word that Fenny and the others were even there, let alone chancing to be looking down on them as they made their way past the place. He wished vainly that he'd found some way to let her know that he loved her. He had known girls in Ripa but never anyone like her who smelled of sunlight, and whose skin was softer than a downy nestling. He had never done more than touch her hand, but his senses had anticipated that it would be so.

He held his anger against the unfairness of it all tight inside him for if he must do this thing, then pride demanded that he do it well. It was what he had been born for, he could see that now, the stalking horse whose purpose was to ensure that Darien survived to bring the

Goddess's plan to fruition. I will be no god's plaything ever again, Jekka had said, and yet in the end he had died still serving the Great Ones. Perhaps he had even known it as the blade sliced into his neck, another soul sacrificed so that he, Marric, could die today? Jekka too had been manipulated and cheated of life, so it wasn't as if his own case was in any way unique. His mother's had been another. Marric hoped that the world his twin would build was worth the lives it was costing.

***

The water carts had been busy in the streets and dew still dripped from railings and roof edges. There were no women to be seen abroad, though some may have ridden in the closed carriages that passed them. Guards liveried in green let them through a set of tall gates and they crossed a wide courtyard where a series of long pergolas covered with flowering vines promised coolness against the midday heat. Glimpses of sky were visible through the lush growth, as was the distant volcano, its red crown limned against the hovering clouds that seemed as much a part of the land as its ubiquitous fecundity.

Marric had been so busy with his thoughts that the separation of himself from his party happened without his awareness. They were within the palace by then, having entered what he presumed was an audience hall, a long chamber, vast in its dimensions, with a raised dais at one end on which a heavily ornamented chair stood. There were no other seats and both sides of the room were lined with ranks of standing men, dressed in white robes that were topped with short, brightly coloured tunics. When he chanced to glance around Marric saw his four companions being herded aside to stand amongst them, behind a thin screen of guards. Osram, he could see, was protesting, trying to push his way to his side. Marric caught his eye and shook his head then had to look away for Doku was speaking.

'Here. You stand here.' The Manat led him to a circle painted onto the tile floor no more than ten paces from the dais. The paint looked fresh as if only applied the day before. Seeing his puzzlement the Baratan Prince spoke quickly, 'Stand within. You may not leave it. These men,' he nodded at his remaining escort now shrunk to three, 'are here to see that you don't. Kneel now, the Manata comes.'

The crowd within the hall was sinking to the ground, including Doku himself. Marric copied him. The Manata of Barat wore power like a cloak, he thought, as he rose again to his feet when the rest did so. He stared across the short distance separating them into the fleshy, intelligent face that might have been chiseled from black marble. Dark, hooded eyes stared inimically back at him and the powerful body beneath the rich robes seemed to swell with some deep emotion. The rounded dome of the man's skull was covered with a tight grey cap of curls, and wide bands of red gold cinched his muscled forearms. Doku had called him an old man but Marric wondered now if that was ambition speaking. He looked fit to reign for many years yet. On the dais behind the huge chair two almost naked servants knelt, their eyes fixed on the back of their master's head.

Ignoring the crowded rows of courtiers and spectators the Manata made a sign to his grandson still standing beside the foreign prince. Doku, performing another deep obeisance, cleared his throat and launched into a measured speech in his native tongue. When he finished he bowed again. Silence followed while Marric wondered what had been said. Then the king leaned forward and began to speak in a deep, accusatory voice, eyes flashing with a bitter light as he bit his words off, spitting them at the figure brought to trial before him. When he ended Marric looked to Doku for a translation. The Prince facing rigidly forward must have felt his gaze. 'Kneel,' he said tonelessly, 'and I will tell you.'

So it was on his knees within the painted circle that Marric heard his fate pronounced in flawless Rhutan in Doku's melodious voice.

'The Manata sentences you to death for the crimes of your people and the outrages visited upon his family. He says: Your people made war on his without provocation or honor. Many of his peoples' lives were lost and their shades cry out for vengeance. They shall have it. He says: Because you have brought his grand-daughter back to him he grants this boon: you will not be strangled as a common criminal, and your body will not be despoiled as is the custom with common murderers. Also your companions are free to leave. Thus all debts owed are paid.' He stopped speaking, bowed again to the angry old tyrant in the chair and murmured, 'The Manata has spoken. You may rise.'

Marric did so then looked at the man beside him glad that he could command his voice. 'If not strangling then —?'

'The sentence is immediate. I am truly sorry but know that it will be quick. Already one brings the jar.'

Gods! Here and now. He had not expected that in front of this vast gathering. Numbly Marric watched Doku step outside the circle, saw the three guards unsheathe their curved blades. One stood to the left of the painted ring, another to the right, and the third behind him. All three looked faintly uneasy and he wondered if they expected him to bolt rather than drink whatever potion they were bringing him. Now that the moment was upon him he felt preternaturally calm, then he saw the sweating face and frightened eyes of the servant straining under the weight of the large clay pot he was bearing. His mind froze. Not poison then. Not unless they planned to drown him in it.

'What is it?' He pitched the question softly at Doku already a few paces withdrawn from him.

'A snake,' the Prince murmured, 'very deadly. It is the reason they,' he nodded at the nervous guards, 'are here. It can be difficult to secure them again afterwards. You must open the jar and place your hand within. The creature will strike at the movement; you will not suffer long.'

'Very well.' A lightness suddenly coursed through Marric causing him to wonder if the imminence of death always carried with it this drifting, dreamlike quality. He glanced once at the Manata's implacable face and dropped to his knees beside the vessel. He fancied he could smell the serpent through the semi-transparent covering securing it. He could certainly hear a faint movement within the jar as the snake's scaled body moved against the hard clay. Death that came in the guise of the Mother, he thought then, could not be beyond bearing, even if it meant never seeing Fenny again. And that too might be a blessing for he would not have to see her as his brother's bride... Steadily, without hesitation Marric tugged off the cord that bound the cover in place and lowered his right hand and arm deep into the jar.

A great stillness had fallen upon the audience hall. The Manata leaned a little forward, his stony gaze on the condemned man's face, and for an instant Doku's breathing checked. One of the guards gulped and shifted his feet, blade rising in readiness as they all waited for the foreigner to jerk back and perhaps fall, and the serpent to surge free of its prison. The closest section of the crowd began to edge slowly back, as if regretting their foremost places.

The snake from the god's mountain was known for its savagery, some victims were bitten a dozen times in the first few heartbeats. It made for a quicker death but also a nervous audience. Then the long drawn tension was broken by a universal, 'Aaaah,' from the onlookers as

Marric rose slowly to his feet drawing his arm after him, and with it the seemingly endless coils of a black snake nearly as thick bodied as his own wrist.

It was a large snake and heavy. The guards shifting carefully back could see the muscles of the foreigner's arm quiver from the strain of holding it steady. Then the wicked head with its two bars of yellow colour slid level with the man's chin as the reptile looped itself about his shoulders, tongue flicking past one ear to take his scent. The stranger's free arm rose (the nearest guard shuddered) to arrange a coil, then the foreigner's mouth opened and they heard their own tongue issue from it.

Osram's hand involuntarily made the sun sign. 'God's balls! What —?' and felt Tranche's fingers dig into his arm.

'Quiet! The Goddess is with him. Look at the king.'

The Manata of Barat was on his knees, head touching the tiles of his audience hall, as was every one of his subjects. Only the four of them were left standing and then only Osram as Tranche and the two Laker men also dropped to their knees. The big man prudently lowered his head but kept his eyes open for it went against his training to be blind in unfamiliar surroundings. And the voice, deep, authoritative, nothing like the Rhutan Prince's, boomed on.

So it was that when the voice stopped he alone saw Marric stagger a little, catch himself then slowly squat to coax the snake back into its wide mouthed pot. His face was screwed tight in pain, his eyes mere slits in the chalky whiteness of his features. He spoke, for his mouth moved as he fixed the covering in place and that done, he bent slowly forward and slid, insensible, to the floor.

Osram's heart seemed to stop. 'Asher's Light!' he moaned inwardly, 'He's been bitten after all.' He was running, shoving bodies aside to reach the Prince, the impossibility of what he had witnessed, warring with dread and duty. Hope revived, was the more bitter for being denied a second time.

***

Marric roused slowly to the familiar pain, as if an axe had been buried in his skull. There had been a snake, he remembered, and agony as brutal and immediate as any he had ever experienced. The memory of it made him cringe. He squinted down at his body, half surprised to find it still whole. She had used his frail flesh, the Mother, and though the serpent's bite would have been kinder, he still lived. The touch on his shoulder made him wince.

He murmured, 'Fenny,' but it was Osram's frowning brow he saw. With an effort he focused mind and eyes and came fully awake.

'What?' He put a hand to his splitting head, unable to stifle a groan. 'Am I not dead?'

'The Lady had other plans for you, it seems.' That was Tranche.

Osram asked urgently. 'Where are you bitten? Your neck? We have looked but I cannot see a mark-'

'No.' Carefully, hoping he wouldn't vomit before them all, Marric eased himself into a sitting position, realising that he was no longer in the palace but back in the guest building where he had slept. 'It's just my head. What happened?'

'Don't you know?' Osram asked blankly.

Tranche was more helpful. 'The Goddess took over your body. I have seen it once before, many years ago, with the Lady Linna. The Great Mother spoke through you.' He shook his head, still dumbfounded. 'They fell on their knees Marric, even the king. I couldn't follow much... You could smell Her power, like the burst of a lightning bolt. Then She left you. You put the snake back and keeled over. I thought for sure you had been bitten then. They fetched a cart and brought you here. They are bringing the women to join us too, apparently, and they've taken the guards from the doors. Whatever you said —' He lifted his hands.

His words brought it back, but dimly, as something glimpsed through moving water. The feel of raw power ripping through his body, pitiless in its strength, the ecstasy of joining with the Goddess's presence, iron edged with ice, allied to the crippling pain of supporting it. 'What did I say then?'

Osram shook his head. 'We don't know. But it had a powerful effect on the Manata, whatever it was.'

'I see.' He made to rise but collapsed back onto the pillow instead with an arm over his eyes. Jagged flashes of light filled his vision. He thought longingly of the herbs that would ease him, but this time he would have to do without. 'Leave me,' he gasped through the blinding pain. 'I will be better, presently.' He shut his eyes and rode the pulsing pain into blessed darkness.

When he woke again it was to find a wet cloth on his head, and Fenny sitting beside the bed. The pain had eased a little. She greeted him with an anxious smile. 'Is it any better? I tried, but Uncle couldn't make them understand what herbs I needed. Perhaps they don't grow here, or they have a different name for them.'

'It doesn't matter, I'm much better, thank you.' He gloried in her nearness, the concern in her face. 'Nobody has come? Not Doku?'

'No. Osram told me they were going to kill you! And that you were going to let them.' She looked aghast at the idea.

'I couldn't have stopped them,' he pointed out. 'Besides, I thought it was the price the Mother would take in return for granting Darien the throne. I was wrong it seems.' The giddy relief of it was overwhelming.

She sounded quite angry. 'You give too much, Marric! Darien would never ask that of you, never! And nor would the Lady.'

'I am Her servant,' he returned gently. 'What She wants I must give.'

'Well you are not your brother's! Do you think so little of your own worth because you are a second son? You were gifted with life. It is a sin, Marric, to hold such a legacy so cheap as to be eager to throw it away. Nor would the Lady condone it! She would have her children celebrate life. Your mother would not have valued you less than your twin, so why would you cast such a gift away like a — a rag you had done with?' Moisture sparkled in her eyes as she caught a ragged breath.

Astonished by her vehemence he struggled into a sitting position. 'It's not like that, not at all! And of course I don't doubt my mother's love for me! I saw her, Fenny! Only last night she came to me in a vision; I know well she loved us both and moreover, approved of what I was doing. Oh, my dear, you surely do not th...' Too late he halted his betraying tongue to find her staring at him.

'What did you say?'

Marric flushed. 'My apologies, Lady. I have no excuse. You told me yourself that you are betrothed to Darien. I would beg of your kindness that you forget you heard that.' That she should never suspect his feelings for her was, he had long decided, the only way left to him to handle the situation. And now his bleary state and foolish tongue had betrayed him.

Fenny was regarding him with the deepest surprise. She said, 'I told you that? When?'

'When we spoke of making the trip. When I said it would be too dangerous for you,' he floundered seeking to recall her exact words. 'You said you came for love of him. So I knew I had no right to speak so. Believe me I would never —'

She broke across his stammering to say distinctly so there could be no mistake. 'Darien is my brother! My mother fostered him. Of course I will do anything for him that I can. It was a sisterly love I spoke of.' Her cheeks had pinkened but she met his gaze squarely.

'Sisterly?' Marric felt a great rush of gladness that lifted him to his feet, headache forgotten.

'Well of course,' she said demurely. 'Foster-sister — but that doesn't mean that you and I are related.'

'No,' he agreed gladly. 'Then if I was to tell you that I find you entrancing, that I cannot take my eyes or thoughts from you — you would not view me also as a foster-brother?'

She pretended to consider the matter, the grey eyes narrowing a little. 'Well, we weren't raised together so truthfully I could not. And do you?' she enquired suddenly. 'Find me entrancing, I mean?'

His breath came short and he longed to hold her. 'I think I love you, Fenny. I think I have from the first moment I saw you wrestling with that old woman in the smoke and flames.'

'Mmn, only think?' She was teasing him now. 'Would it take you long to be sure?' she asked and his heart sang.

'Well, I could kiss you,' he offered, 'if that could be arranged —'

With an untimely rattle the door opened to admit Prince Doku. Marric swore softly and Fenny, who had unconsciously inclined her body towards his, stifled a giggle, saying softly, 'Indeed? Is there no other way to be sure?'

'I doubt it, but we shall see.' He pressed her hand for a moment then stepped forward to deal with the now unwelcome intruder he had but a little while before been so impatient to see.

22

The Manat of Barat stood waiting as Marric came towards him but made no effort to step closer. His eyes were wary and he held himself very much like a man who would rather be elsewhere. He said quietly, 'Nobody survives the yellow barred one. They shake the pot you know, the slaves, to anger it before it is brought in, but still it came to you as if tamed, and did no harm.' There was a question in the flatly delivered statement.

'When we spoke of the gods I told you of mine,' Marric answered neutrally. He felt in no way threatened but a little insurance, a gentle reminder of the power behind him couldn't hurt either. 'The Mother's hand is over me. She holds all life within her grasp. And as I am Her servant nothing may harm me without Her consent. When She chooses I wield Her power.' He searched the other's face. 'It was for that purpose that I came. So will you tell me now what it was that She spoke of to your king?'

'You don't know?' Doku look astonished.

'I cannot speak your tongue.'

'No, of course not. Well,' the Baratan Prince ran a palm across his face and gathered his thoughts. 'She — you are certain She is female? Well, then, yes — She was angry at the Manata: that he had put you on trial and arranged your death. In recompense She demanded that we aid your brother's cause.' Marric drew a startled breath at this, never having envisaged the idea, but Doku was already hurrying on. 'She spoke directly to the Manata, addressing him by his secret name. How could She know that?' he demanded almost querulously, as if it were the last straw in an impressive haystack of surprises.

'The Mother knows all,' Marric returned impassively. 'You say aid us — how? In what manner?'

'That is for the Manata to decide. He is in council now with his generals and I must join him. I came only to say that he is most distressed to have been mistaken in his judgement of you.'

Marric inclined his head. It was enough; a great deal really, given the circumstances. A king could not apologise to a foreigner of lesser rank, but faced with the mouthpiece of an angry Goddess it would be prudent to make a gesture in that direction. Mentally thanking Tranche for his training in merchant's diplomacy he replied, 'It is nothing. I understand. Please tell his majesty it is already forgotten.'

'You are generous,' Doku acknowledged stiffly. 'Please, make yourself comfortable; an escort waits should you wish to go out, and if there is anything you need a slave will fetch it. I shall return when I have news.'

His departure was the signal for the others to appear. Marric repeated the gist of their talk. 'Aid, you said?' Osram repeated the word. 'What does that mean, I wonder? Troops, do you think?' He eyed Marric wonderingly. 'Can this be what it's all about: the girl, our coming here, that bloody snake? Is that possible, Marric?'

'It could be,' he said cautiously. There is a pattern, he had once told Jekka. And he had replied that the acts of the gods were always subject to interpretation. He should have remembered, he thought, that nothing was as it first seemed.

Osram, frowning at his own thoughts was silent but an ugly look had come over his face. 'Does that mean that poor child's ordeal, our finding her, all that, was arranged by your goddess to happen in order to bring us — you — here, so Barat could supply us with auxillary troops? Because if so then your cursed goddess is a mon —'

'No!' Marric said sharply. 'If for one moment I believed such a — The Great Ones do not control what men do; that is their evil alone. They simply shape the results of our actions to suit their own ends. Whether or not you had found Amtee, those responsible for her plight would still have stolen her and used her as they did. We have free will. Does not Asher's teachings tell us so? A man cannot cross the Bridge unless his actions warrant it. But there would be no need of Bridge or Abyss if men were not responsible for their own deeds.'

'Aye. You have the right of that,' the big man agreed slowly, having digested Marric's argument. He looked carefully at the younger man as if seeing him clearly for the first time. 'For one not of our faith you sound very certain of this.'

Marric nodded soberly. 'I serve the gods. Therefore it behooves me to make time to think deeply on such matters. Only a fool would not.'

***

There was time enough in the two days while they waited on word from the palace for many things besides thinking. Marric's party spent them mainly indoors for naturally none of the escort provided them could speak their tongue. If they left their quarters they were simply herded around like so many sheep, Fenny remarked, through the markets or to the pleasure gardens behind the women's quarters. Other routes were never taken though whether the men had orders to that effect or simply lacked imagination as guides, it was impossible to tell. The day they visited the gardens Fenny waved at the balustrade behind the latticed wall.

'She is in there somewhere, poor child, a prisoner of their beliefs. Can you imagine such a life? She will never leave for she cannot marry now. No nobleman would have her, and the Manata's line may not marry a common person. It would have been kinder to have kept her at the Lakes.'

'But then we would not have Barat's aid.' If they were going to get it. The waiting chafed Marric with his dream of Banco's death in the forefront of his thoughts and with it the urgent need to warn Darien. The day was hot, far spent as it was. He held Fenny's hand as they strolled. It was the only public contact, Tranche had told him, permissible between a man and a women — even married ones.

'It's not decided yet, though, is it? How much they'll help, I mean.' Fenny stopped to examine a hibiscus flower. Their escort halted while she plucked it then glanced guiltily at him. 'I suppose that is allowed?'

'They aren't yelling yet. Here, let me.' He took it from her and pushed it gently into her hair behind her ear. 'A much prettier setting than on the bush.'

She dimpled a smile at him and strolled on, pursuing the topic. 'So the aid is worth her happiness?'

'How can we know? Even those of us who See have very limited vision, borrowed at best and mostly misunderstood. Take me — I thought I was to die, and found love instead. I believed you betrothed to my brother and find instead that you love me above him who will be a king, and is a fine warrior to boot. Don't look like that or I shall have to kiss you, and the Mother only knows what that might bring down on us. After all my mistakes I wouldn't even try to foretell what Amtee's future might be. Only two days ago mine didn't look very bright, either.'

She laughed, grey eyes in a crinkle of fine skin faintly sheened with moisture as they turned back, her hair golden in the sun. 'Perhaps,' Marric hazarded, 'Doku will be a less tyrannical ruler than his grandfather. He has seen more of the world and understands that different customs prevail in other countries. When his time comes he might relax some of the old ways. That could help his sister's situation. And, who knows? The poor child may have no wish now to ever share a bed. Her seclusion may be what she most desires.'

***

As if speaking his name had conjured him they found Doku waiting for them at the guest house, straight-bodied even in repose, the afternoon light glinting off his heavily embroidered tunic, and the high ridge of his cheekbones. He greeted them both with courtesy and Marric immediately asked his question.

'The Manata has decided then? You have news?'

'As you say, Prince Marric,' he responded formally. 'We are to send five thousand of our cavalry to your brother. This is the number we can field tomorrow. Should you require more it will take longer — much longer to muster and equip them.' The dark eyes shifted slightly and Marric knew that he lied in that particular. Unwillingly perhaps, from fear of the Goddess, but following his grandfather's orders, as he was bound to do.

The Manata would be gambling that the mention of delay would cause him to accept his first offer. Merchants used similar tactics to close a sale. Still, five thousand hardened fighting men! It was beyond wonderful. Add them to Arn's two thousand archers that must even now have reached the Lakes, and it made for an enormous boost to Darien's numbers. Then there was the effect the Baratans would have on the forces they had just beaten. The blow to their enemy's morale should be worth another thousand at least.

Marric bowed. 'The Manata is most generous; he has my brother's thanks and gratitude. I have just remembered that Darien sent a trifling gift to him, a token of his esteem. It was in our baggage. In forgetting it I fear I have been a poor ambassador for my country.'

'It will be there still,' Doku assured him. 'And you have had other matters to think of. My men will leave this afternoon and we shall follow in the morning, if this is agreeable to you?'

Marric was startled. 'You will accompany us?'

'They are my men. I command, therefore I lead them. Besides, none of them have your tongue.'

It was a hurdle he hadn't considered but still Marric demurred. 'And if you should fall? Am I to be responsible for another death in your line?'

Doku grinned then, suddenly losing much of his stiffness. 'But we are brothers now, not enemies, so there can be no blame. I shall enjoy the venture. I grow weary of court and government. It will be good to be a simple soldier for a while, and a traveller in a new land. Come,' he clapped his hands and a slave entered. 'I have wine. Let me but give the order to start the men then we shall drink to the joys of adventure, and the battle that will vanquish your brother's foes.'

***

It had sounded a fine sentiment, Marric thought morosely the following morning as he rose from his bed with a thundering head, and a foul tasting mouth. Doku's wine had flowed with princely largesse the previous evening. They had dined sumptuously, and their cups had never seemed empty. At first it had been impossible not to respond to the many toasts of fellowship and amity between their two countries, then later it hadn't seemed to matter. A shred of habitual caution had told him he was behaving foolishly but he hadn't listened.

Now, holding his aching head, he wished that he had. Groaning, he drank copious amounts of water, shuddered at the food a slave presented, and was pleased to see that Doku, when he arrived, was similarly discomforted. Fenny was unsympathetic. She hadn't been included in the dinner party, it not being customary in Barat for the sexes to dine together.

'It serves you right,' she observed tartly. 'Men!' She mounted on the word, reining her mare beside Kata and ignoring Marric as they set off, the horses' hoofs ringing loud in the all but empty streets, and raising a corresponding thunder in his head. It felt obscenely early, the sun still hidden behind the mist filled mountains.

By noon he was feeling better and Fenny had recovered from her pique enough to be planning for the trip ahead.

'When we join up with the cavalry,' she said abruptly, twiddling beneath her nose the flower he had plucked from a passing tree and handed to her.

'Yes?' he encouraged, his eyes on the perfect line of her throat and jaw. He could see the pulse throbbing below the pale skin of her neck and longed to touch it.

'You are not planning anything tiresome for then, are you?' She shot him a look, eyes narrowing over the top of the petals. The flower was the size of her hand, scarlet throated with long, golden tipped stamens, the pollen from which now lay dusted across her cheek. He leaned over to thumb it carefully away.

'Like?' He knew what she meant and hardened his heart against argument and pleading.

'Like leaving the women behind, to keep them safe? Because it is not going to happen, Marric. Not to me, anyway. I am coming with you. No,' she held up a minatory hand as he opened his mouth. 'I can keep up. And I'll be much safer with thousands of you than trundling along with a couple of guards, which I do you the justice of supposing you would leave with us. Not my uncle, you'll need him, which means Barb and Stoner, who would ensconce us in the first town then catch you up. That's what you've planned, is it not?'

Marric opened his mouth again, and was again forestalled.

'Besides, Darien put me under your protection, you know he did.'

'Fenny!' he protested helplessly, 'You can't! There might be fighting.'

'They would be very stupid bandits that attacked a camp of five thousand!'

'Of course they wouldn't. I meant when we get back.'

'But we'd be back, wouldn't we?' she asked reasonably. 'And I'd go home then just as you would wish.'

Unwisely Marric tried another tack. 'Fenny, Darien needs these men. They could well make the difference between the throne and defeat. We must reach him without loss of time. You said you wanted to help? Well, what you don't know is that one of Tranche's men has been tortured and killed since we left. So Temes could be marching on the Lakes as we speak. Darien might already be fighting there. There isn't a moment to waste.'

'You think I can't keep up?' She glared at him, insulted. 'You have much to learn about me, Prince Marric! I will be there at the end of every day, and not the last either, as you shall see. Still, you're right about the others. Kata and Ema must travel separately. Arrange that for them, but not for me.'

'Then it won't be possible,' he said with finality. 'You cannot travel alone in a party of men without a female duenna.'

'My uncle will be chaperone enough,' she declared haughtily. It was her final word and with it Marric knew that he had lost.

***

They rode all day at the demanding cavalry pace of walk, trot, and walk again and spent the night at the traders compound where the Baratan Prince and the foreigners made use of the houses there. The troops, sent earlier, had already constructed their own bivouacs, erecting oiled sheets against showers and night dew, with a campfire shared between every ten men.

'Your men are well organised,' Marric said admiringly, watching the glow of myriad fires in the soft darkness. They spread even beyond the spacious compound, the fires of those outside largely masked by the forest. He had given Barb and Stoner their orders and explained to the two priestesses why they wouldn't be riding with them. Kata was frankly relieved, claiming that another day at a similar pacc would be the death of her.

Cravenly he had left it to Fenny to break the news that she was going on ahead with the men. Well, she had brought it on herself, he reflected. Half of him, the giddy half enthralled by her, was thrilled not to be parting from her on the morrow, while the sober side of him was appalled, imagining skirmishes in which she lay injured, possibly dying, far from help. He wondered if all lovers suffered in this way, fashioning terrors to frighten themselves with as a measure of their feelings. Engrossed in his own thoughts he almost missed his companion's reply.

'We train hard and often,' Doku agreed. 'The cavalry are our main strike force. Very few foot soldiers will withstand a charge from them. Has he cavalry, your brother?'

'No more than a thousand. But they are the cream of the old king's army. They call themselves the Green Corps, for the colour of their cloaks, I think. Without them I doubt we would have a chance of winning. Seasoned fighters all, they were the backbone of Cyrus's army.'

'A thousand?' Doku sounded sceptical.

'They were ten times that number once, but Temes wasted them deliberately against the southern barbarians. He distrusted their loyalty, you see. With reason for they knew him for a usurper who had murdered his own family to gain the throne. He feared they would turn the army against him. The few that survived those hopeless battles fled to my brother and he made them welcome.'

'As you would.' Doku agreed. The two men stood for a moment, quiet in the dark. Behind them Marric knew that the fire from the mountain still flared though he fancied its glow had lessened. Distance perhaps made it so. In the trees off to the right brief pinpricks of light flickered off and on. He stared at them then asked his companion.

'Fire flies. Do you not have them in your land?'

'I grew up on the high plateau. A place of snow, and oak and birch trees, and the occasional wolf, but no lights such as those.'

'They are common enough here.' Doku said dismissively. 'So, you said the need for my men was pressing. Given that he cannot know we are coming, when does your brother plan to move against the Appellan king?'

'Perhaps he already has.' Marric explained about Onli's ability to wrest secrets from his victims. 'My friend died under his hand very recently, a handful of days ago at the most. He was not a part of the rebellion but it is possible that he knew, or guessed things that could point to Tranche. And from him it is but a small step to my brother's base in the Lake Country, besides providing a dozen more victims for torture, who would have real information to give.' He lifted his shoulders, let them fall. 'It is even possible we will come too late, but I dare not let myself believe that.'

Marric felt rather than saw the other man stiffen. Doku didn't step back from him but his voice was suddenly wary. 'You know this to be so?'

'Oh yes,' he answered firmly. 'My life on it being true.'

In an uncanny echo of Fenny's earlier complaint the Manat grunted, a disparaging sound that came from deep in his throat. He said dryly, 'It seems to me that you are overly careless with your life, my friend. But having seen what I have, I believe you. Speed then shall be the order for tomorrow, and however many days it takes until we arrive.'

23

Three days of hard riding brought them to the site where the bandits had struck their camp. Fenny, Marric found, was as good as her word when it came to maintaining the pace set by Doku's cavalry. Tranche appeared to suffer most, falling grey-faced from the saddle each evening, scarcely able to hobble between the camps already springing up around him.

'We are halfway there,' Marric encouraged him, 'a few more days will see us home.'

'If I am not dead first.' Holding his back Tranche swore tiredly. 'I am too old for this.'

'Too fat is what you mean, Uncle,' Fenny said hard-heartedly. 'It will toughen you up again. What about all those tales of your trading days that you spun us as children? The storms at sea, the pirates you fought, the time you were shipwrecked. Did you moan about that too?'

'The sea,' Tranche sighed, looking with loathing upon his saddle, 'now that is the way to travel. A leisured, proper way — not this mad gallop across half a landscape. A wise man,' he said with dignity, 'knows his strength and mine was ever my head. I learned early to leave the physical stuff to those less skilled who are more suited to it.'

'Do you suppose that was aimed at me?' Marric asked as they left him groaning blissfully on his bedroll. In the drylands they slept under the stars, Fenny alone being granted the luxury of a tent to which he was now escorting her. He paused near the entrance. 'Shall I bring you some water?' Her hair was a dusty tangle and she looked tired, but he was himself after the distance they'd ridden that day. 'It's not too much for you, is it?' he asked anxiously. 'Because I can still find a place for you somewhere if you want to stop.' He didn't know where, but he would.

'No. I'm just tired, but a night's sleep will cure that. Washing water would be wonderful though; you are thoughtful, Marric.' She was standing very close to him and now she leaned a little allowing her lips to brush his ear, as much physical contact as she dared risk in the teeming camp. The touch ignited his nerve ends and he had to force his hands away from her. He groaned in frustration causing her to giggle breathily against his cheek.

'You sound as bad as my uncle.'

'Unsympathetic wench. You are too hard on him — and me.'

'Nonsense,' her eyes glinted teasingly in the gloom. 'A little gingering up is good for you. And he's just feeling sorry for himself. Off you go and fetch my water, if you please. And do make sure that Tranche doesn't fall asleep before he brings my supper.'

Glumly, cursing the strict Baratan customs that forbade a woman sharing food with any but family members, Marric went.

The following days were more of the same with the dusty miles and barren landscape slipping by. It was bad grazing country for their mounts and general relief prevailed as the surroundings gradually changed, rock and sand being replaced first by sparse dry grass, then more plentiful clumpy varieties that the horses made best use of during the noon break.

'We're getting close now,' Marric commented. 'If I might make a suggestion, my lord?'

'Yes, of course,' Doku replied. 'It is many years since I visited Ripa and then only briefly. Your brother's land lies south-west of the city, does it not?' He drew the short dagger from his belt and scratched a diagram in the dirt, shifting his feet apart to make room. 'By my reckoning we are hereabouts, yes? So what would you have me do?'

'I know you have scouts out, but might I suggest sending two of my party further forward again to see how the land lies? There is no point in our riding the extra miles to the Lakes if Darien has already marched from there. It would be useful also to know the whereabouts of the king. Whether he is still in the city, or has brought his army into the field. My men can question the farmers. Which is more than your lot can do. Besides, if they're seen the locals are likely to think that Barat has invaded them.'

Doku gazed around assessing the ground. They had stopped not far from a creek, one of the many anabranches that fed into the Great River, itself still half a day's ride to the east of them. He nodded, 'It's a good plan. We'll camp here. The grazing is fair and the horses will be better for the rest. I'll send out hunting parties while we wait. Fresh meat will help spin out the rations. How long would you estimate for your men to make contact somewhere and report back?'

Marric considered. 'I'd give them a day. Till dark tomorrow, say. They should each lead a spare mount for speed. Better to wear out another horse at this juncture than waste our time heading off in the wrong direction.'

'Let it be so,' Doku agreed, and spoke briefly in his own tongue to the nearest captain, while Marric gave Stoner and Barb, who had rejoined then two days before, their orders.

Then there was nothing to do but wait. The cavalry mounts were hobbled to graze and the men found pursuits for themselves, bathing, making running repairs to their gear, or simply resting in the shade. A few parties set off to hunt with instructions to avoid the isolated farms spread widely across the region. Tranche, Marric and Osram escorted Fenny to where her tent had been pitched on the creek bank, and stood guard while she bathed and washed her riding apparel.

'It feels so good to be clean again,' she said when she was rubbing her hair dry. 'I'll wait in the tent if you want to bathe too.'

The water was cold but they all took advantage of the chance the temporary halt offered before returning to re-pitch her shelter in the crowded camp ground, and gather wood to cook the evening meal. Some of the hunters had found success with a mixed bag of rabbits, wild goat and a half dozen sucking pigs that ended up at the commander's fire. Marric suspected the pigs at least were more the product of barn than forest, but it was too late to worry about that now. They ate, enjoying the fresh meat, and on Doku's orders immediately extinguished the fires. The night was warm enough even for their tropical blood not to need them, and it was best, he remarked, to keep the element of surprise — though that would grow more difficult the longer they were forced to wait.

However sparsely populated the land hereabouts, a force of five thousand was not easily overlooked for long. The last thing they needed was to have one of Temes's patrols stumble across them. However it was but mid afternoon of the following day when a sentry's warning call had them all scrambling for arms, though it proved to be a false alarm. The three riders approaching the camp were not enemy outriders but Stoner, and with him, Darien and Rissak, both dressed for war in battle caps and leather jerkins.

Darien's smile was wide and relieved as he gripped his twin's forearm and thumped his back. 'I am so glad to see you whole and safe! Stoner has been telling me. I swear my heart all but stopped!' He shook his head, 'And Fenny and the others, safely returned as well. You have repaid my faith in you a thousand times, but this —' his eyes travelled over the camp of thousands now openly staring or turning reluctantly back to their interrupted business. 'In my wildest dreams I could never have imagined you would bring me this!'

'The Goddess's doing, not mine,' Marric said modestly as he nodded a greeting to Rissak. Those moments when he had stood without hope in the circle of death would be with him always, buried deep, something never willingly remembered or spoken of. 'Come, let me introduce you to their leader. He is the Manat, grandson of the ruler of Barat. Prince Doku,' he bowed respectfully, 'may I present my brother Darien, eldest grandson of two kings and rightful ruler of Rhuta and the Lake Country. Darien, this is the man who, one day, will rule in Barat.'

His twin dismounted and pulled off his battle cap as he greeted the tall black stranger whose gaze rose immediately, as did every man's in the vicinity, to his hair. 'Ah,' he exclaimed, 'so you favour the red king. It was our name for Cyrus,' he added in parenthesis. 'Your brother has told me that your Goddess will grant you your throne.'

Darien's eyes widened momentarily at this blunt pronouncement but he only inclined his head, saying gravely, 'Our cause is just, Prince. You are thrice welcome to our company, and we are indebted for your assistance. May it be but the start of a long and useful friendship between our two nations.'

'We came at your Goddess's command,' Doku replied somewhat stiffly, as if the knowledge rankled a little, then he smiled rather wolfishly. 'But we would teach this upstart king of yours a further lesson also. If the two objectives can be accomplished together — well then, all the better. Besides, it is written that we should aid our friends and Marric is more than that; your brother is mine also now. It's complicated,' he added catching the startled look that crossed the other's face, 'an old Baratan custom. But come,' he waved a hand at the rough shelter his men had contrived for him. 'I have only campaign comforts to offer, but sit please. You are hungry? We have fresh meat, if some lack of skill in cooking it.'

Darien's look was wry. 'No difference there, then. Thank you, I could eat. You speak our tongue excellently, Prince. How is that?'

Marric eased himself away judging it best that his brother make his own impression on the Baratan noble. Darien had charm and knew how to employ it, best to give him the opportunity to do so. Rissak and Osram were deep in talk, their rapid exchange condensing the events since the little party's departure into terse sentences. Haran, it seemed, learning of Banco's arrest, immediately it happened had cleaned out the safe at the warehouse and gone straight to Luka.

Fortunately the senior partner's daughters were still absent, 'visiting' their nameless cousins. Forewarned by his trader Luka had filled a small pack then used the river tunnel that exited his cellar to get away by boat. And not a moment too soon either, Haran had reported, for as he rowed away up river Onli's men were already breaking down the front door. Haran himself had taken horse at once for the Lakes, and was currently with the army that had begun its march upon Ripa.

'And the archers from Ansham,' Marric remembered. 'Have they come?'

'Aye lad.' Rissak grinned making his scarred face more hideous. 'You missed your proper calling and no mistake. First Ansham, now this lot. And you don't even speak the language — do you?' he asked cocking his head. 'A man can never tell with you.'

'I don't. But the Prince has our tongue. And the Mother knows them all,' he added without bothering to explain. 'So they turned up?'

'Aye. There's fifteen hundred archers with the army. The rest stayed behind to defend those at the Lakes. Temes's dogs can't kill or burn what they can't reach, and the bows will see they don't. Reach them, that is. The bowmen, or Laketown.'

'Excellent. So where is Temes now?'

'The full army? Light alone knows! I was just telling Osram — his troops and ours have skirmished a bit across the drylands, but so far we've seen nothing but patrols out scouting the country. The biggest lot was a raiding party heading for the Lakes, a few hundred men. That'd be a day or two after Haran brought word that the young trader was taken. We routed them, couldn't hardly call it a battle though, more a running fight, but so far we haven't sighted the main body of his troops.' He looked at Osram, 'Did you have any sort of contact getting here? Anyone at all see this lot?'

Marric answered for the big man. 'No. We had scouts out. We thought the element of surprise could be a weapon in itself.'

Rissak rubbed his hands. 'Couldn't be better. Temes's troops will be shitting themselves when they catch sight of 'em. As for Temes himself, well, Darien forging an alliance with Barat would have to figure in his nightmares. The more so as his army's been seen off by them once already.'

'What of our men?' Osram rumbled. 'Many losses yet?'

Rissak frowned. 'A few. Inexperience mainly, bound to happen. Yesterday it was the cavalry.' A shadow of annoyance crossed his ruined face. 'Damn costly mistake, should never have happened, but that's green troops for you. They clashed with a small group, sent 'em running and disobeyed the recall. Darien was beside himself. Of course it was an ambush. We lost ten men and their mounts, which is almost as bad.' He spat, then sighed philosophically. 'Well, it happens. But maybe Darien can turn the same tactics against them when we finally come to grips. Retreat, then try and manouvre them northwards into the river bend. Could work. The Pretty Boy never had an ounce of battle savvy, and he's murdered most of his experienced generals.'

Osram nodded sagely. 'Force them into battle then box them in with the river at their backs. A sound plan — if it works.'

'If,' his fellow campaigner agreed.

'Speaking of plans,' Marric interrupted, 'I must have a word with Darien for we've hatched one of our own that could scrve us well.' He spoke to Osram, 'Would you ask the Lady Fenny to attend us? She'll be in her tent but as it concerns her as well...'

'She's with you?' Rissak looked horrified. 'What were you thinking of, lad? If you'd run into a fight — Asher's balls! She could've been killed.'

'She wouldn't be left behind,' Marric explained. 'I was hoping to get her back to the Lakes but if there are enemy patrols out that's plainly too risky.'

His old mentor shook his head, his fingers slipping up his jaw to feel the ridged scars there in a way that had become habitual with him, as he eyed Marric. 'Did you really give yourself over to the Baratans to be executed?'

'I had little say in the matter. Besides,' he indicated the cavalry squadron behind him. 'hasn't it turned out to be worth it?'

'Hmmph. I doubt your brother would see it that way. What's this plan of yours?'

'It's Tranche's actually.' He nodded at the merchant who had drifted across to join them. 'If a few of us can get into Ripa to contact them he had the idea of stirring the guilds into action against the City Guards. They'll be the only force left in Ripa once the army is out. If the citizens were able to take the city unaware Temes would have nowhere to retreat to. Because the last thing we want is for him to entrench himself behind the walls. A seige would be the end of us. He could just sit there waiting for his troops in the south to arrive. Darien could then find himself trapped between a second army and Ripa's walls. Not a good place to be.'

Rissak considered the idea then shook his head. 'It's a plan, but it'll take more than a bow and a couple of swords to swing it. You can't take the Guards without arms and plenty of 'em. They may be brutes and rapists but they're trained killers too. All recruited from the army.'

'We have them, the arms that is,' Marric said. 'That's what gave Tranche the idea. There was a shipment that never got sent on, it's cached in Luka's cellar. Yes, the Guards came to the house hunting him but it's unlikely they found the cellar. Why would they even look? The moment they realised he'd given them the slip they'd have been baying through the city seeking him, at the warehouses, the ships, the guildhouse. Anyway, there's enough, Tranche reckons, to arm twenty men; and there'll be other makeshift stuff we can use. The Smith's Guild for instance has hammers, bars — and every Guard we take down will provide more. Don't worry, we'll manage.'

He repeated the assurance to Darien once his twin had expressed his astonishment at Fenny's sudden appearance among them, and then his horror at Marric's stated intention of letting her accompany them into the city.

'You cannot!' he cried aghast. 'Fenny, you're not thinking straight —'

She patted his arm. 'I am, because the alternative is a battlefield. You will be fighting, all your attention needed for the battle. Don't worry. I will be at no more risk than any of the women and children in Ripa. In any case Marric will look after me.'

Marric smiled wryly at his twin. 'I shouldn't waste my time. It gets one nowhere. If it did she'd still be back in Barat. And something else before we part. I want you to have this.'

Osram had long since returned the dagger to him and now he pulled it from his sheath and offered it, hilt first. He'd stripped the concealing leather from it but the silver lions were dull, almost black, for he'd found no time to polish them since leaving Barat. Osram glanced curiously at it then caught his breath.

'Is that what I think it is?'

'Aye,' Rissak's one eye was on Marric and he nodded fiercely. 'The King's Luck.' To Darien he explained, 'Your grandfather sent it to your brother just before he was killed. To mark him to the army as his chosen heir, but Temes moved first. That's a powerful symbol you are holding, my Prince. One the Green Corp knows well. All swore their oaths of service upon it.'

'And you give it to me.' Darien flushed. 'You are too generous, Marric. I am already forever in your debt.'

'You are the rightful heir.'

'But you —' His glance spoke the words he couldn't find of all that his twin had ceded to him. He coughed then, and turned the dagger in his fingers to admire the workmanship. 'I have heard Nannik and Osram speak of this, but I had no idea — Rissak never mentioned it.'

'I thought him dead; what mattered beside that?' Rissak reached to touch the sculpted lions and nodded at Marric. 'Do you remember, lad, the day I brought you to Cyrus? Teach him well, he said. You have done me proud, Prince Marric. Were your grandsire here now he would think so too.'

'Thank you.' It was Marric's turn to flush, made uncomfortable by the praise. To Darien he said, 'It's rightfully yours. Our mother hoodwinked them all, did she not? Even the Great King. And now we must prepare for we need to cross the river and reach Luka's cellar while the night lasts. If — when we succeed we'll raise a flag above the gates and you will know the city is secure.'

Darien looked torn. 'I would wish that my sister was well out of it, but you are right, she is no safer with us. You will be careful, Marric? Take no unnecessary risk. Osram, guard him well. And Uncle,' he shook his head forebodingly, 'are you sure about this? The Guards must already be seeking you.'

'As Temes will be seeking you, my nephew, and he has an army at his back. Mind yourself and we will do the same. I have my reasons as you know and nothing will keep me from striking a blow at the tyrant wherever and whenever I can.'

Darien nodded, embraced them all and stepped back. Marric bowed to Doku. 'We will feast you in the city, my lord, when the battle is done. You and our new king. Fare safely, Darien.'

'And you, my brother.'

A last word to Rissak, the feel of his old mentor's grip on his arm for luck, then Marric took up his bow, let his glance gather up his three companions and led the way to the horse lines. 'One more ride, not a long one,' he said softly, taking Fenny's hand to help her onto her mount. 'Stick close to me, my heart. And please, do as I say.'

She heard the worry and entreaty in his voice and dimpled a smile. 'Just this once then, I will.'

24

They rode at a steady pace until the greenery fringing the banks of the Great River hove into sight.

'Close enough,' Marric decided, reining in and swinging down from his mount. The scene they viewed was a peaceful vista of farmland: some green crop in the fields immediately before them, and the distant hump of cattle lying beneath a solitary tree. 'We'll wait here for darkness.' They hobbled their mounts and found shelter in a timber-lined ditch edging a field. Here they waited for nightfall. Fenny had thought to command a parcel of food for her saddlebag, cheese and some of the flat, hard bread that Doku's cavalry carried.

'Bless you!' Marric was starving. Osram too, helped himself liberally, only Tranche ate little; he was silent, shut in on himself, his gaze remote. Marric wondered if he was having second thoughts but when her uncle moved off to relieve himself, Fenny shook her head at the idea.

'Never. He carries such rage and guilt over the death of my aunt and cousin, even though there was nothing he could have done to save them. Mother has tried, many times, to make him see that but he never listens to her. I think he lives only to kill those he hates.'

'Onli.'

'And the king.'

'He'd best get in line then. Half Ripa must feel as he does.' Marric stared into the gathering gloom, his expression grim for he had his own scores to settle, not least the death of his friend Banco. The light was fading on the river, darkness pooling first beneath the timber along its banks. A misty vapour began to rise ghostlike over the water, thickening as they watched. 'Fog,' Marric murmured, 'perfect. Now if we can find a boat...'

'I'll go look.' Osram slipped from the group and vanished; for a big man he moved silently, but then he had been a scout. Marric didn't anticipate difficulties in the man finding what he sought. River dwellers, even farmers, needed water transport. Nor was he disappointed. In a little while Osram was back beckoning them to follow. They tramped after him, inadvertently stumbling on a roost of wild ducks amid the reeds. They took off with a great flapping of wings, calling loudly, but nothing else was disturbed and the farmhouse, to which Marric assumed the boat belonged, remained silent and lightless.

The craft's bottom, when they felt it, was dry, and the oars lay waiting inside it, the craft rocking gently as they boarded. Osram pushed them off with a powerful thrust of his shoulders then sprang nimbly aboard, the stink of river ooze rising from his muddied boots. A few strokes of the oars had them clear of the bank, and from then on the current did most of the work. Even so, once they had coasted far enough downstream it was a long, hard row to the far bank.

Fenny, shrouded in damp fog, listened to the squeak of the rowlocks and the low murmur of Tranche's voice giving directions. He called Marric Matto once, as if being in charge carried him back to earlier times, and even spoke sharply to him to correct his rowing. 'Sorry,' the culprit grunted, 'you missed out that bit in my training,' and the girl was surprised to hear her uncle chuckle.

The fog had vanished from the water and the moon was high when the boat finally bumped against the jetty at the foot of Luka's garden. A torch burned near the back entrance, a sullen glow in the darkness, and one of the few lights visible along the river. Sight of it froze the boat's occupants. They watched unmoving from the darkness amid the darker shadow of bank and pilings, staring fascinated at the flickering flame.

'I don't like it,' Osram muttered, tensed beside Marric. 'Luka has fled, you say, so why the torch?'

'A trap?' Marric bit his thumb. 'They can't know that we know about Banco.'

'We'll go in through the cellar as we planned,' Tranche breathed. 'They'll not expect that. It means letting the boat drift though, in case they take it into their heads to inspect the jetty. I'll lead, the rest of you keep low and not a sound. If it's a trap they'll be inside. Fenny, you come last.'

The tunnel entrance was concealed in the low wall that formed a revetment for the mound of earth planted over with brambles. A short, bricked tunnel opened into a vaulted cellar also lined with brick, and they immediately heard the lazy tones of two men, muffled as if by distance. Marric fumbled frantically to shut the slide on the dark lantern they had found and lit at the tunnel entrance but Tranche was unperturbed.

'They can't see it. This cellar's behind the one they're in. I'm surprised you don't remember it.' He and Haran had brought Marric this way as a prisoner, but it had been a quick extraction and he had been both physically and mentally dazed at the time.

'It dates from King Waltu's father's time. Smugglers built it and I doubt there's six men living that know it exists. Here are the arms.' He pointed to a bale dumped to one side, its tarred outer covering still bearing the ship's labels and a stamped ticket attesting that dues had been paid on the contents. Stepping quietly up to the dividing wall Marric pressed an ear against it and heard a rolling clatter that was teasingly familiar.

'You have all the luck, damn your eyes,' a voice said, and suddenly Marric had it. They were dicing to pass the time. Somebody sighed as they yawned and a second voice spoke.

'How much longer? Mais is always late, damn his idle hide. The whole thing's a crock anyway. It's been half a moon since the old man fled — who's gonna turn up now? I tell you the captain's losing it.'

'Try telling him so.' A boot scraped on the floor and the dice rattled again.

Tranche had heard as well. He let his breath go in a gentle sigh of relief. 'Luka's safe then. The question is where?'

'Would he go to the Lakes?'

'He'd have needed a horse. More likely stick to the river — or maybe he circled back and is hidden in the city still.'

Marric snapped his fingers. 'Chera — Banco's wife.'

Tranche shook his head. 'Never. He'd not endanger them.'

'No, but he may have sent word to her because he'd know if you returned that you'd visit her.'

'Tell me how to find her,' Fenny suggested. 'Even if I was seen nobody would suspect me.'

'No!' Marric's denial was instant.

'I'm just a woman, a neighbour with a sick child say, what's suspicious about that? Women seek companionship when they're worried. Who better than a neighbour?'

'There's a curfew,' Marric said in exasperation. 'And the City Guards suspect the very alley cats.'

'Really? What of?'

'Of being cats, I expect. We'll all go.' And she could shelter safely there with his friend's widow, posing as a cousin come to help in her bereavement, perhaps. 'How do we get out of here unseen, Tranche?'

'Wait till their relief comes,' Osram counselled, 'shouldn't be too long by the sound of things.'

***

An hour later the four of them stepped cautiously into the street in the wake of the footfalls of the departing Guards. Eager to end their shift both had left the cellar the moment their relief banged on the front door.

'Sloppy,' Osram muttered in disgust but the men's carelessness served the party well. They had flitted from the cellars into the house then out through the back door while the relief Guards settled in, then they'd waited, pressed against the boundary wall of the property until they judged it safe to move.

The moon was high above the sleeping city which lay in darkness, both a help and a hindrance, for if the shadows cloaked them it also obscured the shapes of the occasional patrolling Guards. They almost blundered into one pair and only a frantic sprint to a handy recess in the corner of a wall, saved them. The householder's gate gave creakily to Osram's touch and they crowded through, flattening themselves against the wall, and praying they hadn't been seen. The gods smiled on them; the Guards passed by, and they continued cautiously through the streets until they reached the small yard of Banco's house, there to be faced with the task of gaining entry without rousing the whole street.

Tranche had another pressing problem. Whispering, 'Wait,' he left the wall's shelter for the deeper gloom of the tiny yard where an olive tree overhung a shabby outbuilding. With a sigh of relief his hands moved to his breeches but had scarcely touched them when a voice spoke with shattering loudness behind him.

'Make a move and it'll be your last. Show a light, Tran — let's see what we've caught ourselves.'

Tranche stood frozen, too shocked to react even when the slide on a dark lantern opened to show the silver facings of the City Guards. He stared dumbly into the self-satisfied features confronting him.

'It's the fat one,' the first speaker said. 'Him they wanted most. Well, I reckon the captain'll be —' The words cut off as his face fled backwards driven by the force of the arrow that had taken him in the eye. As the man collapsed the lantern crashed to the ground and the second Guard followed his mate. Tranche, still holding his frozen pose, glimpsed the knife buried deep in the man's throat before Marric and Osram were dragging the bodies into the shed. Fenny had given one little cry that she immediately muffled with her hand.

The merchant's mind started up again, all thoughts of his bladder forgotten. 'If she's still here we can't leave her with two dead men to account for.'

'I know.' Marric heaved the door shut and retrieved his bow. 'How many more places are they keeping watch on, I wonder? They must really want you, Tranche.'

The merchant shuddered at the reminder. 'She'll have to come with us,' he said speaking of Chera. 'That means the baby too. We'll be taking it into danger.'

'And maybe sooner than you think,' Osram said. He jerked a thumb at the shed, 'Light knows when they're due to be relieved so we'd better make this quick.' He suited the action to the word, walking boldly up to the house where he punched his wrapped fist through a window, clearing the glass from the frame in two quick sweeps with the back of his sword. Marric eeled through the aperture to find and undo the bolt on the back door. With the Guards' lantern uncovered he turned round and got an arm up just in time to deflect the descending poker.

Chera's face was white and desperate. She wrenched vainly at the metal he grasped then her hand fell away and she said disbelievingly, 'Matto? It is you! What — why — ?' Her eyes flew from his face to Fenny's, to the big, fair stranger behind her, then settled on the merchant. 'Master Tranche!'

'Hush, my dear. We've come to take you away, you and your daughter,' he said swiftly. 'Did you know the City Guards are watching your house?'

'They're here every night,' her voice was thin, stretched to breaking point. 'They think I don't see them. It started the night Banco didn't come home.' A tearless sob escaped her and her mouth trembled. 'They killed him, Matto, and hung his body from the Tower. His dear body. They wouldn't — I couldn't —' she stumbled into his arms and he held her as she cried, Fenny compassionately stroking her hair.

'I know Chera.' It was part of Onli's cruelty that the bodies of his victims were never returned to their loved ones. He said, 'Both the men are dead. Can we sit down?'

'Oh, yes. I'm so sorry. Can I get you something?' She looked vaguely around, 'A — a drink?' She wiped her eyes on the sleeve of her sleeping gown. 'This is a poor welcome for you Master Tranche, and you were so good to Banco. Master Luka came, you know. He told me you were away but he said when you returned I should tell you that he had been, because you would be worried about him. He was so kind.' She swallowed another sob and Fenny put her arm around her.

'It's all right, my dear,' she said. 'Tranche is my uncle. I'm so sorry about your husband.'

'Thank you.' Chera seemed to have lost the thread of her story and Marric prompted her.

'This is important, Chera. Can you remember exactly what Luka said you were to tell Tranche? Please think carefully.'

She frowned down at her thin hands, her gaze inward. 'He said, *My partner will be concerned. If you see him*' she frowned, 'or perhaps it was when — yes,' she nodded firmly to herself, '*when you see him tell him the guild will know how to help.* I — I took it to mean that because he had his turban that Banco's guild would pay the rent perhaps, or — or something like that?'

'Yes, don't worry about it.' Tranche patted her hand. 'It will be paid. But you can't stay here. Get the child and we'll take you somewhere safe. Quickly now, you must get dressed and bring whatever you need. But hurry. Fenny will help.'

The two women hastened out of the room. Osram prowled out the door to survey the street. Tranche bit his fingers while they waited, saying, 'If the guild is already involved it will make our task easier.'

'Can we trust them though?' Osram was back. 'People talk and you can't guarantee them all.'

'We are a brotherhood, all guilds are, sworn to keep their craft's secrets and to help each other,' Tranche sounded indignant that he should doubt them. 'Anyway we have no choice.'

Then the women returned, Chera carrying the sleeping child and Fenny a modest bag. Osram vanished briefly to check for patrolling guards and they slipped quietly back into the street, heading for the guildhouse where they could rest and be safe until morning which, judging by the stars, was not far off. Ferga would be by soon after if his habits hadn't changed, and they could talk in privacy without need to set foot outside. By which time, Marric thought, the dead Guards would have been reported, and the hunt fairly up.

***

Guildmaster Ferga was a big man by Rhutan standards, with a balding head compensated for by vigorous body hair that curled to the very knuckles of his hands, and overspilled the neck of his tunic. This early in the morning his turban lay like a scarf about his neck and he carried a filled bag in one hand. If he was surprised by the appearance of three men, two women and a child in his office he hid it well, nodding politely to the girls and greeting Tranche cordially.

'I see you have finally got here. Luka thought you would be back. Young Matto too. You know the Guards are seeking you both? How did you get in?'

Marric answered for them both. 'Good morning, Master. Through the roof. I am afraid I did a little damage, too.'

Ferga nodded. 'And then the back door, I see. Tranche frequently spoke to me of your initiative, young man. Well, I take it you are not here about your board review?'

'None of us are,' Tranche replied. 'It's a long story; first, the women need shelter. Sorry — this is my niece Fenny, and young Banco's widow and child. And Matto is actually the grandson of our late king, and younger twin to Prince Darien whose army is even now readying to take the field against Temes. And this is Captain Osram, one of the Prince's men. We are here to raise resistance in the city. We have weapons and hope to find men to use them against the Guards and get control of Ripa.' He rubbed his face tiredly. 'I was hoping to find Luka too. The message he left me implied that you would know his whereabouts.'

'Well!' Ferga set the bag down and began absently winding the green cloth about his head. He secured it with a thin band of scarlet that denoted his leadership of the guild. Marric waited tensely, unable to read his face and wondering if they had made a terrible mistake in coming here. Had Luka been wrong to trust the man? Was he even now in the Tower, betrayed by his own Guildmaster? 'Two princes of the blood?' Ferga said. 'That's a surprise to start the day with.' He tucked the final fold into place and patted the end result. 'Is Temes aware of this?'

Marric grinned and relaxed, liking him then. 'Yes and no. He thinks I'm dead. And the gods know he tried hard enough to make it happen! It's why I was living as Matto, the merchant's apprentice. He has no idea though that my brother exists; but he must be aware that somebody has raised an army against him. An army moreover that's just been augmented by five thousand cavalry from Barat. They're across the river with Darien as we speak.'

He paused to collect his thoughts, trying to condense into the fewest words all that pertained to their situation. 'You'll remember sir, that my mother was Bel's Oracle? She foresaw Ripa's future. It's why she sent my twin to be raised in secret in the Lake Country by Tranche's sister. Everyone who knew of it, Tranche, Luka, some of the traders, the Goddess's people, all have worked towards the one task of defeating Temes. Smuggling arms, building an army and training it. We have men from Appella within its ranks, Rhutans, Lakers, archers from Ansham and now the Black Country. The moment Temes leaves the city with his army we need to secure it against him. He must be defeated before he has a chance to send for reinforcements from the south.'

'Baratans?' Ferga said, as if his mind grasped but one fact at a time. 'There's another surprise! Well, if our neighbours are taking part it certainly seems time we helped ourselves a little. Have you eaten, Prince Marric?'

'I — no sir. Does this mean you can help us find Luka? Haran too, he'll be in hiding as well, unless he's been taken? I know he made it out of Ripa once but Darien told me he'd left them again to return to the city.'

'He did. Return that is, and he hasn't been taken,' Ferga replied. 'They're both here. You'd better come along with me. Yes, all of you, women, children, Princes, even clapped out old merchants.' Tranche raised a tired smile at that as they followed him down into the private regalia rooms where the ceremonies for the induction of new guild members were held. Where else, his weary brain asked, could his friends hope to hide within the city save the one place known only to the members of the guild? The Guards would go on searching, and with twice the energy once their dead were discovered, but Chera and her child would be safe here while the men of the city conducted the struggle for Ripa.

25

Luka and Haran rose to their feet as Ferga and his followers descended the stairs into the basement room, surprise plain on their faces. 'What's happening?' Haran's eyes had widened. 'Is it safe for you to be here, Prince Marric?'

Chera gasped at the question, goggling at the man she knew only as the apprentice Matto, her dead husband's friend. He replied, 'As safe as it is for Tranche, or you. We're here to overthrow the City Guards and rescue those in the Tower. That's our first priority, but we mean to make the city our own. The time is ripe for rebellion for Darien's army is across the river and should meet my uncle's soon in battle, today, tomorrow, I don't know... If Temes tries to retreat, turn a battle into a siege, we need to be able to deny him the city. Otherwise we must lose everything — the war, the throne, our lives. It's as simple, and as vital, as that.'

They discussed the situation, canvassing options, Haran as always going straight for the kernel of the matter. 'You'll be using the arms in the tunnel?'

'That's the idea. And the power of the guilds, all the guilds. We need them to gather their members and join the fight. Fenny will make us a flag.' Marric looked an enquiry at her and she nodded eagerly.

'If there is material and thread, yes.' She was eating, they all were, sharing the bag of breakfast Ferga had brought for his two guests. She licked a sticky finger and divided a bun, handing half to Marric.

'Thank you.' He bit into it, chewed busily. 'And every Guard we take will give us more weapons. The Tower will be the difficulty. We must winkle them out of there or we leave our rear open to attack. Of course they'll lock us out the moment they realise what's happening,' he paused to swallow, 'but I've been thinking we might get in through the cisterns.'

The channels that carried the city's water supplies ran like underground roads beneath Ripa. The sluice gates could be closed to drain the channels but they would need to discover which branch led to the Tower, and where egress to it could be had. He said as much, adding, 'Somebody must know. The system is old, it would need maintenance, surely?'

'The Masons' Guild would have the records,' Haran said.

'It's a good idea,' Luka agreed. 'Risky, but it's probably the only way in.'

Osram, once the layout was explained to him, quickly grasped the possibilities it presented. 'Ideal! How tall is this tower, how many floors are we looking at here? And how many men can we get inside before we're crowding each other out?'

The planning continued until the meal ended, then Ferga drained his cup and rose. 'Time for me to start my calls then. Luka's made a list of the guilds so I don't miss any out. Meanwhile I think that Chera and her daughter should come home with me; it will be safer for you all. If the child were to cry and somebody heard...'

Marric agreed. Anybody could enter the upper rooms throughout the day. 'You would be welcome too, Lady,' the Guildmaster added, but Fenny refused. 'As you choose of course,' he said. 'There would be no risk to you, or mine. I have six brats, one more won't be noticed, nor extra women in my household.' He looked at Haran. 'So, what can I promise our fighters about weapons?'

'Pikes and swords, no armour. That they must get themselves from the Guards they kill.'

'Right. And a meeting point?'

'Our warehouse?' Haran suggested. 'The bastards torched it so there's just a shell left, but it will do to conceal them. Tell them to come at dusk; to bring food and wait until we fetch the arms to them. That suit you, Prince Marric?'

'The warehouse is as good as anywhere. What about the curfew?'

'Split them,' Luka suggested. 'Tell some to be along the river before curfew and to head for the warehouse then, the rest must slip in after dark. We can't have them all herding together at once.'

Marric looked to Osram as the one with the greatest experience. 'A dawn attack do you think?'

'Aye, catch them coming off shift. We'll need transport to shift the weapons though. Could you lay your hands on a cart?' he asked Ferga.

'Too noisy,' Haran objected. 'Pack animals?'

The Guildmaster sighed. 'Mules then. I'll see what I can do.'

***

It was a long day. Ferga returned briefly with more food, material and thread and Fenny settled to her sewing. Haran, restless from confinement, paced the room, flinging questions at Marric until he had the whole tale of Barat's missing Princess and her subsequent return home. He wanted a detailed account of all they had seen of the country, and a description of the city and its markets, but for those he applied to Tranche.

'He'll never rest now until he gets there,' Marric told Fenny whom he'd gone to sit beside to watch her stitch. 'He's a Trader's trader, constructed as we say, from mud and dust, with gold for blood.'

'You love it too though, don't you?' she replied. 'When this is all over and Darien is king, how will you ever settle to just being a prince?'

He smiled at her. 'Badly, I suspect. I daresay there will be land to occupy me, or a province to govern, with a great number of secretaries to keep happy,' he pulled a face. 'And dozens of boring committees and dinners to attend. On the road one's meat has the salt of hunger and there is real, not paid companionship.'

'And if you were not alone?' she queried. 'Would that make it more bearable?'

'With the right companion? Oh, I think so. Even the secretaries wouldn't bother me then.'

Her gaze was downward following the careful stitching with which she was outlining the swan, but he saw her lips curve in a little smile. 'That's good news, for the secretaries, I mean. What do you think Darien is doing now?'

'Luring Temes out to fight, I hope. Tell me about growing up with him — was he a kind brother?'

'Oh yes. Of course he would rather I had been a boy, he missed not having you with him, from the day my mother told him the truth. Then Rissak came with his news of your death. That was bad for him. He had always dreamed of finding you one day, you see, and then suddenly that dream was gone and you with it.'

She was silent for a little while, remembering, then she gave her head a little shake. 'But you were asking what he was like. He was caring. He looked after me, and I liked that, because we were close and I never had a father. Children of the Shrine don't, of course. But I think a little girl needs someone male in her life, to feel secure.

What about you? Did you miss not having anyone close?'

'I had Taba,' he said softly, 'and Arn, but no boy of my own age for a friend. There was a time when I hoped that Tardi, my father's other son — I tried, but he hated me too much, for being older, for being there. He thought it was his place alone. Still, there was Dura.' He told her then about his childhood companion, and something of Arn, and Taba and plump Larky who had fed and cosseted him in the kitchen at Valleyfield. The important figures in his young life that, with kindness and care, had guarded and shaped his growing. He spoke of Rissak too and, for the first time, of the winter preceding his supposed death.

'How you must have missed him!' Fenny touched his face, her fingers a caress. 'Do you mind very much that he has become Darien's man?'

'A little, at first,' Marric was honest. 'But I have come to see that he is better suited to my brother's service. He was always a king's man, Rissak. And he is foremost a soldier, something I will never be.'

She said warmly, 'You are much more. You do what no other can.' Her eyes searched his as she sought to impress the truth of her words upon him. 'Being the Lady's servant is no task for a weakling. What did you think, truly, when the Manata passed sentence on you? Did you hate Her then?'

'I thought of you. And how much I regretted never having done this.' Cupping her face in his hands he raised it and brought his mouth to hers, his lips urgent until hers softened and parted for him so that he tasted the essence of her. She kissed him back, then remembering the others flushed rosily and pushed him away, her gaze flying to Luka's oblivious form.

'Not here.'

'Upstairs then?'

'Should we, is it safe?' But she was bundling her sewing as she spoke and followed him willingly up the steps, her hand in his. Their pulses jumped together and the concealed trapdoor was scarcely shut behind them before she was in his arms. The blue and silvery-white of the bunting fell forgotten at their feet as he slid his cupped hand up the smooth curve of her arm to the rounded swell of her shoulder, her skin as soft and smooth as he had dreamt it would be.

'You are so beautiful,' he breathed. 'I think I could die now for love of you.'

'Please don't,' she dimpled, 'die, that is.'

He kissed the hollow of her throat sending spasms of pleasure through her. She raised her arms to thread her fingers through his dark hair and gave a little sigh, languorous and warm in his arms. Kneeling together on the edge of surrender she nuzzled his neck then produced a breathy giggle.

'What?' Marric murmured cupping a breast.

'Just — if Ferga were to come back now.'

He pressed his mouth to a nipple outlined against her robe. 'Don't even think it.'

Later he frowned at her with mock displeasure. 'You would think the guild could at least supply us with a bed.'

Fenny laughed. 'Because they are merchants? Dear Marric, we have the flag. Though there is still a needle in it somewhere.' Drowsily she stretched a naked limb and ran a hand up his bare chest. Her toes were lapped in blue bunting and the wrinkled shape of a swan's neck lay crumpled behind her left ear.

'Thanks for the warning, my love, though it comes a trifle late. What would Darien think, I wonder, of the use we are putting it to?'

'Don't!' She clutched him suddenly, hiding her face in his chest so that her voice came muffled and fearful. 'This is our time. Don't spoil it, Marric! I won't think of war, or of Darien, or of tonight when you will be putting yourself in peril — again! I cannot stand the thought of losing you.'

'Hush, hush, my love. It will be all right. I will be all right.' He kissed away her tears, murmuring assurances they both knew he couldn't keep, until what started as comforting strokes turned to something else, and they travelled again the road of ever heightening pleasure to its ultimate reward.

***

Ferga returned at nightfall. He brought wine and cold meat, and sweet loaves from the bakery. His robe bore the dust of the streets and he sank thankfully into a chair, and took a mouthful of wine before making his report.

'First, the army has marched. The companies have been gathering all day outside the city walls. Temes and his household joined them this afternoon. He has stripped the city of provisions to feed them all, so enjoy the bread, my friends. I doubt there is a panful of flour left in Ripa. And I swear that even the water carriers have lost their carts to the army. The mules I have secured for you are lame, spavined, and old. The best, indeed the only ones I could find. Everything else with four legs has been requisitioned for the war.'

'That's good news that Temes has left,' Marric said. 'He's Darien's problem now. What of the rest?'

'Well, we have no shortage of volunteers. Ripa is buzzing with talk about the Prince. The other one, nobody knows about you yet,' he assured Marric. 'I don't know where the talk started but once the army mustered for war it really took flight. Nobody is sure where he comes from but all seem convinced that he is a true descendant of our own king. Somebody has remembered the old story of Cyrus's oath and they are saying that Bel has somehow saved, and returned him to us. They mean you, Prince

Marric, as nobody knows that your brother even exists. At any rate, the guilds are with us. Their masters are organising their men and all know the rendezvous point and the time. The smiths will have their tools, the rest whatever they can find, an axe, a spade, a garden fork.' He gave a humourless chuckle, 'A brick to throw...'

'And the mules?' Osram prompted.

'Ah, there will be three of them in the lane behind the Weavers' guildhouse. It's a dead end so the patrols shouldn't bother with it. You will find you have far more men than there are weapons for. Informers are a risk as you know, but maybe not such a great one now.' He rubbed his bald head, considering how to proceed. 'It's hard to put a finger on,' he confessed, 'but there's already a — a feeling of change abroad. The barracks have emptied out, the king's gone, there are only the Guards, and not so many of them really. I think a company or two might've been yanked back into army service for the duration,' he added in parenthesis, 'so people are restive, more than ready to rebel. Oh,' he raised a brow at Marric, 'and I did what you said, told them about the troops from Barat joining us.'

'It will put heart into them,' Osram nodded agreement, 'Remember, they're not trained for battle. Good thinking, Marric. What time is it?'

'The sun's down.' Ferga adjusted the smoking wick on a lamp and shook it to gauge the level of oil remaining. 'They found your dead Guards, by the way. They tell me that part of the city had patrols back and forth through it all day. A few doors were kicked in but nobody seems to have been picked up yet. The Guards are on high alert though, so take care how you go tonight.'

Marric nodded soberly. 'We'll do that. No word on the army's movement so far?'

Ferga drank again. 'No, but there's scarce been a soul through the gates since the last man marched out. I asked a vegetable seller that keeps a stall close by. Is that good or bad?'

'Could be either.' Marric felt a flutter of unease. What if they were to succeed in their part and Darien's smaller army was overwhelmed? No way could they hold the walls against Temes with a handful of looted weapons and untrained men. Resolutely he put the thought from his mind. 'Right. Here's the plan we've come up with.' The entire day hadn't been spent in dalliance, he and the other four men had done some concentrated thinking while waiting for the hours to pass. 'We'll eat first, then we four,' he indicated Osram, Tranche and Haran, 'will leave to retrieve the weapons. If — when, we've delivered them we'll time our attack for dawn. By then there must be plans in place to guard the key points of the city against Temes, should the need arise. Luka's working on that now. Let's hope they won't be needed but it's as well to be prepared.'

Fenny spoke. 'What about me? What do I do?'

'There will be wounded to care for. We'll make this our aid post. Upstairs, I mean.' She pinkened faintly under his gaze. 'We'll pass the word that the injured are to be brought here.' He glanced at Ferga. 'She'll need help, other women, and supplies. Could you organise that?'

'My wife can,' the Guildmaster said. 'Leave it to her. Trust me she could organise rain in a desert. I won't be here, anyway. I'm joining the fighters.' He rose to his feet then. There were still a few swallows of wine in his glass, which he raised ceremoniously in a toast. 'To a successful night's work gentlemen; and the rise of a new dawn for Rhutans under the aegis of our true king.'

'I'll drink to that,' Osram said, collecting cups and busying himself pouring wine.

26

Curfew had fallen by the time Marric and his three companions slipped out to make their way across the city to Luka's house. They met nobody enroute but twice saw Guards passing in the distance. The only other living creatures abroad were stray cats and the odd scuttle or squeak that told of a passing rat. One of the promised mules was missing; cursing to himself Marric made a quick reconnaissence of the lane and found it at the far end, lipping at weeds growing through a pile of discarded bricks. He caught it, switched the bow to his left hand, and started back.

Either the Guards watching Luka's place had been recalled or were already inside. There was no way of telling and no point in waiting. Stealthily they slipped into the river entrance of the tunnel, carried the heavy cargo out in pieces and loaded the mules, one of which was less tractable than its mates. Haran, swearing in a low mutter as it shied and kicked was trying to balance the load when the beast shattered the night with a bray.

'Shit!' Marric snatched an arrow and laid it to his string. An armload of swords hit the ground with a noisy rattle even as a voice challenged them from behind.

'Halt! Who's there?'

Marric glimpsed a shadow, and heard the snick of metal as a blade was drawn. 'Stand!' the Guard shouted. 'Make yourself known.' He stepped forward into moonlight sword in hand, and the arrow took him in the throat. All four of them froze then, eyes scanning the night but the sentry had been alone, his challenge unheard by his mate who must have been inside. Osram stripped the body of armour and weapons then hoisted it over his shoulder and padded away to drop it into the cellar. The man's blade and leather tunic was added to the loading, and with urgent proddings and muffled oaths the mules were urged on their way before anybody came looking for their man.

'Nice shooting. Let's hope his mates think he's gone for a piss,' Haran muttered. The excuse however could only work for so long, and by the time the house was well behind them Marric felt as if he hadn't breathed properly for days. It was past midnight when the mules plodded through the entrance to the familiar yard at the docks where everything looked different, from the gates hanging drunkenly askew to the roofless shell of the warehouse. Ferga, who had been keeping watch, greeted them with relief.

'You've been so long I thought you'd run into trouble.'

'A bit. There was a Guard posted outside the property. He saw us before we noticed him,' Marric said. 'It's given us an extra blade. And these damn mules aren't just lame, they're practically legless. Is there some sort of light?'

Ferga brought a dark lantern and by its dim glow the weapons were unloaded and laid out, the gathered men crowding about to receive them. Ferga, who had an easy authority and was known to many of them, divided the gathering into three companies, then calling for quiet, introduced them to their leader, Prince Marric. Brother to the man, he said, who would be their new king.

Marric eyed the dark mass before him, fitfully lit by half a dozen flickering wicks, who stared curiously back at him. 'If we win,' Ferga warned, 'he will be king. This is no time for half measures. There won't be another chance, for us or for Ripa. If we can't take and hold the city our friends outside could find themselves caught between its walls and the southern army. I'd wager that Temes has already sent for them, so it's now or never for every man of us here tonight.' He paused to give his words weight, searching the rapt faces of those he could see among his audience.

'Some of you will know Prince Marric here, as Matto, the Merchant Tranche's apprentice. And a sharp and lively lad he was with a good head on his shoulders. He'll be using that now to lay out his plan for the attack, first on the Guards patrolling the city, and then on the Tower. We aim to be rid of the one and to save whoever still lives in the other. That's what we're here for.' He stepped back then, motioning his companion forward.

Marric had not envisaged a speech so kept his words brief. 'Guildsmen, brothers, tomorrow we have the chance to avenge every one of our friends and citizens who have suffered and died under Temes's rule. My plan is that we start at dawn within a street or so of the Tower and work outwards from there, catching the Guards as they come off shift. We must not allow them time to consolidate with their fellows. We haven't weapons enough for you all, so we must take them from the enemy. Attack them as they straggle back to their base, there are usually no more than two together, take their weapons and armour and pass them to those without. The longer we can prevent word of us getting back to the Tower, the more chance there is of them sending others out to learn the reason why nobody's coming in. That's about it...Oh, the Merchants' guildhall will be the aid post. Take the wounded there. And may the gods grant us success and an end to that monster, Onli.'

'I'll drink to that!' somebody roared enthusiastically.

A clear voice grumbled, 'You'd drink to anything, Pran.'

It brought a laugh, followed by a hubbub of conversation. Marric squatted against a pillar amid the rubble and shared the food others had brought, and thought of Fenny, and worried about Darien and the battle before him. He didn't envy his twin the task. At least if he died tomorrow he had loved Fenny. Mind and body he yearned for her presence and in the same breath feared for her safety. Osram, dropping down beside him said, 'You realise if Onli gets wind of this he could barricade that Tower against an army? I've been quizzing Ferga. He says it's as solid as a fortress.'

'Because that's what it was, generations back. It's why we'll go in from below. I've been thinking about it and yes, it'll keep an army out but there's really no way to actively defend it. There's just the one door they couldn't risk opening and a couple of narrow windows high up. Useful if you had bowmen, which we know Onli hasn't. They could tip heated oil down if they had any, or throw rocks maybe...'

'So his best bet is to bar the door and sit it out, hoping that Temes will win?'

'Yes. So we've two choices. Wait him out or go in after him. And because he's got prisoners it means we have to go in. He's quite mad by all accounts; he could do anything to them. What?' he asked seeing his companion shake his head.

'With this rabble? Your pardon Marric, but close quarter fighting? It's a job for trained soldiers.'

'I know. But if Onli's lot were kept busy above ground while we came at them from below?'

'How? You're not going to batter that door down. Ferga says it's oak, a handspan through.'

'Build a fire against it. Get ladders up and pour oil in through the windows and set it alight; anything to keep their attention off the cells. They're underground, Luka said. Temes arrested a slew of guild members way back, before his crowning, when he first governed the city. They enjoyed a few days in the cells then. So anything we do above ground is unlikely to harm the prisoners. Either the Guards open the door to save themselves or the fire will cause enough confusion to give us an edge —' He stopped because the big man's face had cracked into a grin. 'You think it could work?'

'I do, Prince Marric, I do.'

***

The day the city of Ripa rose against the tyranny that had held it in thrall since Temes first governed there, was also the one in which the king set out to crush the incipient rebellion from the Lakes. At first he had paid scant attention to the tale Onli brought him from the Tower, of weapons smuggled into the city by ship. None had been found, after all, and beaten men Temes knew, hatched dreams as an antidote to their own helplessness. While whatever Onli might believe about the worth of truths learned in his dungeon, Temes also knew that torture made a man say whatever he thought his oppressers needed to hear.

Still, the king was no fool. He might despise his Rhutan subjects but even merchants could, in theory, organise an uprising, which was why the City Guards were there. A constant reminder in the blood and suffering they generated, of the futility of such schemes. Onli, Temes couldn't help but notice as the years passed, had become a little crazed as a result of his calling, which was why he had tended to dismiss the trickle of babbled information, inconclusive but persistent, of the existence of some shadowy prince. He knew it to be untrue.

Those suffering Onli's ministrations would claim anything to stop the pain, and more tellingly, none it seemed, so far as Onli could establish, had ever personally seen the man they claimed existed. But when the tale became one of smuggled arms, unease had niggled at him. He'd agreed that Onli should make further investigation into the unwilling informant's work associates. The first real pricking of disquiet had come when his captain reported that all the principals in the business had vanished.

Temes's attention had then become focused on the lives of Luka and Tranche, the now dead man's employers. It had taken no time at all to establish that the latter was a Laker from the reclusive province to the west, where the unsettling goddess his forefathers had banned from Ansham, was worshipped. His treasury regularly received a hefty tax from the place but in twenty seasons he had never bothered to visit what he imagined to be a string of fishing villages built over the water he had heard they lived upon. Perhaps it was time to remedy that. Temes thought about it then sent a scouting party instead.

The soldiers, who shared their king's opinion of Lakers as unimportant peasant folk had expected only dumb and sullen compliance to their demands, which in a fishing village they had agreed, wouldn't garner them much. It had been a surprise to run into an armed and mounted patrol, which however fled at the first glimpse of army green. Expecting sport the Appellans had thundered in pursuit through the straggling scrub that denied a clear view foreward, and had run straight into a torrent of arrows. Half a dozen saddles had emptied before their captain understood they had been ambushed; then, moments later and before he could re-organise his demoralised troops, the fleeing patrol returned. They swept through the rattled survivors cutting them down almost at leisure until those still able to do so, gathered their wits and fled.

'Like a knife through cooked fish and with no more resistance,' a delighted Buka had announced, exuberantly shaking hands with the dour leader of the ambush.

Keelin, busy cutting an arrow from a corpse he had made permitted himself a grim smile. 'They do not look so powerful now. Think you they will be back, brother?'

'Not them, not soon.' The Laker made a rapid count of the visible bodies. 'I would put their losses at a little under half their strength. Their leader will report it first. Then, my friend, they will come in greater numbers and your bowmen will have a real workout.'

Keelin had spat, unimpressed. 'Let them come. We will be ready.'

***

Temes had received the news the captain of his routed scouting party brought him in thunderous silence. His rage had flushed his face scarlet in a tide that rose up his neck to throb visibly in the veins at his temple.

'Arrows?' he said dangerously, 'How can they have arrows?' Without turning his head he snapped, 'Get one of them here. Now!'

'Here?' the slave repeated blankly. 'Yes, Sire, at once. Only — who, my lord? Who is it your Majesty desires me to bring?'

'Find me a whoreson of a Laker, you idiot!' roared Temes. His court waited in fearful silence, moving noiseless feet and wishing themselves elsewhere, until the sweating slave returned with two soldiers hustling a scared looking man between them. Him they flung at the king's feet.

'Laker born, my lord. Been here ten seasons, he says.'

The man, the armpits of his tunic wet with the sweat of terror grovelled unhappily. 'Yes, my king. I was born on the Lakes. But I have never been back. Not once! I am loyal to you and the city, I will swear it by the Lady. I —'

'Shut it!' One of the soldiers kicked him and his babble died.

'So tell me,' Temes said, 'do your people use bows?' And as the man gaped at him. 'Well? It's a simple question. Have-you-ever-seen-a-Laker-with-a-bow-and-arrow?'

'I — yes, my lord.' Seeing the king nod encouragingly he gained heart. 'Only — only small ones. T-they use them for birding, my lord. Not often, nets are better, but to take swans they will use bows.'

'So,' Temes glared at the leader of his scouting party. 'You were chased from the field by a weapon used to slaughter birds for the table.' He nodded at the soldiers who had brought the Laker in. 'Take them both to the Tower. Neither are of further use to me.'

'My lord, no!' the Appellan shrieked. 'Please — I have not — Those arrows killed men, they knocked them from thc saddles. No birding bow —'

The soldier dragging him off, the same one who had kicked the Laker, pulled up long enough to punch him in the face. 'Shut it, sunshine,' he said conversationally. 'The Tower, the King said, so the Tower it's gonna be. On your feet or on your back. Makes no difference to me.'

***

The next investigative party sent out was larger, its captain more cautious. They rode warily expecting an ambush, with raiders scouting ahead of the main body, and it was one of these who returned, goggle-eyed, to report that there was an army ahead of them.

'Shit!' The captain, having checked the veracity of his scout's report, chewed his lip in indecision. 'Where'd they spring from? Not Rhuta; the bulk of them are under the king's eye in Ripa, the rest only farmers. Besides, they're thousands of the bastards! The Lakers are only fishermen. Nor does it make any sense for the Meddii to field an army. Besides how would they get here? ' He broke off, thinking furiously, aware of the royal displeasure this report would arouse. Meddia was east and north of them while the unknown army appeared to have come from the west. 'They've got to be from the Lakes,' he decided unhappily. 'The king is never going to believe it.'

And so the long held secret was out and Temes prepared to take the field against his unknown challenger. Once he had mobilized the forces he had on hand he sent a messenger pounding to the south to alert the closest garrisons. These were at Valleyfield, and Nandon, which was situated midway between the pass and the port of Chade. Nandon was close to the frontier of the Grass Country and shared the unenviable task of keeping the barbarians within their own boundaries, with a sister garrison at Byfield, a military town roughly midway between Chard and Nandon. Stripping the Nandon garrison would leave the northern part of Appella exposed to raids, but that couldn't be helped. The Byfield forces would have to take up the slack until the malcontents from the Lake Country had been dealt with.

It made Temes grind his teeth to have had no warning of the incipient rebellion. It couldn't have come at a worse time, following as it did on the heels of his loss to the Black Country. That exercise had cost him men, equipment and prestige. And could even be the indirect cause of the challenge he reasoned, making his army appear as a force that could be beaten. Unthinkable though such a thing would have been in Cyrus's day.

The knowledge was infuriating, and his veins swelled with rage at the truth of it. He would raze every village on their stretch of water and throw their priestesses into the Tower. Every man not slain on the field would be sold as a slave. He would give them rebellion! Henceforth they wouldn't breathe without permission and — the thought appeased a little of his wrath — the profit raised on the slaves would help compensate him for the cost of the Baratan fiasco.

His temper cooling he considered matters. The messenger he'd sent was very likely unnecessary. It might even be worth recalling him; a bird sent to Winno would do it. Because it was probably more mob than army heading towards him; chances were they'd fold or run with their first taste of disciplined troops. One brief clash and it would all be over. He could hang the leaders in the field, round up the rest, then send a few companies into the homelands to destroy the dwellings and gather up the women and their brats. Even children could be trained into tolerable slaves. Cheered by his reflections the king shouted for his secretaries and began dictating the orders to recall his messenger and set in train orders that would see him march to war.

***

The overthrow of the City Guards by Ripa's populace that was to become the stuff of legend, worked very much as Marric had planned. The sheer unexpectedness of the first few attacks built a momentum that carried his small force past the initial shock and losses of the battle they waged through the streets. Casualties were heavy at first; naturally so, for men who had never held a pike or blade before were easy prey for experienced fighters, but long held hatred and the survival instinct made wonderful teachers. The Guards' original complacency in their own superiority helped too.

The very first one to confront a frightened citizen carrying a pike laughed and beckoned him forward with a wave of the blade he'd drawn. The man's courage wilted and he hurled the pike clumsily from too great a distance, knocking the startled Guard down without inflicting a fatal wound. But the pikeman's mate, who belonged to the guild of butchers, dispatched the bleeding Guard with a single blow while his erstwhile assailant was being sick.

The butcher then collected the dead Guard's sword and helmet, handing the one to his mate and clapping the other on his head.

'Bel's scaly hide!' The pike man held the blade as he spat the taste of vomit from his mouth. He made a tentative swing at the air. 'We did it and we're still alive!'

'Aye,' agreed the single-minded butcher. 'But they're always in pairs. Best we find t'other and do 'im too.'

Marric, busy with his bow, led his own small band west towards the temple. He killed one Guard that took the leg of a mason's apprentice from under him, while a quick witted youngster dropped the blade he had no hope of using, to hurl a chunk of masonry at the other who was slashing open the arm of his friend.

The apprentice bled to death in the street before they could reach him, but they wrapped the cut arm of the other in the tunic of the youngster who had defended him, and sent both off with instructions to find the aid post. The dead men's weapons were handed on, one to a baker still wearing his apron, and the second to a water-carrier early abroad, who had dumped his barrel and string of cups and joined them with a single nod of assent. It was happening everywhere across the city. Men, who had not known of the rising, downing their tools to be part of the fight.

By the time the sun rose the Guards knew themselves to be hunted. Howls of rage would rise at sight of them. The foolhardy among them stood their ground to fight, the prudent fled, emboldening their pursuers. The running battles spilled into taverns and shops and even the private homes some desperate fugitives broke into, looking for refuge from men seeking vengeance for years of repression and murder. Marric and a half dozen others chased six into the temple forecourt and there lost them. They cast about like hounds amid the statuary and elaborate frescos, then hammered at the great bronze doors, but no priest came to open them.

'They're inside,' Marric beat futilely on the metal. 'There's nowhere else they could've gone.'

'Then we'll have them out,' Trent the smith, said. He had the shoulders of his trade and fought with a heavy, long handled hammer. 'Open up, priests!' he roared and with a single blow smashed in half the statue of the fish god beside him. Some of the others flinched from the sacrilege. 'What? You reckon the priests didn't let 'em in?' Trent growled. 'Course they did! Been hand in glove for years with the Guards, ever since the old king died, Bel bless 'im. I can keep this up all day,' he bellowed, and began systematically wrecking his surroundings.

The forecourt was a litter of smashed tiles, the mosaics ruined, before one half of the door inched open and an outraged voice cried, 'Stop! What have you done?'

'Got your attention,' Trent growled. 'We're coming in.' Shouldering his hammer he grabbed the door and jerked it wide, which left the man pressing forward behind him to take the waiting blade full in his body. He shrieked and died even as Marric shot and killed the Guard who had been lurking beyond the priest. Trent with a roar of fury flattened the latter as he clung wide-eyed to the door handle, then whirled to smash in the skull of the second ambusher who was waiting with raised sword, to spit him.

Another Ripan fell to a Guard's weapon before sheer weight of numbers carried the day and Marric's men stood panting amid the bloodied bodies in the sudden stillness created by wholesale death. The priest that Trent had felled had regained his feet and was scuttling for an inner door when Marric stepped in front of him, the point of his blade at the man's throat.

'You. Where's Fevran?'

'I — I don't know.' The priest, young, eyes starting from his head, spoke in a squeak. His robe with its pattern of stylised scales was spattered with blood, another's, not his own.

'That's a pity. I might as well kill you then,' Marric said conversationally, 'for sheltering the enemies of your new king. The penalty for treason is death.'

'W-what — Who —? You can't!'

'Yes I can.' Steely voiced he advanced the blade until the point dimpled the priest's jerking Adam's apple. 'I'm Prince Marric and I have an old quarrel with your master who murdered my mother, the Princess Leona of Rhuta. Before your time, I would guess, but the thing is I don't care how many priests of Bel I kill to find him, because find him I will.'

'I — don't, please — I'll get him,' the man gabbled.

'You do that.' Marric slid the sword back into its scabbard, 'and you might live. Otherwise I can promise you that you won't.'

Trent, stripping the dead of their weapons paused to eye him as the priest hurried off. 'Is that true, that the high priest killed the Princess? We — the city I mean — always blamed Temes's lot.'

'It's true. Temes's slave told my grandmother, Queen Quan how it was done. See our dead carried out of this place.' Marric glanced around the opulent room that now reeked like a slaughterhouse. 'All this while the poorest starve! Pah, the priests have made a midden of the god's house.'

The high priest appeared then flanked by eight of his followers giving Marric his first sight of the man responsible for the deaths of both his mother and her cousin. He was tall for a Rhutan, a clever faced man with a high brow and a straight nose. He would have enjoyed at least sixty seasons of life, Marric calculated, while his mother had barely eighteen. His head was completely bald, but the flesh of his arms exposed by the sleeveless gown he wore, with its double blue band to proclaim his rank to the world, was still firm. Nor had age spots marred the slender, soft skinned hands, one of which Marric saw hung oddly, the thumb strangely withered. The man was plainly in a towering rage, dark eyes snapping, his cheekbones mottled red as he launched at once into a tirade against the invaders.

'You filthy rabble! What is the meaning of this? How dare you desecrate the god's temple with murder? Get out! I'll see you all die in the Tower for this.'

'Will you?' Trent's brows lowered dangerously. 'You seem a bit over ready to threaten fellow citizens. How many others have you sent there, I wonder? Do we take him in, Marric?'

'That won't be necessary,' the sudden iron in the Prince's tone chilled the smith's blood. 'I'm going to kill him where he stands.'

Fevran stared at him. 'Who in Bel's name are you?' He sounded more puzzled than fearful. 'I am the God's priest; harm me at your peril.' He gestured angrily at the ruined room. 'What is going on here?'

Marric looked him up and down. 'Your past is catching up with you, Fevran. Did you think Bel would let you murder His Seer and never exact payment? You were wrong, priest. You shouldn't have had her killed or she could have told you that this day was coming. You know who I am, don't you?'

'Had who killed? What are you talking about, you madman?' But Marric recognised bluster for he had caught the flicker in Fevran's eyes at the word seer.

'Princess Leona. My mother. And the mother of your true king who is presently bringing an army to put down my uncle, the usurper. I am Marric. Remember him? The baby you sold to Temes. The foster child of the woman he had tortured and later killed. Or was the poison your doing? Oh, I see you remember now. Have you anything to say, traitor?'

The red had gone completely from Fevran's cheeks; shock had turned them white. He stammered, 'You're dead! Temes had you ki —' and shut his mouth on the betraying words, his hands clenching on his robes.

'Yes, he thought so too, still does; if he yet lives that is.' Marric had forgotten his surroundings and his companions. He said reasonably, 'Men have no business trying to prevent the fulfillment of oaths made in good faith to the gods. They are jealous masters, Fevran, as you would know if you had ever truly dealt with them. Yes,' he smiled slowly, cruelly, at the man before him. 'I inherited my mother's gift. Neither past nor future is closed to me.' It was only a slight exaggeration he reflected, watching the horror dawn on the face before him. He smiled again as he opened his bow.

Fevran shrieked and dropped to his knees. 'No! Mercy. You cannot —'

Reasonableness vanished and a mist of rage clouded Marric's vision. 'There was no mercy for Taba, just poison and a cruel death.'

Too late he saw the priest's arm jerk and the flash of the knife spinning across the space between them, but Trent had been watching like a cat and his hammer smashed it aside as Marric released the string. It was not his best shot; Fevran, twisting to rise and run, took it low in the back, to the left of the spine. It pierced through his body, the barbed head penetrating a hand's breadth through his groin. He lay where he fell, scrabbling uselessly at the expensive, blood spattered tiles, and as the shock wore off began to shriek.

The priests, inching together for protection, stared open mouthed. Trent wet his lips, the hammer dangling by his side.

'What have we done? He is the high priest!'

'And a renegade who betrayed his calling and his people. It's no thanks to him that I still live,' Marric said. 'Now come. The work's not finished yet. Not by a long shot.'

***

By mid-afternoon the hunt was over. Any surviving Guards outside the Tower were so well hidden as to make seeking them a waste of time. The city gates were closed, a small guard posted to see they remained so, and the blue and white flag of the Lakes hoisted above them.

'We've done well, even if the hardest part's ahead of us still,' Marric observed, 'but I don't like it that we've heard nothing from either army. Surely battle has been joined by now? Darien was practically here, yesterday. There should be something — a message from him, deserters, or wounded men from Temes's side trying to return?'

'There'll be word before dark.' Osram spoke stolidly. 'The one certain thing about a battle is that nothing ever goes to plan. Darien was going to lead him away to the riverbend, wasn't he? Well, that takes time, and care, moving that many men about without leaving yourself unprepared for a sudden attack. No use fretting, Prince.'

'You're right.' Marric cast one last look at the flag then turned to lead the way back. He met Haran instead whose party had been detailed to ensure the Tower remained sealed. There was a stained bandage on the trader's left arm and a swelling welt across one cheekbone.

'There you are,' he said. 'Half our force seems to be at the Tower. They've been straggling in by twos and threes and I sent 'em over there. Reckon there're no more Guards to be found outa the Tower. I've got some of my boys carting wood to stack against the door. Our best guess, which could be very wrong mind, is that there's maybe fifty Guards inside. Onli hasn't been sighted so we assume he's in there too. Luka's been trying to organise transport for the prisoners inside but all he could find was a cart with a busted wheel. The smiths are making repairs as we speak. We'll have to pull it ourselves, unless you can find those mules we had earlier. So what's our next step?'

Marric rubbed a cheek that still stung from where he'd slammed it against a brick wall dodging a thrust from a blade that had almost killed him. 'The plans for the water channels. Did Luka find them?'

'Here,' the old merchant spoke from behind him, having just come up with the party. He knelt on the cobbled street and spread the long roll of parchment he carried, Marric, Osram, Haran and Trent squatting to hold the corners down. 'Luckily the masons keep extensive records. The Tower is one of the oldest structures in the city so it's actually built on the main water channel. This one here.' He tapped it, the shadow of his turbanned head falling across his fingers.

Squinting, Marric saw that the system was like an arterial road running beneath their feet. The largest channel traversed the city running directly beneath Tower, Temple and Palace, with numerous smaller, feeder channels entering and leaving it. 'You'll have no trouble following it, just don't get turned round once you're in it. It should be drained by now because I sent to have the sluices closed this morning.' His stern features relaxed into a rueful smile. 'There'll be housewives all over the city cursing me, but I had all the barrels I could lay hands on filled, so people can drink, and the wounded aren't short either.'

'Good work,' Marric said absently, tracing the route with his eye. 'How do we get in?'

'Your closest entry's here.' Luka tapped the map. 'It's an inspection point back up the street the Tower's on. They're the only ones large enough to take a man. The rest — the public openings, like the hatches within the buildings, were only designed to take buckets.'

Marric looked at him in consternation. 'Then how do we get out?'

'Fortunately there's another inspection point under the Tower. Perhaps they were worried about weakening the city wall with their tunnelling and wanted to keep an eye on the foundations? The lower part of them is the wall, you see.'

'So it is.' Marric considered they distance they would have to traverse. 'Not too bad. Difficult coming back though if we have to bring the prisoners out that way, they'll be in no shape for it.' He looked at Harun who was to lead the assault on the door. 'You've got everything organised? What about ladders?'

'In hand. And we've got a ram. One of Trent's lads is fetching a metal shoe we can fit onto it. I had him shape the end to a dull blade, don't want it to jam in the oak, but gouging might work better than battering. The metal should protect the head of the ram from the flames — that's the idea, anyway.'

Osram grunted approval. 'Good thinking. Even if you can't get through the noise should unsettle 'em and keep 'em focused on the door. That and the smoke. So who comes with me and the Prince? You up for it Trent?'

'Bel's life I am.' the big smith grinned and hefted his hammer, biceps swelling.

'And me,' Tranche said. Marric's protest died unuttered before the fierce challenge of the merchant's stare.

'Right, sir. I'll find the rest, shall I?' Osram asked. 'Fifteen of us should do the job. Too many and we won't have room to move, too few and they could push us back. Might be good to get the fire started before we leave, Haran? Oak burns slow and it should help keep their attention away from anything happening below.'

***

In due course they were ready. Marric sent all the extra men to help out at the Tower while the chosen fifteen lined up at the inspection hatch, nervously fingering their weapons, for nobody expected the task to be an easy one. He had given his bow into Luka's care knowing it would useless in the close quarter fighting within the Tower. Now he loosened his own blade in its sheath, swallowed and took a last look around the street. It was growing late, those prisoners who had survived would, when it was over, be emerging into darkness, but at the moment their every move he saw would be visible to anyone who, standing at the Tower windows watching the bonfire below them, happened to glance up the street.

He beckoned to Luka who nodded once as he spoke, then issued instructions to the crowd of armed men. They immediately began to mill about forming a screen behind which Marric's party began to drop through the open hatch. A couple of lighted torches were handed down, with a spare, then somebody above ground slid the hatch closed, leaving them to gloom and ankle-deep water below the street. Half Ripa's population seemed to be above them but Marric's thoughts were with only one and she was not among them.

He had seen her briefly at the guildhall enroute from the city gates, and watched her eyes light up as they met his across the body of a wounded man who was bleeding out despite all her frantic hands could do. Fenny's face was smudged with dirt and soot, for fires were burning in the city, and her gown was splashed with dried bloodstains. She looked wonderful. He had kissed her quickly. 'All right, my life? I can't stop. Stay safe.' His gaze swept over the organised shambles of the aid post. Other women had joined her; there were buckets, gory dressings, piles of torn linen and men's bodies, half clothed, groaning, comatose and dead. 'We're winning,' he assured her briefly. 'Only the Tower to clear now, then I'll be back.'

'You will take care?' She lifted a bloodied hand to him, hesitated and lowered it again, biting her lip. 'Come back to me,' she whispered fiercely as the body she was tending slackened into sudden death.

'Of course I will.' Another quick kiss as he rose and he caught the wink and grin of a man with a bandaged leg, and left her there. He wished now he'd taken the time to hold her, and assure her of his love, but the urgency driving him would not permit it. Only, those few precious moments might be the last he ever had with her...

With an effort Marric dragged his mind back to the present, to the water channel and the men he was leading, and the task before them.

27

The main channel was wide enough for three men to walk abreast. It echoed hollowly and the wavering torchlight threw bold shadows across the brick surface of the tunnel. Marric marvelled at the labour and the expense involved in creating the system, but Ripa had known great wealth he knew, and been ruled by mostly humane and progressive kings who had used their resources wisely for the good of all.

A pervasive damp came off the bricks and the water sloshed noisily under their many feet. Amazingly there were bats, minuscule fleeting shapes that darted past their heads. Somebody slipped and swore as his buttocks touched the water before a companion hauled him erect. A laugh, quickly smothered at the clumsy one's expense, and the repetitive sloshing continued. Marric wondered how far it could be heard. It would be fatal, the worst possible outcome, if their ambush were prematurely sprung by the simple expedient of some trooper letting down a bucket at the wrong moment and hearing them. That was all it would take, or of course, the discovery that the water had vanished. Only one conclusion could be drawn from that.

He breathed a voiceless prayer to the Mother, turning his head aside from the streaming smoke of the torch, for air moved through the channels, enough of it to send the torch flames peeling backwards. He was wondering about its origin when his eye was snagged on a shape incised into a brick. Peering more closely he saw it was the outline of a crab, and then that every tenth or so brick held a watery symbol — fish, shells, river weeds, waterbirds — all the varied life forms of the Great River shown here in a few incised lines, that flowed as sinuously as the water itself. All carved to be hidden and forgotten, thousands of them — and that supposing they were only to be found in the main channels. The scale of it staggered him, mirroring as it did the faith of the artists in their god, and ultimately their city.

If it was not an answer to his petition it was an example of the trust such men had felt in their deity, and the knowledge heartened him. He strode on more confidently until the torchlight gleamed on a blank wall ahead. Then he saw the ladder, as corroded as the one they had descended, and halted, waiting for the tail of his group to close up around him.

'No talking from here on,' he said softly, 'no noise at all. The basement is probably empty but sound echoes in stone buildings. Trent, you go up first with the bar in case the hatch is locked. Me next, then Osram, then the rest of you. Once up we wait for the last man. The cells are our priority. We open them but the prisoners are to stay put till the Guards are dealt with. Everyone got it? Right, up you go, Trent.'

Above their heads the hatch rose and fell back with a thud that set every man's nerves on edge. Trent heaved himself through and the rest followed, the torches flaring over a stream of shuffling, pushing men, and glinting off the weapons they carried. Every clink and footfall echoed hollowly back from the stone. Marric made for the door but Osram put out an arm to hold him back. The big man checked the corridor outside then beckoned them on with a jerk of his head, taking the torch from Marric to light the way.

They climbed steps so old the stone was worn in the center from use. Afterwards it seemed they had spent an age, dry-mouthed and fearful, toiling up the endless spiral stair until they reached the level of the cells. There were ten of them; lightless, stone floored apertures with doors of thick oak. Trent, thoughtfully studying the first lock shook his head, his voice a soft rumble in the breathing silence.

'Take me all day to chisel through that.'

Marric hissed, 'Bel's balls, man! We have to get it open. Use the bar.'

'How?' The planked door fitted smoothly into its socket of stone. 'On t'other hand,' the smith fingered the hinge pins, a horny thumbnail scraping through layers of rust. 'These are as old as the stone.' Wedging the blunt tip of the bar between wall and hinge he heaved and with a dull crack! the top pin snapped. The lower one followed and Tranche wrenched the oak back against the lock. Within, torchlight fell on a huddled shape dragging itself backwards into the corner. Dried blood crusted the feet crushed out of shape, and the distorted mouth made little whimpering noises at them.

Tranche swore loudly until Osram gripped his arm. Shock held the rest of them dumb.

"S all right, mate,' the smith said gently. 'We're getting you out of here. Stay quiet and we'll be back.' He moved onto the next cell and the next. All ten were occupied and with each the rotten metal gave easily to the bar's force. Each tiny room held the tortured remnants of a man, save the tenth where it had turned into a corpse. The body had lain there longer than a day, Marric thought. The stone floors and tainted air reeked of human waste, of degradation and death. Nobody spoke, but the combined anger of the raiding party was palpable in the silence. The prisoner in the second last cell was the newest. His face was a mess and one arm hung crookedly but he met them on his feet with a leap of hope in his blackened eyes, painful in its intensity.

Marric said quickly, 'You have to wait here. Help the others if you can. What can you tell us about what's above?'

The man spoke through mashed lips, 'Guards' room on the ground floor, cells underneath. They throw us down the stairs, it's how I got this,' he indicated his broken arm. 'Onli's got his quarters higher up the Tower. What's happening?'

It was Trent who answered him. 'We're taking over the city. The new king is on his way. This here's his brother.' He jabbed a large thumb at Marric. 'You look out for those poor bastards in the other cells and we'll be back.'

There were yet more stairs and a door at the head of them, unlocked. Osram, pulling it open sniffed and grinned fiercely. 'The fire's got a hold, I'd say. How long before one of 'em remembers the cisterns?'

'Most wouldn't know about the hatch,' Marric whispered back, 'but you're right. If they go down for water they'll see the cells are open. We have to deal with them first.' The smell of smoke was strong and he fancied there was a vague blueness in the air. Haran must have got something in through the window slits for he could hear boots stamping about above their heads. 'All together,' he told the men crowding his heels, then Osram was charging down the corridor and he followed, aware of the rest pounding behind him.

They burst out of the short corridor into a room with a mess table and chairs, and hammocks slung against the curvature of the outer wall. A wide hearth containing ashes lay opposite with more stairs rising beside the fireplace, then a short entrance closed by leaping flames where the burning oaken door stood. Several men, all that could come at it at once in the confined area, were attempting to smother the flames with blankets, but losing their labour.

A quick glance at the table showed they had been disturbed at their meal, then one of his men shouted a warning and Marric whirled to see three guards carrying buckets coming through a door he hadn't even noticed. A brief melee while the three tried to divest themselves of their load and reach their weapons but went down instead under the force of numbers. The clash of steel brought the firefighters spinning about and suddenly Guards were swarming at them from all directions, just as the first thud of the ram sounded against the burning oak.

After that it was every man for himself. Marric was peripherally aware, through the screech of blades, the shouts and laboured breathing and stamping boots, of Trent's fearsome hammer clearing a path to his left, and of Osram at his right shoulder. The big man fought with a sword in his right hand and a dagger in his left, and twice that Marric saw, fended off blows that, had they landed, would have maimed or killed him. The first time he stabbed the neck of the Guard who had easily beaten Marric's blade aside, and on the second occasion slashed the dagger across a crooked elbow, severing tendons. Marric thrust his disabled enemy through and gasped his thanks.

'Rissak was right, Prince,' Osram, breathing easily, spoke without taking his eyes off the fight, 'you really are shit at this. Beside you!'

Marric ducked and swung and the danger passed. Trent had got separated from them, but another man, a shipwright's apprentice, he thought, had stepped into his place. The lad's head was bleeding but he seemed unaffected by the cut. Searching blindly for the smith Marric realised that the smoke had thickened alarmingly. Men were coughing within it but the furious clash of metal and the odd shriek as a blade bit home, never ceased. Behind it all roared the fire and the furious thump-

thump-thump of the ram against the oak. Then Osram yelled, 'Watch out!' and he snapped back to the business of staying alive.

There was fighting on the steps beside the fireplace. Somebody crashed into the table, sprawling across it on his back and the brief glimpse he caught showed it to be one of their own. The body had fallen from the stairs and the man who had sent it plunging downwards, squat as a toad, the silver facings of his coat smeared with blood, suddenly flung back his head and bayed, 'Oooow, oooow, oooow,' the long drawn howls ripping through a space less crowded than before. 'Who's next?' the mad, high cackle that broke from his mouth was a sound those in the cells learned early to dread.

Osram barked, 'Light's sake! What —?'

'Onli.' It was Tranche who shouted the name and started forward. Trent sprang after him just as a renewed surge flung half a dozen Guards in Marric's direction. His brief stocktaking had shown him that the last furious moments had cost them dear for there seemed to be no more than six of his men still standing. Osram had also noticed. He thrust at a sword arm then sprang sideways to hack down at the back of an exposed knee, his expression grim.

'They better get that damn door down soon.'

Somebody fighting near it was forced back shrieking into the flames, then as suddenly catapulted forward, hair on fire, as the ram shoe burst through the oak. It withdrew and hammered again and a faint cheer rose from outside.

He saw Trent fall into the smoke and heard Onli bay again in triumph. His eyes were streaming and his throat on fire, his sword arm weighted with lead, then miraculously he could breathe again as with a great blast of air the door crashed down, and men in Laker blue poured through the opening. He saw Darien and Nannik killing with contained rage as they pushed deeper into the room, others, including Rissak, entering behind them.

Beyond the flames the sky was black. It seemed only moments since they had entered the cistern but it must be more like hours. That Darien was here could only mean that he had won the day, and come through the battle unharmed. Awash with relief Marric turned just in time to see Tranche sliding slowly down the wall, the sword dropping from his hand.

He shouted in rage and despair and Darien checked at the sound, turning towards him. Later, when there was time to think, he saw that Onli must have seen his twin's hair, and made the leap to his identity for the captain of the City Guards made straight for him, casually beating aside the blades that tried to stop him. He was already wounded, left arm hanging limp, but his strength seemed unimpaired as right-handed, he raised his sword high to drive it into the Prince's unguarded back.

Darien saw the horror on his brother's face and was turning, blade rising even as Marric lunged to knock him aside, then thrust with all his strength, careless of laying his own body open for the riposte. He felt his weapon penetrate deeply and the answering stab of Onli's sliding into his own flesh. His foot slid on the gore spattered floor and even as Onli fell, gaping mouth blooming suddenly crimson with a rush of blood, he joined him on the floor, the fire in his own ribs leaving him too busy to wonder how he had got there.

Somebody roared his name. He pushed weakly at the loathsome flesh beneath him, hands sliding in gore, then Darien's arms were under his own, lifting and turning him, and Osram's face was hanging upside-down above him, while hands carefully wiped his red-spattered face. Around them the stamping and clashing continued as Darien ripped off his shirt to bunch against the wound pouring blood from Marric's side. His hair looked suddenly redder against the bone-white of his face.

'How bad is it?' he asked urgently. 'Does it hurt to breathe? We'll get you to a healer.'

'I don't think it's bad.' Marric caught his breath and slowly sat up. Pain burned in his ribs as he pushed exploratory fingers into the hurt place. Blood covered his hand when he withdrew it but the wound itself seemed shallow, the blade hadn't penetrated his ribs. Cautiously he breathed in. The air stank of charred wood, of smoke, and the sickly reek of blood, but he drew it easily into his lungs. He pressed a hand to the impromptu wadding and lifted his other arm. 'Help me up. It's just a slash along the bone. But Tranche is hurt.'

'You saved my life,' Darien said.

'So? You're my brother.' And suddenly it was as simple as that, the bond between them greater than anything else. Marric steadied himself against his twin's shoulder then, favouring his wounded side, headed for where Tranche lay. Osram was before him, straightening the merchant's body and closing the sightless eyes; he shook his head at them.

'He's gone.' A nod indicated the deep slash in the dead man's side. Onli's sword thrust must have found his heart, his life's blood had poured from his punctured chest and was already thickening where it pooled. With careful hands Osram slipped the blue turban from Tranche's head and began to unwind it.

'What are you doing?' Marric demanded, then had his answer as Osram stepped to his side using the material to bind the bloodied shirt to his lacerated ribs.

'He has no need of it now,' the big man said simply.

Guilt tore at Marric along with a burdening sadness. 'I shouldn't have let him come. He was a businessman, not a fighter. He deserved a better ending than this.'

'Who doesn't?' Darien's sigh was weary. 'We lost our share today. Much grief lies in store for those waiting in Lake Town.'

Marric remembered the battle then. 'But you were victorious. What of Temes? Is he dead?'

'Aye.' Rissak had come up behind them. 'Not hurt bad, lad?' He wiped his blade before sheathing it. 'That's the last of 'em accounted for, my Prince. No quarter granted. The last one went head first through the top window. He was skinny enough for some crazy Rhutan to toss him out. The Pretty Boy,' he added, reverting to Marric's question, 'ain't quite that now. That black mate of yours slaughtered him; something about a debt owed to his grandfather.' He shook his head at his old pupil. 'You're lucky you're still standing. I saw it all from across the room. How many times have I told you about leaving yourself open like that to a counter thrust? Asher's Light! A child coulda killed you, let alone a mad bugger like that.' He nodded at Onli's corpse.

Marric grinned tiredly. 'If it comes to that where were you?' Then, seeing the mortified look cross the scarred face, regretted his levity.

'Aye, you're right enough. I shoulda been there beside my Prince.'

Trent, though pale from blood loss, still lived, one of the remaining four of the fifteen men who had entered the cisterns. It had been a costly victory that only the timely breaching of the door had cemented. Once they had seen the smith lifted and carried out of the charnel house the Tower had become, Marric remembered the prisoners.

'I'll see to it,' Osram promised. Kindling a torch from the dying fire he went off shouting for men to help carry the survivors up from the dungeons that had cost them everything but life itself.

Darien stood, seemingly irresolute beside his twin, rubbing a hand through his sweat matted hair. Marric wondered what had become of his helmet but was too tired to ask. 'What next? You realise you're king now?'

'Yes. It's happened so fast... After all the planning, I thought — But there's a million things to be seen to first, the wounded, the dead. I'll have to speak to the people. The Guildmasters would be the best channel I suppose. Tranche could have —' he shook his head, sighed. 'I thought of him as my real uncle, you know. And he was Fenny's, she'll be — Where is she? Is she safe?'

'At the merchants' guildhouse, with the wounded.' Mention of her roused Marric to new life. 'We need carts, wagons — apart from the likes of Trent there are the prisoners. They're in a dreadful state, Darien. They cannot walk, some will certainly die still. They need food, a healer. There's scarcely a vehicle left in the city: Temes commandeered them all.'

'You need a healer yourself,' his brother chided. 'Don't fret, I'll see to it.' He gave brisk orders before turning back. 'You know the city. Lacking Tranche, whom should I seek advice from?'

'Luka,' Marric said promptly. 'Have him gather the heads of the guilds, then form a council from them. That was how our grandfather ruled, according to Taba. The king at the head, his sons, representatives from the guilds, and the high priest to make up the working body that decided all governing issues. Which reminds me. You will be needing a new high priest because I killed Fevran.'

'Did you so?' Darien's eyes widened. 'It was a task I had earmarked for myself. No matter.' He gave his twin a rueful sideways look. 'Rissak said you were full of surprises; he also said you weren't soldier material. You've proved him wrong today.'

'I'm not,' Marric said, 'a fighter.' There was a sudden edge to his tone. 'Neither was Tranche but sometimes you have no choice. I had fifteen summers when I killed my first man. I have heard it said it gets easier after that but I have never found it so. Though I will lose no sleep over Fevran.'

'Neither you should,' Darien agreed. The sound of wheels over cobbles brought his head round. 'Ah, transport at last.' Somebody, thinking ahead, had thrown pallaises into the cart's bed. There was a mule between the shafts and willing hands lifted Trent and two other badly wounded men.

'There's more coming, sir,' the driver said. He wore Laker uniform and one leg of his trousers was stained with blood, black in the shifting firelight. 'A wagon for our dead and a coupla carts. Capt'n Manna said he'll send a surgeon. On'y one; orl he can spare.'

'Very good. Take a local, this man,' Darien picked one at random from the bystanders. 'Show him the quickest way to the merchants' guildhall,' he instructed. To the Laker he added, 'Come straight back, there will be more to transport. You'll find me here for the present. Merciful Lady!' his mouth fell open. 'What's this?'

Two of Osram's volunteers were emerging through the smoke blackened entrance chairing one of the prisoners between them. It was the hollow faced, emaciated man with the crushed feet. A horrified murmur ran through the crowd until a woman who had been elbowing her way urgently through it suddenly screamed, her hands flying to her face as it to shut out the sight of the survivor.

'Sano!' She began to keen. 'Oh, dear Bel — what have they done to you?'

Fortuitously the wagon intended to transport the slain arrived at that moment, and Darien waved imperiously to the two bearers, bidding them lay him in it. Other couples now appeared with their dreadful burdens slung between them, each skeletal wreck testimony to the grim fate of those incarcerated on Temes's order.

The onlookers' repugnant horror at the sight was echoed in Darien's face. Staring with sick disbelief he said forcefully for all to hear, 'That such evil has existed! Brick by stone that Tower is coming down! It will be my first act as king. Should you go on the wagon too, Marric?'

'I can walk.' He moved to follow the wagon, Darien stepping beside him, ready to grab or steady him.

Marric said, 'Our grandfathers would be pleased, I think. Both of them.' The clear dark sky with its burden of stars seemed very precious after the terror and blood of the Tower. 'There is a new purpose in the people already. I sensed it this morning. They look — free.' It wasn't what he meant but he was too tired, and his side pained too much to find the right words to describe the dazed, unbelieving looks on the faces that, patched by smoky torchlight and shadow, watched the two Princes pass. He couldn't remember when he had last slept. 'I wish Tranche had made it, though.'

'I, too,' Darien replied. 'The Laker flag was a nice touch. Where did you get it?'

Marric smiled. 'Your sister made it.'

'Will you marry her?' He smiled at his brother's surprise. 'I didn't notice but Tranche told me. He was like that. He always saw below the surface; it was what made him so valuable to our cause.'

'It's a skill a merchant learns, that and acting.' Marric smiled wryly. 'He told me so often enough. Listen for what's not said. Look for what's not there. He was a good man, a good master. I shall miss him.'

'So will you?' Darien persisted.

'Marry Fenny? Oh, yes.'

'She will be the first lady of our new kingdom then, a position she will grace.'

'Until you marry yourself. Which I had rather you did sooner than later. Rissak,' he slanted a look at the man walking at his brother's other side, 'will tell you I have no taste for the throne.'

'You will be first minister in my council,' Darien said but Marric wasn't listening for he had spotted a fair head moving rapidly towards them. A turbanned figure holding aloft a lantern, bobbed behind her. Haran; he would have told her that the door was down and the Tower taken. He wouldn't yet know about Tranche, nor would Luka... Somebody should tell them; they had been a team so long, the very heart of the rebellion against his uncle.

Marric was suddenly exhausted, as much from his wound as the thought of all that had still to be done. So he simply stood and waited for her to come to him. She saw him then and quickened her pace until something in his stance checked her impetus. Her face paled and she gasped at the sight of the bloodstained turban wound about his body. He stepped towards her and her arms went gingerly around him.

'What?' she said fiercely. 'Tell me!' And with desperate hope, 'You wouldn't be standing if it was bad.' He read the terror behind her forced calm and stopped it with a kiss.

'It's nothing. A cut on the ribs, that's all.'

'He got it saving my life,' Darien interposed, but she brushed his words aside with another fierce question.

'You're sure?'

'As of the sun rising tomorrow on our new king, my love.' His heart sickness over Tranche and the weary drag of his body was momentarily lifted by her presence. He closed his eyes and rested against her, nose buried in the softness of her neck. Her hair smelled of sunlight and lavender, overlaid with the smells of her work among the wounded.

'Let me see.' Her hands moved gently, loosening the stained coverings over his hurt. 'Thank the Lady the bleeding has taken up! Darien,' she said imperiously, 'he shouldn't be on his feet. Find a cart or something to carry him to bed.' She stamped her foot. 'What is the use of winning battles if he bleeds to death standing here?'

'I'm not,' Marric protested. A yawn cracked his face wide open. He rubbed his mouth feeling the scratch of stubble against his palm. 'By the gods I'm weary though.'

'Then sleep,' Darien said. He raised an arm to signal the driver of the cart trundling towards him. 'Take him away and tuck him in, Fenny. Send the cart back, there are still wounded to move.'

'Thank you.' She wrinkled her brow, 'But where? The guildhall is overflowing with wounded already.'

'To the palace,' her brother said. 'I will find you there later. Osram,' he beckoned to the Appellan, 'will go with you, though I cannot think there will be trouble. Our uncle's slaves must have hated him too.'

'Come then, my dear.' Marric needed little coaxing; it took a conscious effort to keep his eyes open. As they were leaving Fenny called back to Darien. 'I forgot; a bird came from the Lakes earlier. Mother is on her way with her priestesses to help with the wounded from the battle. The Ansham archers are escorting her. Some of them will have herbal knowledge too.' Her face clouded. 'So many of our people have died.'

'I know,' Darien said. 'War takes its toll from all. Tranche was among those who fell, Fenny. I am so sorry.' He leaned over the cart's side to give her a comforting hug. 'Now I must go. I will come when I can.'

The cart tipped as Osram swung his frame up beside the driver and the mule plodded slowly off, the elderly vehicle rocking over the cobbles.

'Not quite a royal progress,' Fenny said, squeezing Marric's hand. 'We must manage something better for Darien's coronation.'

'And we will.' Marric spoke with quiet certainty for it had come to him in a moment of revelation, as if blinkers had been pulled from his eyes, that this was the fullfilment of the first vision the Mother had sent him, that day by the river when he was but a child. Today — tonight — he corrected himself, here under a sky still stained with the smoke and terror of battle, was the culmination of the route the goddess had shown him then. The journey had been arduous, its ending entirely unexpected to say the least, bringing with it the brother he had lost, the love he had found, and a future that would at last allow him to take his proper place in the golden city of his birth.

Not that it bore much resemblance now to the powerhouse of commerce it had been in his grandfather's time, but all that would change under the rule of Rhutan's rightful king. Rhutans were resilient folk, he thought drowsily; a man, or a race, that lacked persistence, never attained greatness. The burned out warehouses would rise again, Darien would cement the ties already formed with Ansham and Barat and no matter who claimed the Appellan throne, that fact alone would prove a powerful deterrent against future trouble, should one ever be needed. Meddia, given their example, might even throw off the yoke of their overlords. There would never be a better time for it than now with the power vacuum Temes's death had created.

It was an exquisite irony, he mused, that Cyrus's grandsons should be the force behind the break-up of the empire he and his sire had amassed. Truly the gods moved their human pawns in ways no man could predict. For himself he was just glad to have come home at last.

Fenny was peering at him, reaching to feel his face. 'Are you all right? You're very quiet. You're not bleeding again, are you?'

'No, just thinking. I — we — were born in the palace. Seventeen generations of the kings of Rhuta have ruled there, did you know that? Something Taba told me. Darien will be the eighteenth. And our grandmother can now return to her home.' He yawned again and apologised. 'When I have slept I will propose to you properly. Ours could be the first wedding to grace my brother's reign.'

'Indeed? I have heard it's a tradition of Rhutan royalty that younger sons must postpone matrimony till their elder brothers have wed.'

'Lucky we are half Appellan then. They have no such foolish rules.'

The cart lurched, thudding down onto a smoother level as they reached the Processional Way. The mule picked up its pace ignoring the bobbing lanterns of the Ripans who had wandered into the square to celebrate their newfound freedom. Nobody, it seemed, wanted to waste the night in sleeping.

A bonfire burned in the market place and flashes of Laker blue and Baratan green were caught in the glow. Marric saw wine being passed and smelled roasting meat; he wondered how Doku's men were making themselves understood, but guessed that goodwill engendered by victory was probably language enough. There would be sore heads tomorrow when it would be time enough to mourn fallen comrades. Tonight was for the survivors and the victory they had won.

The palace gates were open and unattended and only one light burned in the deserted hall. Osram, shouldering his way through the door to investigate, returned after a short time carrying the lamp, to report.

'The place is deserted. Looks like the slaves have fled, or hidden themselves. No sign of the court either. Probably heading for the hills with whatever they can carry.'

'Probably,' Marric agreed. Temes's Appellan sycophants would find no sympathy in the city. Leaning lightly on Fenny's shoulder he followed the big man into the palace. 'Can you find more lamps? And locate the kitchens and a cook? There will need to be food ready, and wine.' He stared around at the spacious hall with its inlaid panels and ornate decoration, finer than anything he had ever seen. 'Darien will be coming later, and his officers, I expect. The Baratan Prince as well. They must find something better awaiting them than lightless, deserted rooms.'

'I will see to it, Prince Marric,' Osram said formally. 'You may leave it to me.'

Marric was glad to do so. He stood in the wide hall remembering the day he had taken the boat up-river for the purpose of glimpsing the place where Taba had been raised. It was hard to imagine himself as a baby in this setting, or Taba as a young princess, which her marriage to his uncle would have made her. Fenny, as she increasingly seemed to do, uncannily divined his thoughts.

'You have come home, my dear. I wonder if they know it, the shades of those who loved you? How pleased your grandfather would be to see this day! After all your struggles, Marric, how does it feel to have won through? For it is your victory too, you know, as much as Darien's.'

'It feels strange,' he responded. 'Like a vision. Nothing seems quite real though you know it must be. To have travelled so far just to return to where it all began.' He shook his head tiredly, and recalled to her purpose by the action, Fenny tugged him forward.

'Sleep. But first I will clean that cut.' There will be time enough later for everything else.'

Marric kissed her. 'And for us. With the war over and the rightful king on the throne, the time will finally come for us.' Grimacing, he raised his arm to stroke her hair. 'We will find our own place, and our own life. We will marry and have children who will share their lives with Darien's sons and daughters...'

***

And somewhere, beyond their joint imaginings and hearing, the listening gods must have laughed.